BREAKING AWAY

THE BREAKING SERIES BOOK 2

JULIANA HAYGERT

COPYRIGHT

English - Portuguese

For a complete list of words used in the series <u>click here</u>!

Note that some words and expression don't have a perfect literal translation. The translation you see here is the one that fits the context of my novels.

Ai – ouch

Ainda bem – thank goodness

Até depois – see you later

Beijinho – a sweet made with condensed sweetened milk

Bem – fine, good, well

Boa noite – good night

Boa sorte – good luck

Boa tarde – good afternoon

Bom – well

Bom dia – good morning

Bomba – item to drink chimarrão with

Bombacha – typical pants used by gaúchos

Branquinho – same as Beijinho

Brigadeiro – a sweet made with condensed sweetened milk and cocoa powder

Café colonial – continental breakfast

Calma – calm down

Carreteiro – typical dish made of leftover steaks from barbecues

Chato – a name for someone who annoys you

Chimarrão – herb-based drink from the south of Brazil

Churrasco – Brazilian barbecue

Churrasqueira – a type of a grill where Brazilian barbecue is made

Claro – of course

Credo – jeez/damn

Cuia – kind of cup to drink chimarrão with

Dança folclórica gaúcha – typical dance from the south of Brazil

De nada – you're welcome

De novo – again

Delícia – delicious

Desculpa – sorry

Deus do céu – Lord above/Oh my God

Droga – crap

E aí – what's up?

É assim – this way

Eita – whoa

Então – so?

Eu não vou me atrasar – I won't be late

Eu te amo – I love you

Eu vou te matar – I'll kill you

Feijoada – dish made with black beans

Feliz Páscoa – Happy Easter

Filha da puta (daughter of a bitch), mimada (spoiled), china (it's like *prenda*, but in a bad way), rapariga sem vergonha (girl without shame), invejosa (jealous) – insulting names for women/girls

Filho duma puta – son of a bitch

Gaúcho(a) – people from the south of Brazil

Graças a Deus – thank God, thank goodness

Grande coisa – whatever

Guria – girl

Idiota – idiot

Irmã – sister

Irmãzinha – little sister

Mãe – mother

Me dá – give it to me

Me deixa em paz – leave me alone

Merda – shit

Meu Deus – my God

Morena – brunette, but in Brazil this term is used in a caring way, like darling or sweetie

Não – no

Negrinho – same as Brigadeiro

Nossa – wow/whoa

O que – what?

O que é isso – what is this?

Obrigado (a) – thanks

Oi – hi/hello

Ótimo – great

Pai – father

Pão de queijo – cheese bread

Parabéns - congratulations

Peão/Peões –cowboys in Brazil

Perfeita(o) – perfect

Pois então – well/you see

Por favor – please

Por que/por quê – why

Porque – because

Porcaria – crap/jeez/damn/shit/bad stuff

Porra – fuck/shit

Prazer – Pleasure, a short way of saying "nice to meet you"

Prenda – just like a gaúcha

Presta atenção – pay attention

Preta – black

Puta merda – fuck/shit/bullshit

Puta que pariu – goddamn it, holy shit, fuck

Que droga – crap/jeez/damn/this sucks

Que foi – what?

Que mentira – what a lie

Que nada – nonsense

Que porcaria é essa – what the hell is this?

Querida – dear

Rio Grande do Sul – southernmost state in Brazil

Sem rodeios – without rodeos, means without dillydallying

Senhorita – miss

Sério – really

Sete de Setembro – Brazil's Independence Day

Sim – yes

Tá bom/bem – okay

Tá tudo bem – it's okay

Também – too/also

Tchau – bye

Tche – common expression used by gaúchos – it can mean many things. A salutation, an exasperated exclamation, or even addressing someone

Te amo – I love you

Te comporta – behave

Tia – aunt

Tio – uncle

Tudo bem/Tudo bom – how are you?

Um minuto – one minute

Vai com – go with

Veado – deer. In Brazil, it's a nickname for homosexuals. Between friends, it's used as a friendly, teasing name.

Vestibular – an extensive and hard test Brazilians take to enter college – each college has its own vestibular test and if the student doesn't pass it, he/she doesn't enter that particular college.

Você – you

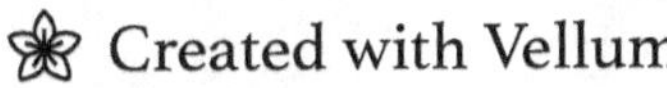 Created with Vellum

AUTHOR'S NOTE

I hope you enjoy reading *Breaking Away*!

Don't forget to sign up for my Newsletter to find out about new releases, cover reveals, give-aways, and more!

If you want to see exclusive teasers, help me decide on covers, read excerpts, talk about books, etc, join my reader group on Facebook: Juliana's Club!

1

LEAVING SOME THINGS—OR PEOPLE, OR HORSES—behind was harder than I thought it would be.

"*Tá tudo bem*," I said, patting Preta's long neck. My beautiful gray mare tilted her head to me and nudged my shoulder with her wet nose. Smiling, I leaned over the stall door and hugged her. "Hannah will take care of you." In the next stall, Argus nickered. I turned to him. "*Sim*, you better take good care of her too."

"I know he will," Hannah said, entering her ranch's stable. She had a sweet smile on her lips, but her dark green eyes looked at me with concern. That was how everyone looked at me lately, and I was getting sick of it. Hannah stopped by my side and watched both horses. "He's in love."

I scratched Preta's wither. "So is she."

That was the main reason I was leaving my mare here. Because Argus and Preta behaved like an old married couple. Not because my father and I had had the fight of the century two nights ago, and I had left promising never to come back. Not at all.

Hannah leaned on the back wall. "Excited?"

I faced her and rested my butt on the stall's door, allowing Preta to keep nuzzling my back. I needed my mare's comforting and supporting touch right now.

My entire life, I did whatever was good for my brothers' and cousin's polo career. Dropping out of vet school and following them from Brazil to the U.S. a little over a year ago had been the culminating point. We had always traveled all over the world for tournaments and contracts, but we had never talked about moving. Much less to another country.

At first, it was like a new, fun adventure. So much to see, so much to explore. However, after a couple of months, I grew tired of it. All I did was follow them to the club for training, then back home. Even riding by myself, without a time frame or obligations, had been hard to squeeze in with their busy calendar.

I loved my family with every drop of my blood, but I wasn't the type to sit pretty and smile. I would rather run around, muck out a stall or two, get my hands dirty, and feel useful.

My patience had a limit, and I had reached it a long time ago.

"*Sim*. And nervous too."

She nodded. "I know. You'll be fine, though. You're smart and pretty. Girls will want to know all your secrets and boys will fall head over heels for you."

"Boys? Who's talking about boys?" Leo strolled in the stable. As usual, my twin brother wore jeans and no shirt.

"*Eita*." I slapped my hand over my eyes. "Put on a T-shirt."

Hannah laughed. Of course, she was laughing. He was her boyfriend. She probably enjoyed staring at his chest. I didn't.

"Don't change the subject, *senhorita*." Leo halted beside Hannah and put his arm around her shoulders, pulling her close. Most of the time, it was cute to see how much they loved each other. But sometimes, it was sickening. Didn't they get tired of being together all the time? "I'll punch any boy who looks at you the wrong way."

I rolled my eyes. "Leo, we just turned twenty-two. I don't need your protection anymore."

He shrugged. "You'll be fifty and I'll still be watching over you."

"*Meu Deus.* Good thing I'll be many miles away."

His happy demeanor fell through, and a knot appeared between his brows. "Too many miles away."

And I couldn't wait for it.

I whirled around and patted Argus's neck then kissed Preta's forehead. "Be a good girl, okay." I inhaled a deep breath and put on a smile before facing my brother and his girlfriend. "I should get going." After all, I had to drive seventeen hours to get to Colorado.

Without waiting for an answer, I marched out of the stables to the parking lot beside the main house, hearing Leo's and Hannah's footsteps as they followed me.

After I told him of my plans a month ago, Leo decided I shouldn't leave without a car. He said it would be helpful to have my own set of wheels wherever I went, so he gave me a brand new red Grand Cherokee for our birthday. I wanted another SUV, but since Jeep was his sponsor, I had no say in it. Besides, I hadn't set up my own bank account here in the U.S. since we moved. At the time, it didn't seem like a big thing, since I had debit and credit cards from my parents' account and I didn't need to ask permission to buy anything. That changed after my fight with my father. Now, I didn't feel like taking his money for anything, and I depended on Leo's bank account. He insisted he didn't mind, but I did.

I opened the driver's door and stared inside for a moment. I had jammed everything I owned in there, everything I had brought from Brazil and bought here since. It didn't look like much, but the car was about to explode clothes and boots and cowboy hats everywhere.

Sighing, I faced Leo and Hannah. "Thanks. For everything."

Hannah pulled me into a hug. "Drive safe. Call us every time you stop to eat or rest. And call us when you get there. Take care. Have fun. And—"

"Okay, Mom," I teased, breaking the hug. Leo opened his arms and I wrinkled my nose. "I'm not hugging you. Put on a T-shirt first, then we can talk about it."

Ignoring me, he wound his arms around me. "Come here." I squirmed, which made him squeeze me tighter. "Everything Hannah said, okay? Be a good girl."

I stepped back and shook my head at him. "I'm always a good girl." He snorted, but I decided this wasn't the time to start an argument. I slipped inside my SUV and looked at them. "I'll see you soon."

"Farewell," Hannah said.

"*Tchau*," Leo said.

I turned on the engine, closed the door, put on my seat belt, and tuned the radio to a loud country song before driving out of the parking lot, off the ranch, and taking the first step into my new life.

THE UNIVERSITY OF FORT HOWELL, LOCATED IN THE tiny town of Fort Howell, Colorado, just east of Aurora, buzzed with life. Classes started Wednesday, but today the dorms and the registrar office opened, allowing students to get ready and acquainted with the campus, and with new friends.

As I drove through the streets, students walked up and down, carrying boxes, bags, sofas, mattresses. Parents took pictures instead of helping. Cars were parked in non-parking spaces or were doubled parked. There were smiles and tears everywhere.

After driving seventeen hours, not counting

my stops and the nap I took at a rest area during the night, I was so tired that I didn't think I would feel anything once I got here. *Tche*, I was wrong.

Butterflies danced in my stomach, my hands shook, and my palms sweated. A stupid smile adorned my lips, and I knew I looked like a dork. This was it. This was me, living my life, taking charge. Who cared about not transferring almost any classes from the two years of vet school in Brazil? Who cared if I had to take two years of pre-vet to be able to apply to vet school here? I was young. I had time. This was my chance to start anew, to do it better, to *be* better.

Following the campus map, I turned on the Greek Lane and instantly got the name. Large houses lined the street, with lush, green lawns, colorful flowers and tall trees, porches or archways, and big Greek letters flat against a prominent wall.

The famous Greek life. Brazil didn't have anything like it, which made me that much more curious about it.

I slowed down, scanning around. Soon I realized that the left side of the street harbored sororities, and the right side housed fraternities. In the front lawn of the sororities, girls ran to other girls, embracing, squealing, and jumping up and down. In front of the fraternities, guys walked to other guys, bumped fists, shook hands, slapped backs.

At the last fraternity house of the street, marked by the letters BAT, a guy was sprawled on a lounge chaise in the middle of the front lawn, under the shade of an umbrella and drinking what looked like a colorful margarita. Around him, other guys played with a football, throwing it at each other, often bumping each other or stopping to gawk at girls who arrived at the sororities or walked down the sidewalk.

One of the guys pointed to a sorority house. "Look!" he yelled. The others turned, and they all looked at whatever. Despite it all, I looked too. However, before I could see anything, something hit the passenger door of my car. On instinct, I sank my foot on the break.

As I exited my car, one of the guys from BAT jogged in my direction.

"Sorry about that," he said, picking the ball from the ground. "Garrett, there—" He gestured toward a tall guy standing a few yards from him. Wearing a dark brown cowboy hat and cowboy boots, Garrett turned his attention from the sorority house to me. One corner of his lips quirked up and he tipped his hat. "—was supposed to catch the ball."

"But he was busy gawking at the girls across the street," I said.

The guy smiled. "Well, yes."

I shook my head and examined my car. A tiny dent marked the passenger door.

"Great," I muttered.

"Hey, I couldn't help but notice your accent. Where are you from?"

That was always one of the first things anyone said or asked me in any conversation.

"Brazil," I said.

The guy's eyes widened. "Wow. For real?" I nodded. "Cool." Still smiling, he took a step closer to me. "I always heard Brazilian girls were beautiful." His eyes raked me from head to toe and back. He seemed to like my faded jeans, cowboy boots, and tank top. "Glad to know it's true."

I fought the urge to roll my eyes.

"Hey, Jeff," Garrett called. "You're hogging the ball, bro."

"I gotta ..." Jeff pointed back to his friends. What? Did he think I wanted to stand here in the middle of the street, messing with traffic, just to talk to him? "I'll probably see you around. Right?"

"Yeah, sure." I waved him off.

After glaring at the dent in my door for ten more seconds, I marched around my car and slipped inside. I avoided looking at the BAT house as I drove by and turned onto another street.

FROM THE OUTSIDE, THE DORM BUILDING LOOKED like most buildings in Brazil—four stories, with several windows lining the red-brownish walls. Except for the part where there were full apartments inside Brazilian edifices, and here there were tiny bedrooms and common bathrooms. That was going to be hard to get used to.

Since all the buildings looked the same, I slowed down again, reading the banners on top of each main entrance, looking for my future home, the Linda Hudson Residence. It was right beside the Colton Hudson Residence. Go figure.

The parking lot was behind my building, and I had almost given up parking there when I found an unoccupied spot in the back.

Holding my purse and a small bag, I entered the Linda Hudson Residence, climbed up one flight of stairs, and turned right, looking for room number 216. The room door was ajar. A girl stood in the middle of the room, and an older couple sat on one of the beds.

"Look, dear, this must be your roommate," the woman said.

A blond girl with beautiful curls and brown eyes turned to me with a big smile. "Hi! Are you in room 216 too?"

"Yes," I said.

The bedroom wasn't as small as I thought it would be, but it wasn't that great either. If there was a line running across the room, I could say the sides were symmetrical. A wooden twin bed, thin mattress, nightstand, desk and chair, a drawer chest, and a door, which was probably the closet.

Apparently, the girl had arrived here early, because her things were already spread over the right side of the bedroom. Pink comforter and pillow on the bed, pink lamp and alarm clock on the nightstand, books on the desk, and portraits over the drawer chest.

"Come in, then," the girl said. I couldn't help but notice the fitted pink polo she wore and the big Greek letters on the left side. "I'm Molly Stuart, your roommate."

"I'm Beatriz Fernandes." I stepped inside, dragging my bag over the worn beige carpet, and turned to the unoccupied side of the room. "But I prefer Bia."

"Cool. Bia. I like it," Molly said. "I hope you

don't mind, but I chose a side without waiting for you."

I dropped my bags on my bed. "It's fine."

She introduced me quickly to her parents. They were from Denver and had come with Molly for her first day at school. They did that every semester, even though she was starting her third year here. As expected, they asked about my family.

I thought about lying because I didn't want anyone pointing at me with one of three options. A, they loved my brothers and my cousin and were big fans, which meant they would bother me. B, they knew about Leo and everything involving him: his problematic phase and last year's tragic events, in which case they would pity me or be wary of me. C, they knew nothing about polo and never heard of my family before.

Even if they knew who my brothers and cousin were, lying wasn't for me. I was proud of my family, even through the rough patches.

"My brothers play polo and my father is the coach." Then I lied, "They are at a big tournament this week, and I didn't want to bother them."

"That's nice of you," Molly's mother said. "Well, if you need anything, let us know. We'll be in town until the weekend to make sure Molly is okay. We don't mind helping Molly's friends."

"Thanks," I said.

"We'll let you girls get to know each other now," Molly's father said. He kissed Molly's forehead. "We'll pick you up later for dinner. You're invited to come too, Bia."

"Thanks," I said again.

Once her parents walked out of the room, Molly closed the door and leaned against it. She smiled at me, her eyes sparkling. "Let the party begin!"

2

Two hours later, Molly and I had unloaded all of my things, dropping all the boxes and bags on the floor.

"I'm not going to organize this mess right now," I said, sitting on my bare mattress.

"Don't sit there!" Molly shrieked.

I jumped to my feet. "Why?"

"You don't know where this mattress has been, what people might have done on it, with it." She wrinkled her nose in disgust. "If you sleep on it, make sure to put several sheets, but if I were you, I would buy a new mattress ASAP."

I nodded, making a mental note to browse the internet later for a local mattress store. The perks of never having lived in a dorm before. It seemed I had a lot of things to learn.

"Come on." She picked up my purse from the chair. "Let's take a break."

"Where are we going?"

She smiled. "I'm going to show you around. There's much to see."

She wasn't kidding. Molly and I walked around campus, stopping by the buildings where our classes would be; by the gym, which, according to Molly, was a great place to meet hot guys; by the main square, where lots of events happened; by the bookstore, where we browsed for the books we needed to buy; and by a coffee place three blocks from our dorm.

Molly bought a white mocha latte, and I got a cappuccino before we sat at a table by the window.

So far, I had found out Molly would turn twenty-one in two months, this was her junior year too, and she was double majoring in business and French. During high school, she had been head cheerleader and valedictorian and dated the quarterback for almost two years, but they broke up right after prom. Here in college, she was taking it slow. She had a few dates, but nothing too serious.

"Life is a party and I want to enjoy my last two years here," she said.

In turn, I told her where I was from, my age, that my two years in vet school had gone down the drain, though I was able to transfer a lot of core curriculum classes, putting me in my third year of pre-vet here. I also told her pre-vet was something that didn't exist in Brazil, which bothered me to no end when I first found out. I almost gave up vet school because I didn't want to lose a few years. However, I had come to terms with that and I was embracing the American lifestyle.

"So tell me," Molly started. "Is it too different from Brazil so far?"

"You mean, being in college?" I asked, and she nodded. "A little. First, universities in Brazil don't have dorms. You can't live on campus."

"Are you serious? Then what do people do?"

"Live with your parents, or if you're from out of town, rent an apartment."

She blew on her steaming mug. "Interesting. What else?"

"Brazilian colleges don't have a Greek system."

"No way! But that's so fun. I'm in a sorority—" She pointed to her polo shirt. The letters embroidered on it spelled ATN. "—and I love it! My parents belonged to Greek houses, and they loved it too. They met during a mixer. Oh, and they met their best friends there too."

"It sounds like fun."

"It is! You know, tomorrow night is rush night. I'll be at the house helping out, but you should come. You should rush!"

"Um, I thought only freshmen were supposed to do that."

She chuckled. "No. We accept girls from any year. You should do it."

"I'm not sure."

That was when those guys, Jeff and Garrett and the one lounging on a chaise in the middle of the front lawn, strolled past the coffee place, outside the window.

They tossed the football around, chatting. Jeff saw me and nudged the other two. Without slowing their steps, the other two turned their attention to me. Jeff waved, the nameless guy gave me a big, bright smile and winked, and Garrett showed me the same lopsided grin from before.

I stared at my coffee.

"Do you know them?" Molly asked.

"Not really. They hit my car with that damn football when I was arriving on campus. But other than that, I have no idea who they are."

"The shortest one is Jeff Smith, the tallest one is Garrett Blackwell, and the blond one is Jonah Hudson. They're—"

"Wait. Hudson? As in Colton and Linda Hudson?"

"Yes, those were his grandparents. They donated a lot of money to the university back when."

"Oh."

"Yeah. He's loaded, and he's the president of the Beta Alpha Tau fraternity, or The Bat for short. It's the best fraternity on campus."

Well, there were about six fraternities on campus. To me, that was a lot.

"So far, they seem full of themselves," I said.

Molly laughed. "Like most college boys." She pointed to where they disappeared. "But you saw how cute they are, right? Like, super cute."

I shrugged, but the truth was, I noticed. I mean, I wasn't a saint. I liked guys, and being in college meant getting to know lots of them.

I noticed Jeff, the shortest one, but still taller than my 5'7", had an olive complexion and chocolate eyes, with short, dark hair. Jonah was taller than Jeff was, and had fair skin, blond hair cut in layers, and blue eyes. Garrett, the tallest of the trio, had tanned skin, messy brown hair, hazel eyes, and a five o'clock shadow covering his jaw and chin. And the three of them looked like they worked out.

"Yeah, they're cute," I admitted.

"If you rush my sorority, Alpha Tau Nu, you'll be seeing more guys like them." She leaned over the table, and for a second, I thought she would leap over it, clutch my shoulders, and shake me until I agreed. "Please. Come over, even if you're not interested. If someone bids on you later, you can always pass."

"I don't know."

"Hey, didn't you say you wanted the full American experience? It doesn't get much more American than rushing sororities."

She had a point.

Since the idea of going to college here in the U.S. bloomed in my mind, I promised myself I would experiment with new things and try the American way of life. Rushing and pledging sororities were part of it. Still, I wasn't sure it was something I wanted.

"You get a maybe," I said. Then I clamped my hands over my ears before Molly's squeal made me deaf.

I ENDED UP NOT GOING TO RUSH NIGHT. INSTEAD, I went out to buy a mattress, which was almost impossible to carry inside the building by myself. *Graças a Deus* for the girl who was ascending the stairs to go to a party, and took pity on me and helped me out. After throwing the other mattress under the bed—I would deal with it later—and putting my new one in place, I organized my stuff around the room.

When she came back from the house, Molly seemed upset about me not showing up. I tried explaining to her that I didn't think it was for me, but I liked the fact that she was into her sorority. She shrugged and didn't look at me again until the next morning.

"Hello, sunshine!" she said, sitting up on her bed at 8 a.m. sharp.

At least she was in a better mood than last night.

"*Bom dia*," I mumbled before pulling the covers over my head. Two seconds later, Molly yanked the covers away from me. "What the hell?"

"Come on." Molly grinned. "We've got a big day today."

Other than getting our student IDs in the afternoon and buying our books, I had no idea what she was talking about.

I hugged my pillow and turned my back to her. "My bed feels so good right now."

"Come on, Bia!" She pulled my pillow away.

"Hey!"

She chuckled. "You have orientation all morning—"

"That's optional."

"—and we have to get our IDs and buy our books. Oh, and I'm going to introduce you to my friends. You're gonna love them."

After about fifteen minutes of her chipper self, I couldn't take it anymore. I gave up and got out of bed. She hovered so close to me, I thought she would follow me into the bathroom. I would shove her off if she did. *Graças a Deus*, she didn't and I was able to take a shower and brush my teeth in peace. After much thought, I decided to go with my usual ensemble. No need to try to impress anyone, or be someone I wasn't.

Molly looked me up and down when I exited the bathroom. "You do take your cowgirl style seriously, don't you?"

I glanced down. Jeans, a white tank top, thick black suede belt, and my favorite black and white Lucchese boots. If only she knew I almost reached for my black hat, but decided it would be too much. For now.

I shrugged. "Anything wrong with it?"

"No, it's not that." She smiled. "I'm just not used to it."

I looked at her clothes. A not too short jean skirt, a pink blouse with slight cleavage, and high-heeled sandals, and too many rings and bracelets and necklaces. Yeah, not my style.

Molly walked with me to orientation, and I was surprised when she stayed with me for the entire thing. I asked her a couple of times why the hell she wanted to sit through it if it was optional, and she wasn't new to the university.

"Just because," was her answer each time.

The girl probably didn't have anything better to do, or she wanted a favor later, in which case I should be careful with what else she did for me just because.

After the boring introduction and brief tour of the main sites of the campus, Molly took me to a Panera Bread just off-campus.

"Bia, meet Audrey and Sarah." Molly introduced me to two blond chicks who had on too much makeup for my taste. But then again, most American women—or little girls for that matter—wore too much makeup for my taste. She took a chair across the table from Audrey and Sarah. "This is the girl I told you about last night." She gestured to the chair beside hers. "Audrey is the president of my sorority, and Sarah is the rush chair."

I sat and stared at Molly. "Are you setting me up?"

She averted her eyes. "Not exactly."

"She just wanted us to meet you," Audrey said. Her blond hair fell in perfect waves down her back, and I wondered how many hours she spent in front of the mirror to get that effect each morning.

"We're her friends and you're her roommate," Sarah said. She flipped her straight-as-a-board blond hair—this one also spent at least an hour flat ironing her hair every day—and looked me up and down. With her fancy skirt and pumps, I bet my jeans and boots didn't really please her. "She says we'll get along famously."

I was starting to doubt that, but hey, I was the foreigner here and I didn't mind diversity as long as everyone respected each other.

"I'm sure we will," I said. Seeing as Audrey and Sarah were already waiting for their food, I stood. "Hey, Molly, why don't we go order something?"

"Yeah, sure." Molly stood and followed me to the cashier.

I ordered a panini and soda, and Molly got a salad and iced tea. When we returned to the table with our plates, Audrey and Sarah were almost through theirs. Not surprisingly, they were eating salad.

"What brings you to the United States, Bia?" Audrey asked as soon as I sat on my chair.

I had rehearsed this answer several times, because this was another one people always asked me. "My family. My brothers are polo players, and they have a contract with an American club." I just hoped they didn't want more about it.

"Oh." Sarah looked me up and down again. "But Brazilian girls aren't exactly cowgirls, are they?"

I didn't get that question often. "Like here, there are many kinds of girls in Brazil. There are a lot of farms and ranches in the state I was born, and lots of girls become sort of a cowgirl, called *prenda*."

Audrey pushed her empty plate aside. "Interesting."

"How about English?" Sarah asked. "I thought Brazilians spoke Spanish."

I gritted my teeth and counted to twenty. I knew it wasn't anyone's obligation to know which language we spoke in Brazil, but Brazil had a huge rivalry with Argentina, and assuming we spoke Spanish was like saying we were Argentines. Or worse, that Buenos Aires was the capital of Brazil.

"Actually, we speak Portuguese," I answered after calming down. "English is taught in schools, but that's only the basics. There are private language schools in Brazil, and because of my brothers' international career, my father thought it would be a good idea to learn English from a young age."

"That's good, I guess," Audrey said, sounding uninterested.

We talked some more about college in Brazil and here, and how they were different. The same conversation I had had with Molly the day before.

"See," Molly said. "She would be a great addition to the house."

I was about to open my mouth and tell them I had zero interest in joining the sorority when Audrey said, "We have time to change your mind. Meanwhile, you can help us plan our stand for the Welcome Carnival on Saturday. Got any ideas?"

Banners for the Welcome Carnival were everywhere. Apparently, it was a huge evening event in the main courtyard, which happened every semester on the first Saturday after classes started.

Sarah leaned over the table and smiled. "I bet our carnival isn't like your country's Carnival, but I bet you'll love it anyway."

I fought the urge to roll my eyes. One, it

was *Carnaval*, not Carnival, and two, I also bet it was different, but I wasn't a big fan of it in Brazil. Maybe I would like this one better.

I forced a big smile. "I can't wait."

We were getting ready to leave when a girl with red curls stopped by our table. "Hello, girls," she said, her tone a little sarcastic.

"Hello, Gina," Audrey said, her expression closing.

Gina turned a bright smile to me. "Hi, there. You must be Bia, the Brazilian girl." I gaped at her. How did she know that? "I'm Gina, president of the ZTZ. I know you missed rush night, but I want to invite you to the house tonight, so you can meet the girls and me."

"That's illegal," Sarah said. She turned to me. "It's against the rules to rush after the rush night, or to bid on someone before bidding night."

"Oh," was all I said.

Gina didn't lose her composure though. "Girls, let's be honest here. I know you bent the rules a few times, and you know I did too. Besides, I know you're going to bid on Bia, so I'm here throwing my hat in the ring too."

Audrey glared at her. "Take your freaking hat somewhere else."

Unaffected, Gina smiled at me again. "Don't

worry about them, Bia. Just don't forget you have other options. And I promise, our bid will be *good*." She winked before leaving.

Sarah tilted her head to me. "Bia, if you plan on joining a sorority, you should know there's no house better than ours."

"True," Audrey said. "And whatever her bid is, we'll make it better."

I almost told them that I wouldn't join any sorority, no matter what bid I got, but maybe they would launch in an argument and try to convince me about why I should join if I did, and I wasn't in the mood for that. Better to stay quiet.

I just nodded. "Okay."

After leaving Panera, I actually had a good time with Molly, Audrey, and Sarah. We walked around campus, got our student IDs done, bought books for our classes, then stopped by a froyo stand between the science and the English buildings. They told me all about sororities and fraternities. I also found out most girls were allowed to live in the house, but Molly had a scholarship that involved boarding, which meant she had to live in the dorms.

The trio knew everyone around. We would take a step, and they would say hi to someone and call that person by his or her name. If I had to guess, they must have greeted at least three hundred students in the short time we spent together, and they actually knew all of their names. That alone would be a miracle for me.

Some people stopped and started conversations with them. Very polite and cordial, the girls introduced me with flare. Apparently, being Brazilian was an exciting thing, because everyone turned to me saying, "Really? That's so great!" or things of the like. Shame I forgot the name of four of every five students they introduced me to in less than three seconds.

They had been nice to me and, even though we didn't share the same tastes, that didn't mean we couldn't get along well.

3

———

A PILLOW FLEW TO MY FACE.

"*Que porcaria é essa.*" I sat up, lost for a moment.

"Get up or we'll be late for our first class," Molly said, combing her hair in front of the tall mirror she had brought from home.

I looked at her alarm clock—it was eight, and my first class was at eight-thirty—and shot up.

I put on my uniform: jeans, tank top, my favorite cowboy boots, and braided my hair down my back.

"You look cute," Molly said, her voice a little cold. I guess she was still mad at me. After Gina, another two sorority presidents stopped me to invite me over for an unofficial and private rush night.

I shrugged. "Thanks. You too."

In silence, we left our building and walked to the science building. My first class was Biology 201, and Molly had Biology 101 next door.

As soon as we stepped out of our building, a girl wrapped her fingers around my wrist and yanked to the side.

"*Tche*!" I exclaimed, ready to spit my anger in her face, but I recognized her. She was one of the girls that cornered me last night, the rush chair from one of the sororities.

"Sorry," she whispered, letting go of me. She pulled a piece of white paper from her pocket. "Take this. We'll talk later."

I took the paper and she left.

I stood frozen. "What the ...?"

Molly pursed her lips for a second. "It's probably a bid."

"But I haven't even been to their house."

"Well, they might think that by offering you a good bid, you might show up at their house for bid night, regardless of rushing or not."

"That's crazy."

"Yup. They know early bids are illegal, but if

she thinks you'll get better bids from other houses, she might want to be the first."

That sounded ridiculous. Why would they waste their time with me if I weren't going to accept anything? It didn't make any sense to me.

Curious, I unfolded the piece of paper and read the brief note.

We'll wash your clothes, clean your room, and you'll have prime meals in the house.

"That's a nice bid," Molly said, reading it from over my shoulder. "Will you take it?"

"No! I don't care what they offer me." There was no garbage can in sight, so I shoved the paper inside my purse. "Come on. We don't want to be late for class."

With a frown, Molly walked beside me as we crossed the campus. I made a list of things I could comment on or ask to break the ice growing between us, but nothing seemed good enough. I wasn't one for small talk. But being too direct, as I usually was, might not be the best way to fix whatever was going wrong between my roommate and me.

Two steps before I entered the science building, a girl bumped into me, dropping a blue paper in my hands.

"You gotta be kidding me," Molly muttered.

I turned, but the girl was already gone. "Seriously?" Molly shook her head and rushed ahead. "Hey, wait up," I called, following her inside the building. Before I could catch up with her, Molly entered her classroom. "*Merda.*"

I stepped into my classroom and chose an empty seat in the back. I sat down and stared at the folded blue paper, unsure if I wanted to open it.

A girl with shoulder-length, dirty blond hair, and clear blue eyes sat beside me.

I turned to her. "If this is about a bid, I'm not sure I'm interested."

She stared at me as if I had sprouted horns from my forehead. "Hmm, what?"

"Oh." I laughed. "Are you with any sorority?"

Her expression relaxed a bit. "Good gracious, no."

I let out a long breath. "Good."

She opened her bag and pulled out a thick biology book. "Classes just started and you look like you could use a break already."

I smiled, pulling my book from my tote. "Tell me about it." I extended my hand to hers. "Hi, I'm Bia Fernandes."

She took my hand and shook it. "Phoebe Erickson." She tilted her head, still looking at me. "May

I ask where you're from? I'm sorry, but your accent makes it hard not to."

Here we go. "Brazil."

Her eyes widened. "Seriously? That's cool. My uncle goes to Sao Paulo and Rio a few times each year for business. He says it's a great place."

If her uncle liked to talk about his travels, Phoebe probably knew a bit more about Brazil than most people, which made me glad for some reason.

The professor entered the classroom, and I opened my book to the first chapter, turning my attention to the front.

"It can be a great place," I muttered.

I GOT ANOTHER THREE BIDS—TWO BETWEEN MY classes, and one on the floor of my room, which probably had been slipped under the door.

"You're made of honey," Molly said. She tried going for a teasing tone, but I could hear the jealousy behind her words. I hoped that when she rushed, she received these many bids, but by the evil stares she gave me, I doubted it.

As I suspected, Molly spent the evening with her parents. I preferred to think she wanted to take advantage while they were still in town rather than avoiding me.

I was glad to find out I had two other classes with Phoebe the next day. The first one was English 102. As we entered the classroom together, I noticed all the students were freshmen, ranging from eighteen to nineteen, while I was twenty-two. Phoebe was nineteen. I was the only junior in a freshman class.

Maybe it wasn't too odd to them, but to me it was, and suddenly, I felt as if I was ten, twenty years older than them, and all those terrible thoughts and doubts that haunted me all summer came back in a rush.

Que droga. I knew I would be surrounded by students younger than me since I wasn't able to transfer most of my classes. I knew this. I had come to terms with it. I had accepted it and promised myself it wouldn't bother me. After all, twenty wasn't too far away from twenty-two. I hoped that in two years, I would be in vet school, and that difference wouldn't matter that much anymore. I could endure it for another two years.

I took a deep breath as I sat beside Phoebe in the back of the classroom.

"Are you okay?" she asked.

"Yup." I pushed those thoughts away from my

mind and pretended the students were all my age, or that I was theirs, that I wasn't starting again, that this was my first and only time in college.

Our next class was American History 101—another freshman course. What was I supposed to do? We didn't have English or American History in Brazil.

Once more, we sat in the back. I grabbed my history book from my bag, and when I raised my eyes again, Jonah strolled in the classroom. He stopped by the door and looked around. His eyes met mine and he smiled.

I shook my head.

"Do you know him?" Phoebe asked.

I shifted my gaze to her. Better than watching the guy. "Not really."

"Oh. Well, I might be mistaken, but I think he's coming this way."

I looked again, and sure enough, the guy made his way to where Phoebe and I were seated.

"Is this seat taken?" he asked, pointing to the chair beside mine.

"Hmm, no," I answered.

He flashed me another one of those perfect smiles and sat down. "I don't know if you remember me, but I definitely remember you." He extended his hand to me. "I'm Jonah Hudson, president of the Beta Alpha Tau."

I shook his hand. "Bia. And this is my friend, Phoebe."

"Hi," Phoebe said, her cheeks turning pink.

"Hi, Phoebe, nice to meet you." He shook her hand too.

When Jonah lowered his head to his books for a moment, Phoebe nudged me with her elbow and mouthed "cute." I rolled my eyes at her and looked ahead as the professor entered the classroom.

"By the way," Jonah started. "I'm sorry about the dent in your SUV. Since I'm responsible for what happens with my brothers and around my house, I want to pay to have it fixed."

I shook my head. "No. It's fine. Don't worry about it."

He looked at me, those bright blue eyes fixed on mine. "Bia, it's my responsibility. I will pay for it. In fact, we should take your car to my mechanic after class. What do you think?"

I opened my mouth to tell him I could do it myself, but then the professor strolled into the classroom. I pointed to the front. "Class is starting," I said.

He leaned back on his chair with a smile that told me he wouldn't give up that easy.

I WAS ABLE TO DITCH JONAH AFTER CLASS. Actually, Phoebe and I rushed out of the classroom before he could catch up with us, and ran across the courtyard to avoid him.

"Why don't you want him to pay for it?" she asked as we entered the coffee shop at the student center.

"Well, for starters, I can afford it."

"But, girl, he's cute, and he's totally into you."

We stopped by the cashier and ordered our drinks.

"He just met me," I said while we waited for our drinks.

"It didn't seem that way when he smiled at you and sat beside you."

We picked up our drinks, made a beeline to a small round table in the middle of the shop, and sat down.

I told her about how Jeff and Garrett hit my car with the football while Jonah enjoyed the sun right in the front yard of their fraternity house, then that I saw them again while seated right at that same coffee place.

"See? Don't really know him."

She smiled. "It seems to me that he wants to

get to know you. Why don't you want to get to know him?"

"It's not that. It's just ... classes just started. There will be plenty of time and plenty of parties to meet interesting guys. I prefer to have some fun before starting something right away. Besides, he's probably younger than me." And I was thinking of his friend. His cowboy boots told me he was more of my taste.

"One—" She raised her index finger. "—age is just a number. Nobody cares about it. Two—" She raised her middle finger. "—who says it isn't going to be fun. Three—" She lifted her ring finger. "—who says it'll end up in something. You guys can just go out a couple of times, have fun together, and then realize you don't want to be tied up, or maybe you two are too different, or whatever. But do you see my point?"

Yes, she had a point. But come on! It was the first week of classes. I had time to worry about boys later.

"I see your lips moving, but I don't hear anything," I teased.

Phoebe slapped my arm and laughed. "Okay, I'll drop this subject for now."

4

———————

Finally, bid night was past us and I didn't join any sorority—Audrey and Sarah didn't try to hide their disappointment very well.

Saturday, Molly seemed like another person. She smiled at me and treated me like a good friend. It seemed that not joining a sorority had been the right choice for the sake of my friendship with my roommate.

"Are you sure you want to go like that?" she asked.

I spun around to face the mirror. I had opted for a jean skirt, red Lucchese boots, a white blouse, red earrings, and a silver bracelet with a horseshoe charm. "What's wrong with it?"

She shook her head and smile. "Nothing. Like

I said before, I'm not used to seeing a girl wearing cowboy boots all the time."

"But this is Colorado. I mean, aren't there a lot of cowgirls around here?"

"Yes, but we don't run in the same circles."

I stared at her reflection in the mirror. What was that supposed to mean? Whatever it was, I shook it off.

At six, we walked the short distance to the courtyard. It was strange how parties started early here. This one more than most, but even others. By two in the morning, everything was quieting down and closing. In Brazil, everyone would get together for dinner or private parties before going to clubs, and that would happen only after midnight. In most cases, not before two in the morning. The club would keep it going until the sun was up. True story.

I had seen university employees and some students working around the courtyard during the day, but I didn't think they would be able to do too much in so little time. I mean, the courtyard was simple. A big square between several buildings, heavy wooden chairs and tables spread through the vast grass, and a three-foot-tall stage area in the center. But this? This was a miracle. Stands lined the outer circle of the courtyard, selling all kinds of drinks and food. Some were game stands manned by Greek houses. Large pieces of white and blue fabric—the colors of the university— were tied together, creating canopies every twenty feet, like a big tent, and white twinkling lights, like the ones people decorate their houses with during Christmastime, adorned lamps, trees, and the stage. It looked a little overboard, but cute and thoughtful.

"Wow," I whispered.

"I know, right?" Molly said. "It's practically the same every year, but the impact never lessens." She linked her arm to mine. "Let's go find Audrey and Sarah."

She weaved us through the crowd, and I saw every kind of human being alive. White, black, yellow, brown, guys with pink hair, girls with metal all over their face, Asian, Latin, goth, geek, punk, athletes, groupies, the girls who looked like Miss America, and the guys who look like rock stars.

We halted by a stand decorated with pink and gold stuff, and lots of blond girls milling around, in charge of a ring toss game on empty bottles. I had met some of the girls from Molly's sorority throughout the week, but I couldn't remember one name to save face. I just waved and smiled when they greeted me.

The stand next to theirs was decorated in black and orange, and the huge stuffed bat on top of it was a dead giveaway. What shocked me though was the game they had chosen. A kissing booth! The guys were in a line inside the stand, and girls came to them, gave them a dollar bill, and the guy in the line gave her a brief peck on the lips. I laughed.

"They can be so ridiculous," Audrey said, also watching the stand. "Only they could come up with a kissing booth and not look desperate."

"Boys will be boys."

"Exactly." She smiled at me.

I recognized a few guys from the line who the girls had introduced to me earlier, but again I was at a loss for names.

Seriously, I remembered the digits of my parents' first phone number, my first cell phone's number, and also Leo's, Ri's, Pedro's, Gui's, and Gabriela's. I even remembered Leticia's, my best friend back in Brazil. I knew the passport number and driver's license numbers of everyone in my family—things that I didn't really want or need to memorize. However, did I remember the name of the person I met a couple hours ago? No. What a waste of memory space.

I looked around. Students were everywhere.

Some giggling girls walked past us. A bunch of boys yelled and bumped fists. Two couples played at the stands, girls versus guys, and they laughed each time the other team missed. Some girls from the other sororities stopped by and hugged Audrey and Sarah as if they were besties. Another group of girls sneaked past us with a hidden bottle of vodka. Another group of guys ran by throwing a football and laughing. A few couples strolled around the courtyard, holding hands and sharing starstruck gazes. By my side, Molly, Audrey, and Sarah seemed content, chatting and observing the crowd.

Once more, a warm sensation spread through my chest. I was here, and this was going to be great. I just knew it.

"You're over twenty-one, right?" Audrey asked. I nodded. She turned to a guy from The Bat and whispered something in his ear. He disappeared inside the orange and black stand. She just smiled at me. Five minutes later, he came back with three plastic red cups. "Thanks," she said, taking the cups from him. She gave me one and handed the other to Sarah.

"Thanks," I said, looking inside the cup. Beer, of course. Molly pouted at us and I smiled. "Soon."

"Yeah, that's what I keep telling myself," Molly said.

For a second, I considered giving my beer to Molly and telling her to pretend it was soda. I mean, who could guess what it was with these red cups. However, that wasn't right. I didn't want to start our friendship by shoving beer at a minor.

But I didn't want it either.

The same guy walked by us, and I touched his arm.

"Oh, hello there, beautiful," he said, flashing me a big smile. "Haven't seen you around here. Are you with them?" He gestured to Audrey, Sarah, and Molly.

"She's with us, Robbie, but she's not at the sorority," Sarah said.

"What's your name?" the guy asked.

"Bia."

"Do I detect a hint of accent there?"

"Yes, I'm Brazilian." His eyes went wide, and I saw his jaw working. He would ask the many questions I always got, so I cut him off. "Listen, are there more drinks back there?" I gestured to the beer and the stand.

"Yeah, we have a full bar. Want me to get you anything?"

"No, thanks. I can get it myself." I turned to the girls and said, "Be right back."

I walked to the narrow alley between the stands. I had to tiptoe around a girl from the ATN and a guy from The Bat, who were leaning against the wall in a full make-out session. I averted my eyes, not from embarrassment, but because I wanted that too. I mean, I wouldn't kiss just any guy—that wasn't me—but I missed it. I missed flirting; I missed being held and kissed. I sighed, reminding myself that I was here now, away from my father and my brothers. What better place was there to flirt and go on a couple of dates than during college? If it was like in Brazil, this was the best place to get my heart broken a few times. After all, that was all part of life, right?

I entered through the back door and halted. Robbie wasn't kidding. They had a tall shelf filled with bottles, a mini-fridge, and three coolers in the back of the stand.

I threw the beer in a garbage can, found one of the many bottles of whiskey, poured a good dose in a red cup, grabbed a can of Coke from inside the fridge, and dumped half of it with the whiskey.

"My kind of girl."

I jumped and nearly dropped the cup. Bah, if I

had dropped it, my boots would have been ruined and I would have killed the jerk who—

I turned around, ready to yell at whomever, but shut my mouth when I found myself face-to-face with Garrett.

He sidestepped me and poured himself some whiskey. No Coke. He extended his cup to me. I just watched it. One side of his lips twitched up, and he wrapped his finger around my wrist and moved my arm until our cups bumped into each other. "Cheers." He let go of my arm and took a sip from his cup.

I cleared my throat and drank a big gulp.

In silence, we watched the guys lining up to kiss random girls through a small glass window in the center of the front door. One of them walked away from his turn wiping his mouth, and I laughed.

However, when I heard Garrett's low chuckle, I remembered I wasn't alone and shut my mouth. I hadn't been this nervous around a guy in so long. But then again, I hadn't been alone with a guy in so long.

"I like your boots," he said, breaking the ice.

I glanced at him. *Meu Deus*, the guy was tall. His hazel eyes fixed on me. All right. Wasn't I just complaining that I missed flirting?

"I like them too," I said. These weren't my favorite, but they were close. Seeing he was wearing cowboy boots, I pointed to his feet. "I like yours too."

He glanced down and shrugged. "Are you a real cowgirl, or is it for show?"

I raised an eyebrow. "Are you a real cowboy, or is it for show?"

"Do you always answer questions with more questions?"

I smiled. "Do you?"

His lopsided grin faded, and the shine behind his eyes darkened. My heart skipped a beat, and I held his stare. I wouldn't be the one to break this showdown.

"You—"

"There you are!" Jonah barged into the stand. "Oh, the Brazilian girl." Really? I suppressed a groan. "Good to see you again." He grabbed a beer from one of the coolers.

"Hey," I said, feeling like I was in the wrong place at the wrong time.

He put an arm around Garrett's shoulders. Garrett had about two inches on him. "I see you met my bro."

I frowned. "Your bro? As in big brother, little brother from the fraternity thing?"

"No. Garrett isn't in the fraternity, not anymore. He's my half-brother."

Garrett took a long swallow of his drink and looked out the window to the front.

What did one say to that? Cool? Nice? Oh? I decided on, "I gotta get back to the girls." I turned around. Without looking at them, I exited the stand and rejoined the girls. They hadn't moved, though there were two other girls with them.

I squeezed into their circle and soon learned one girl, Evelyn, had joined the sorority last night, and the other was named Jennifer and she had been with the sorority for a year.

In a matter of minutes, I had emptied my glass. I pondered going back to The Bat stand and re-filling my drink, but I wasn't sure about it. What were the odds of meeting Jonah or Garrett back there again? Probably zero. And even if they were there, what was I afraid of? It was ridiculous.

I stepped back and turned around, and ran directly into Jonah. The glass he was holding—beer—washed over my white blouse.

"Fuck," he said, his eyes wide.

Audrey, Sarah, Molly, Jennifer, and Evelyn grouped around us.

"Oh, that's going to stain," Molly said.

"I'm so sorry." Jonah took off one of his shirts

and dabbed at my chest. Audrey shot him a hard look, and he reddened. "I'm sorry."

He let go of the shirt and I took it, not that I wanted it, but it was already ruined too. "It's okay."

Behind Jonah, Garrett walked past, his attention on me. Was this such a big scene? I scanned around and found a few other people looking at us.

"Your bra is showing," Sarah whispered.

I looked down and sure enough, the white fabric was now transparent. I pressed Jonah's shirt to my chest.

"I'm sorry," Jonah repeated. "Your car, now your shirt."

"What about her car?" Audrey asked, narrowing her eyes.

Jonah ignored her and went on. "I want to pay for it. The car and the dry cleaning."

I shook my head. "It was nothing. I can take care of both myself."

"Nonsense." He glanced to where Garrett was standing by the side and nodded at him. He took my hand in his. "I'm serious. I want to make it up to you."

"Don't worry about it."

His blue eyes were all but begging. "We'll talk more about this later," Jonah said. Feeling like a bitch, I pulled my hand from his. Then he smiled, taking his time to look at each one of us. "Excuse me, ladies."

He stepped back and joined Garrett and Jeff.

Jennifer sighed, her eyes following the guys as they walked into the crowd. "He's so dreamy."

Sarah chuckled. "If you say so."

"Who?" I asked without thinking. Maybe I shouldn't stick my nose in Jennifer's business, but now it was too late.

"Garrett," Jennifer said, her voice mellow.

I frowned. "Oh." Wait. Did she like him? Did he like her back? Before I could ask her more about it, Audrey stepped into my line of sight.

"What happened with your car?" she asked, her tone flat.

I told them what happened, and how I was being lazy by not getting my car to a body shop.

"He'll bother you until you let him do what he wants," Audrey said. Her eyes hardened. "If I were you, I would get your car fixed ASAP. And your blouse."

The blouse was ruined. No dry cleaning would be able to take out the stain. As for the car, I wasn't in a hurry. It was such a small dent and I barely used my car. A few days or weeks until I took it down to a shop wouldn't make any difference.

The girls shifted in conversation—back to sororities and all the fun they had and would have —and I stepped back, wishing to go to my room so I could take a shower and change out of these clothes.

"I'll clean up," I said to no one.

But Audrey heard me. She glanced my way, a crease between her brows. "No need to hurry."

What did that mean? Without another word, I walked out of the courtyard. A great day had taken a wrong turn, and suddenly, I felt completely out of place.

5

Sunday evening was my first laundry day. Ever.

Loaded with a basketful of dirty clothes, I descended the stairs to the first floor, where the common laundry room was, feeling kind of stupid that I had never done my laundry by myself before. I mean, I knew what I had to do, what kind of wash for each type of clothing, and if the machines were older models, I should separate colors and all, but I had never done it. Being born into a family with money, we always had a maid who did it all, even here in the United States.

I wasn't spoiled though. Yes, I could buy almost anything I wanted, but I also was hard working and never minded getting my hands dirty working with horses. In fact, I liked it and wouldn't change that for all the money in the world.

I entered the laundry room on the corner of the building, and the three girls inside stopped talking. They glanced over me, their eyes appraising.

"Hi," I said, turning toward the free machines in the corner.

They nodded, but didn't really greet me.

As I loaded two washers, they resumed chatting, but their voices were lower, and when I looked over my shoulder, they were watching me.

What the hell?

I put a hand on my hip and stared at them. "Did you lose something?"

The blonde with a pink headband gasped, the short brunette with silver glasses put her hand over her mouth, and the black, pixie-haired one glared at me.

"Are we bothering you?"

"Not yet," I retorted. "Keep watching me and you might."

She humphed and flipped her hair to me. They exchanged a few words before walking out of the laundry room.

I sighed. These people were weird, as weird as the fact that they left with the machines on, filled with their clothes. If they were in Brazil, the clothes would be gone by now. Nobody left cars unlocked or anything of value inside their cars. Here, people left the windows of their cars rolled down while they were inside malls or grocery stores. Wasn't anyone afraid his or her car wouldn't be there when he or she got out?

Hannah laughed each time I had a mini crazy-attack when she did stuff like that. I would never get used to it.

I had brought my iPad down, so I could sit around here and pass the time while waiting for my load to be done, but maybe it was time to try it out. To relax and let it go. To do what an American would do. Like an experiment. If it didn't work out, if my clothes got stolen, I wouldn't be too upset. My favorite jeans and shorts were in there, but it wouldn't be the end of the world. I was sure Leo wouldn't be mad at me for buying new ones.

Which would be totally unnecessary if I didn't let them get stolen in the first place.

Shaking my head, I turned on the machines. I whirled on the heels of my pretty boots and walked to the half-closed door. I was about to step out when I heard hushed voices directly behind the door.

"She's in there?" a girl asked.

"The Brazilian girl, yes," another one answered.

"How do you know it's her?" the first girl—girl A—asked.

"Her accent," girl B said.

"Is she as pretty as they say?"

"Yes. More than I thought she would be. Tall-ish, long legs, round butt, tiny waist, long brown hair a la Victoria's Secret, and bright green eyes."

"They were blue."

"I think they were green."

"No, blue."

"All right, I get it," girl A said. "Is she like they say she is? And I don't mean her beauty ..."

"I-I don't know," girl B said. "She was pretty ballsy though, confronting us while everyone else would probably pretend nothing happened."

I smiled. Damn right. To prove to them how ballsy I was, I opened the door and walked out, strolling past the three girls who had been inside with me, and two others, who had joined them. I didn't need to look at them to know they were glaring at me.

An urge to stop, face them, and ask them what their problem was burst in me, but I held on to it. Being ballsy was one thing. Being aggressive and sounding like a bitch would get me zero friends.

I stepped onto the stairs, and once out of sight, I slowed down.

"Told you she was ballsy," girl B said.

"And beautiful," another one said.

"Whatever," girl A said. "I don't give a damn. She's Brazilian, and you know how Brazilian girls are. We're way better than her."

What the hell did that mean?

Before I could ponder, I heard their footsteps closing in on the stairs, so I rushed up two steps at a time, and ran to my room.

Sometimes I hated being Brazilian.

MY SECOND WEEK IN FORT HOWELL WENT WELL BY all accounts. I was better now. Things were going fine. Molly had stopped bitching about the sororities, and she was back to her excited self. Audrey and Sarah seemed okay with my choice too, Phoebe was great so far, and there was plenty of eye candy around. The doubts that haunted me all summer about practically starting over in school, about being among younger students, about being away from my family for the first time, about leaving Brazil—none of that bothered me anymore. Not as much as before anyway. I tried to think that the two years of vet school in Brazil hadn't been wasted. After all, I got credit for a few classes. I even got credits for foreign language with Portuguese. One less thing on my to-do list.

Jonah was still throwing his charms at me during class and out of class too. I had seen him a few times around campus with his half-brother, Garrett, and their friend, Jeff. He always stopped to say hi and smile at me. It was kind of flattering.

During the few times I was around the ATN house, I overheard conversations and learned Jonah's father owned a huge cattle ranch in the area. He was in the last year of business school and would apply to an MBA right after, so he could take over when it was time. I also learned he and Garrett shared the same father, but he preferred using his mother's last name. Garrett had gone through pre-vet school, though he took six years to finish it. He hadn't gone to vet school—yet—and the girls didn't think he would. Instead, he spent most of his time around The Bat with Jonah and Jeff.

Thankfully, Jonah didn't bother me about my car anymore. Counting that I wouldn't need to drive off campus anytime soon, I took my car to a body shop close by to be fixed. It didn't look like the greatest place, but I didn't really think any body shop did. The mechanic promised to have my car ready by Saturday. Alas, when I arrived to pick it up, he said it would take him at least another two days.

I could do this. I could follow my plan. I could make friends, enjoy life, be happy, party, be free.

Because she was in such a good mood, I let Molly convince me to go to a mixer at The Bat on Saturday night. She put on a little black dress and pumps, fancy for a fraternity party, and I opted to be me. Dark blue Lucchese boots with custom hardware—pretty, swirly lines made of metal on the boot's tip, sides, and heel—and a white shoulder dress with a flared skirt. It wasn't too long, but it certainly wasn't too short either. To match, I had put on my blue leather earrings and bracelet that I had bought to wear with the boots.

She gave me an are-you-really-going-like-that look, but I waved it away. I wouldn't change to please her, or anyone for that matter.

Molly and I walked to The Bat house together. Outside, it didn't look like much was happening, but once inside—in the big brown foyer and beside the L-staircase—I noticed the loud music vibrated through the walls, and the people milling about, some already falling or swaying with the quantity of alcohol in their veins. *Credo*, the party had barely started.

We found Audrey and Sarah in the living room. They were seated on an ottoman in the center, and other girls—all from their sorority—were around them.

"Hi, girls," Audrey said, sporting a flashy smile. "Molly, why don't you join us for a moment?"

Molly looked at me. "Sorry. Sorority stuff. Probably won't take long."

"No worries."

She stepped into the living room, and I turned to the other side. Curious, I walked around the house's first floor, admiring the beautiful architecture of the place. Besides all the Greek stuff—symbols and Greek letters everywhere, T-shirts, jerseys, paddles, trophies, and such—the house held its charm. The walls in each room had different colors, all warm and inviting. I stopped by the dining room, where a huge table for twelve took over the center of the room. However, what really caught my attention was the professional bar against an entire wall. Long counter, barstools, and lots of options. And a bartender wearing a white shirt and black vest.

I sat on the last free stool and was about to ask for a drink when Garrett halted by my side, holding two glasses. He handed me one. "I like your boots."

Smiling, I took the glass from him. It was whiskey and Coke. "I still like yours too." In fact, I liked everything he was wearing, from the faded jeans, to the black shirt, and the boots. Missed the hat, but I understood he wasn't wearing it to a party.

"I think this is the third pair I've seen you wear in a little over a week. How many do you have?"

Wait? He was paying attention to my boots? Why? Oh crap, he wasn't gay, was he? "You know those girls who are crazy about shoes and have like two hundred pairs of sandals, boots, pumps, flats, that they need a closet bigger than their bedrooms?"

He chuckled. "Not really, but I have an idea."

"Well, I have almost that many, but 95 percent of those shoes are boots."

"And you fit them all in your tiny closet in the dorms?"

I raised an eyebrow at him. "I thought you lived in this house while you were in college."

"I did, but that doesn't mean I have never been to the dorms."

I wondered how many girls he had gone to the dorms with during college. With his looks, too many. For some reason, that made me frustrated.

"I didn't bring them all," I said, my voice much lower than before.

"Hi, Brazilian girl," Jonah said, coming into my view from beside Garrett. "I'm glad you made it to our party."

"Hmm, yeah. Great party," I said.

Jonah asked the bartender for a beer then turned his charming smile to me. "How are you liking it so far?"

"It?"

"College, campus, being around us?" He winked.

"It's fine. Good."

"Is it very different from Brazil?"

"Yes."

"How?"

I told them the same thing I had told Molly, then Audrey and Sarah. That Brazil didn't have a Greek system, that there were no dorms on campuses, that there was no such thing as pre-vet, premed, or pre-law. Vet, med, and law schools were like any undergrad major, though lasted one or two years longer. I also told them about *vestibular*, a hard exam you had to take to be accepted into college. It wasn't like the SATs. Each college had its own exam, so if a student applied to three colleges, he would have to take three different exams, and for some colleges, those tests were actually a series of tests that could last for days.

"Wow, that's strict," Jonah commented. "Very interesting. What else is different there?"

Garrett took a big swallow of his glass, finishing his drink. "Excuse me," he said, stepping away from us. I watched him.

Jonah leaned on the bar counter, where Garrett had been a second ago, blocking his half-brother from my view. "I want to know more," Jonah said.

A guy wearing khaki pants, a polo shirt, and flip-flops walked past us. I concentrated on that detail and babbled on, "Okay, you want to know a few things I find odd? Everyone wears flip-flops everywhere." I gestured to the guy who was now greeting some friends. "I only wear them to go to the beach or the pool or to stay home. You'll never see me in flip-flops in class or at the mall or grocery shopping, I assure you. Another one is makeup. The girls here wear too much makeup. They are in high school and their faces are thick with makeup. I can't understand that. I rarely wear makeup."

"You're wearing it now."

I rolled my eyes. "Because this is a party. I only wear makeup at parties, or formal dinners and events. Even so, it's only a little. Other than that, maybe only lip gloss here and there. Nothing more."

"What else?"

"In Brazil, we start partying much earlier. I was fourteen and already going to clubs all night."

"Seriously?"

"Yeah, but see. Here, when kids leave their parents' place, they are so eager to try it all, they go crazy and sometimes abuse it. Since Brazilians are used to being around it at a much younger age, it isn't a big deal and we don't rush to try everything and do crazy things, you know. I mean, there are the crazy ones that *always* abuse everything, but then, there are crazy ones in any corner of the world."

"True." He gestured to my glass. "What about drinking? You were fourteen and drinking?"

"Well, I wasn't supposed to. In Brazil, you can drink when you're eighteen. When you're underage in clubs, the bouncer usually puts a plastic bracelet on your wrist, so the bartenders can't sell you alcohol, but that never stopped older friends from handing you a beer."

Now he probably thought I was an alcoholic

since my early teenage years. It was hard to explain things like this to people from another country, just as it was hard for them to make me understand American customs.

Some girls walked by, glancing at me and whispering.

Not interested in drama, I averted my gaze and gulped my whiskey.

"Easy there. You don't want to get drunk fast, do you?"

It took a lot more than a shot of whiskey to get me drunk. Shaking my head, I raised my arm and called the bartender. "Can I get another one, please?"

"What is it?" the guy asked.

"Whiskey and Coke."

He smiled. "Nice." He turned around to prepare my drink, and I looked at Jonah again.

"I'm really glad you came," Jonah said, his tone more serious.

I cocked my head to the side and looked at him. He was handsome, in a boyish kind of way. Blonds weren't my thing, but come on, Chris Hemsworth was blond, and ninety-eight percent of the female population would go for him, given the chance. Why not let this blond try to charm me?

Sure, Garrett was more my speed, but Jonah seemed way more interested in me.

Unsure about that yet, I nodded to the space around us. "Is it always this slow?"

"It's early yet, and Audrey still has all the ATN girls in the living room. Once the lionesses are released, the party picks up."

I laughed. "Lionesses?"

He shook his head. "Yeah, I tease them about it. They want to be like lions, the kings of everything, or queens in their case. I don't mind most of the time, but I hate it when they come into my house—" He pointed to the floor. "—and start messing with our rules. Speaking of rules, you probably aren't aware, but it's rare for a girl outside the Greek system to hang with a sorority. They must like you a lot."

I didn't know that. A warm feeling filled my chest. They liked me. A lot. It was never hard for me to make friends, but things had been different this last year, living in my brothers' shadows. Besides Hannah, I hadn't made any friends, and for some reason, I believed I wasn't good at it anymore. But here I was, making friends.

I smiled. "I'm honored."

"You should be. Audrey and Sarah are hard to

please. If they want you around, it means you're special." He fixed those blue eyes on me.

I stared back at him, trying to figure him out, trying to understand why my insides weren't twisting and curling when he looked at me that way. Hadn't I just established he was handsome? For flirting, that was enough.

Garrett stepped between us and put my glass on the counter with a loud thump. "There you go."

Wait. What? Why was Garrett bringing this over? I glanced at the bartender. He was busy concocting other drinks. Facing Garrett again, I opened my mouth to thank him, but he turned and walked away before I could utter a syllable.

"What was that about?"

"That's just Garrett. He's moody. Sometimes I think he must have PMS or something."

I laughed. Again, Jonah stared at me with intent. "You should smile and laugh more. It illuminates your pretty face."

I brought my glass to my lips and took a big swallow, unsure what to say.

Jonah glanced to the doorway. "Here comes the lionesses," he whispered as Audrey and Sarah walked into the dining room.

With a plastic smile, Audrey stopped beside us. If it was anyone else, that plastic smile would have thrown me off, but I was starting to believe it was normal for her.

"Bia," Audrey said. "How are you, dear?"

"Hey, Audrey. Nice mixer."

"Thanks." She put a hand on Jonah's arm. "It's great that the guys let me do what I want." She winked, and Jonah raised his eyebrow in a see-what-I-told-you way.

I bit back a laugh.

A slow song started playing and several couples started dancing.

Jonah offered me his arm. "Would you like to dance with me?"

I gaped. Hmm, I always found it odd when people slow danced anywhere outside the dance floors of clubs or balls.

Audrey lost her smile. "I don't think it's her thing."

Wait. The few times I had been around Audrey and Jonah, she was always tense. Oh, something was going on between them.

"You don't know that," he said, not looking at her. He nudged his arm toward me again. "Let's dance?" I glanced from him to her and back to him. "I don't bite. Unless you ask." He winked.

Droga.

"I'm ... I don't think it's a good idea. I'm a terrible dancer and I would only embarrass you."

He laughed. "Nonsense. Just hold on to me and I'll guide you."

"Sorry," I whispered.

He leaned closer to me. "You do realize that I'll ask again when the next slow song starts, right?"

I wasn't one to back away, but apparently, Jonah and Audrey had unresolved issues, and seeing as I was trying to make friends, I decided not to give her a reason to hate me.

I stood from the stool. "Excuse me."

Not looking at either of them, I walked out of the dining room, but not before hearing the harsh tones being exchanged between them.

Great. I was now a thorn between a couple, or whatever they were. I hoped that Audrey would notice I had done nothing, no more than talk to him, as if he were a friend, and she would be cool with it. I hoped that she wouldn't be one of those touchy girls who went crazy whenever her guy talked to another woman.

In the foyer, Molly leaned over a guy, speaking slowly and smiling in a let's-do-it way. Well, at least one of us was in a good mood and might get lucky.

What was I thinking? I wasn't here to get lucky.

I mean, if it happened, good for me, but that wasn't my focus right now.

Sipping my drink, I walked around the house again. In the kitchen, several guys grabbed beer from the fridge and food from the island, and Garrett prepared another glass of whiskey.

I noticed several of the other guys looked at me as I made my way to Garrett. He saw me too.

I showed him my empty glass. "Would you mind?"

He shook his head once and took the glass from me. He refilled half of it with whiskey, then grabbed a Coke from the fridge and filled the rest of the glass. Still silent, he handed me the glass and I smiled.

"Thanks," I said. He nodded, placing the cap back on the bottle. "Cat got your tongue?"

One corner of his lips curled up. "Something like that."

Meu Deus, he was handsome.

Sarah and Jennifer rushed into the kitchen.

"There you are." Sarah wrapped her fingers around my arm and pulled me with her. "Come. Audrey has something to show you."

I glanced at Garrett. Jennifer stood right in front of him and batted her lashes at him. It looked like it was working since he had his eyes on her. Something like disappointment made its way into my chest.

"What is it?" I asked, letting Sarah take me back to the foyer.

Audrey stood there. "Bia, I'm glad Sarah found you."

I frowned. "What is it?"

She laughed. "Relax, dear. I have a surprise for you. A good surprise." She turned to the office door and pushed me inside.

A guy was seated on of the chairs around the desk. "Hello," he said, sporting a smile.

Audrey gestured to him. "I've found someone for you."

I gaped at her. "What?"

She continued, "Mike here is handsome and rich, and he showed interest in you the moment I said you were from Brazil."

"She's beautiful," the guy said, devouring me with his eyes.

"See? He's into you, and you should totally do … your thing with him."

I placed my hands on my hips and glared at her. "Do my thing? What the hell are you talking about?"

"Oh, dear, you don't need to feign innocence with me. I know how Brazilian girls are." She stepped back and turned off the lights, making the room look eerie with only a lamp over the desk shining through. "I'll let you two be. Have fun."

She exited the room and closed the door.

The guy stood. "Come here, Brazilian girl. Let's have some fun."

What. The. Fuck.

I flipped him off and marched to the door. I threw it open and found Audrey in the hallway, whispering with Sarah.

"What's your problem?" I asked, putting my hands on my hips.

"What?" Audrey narrowed her eyes at me. "Didn't like your gift? Considering where you're from, I thought it was a nice gift."

Ignoring the attention we were starting to gather, I asked, "What's that supposed to mean?"

Audrey lowered her voice. "Come on, Bia. Girls in Brazil walk around wearing bikinis all day, or those barely there carnival clothes. Oh, and top-less at beaches."

"It's *Carnaval*, not carnival, and that damn party is five days long, not the entire year, and those clothes are called costumes. Nobody wears those things on regular days. And there's no such thing as topless beaches. That's illegal."

Audrey looked at me as if I had dumped my

glass of whiskey over her head. "Right about now, I'm glad you didn't rush, otherwise I would be expelling you from the sorority."

"What? For not being a whore?"

"Dear, this is why we wanted you in our sorority. That's why every sorority wanted you. So we would have our own bimbo to offer to the guys at The Bat. Or any other guy we wanted to impress."

Ice ran through my veins. They wanted what? "You're crazy." I walked around them, toward the door. If they were those kinds of "friends," I didn't want to spend one more second with them.

"Beatriz Fernandes," Audrey called. "Don't be a fool. You walk out that door and we won't be your friends anymore."

I glanced over my shoulder. They had never been my friends. "This is me *not* being a fool."

I flipped my hair and stepped into the foyer. I paused outside the door, taken aback from the number of students watching the hallway with wide eyes. I had no idea if they had heard everything Audrey and I had discussed, and I didn't care.

I spotted Molly with Evelyn in a corner. My roommate looked at me as if I had stabbed her in the back, and Evelyn had taken her pain. Jonah, Jeff, Garrett, and Jennifer, who still was all over

Garrett, were also there, looking more curious than anything else.

Whatever. The show was over.

I inhaled a sharp breath, raised my chin, and walked out of that house.

6

"THAT'S IT? YOU'RE NOT TALKING TO ME?"

Molly came back to our room well past midnight, tripping on her own feet, and didn't even acknowledge me. On Sunday, she slept in, but once she was up, she left the room and didn't come back until late. Monday morning, it wasn't any different. She didn't even look my way as we got ready for class.

I sighed. Whatever. I wasn't going to beg her—like she had done to me so I would join and put up with her sorority.

Having the first Monday morning class with her didn't help. Actually, we walked together but not together from our building to the class, which seemed downright ridiculous. However, once we got to class, I took my usual back seat and she went to the front. Far away from me.

Things got more complicated when I noticed several girls, and a few guys, peeking at me and whispering. *Merda*. By now, the entire campus knew about what happened Saturday night.

I met Phoebe for lunch at a sandwich place inside the student center. She was already seated at a table close to the window, looking at the menu when I got there.

"Maybe you don't want to be seen with me," I said, sitting across the table from her.

She set the menu down. "Well ...?"

"*Meu Deus*, what?"

"I heard a few things, but I would rather hear it from you."

"What did you hear?"

"That during the mixer two nights ago, you made a move on Jonah, and when he refused, you threw yourself at another guy. Then Audrey tried stopping you from making a mistake, and you exploded on her. You insulted her, advanced on her, almost hitting her."

I stared at her, my jaw hanging open.

"From your expression, I gather it wasn't exactly like that?"

"I— It was nothing like that."

She sighed in relief. "Oh good. I mean, when I first heard it this morning, I thought it couldn't be true, but then nobody shut up about it. I had to know."

"*Meu Deus*." I buried my head in my hands.

"Do you want to talk about it?"

"Not really." I lifted my head and looked at her. "But I want you to know the truth." So, I told her. About everything. The bidding, the insistence on joining, the way they treated me from the beginning, Saturday night's events, and how I walked out of there before I punched Audrey.

"I knew there was more to it than the lies they are spreading." She reached over the table and squeezed my hand. "I'm sorry."

"You believe me?"

She looked at me with an are-you-crazy expression. "Why wouldn't I?"

"Thanks for the vote of confidence, but I totally understand if you don't want to be seen with me. At least for a while. I get it."

She smiled. "Don't be silly. I don't care about what others think. I just—" She closed her mouth, her gaze fixed somewhere behind me. "What are they up to?"

I glanced behind me, to a corner table where

three guys huddled together, looking at me and scribbling something on a piece of paper.

"*Ótimo.*"

I turned back to Phoebe. "What the hell do you think they are doing?"

"I have no idea."

We watched as two more guys arrived, halted in front of the door, looked at me, smiled, then rushed to the other three guys and joined in the talking and scribbling.

"What the hell?" That was when I noticed everyone in the restaurant was looking at me. "*Merda,*" I muttered, standing. "I better leave."

"But you haven't eaten anything yet."

"I'm not hungry anymore."

I slung my tote over my shoulder and marched out of the place, keeping my head high the entire time.

***

AFTER FINDING OUT WHAT AUDREY WAS SAYING about me, my entire week was a hot mess. As Phoebe told me, the campus wasn't the largest one out there and Audrey had plenty of influence. Wherever I went, I had to deal with people staring at me, whispering, and the oddest of all? Guys hitting on me right and left. What was that all about?

By Friday afternoon, I was about to explode. Bumping into Audrey on my way to my dorm and hearing her sick laughter didn't help one bit. I ran to my room and opened my laptop, determined to find the one thing that could calm my nerves before I jumped down someone's throat and clawed his or her eyes out.

I googled what I was looking for, but there weren't many options out there.

I had to drive thirty minutes out of town to get to the closest riding ranch, which struck me as odd. I was in Colorado, for Pete's sake. Shouldn't there be ranches and farms all over? Maybe not. Seeing as I was pissed for being labeled something that had nothing to do with me, I wouldn't assume Colorado was made of only cows and horses. Although, at times, it did seem like it.

The Rocky Hill Ranch was bigger than the one my family owned in California, but not as big as the one we owned in Brazil. A large portico with the name of the ranch adorned the entrance. The fences were too white, as if they had been painted that morning and they had never seen rain or too much sun. The stable was a big green building with white framed windows and doors. While I parked in the parking lot, among other cars, beside the building, I estimated a good two dozen horses fit in the barn, if the stalls were a nice size. More, if they were smallish.

A mile or so in the distance, a white manor dotted a small hill. It looked pretty from here, and too damn big.

I stepped out of my car and inhaled. Ah, fresh air, wet grass, and a hint of manure. Probably not the best mix, but one that I knew well and felt comfortable with.

A man who reminded me too much of Jimmy from Hannah's ranch walked out of the stables. He introduced himself as Tom, the manager. He told me that Carl, a stable hand, was feeding the horses, and an instructor was out with a riding group. On weekdays, a trainer came to train a promising group for jumping and dressage.

"I don't need instruction or anything," I told him as we walked into the stable. "Just show me a trail and I'll be okay."

He seemed reluctant as he started guiding me to a horse. "Since I don't know what kind of rider you are, I'm going to give you a calm horse."

I followed him past a couple of stalls until a black horse stuck his head over the stall's door, and I halted. The horse was beautiful.

Noticing I had stopped, Tom turned around. "That's Midnight Dream, a two-year-and-seven-month-old colt."

His coat was a perfect, shiny black, his round black eyes curious, and his black mane luscious. He was probably close to seventeen hands tall with strong legs and a long neck.

"A thoroughbred?" I asked, extending my hand toward the horse with my palm turned down.

"Yes," Tom answered, watching.

The horse sniffed my hand. When he didn't pull away, I turned my hand around and stroked his chin.

"What a good boy," I whispered as if speaking to a baby. I kept eye contact with Midnight Dream and stepped closer to him, running my hand up his neck. He snorted and turned his muzzle into my arm. Tom chuckled and I squinted at him. "What?"

"He's hot blooded and doesn't like strangers. Actually, he doesn't like most of us around here." He observed the horse and me with wary eyes. "He never lets me touch him like that if I'm not armed with a dozen carrots."

"Oh, so you're a bunny," I said in a low tone, as if the horse would laugh from my stupid joke. "Do you like hopping too, or you just stand there cute and move your muzzle side to side?"

"He does," Tom said. I shifted my attention to him. "Hopping, or rather, jumping. He's being trained for show jumping. His first competition is in three months."

I scratched behind Midnight's ears. "Isn't he a bit young for that?" I knew most trainers put their horse up for racing and jumping as soon as they could hold a saddle, but it wasn't the best. My father always said that horses should be trained in equestrian sports only after they were four years old.

"That's not my call," Tom said. He beckoned me to follow him. "Come on. Let me show you your ride."

I patted Midnight's cheek, and he snorted when my hand left his coat. I smiled and waved at him before following Tom to another stall. He introduced me to Pepper, a beautiful brown mare. I petted her while he went to pick up a saddle, but then, to show him I knew what I was doing, I took the tack from him and put it on by myself.

"All right, after that and the moment with Midnight, I think I believe you know what you're doing." He exited the stable and I followed, pulling Pepper with me. "Do you see that gate?"

He pointed to an opening on the white fence to the left. "There's a trail just off it. Follow the trail, and you should be back here in about an hour or so."

Sounded good enough. I mounted Pepper and set out.

Once out on the trail, I let her take control, suspecting she knew this trail by heart, closed my eyes, and enjoyed the wind whipping my hair back.

I cleared my mind and relaxed. I forgot about college, about having to start over again, about sharing my room with a hormonal girl, about the sorority, and about the lies. I didn't care about any of it. These events didn't define me. They didn't have the power to hurt, unless I let them. And I wouldn't let them.

Like my father and my brothers, I was strong. I didn't take shit back home. I dealt with it, I fixed it, or I learned how to live with it. However, I never changed or cowered because of it.

The ranch was beautiful. There weren't many trees, but the trail passed some pretty places, including a small lake and what looked like a picnic area. At a distance, I saw one of the riding groups following its instructor around the lake. Next time, I would bring my swimsuit, just in case. If no one were around, it would be nice to take a quick dip in the lake.

Feeling freer and happier, I kicked Pepper's sides. "Let's see what you got."

She shot ahead in a fast gallop and I smiled, liking the way the wind brushed against my skin. It was a shame it couldn't carry my problems away with it.

Pepper wasn't as fast as Preta, my pretty mare. I missed her way too much. She was more than my horse; she was my friend. At least I knew Hannah and Leo were taking good care of her. Once I got more settled, I could think about bringing her here, boarding her at this ranch, and coming out every day to ride her.

The arena, the round pen, and the stable came into view, and I slowed Pepper to a steady gait.

On one side of the arena, jumping poles had been set up in a course. A girl and Midnight Dream jumped over the obstacles, but from here, it didn't look smooth. A man with a brown cowboy hat leaned against the fence, shaking his head.

The girl yelled something I couldn't hear to the horse. He snorted and kicked his front hinds up. The girl screamed, pulling tight on the reins, and the man—the trainer—ran to her, but before he could get to her and the horse, the girl stabilized

Midnight. As soon as he stopped twitching, she jumped off him and stalked out of the arena. The trainer ran after her.

Alone, Midnight Dream stalked off to the other side of the arena, where several horses circled Tom and Carl with their tack still on. Some people were in the parking lot, entering their cars and leaving. One of the riding groups must have arrived and just dropped the horses there, not caring about untacking the horses or cooling them down.

I liked the policy Hannah had adopted about a year ago: if someone wants to ride a horse, he should be responsible for everything else involved in it. She thought it was a nice way to make people connect with the animals and understand them a bit more.

Hmm, if I became a regular here, I would suggest something like that to Tom.

He was working on untacking the horses, while Carl hosed them down, and another man brought the tack inside the stables. Eyeing Midnight Dream, I dismounted close to them, and started unbuckling Pepper's saddle. If they let me, I would do it all myself. Midnight saw me and slowly approached me. He poked my back with his muzzle while I unstrapped Pepper's saddle.

"You want to play, big boy?" He poked me again, nickering. I laughed.

The trainer came out of the stables, and I froze with the saddle in my arms. Midnight Dream shot away from me, and not having seen or recognized me, the trainer chased after the horse for a couple of minutes until he finally caught his reins.

The trainer turned to bring the horse to the stables and halted, his eyes on me.

"What are you doing here?" Garrett asked. His brows knotted in a deep V.

I forced myself to move and set the saddle on the fence rail. "Riding." I kicked my foot in the air, showing off my black and white cowboy boots. "Did you think these were just for show?" I picked up a hose. "And you're a trainer here?"

Without acknowledging my question, he led the horse inside.

Whatever.

I hosed Pepper off and she nickered in delight.

A moment later, Garrett was by my side. He took the hose from me. "I'm an instructor, a trail guide, a trainer, caretaker, handyman, and everything else in between." He washed Pepper's hot coat. "I work here full time."

"Of all the places I could have chosen to ride,"

I whispered, taking a step back. Which wasn't true. There weren't that many places around.

He finished hosing Pepper, and then pulled her inside the stable. I followed, but only because I had to go through it to reach the parking lot on the other side. However, with Garrett walking right in front of me, it was hard to focus on anything else. He wore fitted blue jeans, a gray T-shirt that showed a hint of the muscles under it, his brown boots, and a hat. There was a small stain of sweat right between his shoulder blades, and I wondered if I could get close enough to sniff him. Not that I liked sweat per se, but a hot guy sweating from hard work? Add that to a great natural scent and I was done for.

I wasn't a slut like the girls from the sorority made me look like, but I wasn't a saint either. I liked boys. I liked staring at boys. I liked kissing boys. I liked … I sighed.

Garrett opened a stall and put Pepper in. He closed the door and picked up a bucket of water for her. I leaned over the door and caressed her long neck.

"Thanks for the ride, girl. I needed it."

I turned and found Garrett right behind me. He stared at me with those hazel eyes, and I wondered what was going on in his mind. He probably had heard about the lies Audrey and Sarah were spreading about me. I wouldn't be surprised if he believed them. Everyone on campus, except for Phoebe, believed them. What could I do? I seemed to have "Brazilian Slut" stamped on my forehead.

"I ... I should go." I turned to the door as the girl sauntered out of the tack room.

She flipped her long, blond hair back and looked me up and down with disinterest before shifting her gaze to Garrett. "Am I dismissed?"

"Yes, Delilah," Garrett said, walking around me to meet her.

The girl, who couldn't be older than eighteen, stopped by Midnight Dream's stall. "Goodbye, M.D." She reached her hand inside, but the horse retreated.

I frowned.

"Hey, if it isn't the Brazilian girl," Jonah's voice filled the air, and I turned toward it. He was entering the stable. "What a nice surprise."

"You have got to be kidding me," I muttered.

"What brings you to my family's ranch?"

"Your family's ranch? I didn't ..." I looked at the girl—blond girl, blue eyes. She was his sister. Which meant, she was also Garrett's half-sister. "I didn't know."

"My father owns this place, and everything

around it." He opened his arms wide. He glanced at Garrett. "Hey, bro."

Garrett nodded and left for the arena.

I frowned at Jonah. "I thought your father was in the cattle business."

"Yes, that's his main business, but we also own ranches like this one." He flashed me his usual smug grin. "So, what are you doing here?"

"I came for a ride," I said. He quirked an eyebrow and I shook my head. Frustration filled me, and it was all I could do not to punch him. Instead, I rolled my eyes and slipped past him. "Don't be a jerk. You know what I mean."

"You know," he said, making me slow down. I glanced over my shoulder, and he smiled at me. "We could go riding together. How about tomorrow?"

What the hell? I flipped him off and he laughed. Jerk.

I marched to my car, wishing I could blink my eyes and disappear from here. Seriously, I couldn't have found another ranch close by? Worse than being owned by Jonah's parents would be if the ranch was owned by Audrey's parents.

Entering my SUV, I looked past the stables and saw Garrett helping Tom and Carl with the other horses. He glanced over his shoulder, and he looked in my direction. With several yards between us, I couldn't be certain if he was looking at me, my car, the horizon, or the house atop the hill.

I chose to believe he was as intrigued by me as I was by him.

7

As much as I wanted to, I didn't go to the ranch on Saturday and Sunday. After finding out it was owned by Jonah's parents, my excitement died down a little. Wasn't I going there to escape the shit happening on campus? But bumping into Jonah at the ranch did the exact opposite.

I avoided leaving my room because of the stares and gossip. It wasn't supposed to be this way. I had come to be free, to make lots of friends, to laugh, to have fun, to go out, to flirt. And now, here I was, holed up in my room and frustrated.

Another one of my fantasies about moving out was my roommate. I thought she would be my best friend in ten seconds flat. Unfortunately, luck wasn't on my side. Molly had taken Audrey's side, and now ignored me most of the time. I was glad she barely stayed in during the weekend. Apparently, her sorority was having a big sleepover, and they were having lots of fun. Yay!

Ugh.

Lying in my bed, I pulled my laptop onto my stomach and opened Facebook. I checked over my friends in Brazil. I missed them and I missed my best friend most of all. I clicked on Leticia's page to check what she was up to. Photos of her in med school filled the screen: in classes, with her white doctor's coat, going to parties with her new classmates. She was having the time of her life, and I was too far away to be a part of it.

Next, I checked the page of my cousin, Gabriela. She was seventeen and already going to parties and having more fun than I was. I hoped Guilherme didn't access Facebook too much, or he would kill his sister the next time they met.

I closed my laptop and put it aside. Browsing Facebook to know about my friends was great for the first ten minutes. After that, nostalgia took over, and I felt sad about being too far away.

My cell phone beeped.

Hannah: *Hey, girl. How is it going? I hope you have one hell of a hangover.*

Me: Oi. *Nope, no hangover.*

Hannah: *You're in college!*

Me: *You too and I don't see you with hangovers.*

Hannah: *That's because I don't go to college parties. Your brother throws me our own private party almost every night.*

Me: *EEEEEWWWW. TMI.*

Hannah: *haha sorry. But seriously, how is it going?*

I thought about calling her and telling her all about it. After all, she was my friend and I needed a friend right now. At the same time, she was with Leo and she didn't hide anything from him. If I told her how bad and lost I was feeling, she would tell him and he would try to do something about it. He would come here and threaten them, or he would shove me inside his SUV and drag me home.

No, I didn't want that.

So I lied.

Me: *It's wonderful. It's better than I thought it would be. Love it here.*

Hannah: *That's great!*

Me: *How's Preta?*

Hannah: *I think she misses you, but Argus is right there all the time. And Minuano throws a fit when they get too honey-like. It's so hilarious! Lol*

Me: *I miss her too.*

I started typing about the ranch, and Pepper and Midnight Dream, but stopped. If I told her about it, she would want details and she would ask me why I wasn't there now, and I was unsure I would go back, so why tell her?

Instead, I kept on lying.

Me: *Gonna go out to grab dinner with my roommate now.*

Hannah: *Great. Have fun!*

Me: *Thanks.* Até depois.

Hannah: Tchau.

I hit the end button and pulled my pillow over my head.

"LET'S TALK ABOUT YOUR PROJECT FOR THE semester," the American history professor said on Monday morning. "This project alone will be 50 percent of your final grade."

He started on the details of the project—a forty-page essay to be researched and written as a small group—while I tried to ignore Jonah. He sat on my left and his right arm was on the armrest we shared, his torso leaning slightly toward me. He found out where I usually had lunch, when and where I went out for a walk to relax and exercise a bit, and the times I stopped by the library to study. Phoebe had nicknamed him The Creeper.

I couldn't say she was wrong about that.

Most of the time, Garrett was with him. I didn't get him. He wasn't in college anymore, and he told me he worked full time at the ranch. So why was he on campus? And always with Jonah?

The professor passed the sheet of paper where we had to sign our groups. Phoebe and I nodded to each other, confirming we were working on this together.

The sheet got to Jonah first. He scribbled something on the paper, and then passed it along to the student behind him.

"Hey," I called him. "Why didn't you pass it to me?"

He flashed me one of his smug grins. "Because you're already signed up."

"No, I'm not. You didn't give me the damn paper."

"Don't worry, Brazilian girl. We're doing it together."

"What? No! I'm working on the project with Phoebe."

"I figured as much and put her in our group too."

Instead of helping me, Phoebe sank in her seat

and pretended she didn't know what we were talking about.

"No. No." I stood and went after the sheet of paper, but before I could get to it, the professor took it back.

"Something wrong, Miss Fernandes?"

"Um." I slowly moved back to my seat. "Yes, well. Mr. Hudson added himself to my group without consulting my partner and me. We would like to remove him."

"Ouch," Jonah muttered.

The professor looked at the paper, then back at Jonah and me. "Well, Mr. Hudson is repeating this class. I guess he could use some help from you and Miss Erickson."

I sat and stared at Jonah. "You're repeating this class?"

He shrugged. "What? Last semester was my first semester as the president of The Bat. I had too many parties to attend, no time for studying."

I shook my head. "But he could endanger our project," I protested.

"Then I suggest you accept this challenge, Miss Fernandes." The professor set the paper on his table. "I won't accept any changes to the groups, and I expect a full report of your essay topics and how you'll approach it by next Tuesday." I opened my mouth to argue more, but he kept going. "Now, open your books to chapter eight."

I glanced at Jonah, who still held that conceited grin. "So annoying."

He shrugged. "Most girls say that before they fall at my feet."

Meu Deus, I needed a mountain of patience or I would strangle him before we even started this goddamn project.

<hr>

SINCE I HAD NOTHING BETTER TO DO, I FORCED myself to study. I was deep into a poetic English essay when my bedroom door opened with a loud creak.

"Here she is," Molly said, entering the room.

Behind her, Audrey stepped forward. Eyes narrowed, she put her hands on her hips and stared at me. "We need to talk."

I glanced over my shoulder. "What did I do now?"

She glared at me. "Why are you after my boyfriend?"

"Your boyfriend? I didn't know you had a boyfriend."

"Don't play games with me, slut."

Anger bloomed in my chest and I stood. "Okay, Audrey, I'm not in the mood for this."

"Why are you after Jonah?"

"Jonah is your boyfriend?" So that was the weird vibe I had noticed at the mixer. There really was something between them.

She pressed her lips into a thin line. "Not anymore. But we're working on getting back together."

Which meant she was working to make him take her back. Okay, now everything else made sense.

"I don't want anything to do with Jonah. He's all yours."

"Then why did you insist on working on a history project with him?"

"*Meu Deus*, woman. I didn't insist. I even argued with the professor, trying to get out of the group. I don't want to do anything with him."

She flipped her blond hair. I swear, if one more girl did that while staring me down, I would punch her fake nose and put her in her place.

"Do me a favor, stay away from him. He's mine, and if he so much as looks at you again, I'm blaming you."

"You can have him."

"You're the one throwing yourself at my boyfriend."

"I'm not! You can have all of him, only for you. I don't care. I don't want him."

"Then stop throwing yourself at him. There's only so much a guy can take from a girl offering herself so freely."

That was the thing. She was afraid that, if I were really into him, he would never say no to me, and they would never have another chance.

I shook my head. "Get out, Audrey."

"I'm not done with you, bitch," Audrey hissed.

"But I'm done with you." I pushed her out the door and closed the door in her face. For good measure, I turned the lock.

She pounded on the wood. "Bitch! We're not done! Open this damn door!"

I leaned on the door and faced open-mouthed Molly. "What? Do you want to join your friend?"

"I can't believe I liked you at first." Molly grabbed a small bag from under her bed and tossed a change of clothes and her books in there. She strolled to the door. "I'll ask to change room-mates tomorrow."

I shrugged. "Sounds good to me."

Molly opened the door, and Audrey's screams sounded louder for a second, until Molly closed the door again. I had never intended to be this bitchy with my roommate, but she started it and I wasn't going to back down.

In fact, I was tired of backing down.

I closed my eyes and channeled my anger. I let out a long breath, imagining my anger and frustration escaping with it. Not that it really worked, but I liked to believe it did.

I was tired but too agitated. I reached for my phone on my nightstand and scrolled through my contact list. Gabriela, Guilherme, Hannah, Hilary, Leo, Leticia, Molly, Pedro, Phoebe, Ri. I wanted to tell someone how I was feeling, what I was going through. How confused I felt, and how any action I took seemed like a hundred steps in the wrong direction. But nobody would understand. Besides, most of them were far away, and the ones closer to me were too busy.

Moreover, I felt weak asking for help.

Once more, I closed my eyes and breathed, clearing my mind. If I were riding, there wouldn't be *trying*. My mind would be clear already.

I dropped the phone and turned to my desk. Since I wouldn't be sleeping because of my nerves, I had better make them useful. I researched topics for the history project. The sooner we did this, the sooner I would be rid of Jonah. And Audrey.

8

A FEW GIRLS WERE GATHERED IN THE COMMON ROOM on the first level of my dorm building. There was always someone there, and Thursday evening wasn't any different. Lounging on the worn couches, reading, studying, drinking—because here it didn't need to be the weekend for students to party and drink.

As soon as I stepped through the front doors, they stopped talking and looked at me. I knew that look. They appraised me and scanned every inch of me. They thought they were superior to me, and they wouldn't be caught near me even if paid a thousand bucks.

Grande coisa.

I didn't look their way, I didn't rush my steps,

and I didn't change my expression. I wouldn't give them the satisfaction of knowing how much they bothered me.

I climbed the two flights of stairs and put my key in my dorm room. It didn't turn. What the hell? I took it out and insert it again, jiggled it a little, but it didn't work.

A sliver of light came from under the door and I heard shuffling from inside.

"Molly?" I asked. As I expected, she didn't answer. "Molly, I can't open the door. Did you leave your key on the lock?"

She would have had to leave her key twisted in the lock so I couldn't insert mine. It was on purpose. She didn't answer. As far as I knew, she had asked to change roommates yesterday, but they told her that if it were possible, it wouldn't be immediate.

I rested my head on the door. "I know you're mad at me, but please, unlock the door. You can go back to ignoring me and pretending I don't exist the next second. Please."

I heard a chair being dragged and the light went off.

"Molly!" I punched the door.

And she still ignored me.

I groaned and marched out of the building.

This time, parading in front of the girls in the common room was harder, but I made it.

Once out of the building, I stopped and took a deep breath, willing my nerves to calm down. I knew I could go to student housing and complain about this, but I wasn't ready for that. In Molly's eyes, I would look weak, and she certainly would love to tell Audrey. No, I wouldn't go running and asking for help. Not yet.

But where could I go? I pulled my phone from my pocket and checked the time. Phoebe was still in class so I couldn't go to her room, or somewhere with her. I hated going places alone these days. Which was ridiculous. I had never cared about what anyone thought before. Why did I care about it now? This was ridiculous.

I took another long breath and strolled to the coffee shop. It was crowded, as usual, but the line moved quickly and soon I had my drink in hand. A small table in a corner vacated as I walked by it. I sat down and pulled my iPad from my bag. I would spend the time browsing the internet, maybe updating Facebook or Skypeing with Leticia. She would understand and she wouldn't tell me to go back to my parents' like my brothers or Hannah would.

I hoped Molly moved that key soon.

Out of nowhere, a guy sat across the table from me. He leaned over the table, a confident smile on his lips. "Hello there. You're Bia, right? The Brazilian girl." He nodded his head, as if we were sharing a secret. I gaped at him. "Tell me, do you have a Brazilian wax under those jeans of yours?"

I blinked. "Excuse me?"

"I would love to see it."

I slapped his face.

There was a low "oooh" all around. I tried to resist it, but it was stronger than me. I looked around and saw *everyone* staring at me. Including Audrey and Sarah, the two princesses seated at the tall bar wrapping around the back wall. They giggled.

"What was that for, bitch?" the guy asked.

Shaking my head, I wrapped my arms around my stuff and stood, grabbing my half-full cappuccino. I approached Audrey and Sarah.

"Poor Butch," Audrey said, still smiling. "When we told him you were Brazilian, he was so eager to meet you."

I took the lid off the to-go cup and dumped my drink over her head.

Audrey gasped and froze, while Sarah put her hand over her mouth to hide her giggle—great friend—and the rest of the students laughed.

"You're the bitch, Audrey."

I marched away from her.

"I'll get you for this!" she yelled.

I paused at the door and gave her my best come-and-get-it smile. "I'm so afraid."

DUMPING MY DRINK OVER AUDREY'S HEAD HAD FELT good, empowering. I almost skipped out of the coffee shop and whistled on my way to my dorm. I felt more like myself than when I first arrived here.

The normal me would go out almost every weekend, drink two or three shots of whiskey, dance, laugh, gossip. The normal me would have tons of friends and maybe one or two guys that I was interested in. The normal me loved boys and missed kissing them; the normal me wouldn't miss the opportunity to make out with a hot guy. The normal me would walk around campus singing and looking like a fun girl. The normal me was the girl everyone wanted to do projects with because, besides being fun, she was also intelligent.

But I couldn't be the normal me. Not right now.

I wasn't afraid of Audrey or Sarah, or any of the girls from the sororities. I just didn't want to give them another reason to spread more lies, to stretch the ones out there. If I went out, they would say I was on the hunt. If I was seen kissing a guy, they would think I had already slept with him —and a couple of others. I knew how a bad reputation could ruin everything, and I didn't want to have a bad one attached to my name. *Bem*, a worse one.

So, when Phoebe asked me to go with her to a bar Friday evening, it hurt me to say no.

"How do I look?" Phoebe asked, whirling around in the middle of her dorm. It was like mine; however, her roommate actually seemed nice.

We had spent the last hour getting her ready. She looked fantastic in a short jean skirt, red blouse with moderate cleavage, and black sandals. I helped her flatiron her hair and put on her makeup.

"You look great. Ready to break a few hearts."

A red tint spread through her cheeks. "Only one will do."

"Kevin will agree with me."

She smiled. Finally, after two weeks of meeting almost every evening at the library, the guy had worked up the nerve to ask her out. He was going to meet her at one of the bars off-campus. She was nervous about arriving alone, hence why she wanted me to go.

She sat beside me on her bed. "I wanted to meet the real Bia. Let her out. Just for tonight."

I shook my head. "I can't. You know what would happen. I would go with you, have a few drinks, have a great time, but the next day, everyone would be talking about how I left the bar with not one, but two guys. I can't risk that."

"Well, the real Bia wouldn't care about all that shit. At least that's what you keep telling me."

"Touché." I sighed. "It's not that easy this time. I'm here for the next two years. More, if I get into vet school." Though I was starting to think it would be better if I went somewhere else. "I'm not sure I can't *not* care about what people say for so long. And I don't want to run away either. I just need to lie low for now."

"For how long?"

"I don't know. One month? One semester? The interest in me and where I am from has to die down at some point. Especially if I behave and don't give them anything to talk about."

Phoebe laughed. "Because throwing your drink over Audrey's head yesterday is lying low."

I buried my head in my hands, but a loud laugh escaped through my lips anyway. "*Meu Deus,* that felt so good. But yeah. It only made things worse. Now she's out to get me."

"As if she wasn't before."

"Right."

I walked with Phoebe to the bar. Like everything, it was just off-campus and lots of students went there practically every evening. On Fridays, they had a live band and Phoebe said Kevin knew the lead singer.

"How about you come in? I bet Kevin can introduce you to the singer. All singers are cute, right?"

I chuckled. "No, thanks. I've sworn off men for now."

"That's silly."

Well, that was my life.

I halted on the sidewalk, eyeing the bar on the other side of the street. "Here we are."

"Thanks for walking me."

"My pleasure. It was a good excuse to get out of my dorm for a little while."

"Text me when you're in your room. I'll be worried about you until you do."

"Sure."

I stayed in place until she crossed the street and entered the bar. I turned to leave as an old truck with peeling dark blue paint parked in the spot by my side.

Not thinking anything of it, I kept on walking.

"Bia."

I halted. My heart sped up a little.

Garrett walked up to me. "Hey."

I turned to him, keeping my face blank. "Hi." As usual, he had his brown boots and hat on. This time he wore dark jeans and a fitted dark green button-up shirt that brought out the green speckles in his hazel eyes.

He pointed to the bar across the street. "Aren't you going in?"

I shook my head. "I just walked Phoebe. She has a date."

"You should come."

I frowned. "I shouldn't."

He cocked his head to the side. *Meu Deus*, what I wouldn't give to know what was going on inside that pretty head.

"You haven't been at the ranch," he said. "I thought you would come back last Saturday or Sunday. I thought you liked riding."

"I love riding. It's the only good thing in my life —" I slapped my hand over my mouth and my eyes went wide. *Droga*, I said too much.

His eyes narrowed. "Audrey still giving you a bad time?"

Of course, he would have heard the rumors. "You can say that."

"One more reason to come back to the ranch and do what you like."

What was this sudden interest in me going back to the ranch? "I'll think about it."

One corner of his mouth curved up. "Good."

He tipped his hat before turning on his heels and walking across the street to the bar.

I watched his backside, taking in how edible he looked. I didn't understand him. He worked at the ranch—his father's ranch—had already graduated college, and yet was always here, especially at The Bat. He seemed to be friends with his half-brother, and he trained his half-sister for show jumping.

Garrett was a mystery—one second he was hot, the next he was cold—and I felt compelled to unravel it.

9

That bold feeling was gone Saturday morning.

I had bad dreams all night about my father telling me he was disappointed in me, about Molly throwing my stuff out the window, about Audrey spreading more lies that everyone believed, and about Garrett and Jonah laughing at me.

I tossed and turned until I finally gave up and shot from my bed at 5:30 a.m. Molly was passed out on her bed. I heard her coming in around two in the morning. Apparently, her nights were fun. Meanwhile, I stayed in and moped.

As quiet as I could, I showered, got dressed, and drove off-campus.

I stopped by a Starbucks drive-thru, got a cappuccino, a butter croissant, and then drove the thirty minutes to the ranch while eating. It wasn't 6:30 a.m. when I parked my car beside the stable, but Tom was already there.

The best part of all? It was too early, and since Garrett had partied last night, I was sure he wasn't here yet.

With a smile, I walked in the stable. Tom was filling a couple of buckets with grain.

"Morning, Tom."

Tom stopped working and looked up at me. "Morning, Miss Fernandes. Isn't it a bit early for you?"

"Not really." I picked up two of the filled buckets. "Which stalls should I put these in?" He squinted at me, probably wondering what I was doing. I chuckled. "Come on, old man. I'm used to working hard on a ranch. Let me do something, please."

He considered it for a second more, and then said, "You can put those inside Mandy's and Sugar Ray's stalls."

I glanced around, looking for the right names on the plates over the stall doors. I quickly found them and deposited the buckets inside their stalls. The horses nickered in thanks and dunked their muzzle in the buckets without a second thought. On the way back to Tom, I glanced over Midnight's stall. He was standing in the back, his head low.

I approached the door. "Hey, big boy, you seem a little sad. What happened?" His ear flicked up and he turned his face to me. His big black eyes met mine and I smiled, encouraging him. "You can tell me." Slowly, he walked to me. I extended my hand, and he buried his muzzle in my palm. "What happened, big boy?"

He snorted and poked my forearm. With a smile, I ran my hand over his chin and scratched his neck.

"I think he's tired," Tom said. "Delilah over-worked him yesterday." There was a hint of re-proach in Tom's tone.

"Has she been jumping for long?"

Tom brought over a bucket and handed it to me. "Since she was twelve, but she hasn't won many competitions." He put another bucket in the next stall, and I put the one he gave me inside Midnight's stall. "She's signed up for several com-petitions in the next couple of months. She's sev-enteen, and Mr. Hudson said that if she doesn't make it before her eighteenth birthday, she has to stop fooling around and get serious about college and working for him."

The horse didn't even look at it. Although,

when I tried to take my hand away from him, he snorted. I smiled. "Cattle business, right?" I asked.

"Right," Tom said. "As you can imagine, she doesn't want anything to do with cattle."

Hilary came to mind. She was Hannah's younger sister, also almost eighteen, and she was wary of horses. Lately, she was better in that department, but she still didn't want anything to do with her father's horse business.

"So she has been overworking Midnight because she feels pressured to win."

"Yes." Tom tsked. "Sorry, I shouldn't be telling you all this."

"It's okay. I won't tell anyone." I winked and he shook his head.

The sounds of hooves stomping rapidly on the ground approached the stalls, and I looked at the door leading to the arena.

Garrett stopped a beautiful light gray mare outside. He jumped off and entered the stables, pulling the mare with him. He paused when he saw me, his eyes wide. His lips curved slightly. "Good morning," he said, tipping his hat.

I kept on stroking Midnight's soft coat. "Morning."

What was he doing here at this hour? He was supposed to be in bed with a hangover until noon.

His gaze shifted from my eyes to my hand on Midnight. Surprise flicked in his eyes. Or was it wariness? I couldn't tell. Feeling self-conscious, I lowered my hand from the horse, but he nickered and poked my arm. Frowning, Garrett averted his gaze and guided the mare to the wash stall.

I turned to Tom. "What else can I do?"

Tom looked around. "You could take Autumn Storm for a quick exercise?"

"Sure."

Garrett was walking the mare, Felicity, to her stall when I pulled Autumn out of the stable, already tacked and ready to go.

After twenty minutes of riding with Autumn through the pasture, I brought him over to the stable through the arena. Garrett was there, standing outside. I slowed Autumn's steps and Garrett walked toward us. He grabbed Autumn's reins as I brought him to a stop.

"You came," he said.

"I did. Weren't you supposed to be in bed with a hangover?"

"I didn't drink too much, and I didn't stay up late. Nothing was interesting in that bar." He fixed his serious gaze on me, and my cheeks heated.

I didn't want to read between the lines, because I was afraid of misinterpreting what was there.

"Bummer," I muttered, stroking Autumn's mane.

"I don't understand." Garrett tilted his head to the side, watching me as I jumped off the horse. "Tom isn't nice, nor is Midnight Dream. How the hell did you get on their good side?"

I smiled. "Honestly, I don't know." He patted Autumn's neck and stared at me. This time, I held his gaze, wishing I knew what was going through his mind. Maybe I wanted to find out what was written between the lines. Boldness surged in me. "I guess it's just my charm," I teased.

His hazel eyes darkened, and I instantly regretted saying that. I averted my gaze and grabbed Autumn's reins from Garrett.

"Excuse me," I said, walking past him.

What was I thinking? He definitely knew about all the shit Audrey had been saying about me, and he probably believed it. Flirting with him would only fan the flame and make everything worse.

I took Autumn to his stall, and then looked for Tom to see what I could do next. I scanned the area, thinking there was a bunch of stuff to be done, but I didn't want to put my paws all over the place. Tom must have his way of doing things, and

I didn't want to upset him enough that he would kick me out of here.

Midnight stuck his head over the stall's door and snorted.

That stallion-wannabe looking at me that way? I smiled and went to him.

"What is it, big boy?" I scratched his ear. He shook his head, showing me he liked that. I leaned into him and embraced his neck. His heavy head rested on my shoulder, and I ran my fingers through his silky mane. He nipped at my hair, tickling me. "You're telling me you like me? Well, you're the only one in this entire state."

"Midnight is a tough guy." Garrett's voice came from the back entrance. "If you won him, I bet you can win over more people."

I turned my face, resting my cheek on Midnight's cheek, and looked at him. Garrett was walking toward us. "Have you seen Tom? I want to ask him what else I can do."

He halted beside me, crossing his arms. "Why are you helping? Don't you have anything better to do?"

"Do you have a problem with me helping? I thought you would be glad since that would mean you have less stuff to do."

Again, one corner of his lips curled up. Didn't he smile? Ever?

"Oh, believe me, I don't mind you helping. One —" He raised his index finger. "—yes, I have less stuff to do then. Two—" He raised his middle finger. "—there's something nice to look at besides my dear horses." I stopped breathing. Something nice to look at? Was he saying he thought I was pretty? But he wasn't finished. He raised his ring finger and continued, "And three, Midnight likes you. That's a great feat, and I'm wondering if that would help with his training."

"What are you saying?"

He took a halter from a hook on the wall. "I'm saying you should take him for a quick run to get him warmed up. Delilah should be here in an hour, and if he's ready, we can get right into training."

He offered the halter to me, and I felt like the kid who got candy after dinner for having cleared her plate. I suppressed a happy squeal and snatched the halter from him.

"Do you hear that, big boy? You and I are going for a ride." I planted a kiss on Midnight's forehead.

"Kissing a horse?" Garrett scrunched his nose. "That's a damn waste of a good kiss."

I spied on him from the corner of my eyes and

I found his lips curled a tiny more than usual. I didn't know why, but making him show me a full smile felt like a mission I couldn't fail.

MIDNIGHT AND I GALLOPED AROUND THE ARENA.

He was perfect. Strong, fast, confident. I felt like I was flying. I wondered how cool it would be to jump with him. Delilah was lucky to have a horse like Midnight to compete with her. Although, I still thought he was too young for it.

Garrett watched the twenty minutes I exercised Midnight, seated atop the tall white fence. I could see the wheels inside his head turning, and if he had a pad in his hands, he would be taking notes. About what, though? He knew this horse.

In the last five minutes, Tom showed up and hooked his arms atop the fence. He and Garrett exchanged a few words.

"Time's up," Garrett shouted.

I pulled the reins and slowed Midnight, steering him toward the men.

I leaned over the horse and patted his neck. "Good boy." I stopped him in front of Garrett and smiled. "He's amazing."

Garrett nodded, his face serious, and Tom looked at me with a frown.

I was about to ask them what happened when Garrett's cell phone beeped. He glanced at it and sighed.

"Delilah will be here in ten minutes," he said, jumping off the fence. "Can you cool him down, please?"

"Yeah," I said. He stalked off and I glanced at Tom. "Something wrong?"

"When isn't something wrong?" Tom answered before following Garrett inside the stables.

What the hell?

Midnight nickered, bringing my attention back to him. "All right, big boy." I slipped off him. "Let's get you cooled down for your practice."

I didn't take him inside to a wash stall since he would be out here again in a few minutes. I just tied his reins to a fence post, took off his saddle, and turned on the hose on the outside of the stable.

As soon as the cold water hit his hot coat, he advanced on me in a happy gait. I laughed and got out of his way. To let him play, I untied his reins and held them in my left hand, while I hosed him with the right one.

He nipped at my shirt, biting the edge, and pulled me closer.

I laughed. "Hey. Are you trying to get me wet too?"

He nickered and I laughed louder. He tried nipping at me again and I stepped aside, turning around to escape him, and saw Garrett leaning in the stable's doorway, watching us with his arms crossed.

That caught me by surprise, and I came to an abrupt halt, facing him. He held my stare, his expression impassive. I didn't get him. Half an hour earlier, I could swear he was flirting with me, and now he was distant and looking at me as if I had stolen something from him.

Midnight poked his muzzle on my waist, tickling me, and I laughed again. I pushed Garrett out of my mind and turned to the horse.

We played with the water for a while, and he did manage to get my legs soaked. *Droga*, I didn't have any other jeans with me. Next time, I would bring a couple of extra pants, boots, and tops.

I was about to turn off the hose when Midnight bit my shirt again and pulled me back, away from the faucet.

I laughed. "Come on, big boy. We have to get you ready."

"What's going on?"

A chill wave rushed through me. Midnight let go of me and neighed.

I turned around and found Delilah tapping her foot on the ground, her hands on her hips, and her blue eyes about to murder me.

"I asked, what's going on? What are you doing with *my* horse?"

"I was helping Garrett. He asked me to cool Midnight down before your practice." I walked to her, pulling the horse with me. He snorted, not wanting to come, but I jerked the reins with force. I offered her the reins. "Here. He's all yours."

She took the reins, still looking at me as if she was going to jump at my throat at any moment.

"Excuse me." She took a step closer, expecting me to move from her way. Oh, there was plenty of space by my sides. I jutted my chin out and didn't move.

With a huff, Delilah walked around me, keeping her eyes on mine until she couldn't turn her neck any farther.

I watched as she marched to the other side of the arena, fighting with Midnight all the way. He didn't want to go with her, but she pulled him hard and hissed at him. That was no way to treat a horse.

Garrett was going after her, but before walking on, he paused by my side and offered me a hand towel.

"You've got some balls," he said, his lips turned up.

I smiled, using the towel to dry a little of my pants. "I rather think I don't."

He chuckled low, and I swear he almost smiled. Shaking his head, he said, "Gotta make sure the princess is well attended." He tipped his hat and followed his half-sister to where the jumping poles were set up.

After yelling at the horse, Delilah mounted him and set out to practice. She seemed upset and uptight, and the horse was sensing it and hesitating before the jumps, which caused him to bump the poles, and Delilah to scream because of it. I couldn't hear them from here, but Garrett seemed to be trying to reason with her, but she looked like one bossy kid.

"They argue during practice day in, day out," Tom said from behind me. He had a saddled Pepper with him, holding her by the reins.

"It makes Midnight tense," I said.

"Garrett knows that, and I think Delilah does too, but the two of them? I know they care about each other, but they are too different; their styles are too different."

I turned and watched them for a minute, and it was clear. Delilah was harsh, wanted Midnight to do exactly what she wanted, and she didn't actually express it right or all of it. She probably wanted the horse to guess what she wanted. And Garrett was gentle with the animal. He treated Midnight as if he was a precious student, like Delilah. He was considerate and never raised his voice, not near Midnight anyway. With his clenched fists, pressed lips, hard jaw, and flared nostril, he wanted to explode, but somehow managed to keep it all in.

Points for Garrett.

"Since you want to help," Tom started, catching my attention. I faced him and he continued, "Could you take Pepper for some exercise."

Nodding, I traded Pepper's reins for the towel. "Are you ready, girl?" I asked, patting her neck.

She nickered and I took that as a yes.

Laughing, I swung over her. I clicked my tongue and she moved in a slow gait. I brought Pepper back in half an hour. Delilah was dismounting Midnight. She handed the horse to Garrett then rushed out as if the arena was on fire. She entered a sleek silver Mercedes and left before I had reached the stable.

I jumped off Pepper, right beside a lonely dandelion. I crouched and plucked it off the ground. I closed my eyes.

I wish Midnight's owner really cared about him.

I opened my eyes and blew the dandelion. The white puffs flew around Pepper and me as Garrett walked past, taking Midnight into the stable.

He watched me with curious eyes. "What's that for?"

I shrugged. "Nothing."

Midnight neighed and pulled back. Sighing, Garrett extended his reins to me. "Want to trade?"

I looked at Midnight. The horse neighed again, jerking his muzzle in my direction.

"Don't mind if I do."

We traded reins, and instantly, Midnight stopped fighting. With a smile, I walked to the horse and wrapped my arms around his neck. He lowered his head over my shoulder.

"There, there." I ran my hands on his withers. "You're okay now, big boy."

Garrett shook his head. "Seriously, did you give a love potion to this horse? I've never seen him like this and I've been by his side since I delivered him."

I laughed. "I told you, it's my charm."

He locked his gaze with mine. "Can't argue with that." Then he stalked into the stables with Pepper.

What did he mean?

I pulled Midnight into the stables and into a wash stall, right beside where Garrett was tying Pepper. We began cooling down the horses in silence. Being by his side and working with him was comfortable and almost familiar, but there were things hanging in the air that I wanted to clear.

"Is Delilah always this harsh with Midnight?" I asked in a low tone, a little concerned he would pretend he didn't hear me.

"Unfortunately, yeah." He sighed. "She's harsh like that all the time, with everyone, not just Midnight, but because they have to be in total synchrony when they're jumping and he feels how stressed and tense she normally is, he tenses up too, which makes her yell at him more."

"I noticed that." Midnight dug his wet muzzle on my side and I chuckled. A big wet splotch decorated my tank top. "Sorry for saying that, but I was glad Tom sent me out with Pepper. If I had stayed, I wasn't sure I could have watched that for long without interfering."

He nodded. "I know. I think Tom knew that too, and that's why he sent you off with Pepper."

I paused, feeling played. "Oh."

In automatic movements, I turned off the hose, reached for a sweat scrapper, and started wiping excess water off Midnight. After I was done, I took Midnight to his stall and checked the time. Almost noon. I looked around. Garrett put Pepper inside her stall, but there was no one else there.

"Um, any idea where Tom is?"

Garrett shrugged. "He could be anywhere."

"Well, I gotta go. Tell him I said thanks for letting me help."

"I think he'll be the one saying thanks. In fact, me too. Thanks for helping."

I smiled. "You're welcome." Watching him, I gave a step back, and then turned to leave.

"Wait," Garrett said. My heart skipped a beat and I faced him. "You'll be back, right?"

"Yes." If it depended on me, I wouldn't leave this place—even with the potential of running into annoying Jonah. Hopefully, he wouldn't come by too much.

Garrett showed me that cute lopsided grin. "Good."

I MADE IT BACK TO CAMPUS WITH TIME TO TAKE another shower, stop by the coffee shop at the student center so I could grab a quick bite, and then step into the library. Phoebe and Jonah were already there, with their books and notes spread around a central table.

"Hi, Brazilian girl," Jonah said, smiling, when I approached them.

I sat beside Phoebe. "I have a name."

"I was about to call you," Phoebe said. "Where were you?"

"I was ..." I was about to tell them where I had been, but for some reason, I didn't want Jonah to know I was at his father's ranch. "I was busy." I opened my books and notepad. "So, any ideas on topics?"

"I was thinking the Great Depression," Phoebe suggested.

"How about the First World War?" Jonah asked.

I frowned. "But that's not American history. I mean, not alone."

"Yeah, but we can talk about how the Americans swooped in and saved the day."

Typical. Americans and their super patriotism. Nothing wrong with that, until some people got sickly obsessed about it. I loved Brazil, but damn, I was the first one to point out all the bad things in my country without shame. Brazil had a bunch of flaws. Too many even, but I wasn't going to pretend they weren't there because I loved my country.

"Yeah, well," I started. "I suggest we make a list of possible topics, and then we can vote on them."

"I like that," Phoebe said.

Jonah shrugged, clearly dissatisfied. "Whatever."

After fifteen minutes, we had an extensive list. Each of us voted on the topics we preferred discussing, and we ended up choosing the Great Depression after all.

"That's going to be depressing," Jonah joked.

Phoebe snorted, and I shook my head. "Come on, that was funny."

I rolled my eyes. "Maybe a little."

He leaned across the table and stared at me. "Confess. It was hilarious." He reached over and rested his hand on my forearm, stroking his thumb over my skin.

Swallowing hard, I pulled my arm away. "We should make an outline of important facts from the Great Depression to present to the professor next class."

"Right," Jonah said, his tone not hiding his disappointment.

When Jonah lowered his gaze to his notebook, Phoebe widened her eyes at me. I shook my head, hoping she understood not to ask about it. Undoubtedly, she would ask about it later though.

We composed a two-page essay about the other, longer essay we were going to write as our project. Phoebe assigned topics within the Great Depression for each of us to research and write about. The idea was to put all those parts together later and go over it to make sure everything aligned. If it didn't, she said she could smooth it out. So far, this group project wasn't such a bad thing.

Phoebe's cell phone dinged, and she picked it up with a smile. "It's Kevin."

I closed my books and muttered, "Love birds."

Her cheeks flushed as she answered the call.

"Her boyfriend?" Jonah asking, putting his things away too.

"Not yet," I said.

Phoebe set down her phone. "Will you be mad if I bail on our coffee date to go to the movies with Kevin?"

"Of course not." I grinned. "Go out with your guy."

"Thanks." She embraced her books and shot up. "I'll call you later."

"You better!" I yelled as she scrambled out of the library.

A lot of shhhs followed, but I shrugged. I was happy for her. And a little jealous.

"So." Jonah leaned over the table again. "If you still want coffee, I can go with you. You know, as your date." He flashed his trademark grin.

I sighed. "Jonah, Audrey told me about you and her."

"There's nothing—"

I raised my hand, interrupting him. "I don't care. She thinks you two still have something going on. Really, it's none of my business, but I don't want any more trouble, so please, don't ask me out, don't look at me with your stupid grin, or anything else." I picked up my books. "She's already making a mess of everything because we have this project together. If she sees us together for any other reason, she'll go ape shit."

He laughed. "Wow, you do know Audrey."

"Not her exactly, but girls like her. And I really want to stay away from her."

I stood and walked away.

I was a good ten steps outside the library when Jonah caught up with me. He halted in front of me, and I had no other choice other than to stop.

"I'm gonna talk to her," he said, his blue eye shining with determination. "She has to stop this nonsense. I knew she was still hung up on me. I've seen her threatening other girls before, but I thought it was some kind of joke. Now I see she was serious. She is serious."

"Jonah—"

"No, I want to. I'm gonna talk to her. I'll make her understand there is and there will never be anything between her and me again."

I shook my head. "Jonah, you—" I wanted to tell him that even if he did talk to Audrey and she did let him go, I wasn't really into him but he interrupted me again.

"I'm going to do that right now." He stepped into me and kissed my cheek. "I'll call you later."

He ran away while I remained frozen in place for a good five minutes. What the hell just happened?

SUNDAY MORNING, I ENTERED THE STABLE WITH A tray and a large brown bag.

Tom peeked out of the tack room. "I smell coffee."

I smiled and raised the bag. "And pastries."

He whistled. "Aren't you the perfect girl? Pretty, has a way with horses, and comes armed with coffee and pastries. If I was younger, I would be all over you."

"Good morning to you too." I entered his office and dropped the tray and bag on the disorganized desk. There were paper, pens, notes, and folders everywhere. "Um, when was the last time you went through these things, Tom?"

He joined me in the office. "I don't know. I pay attention to the urgent stuff and the rest just stays there."

I tease-glared at him. "That's not a good manager."

"That's what I tell him every day," Garrett said, stepping in the office. He inhaled deeply. "Ah, coffee."

I picked a travel cup and handed it to him. "I only brought plain black, because I didn't know what you like, but inside the bag are lots of cream and sugar."

He took it from me and tipped his hat. "Just black."

Tom opened the bag and took a glazed donut from inside. "I vote you spoil us with breakfast every morning."

"Well, don't get too used to it. I'm only doing it because it's Sunday. During the week, I have classes all day."

"Bummer," Garrett said.

My cheeks warmed. "Where's Carl? I brought coffee for him too."

Garrett grabbed a cinnamon scone from the bag. "He doesn't work on the weekends."

"And you both do?"

"Sometimes, it's twenty-four-seven." Tom bit into his donut and moaned. "Are you planning on spending just the morning?"

I frowned. "I don't know. Why?"

"Just trying to decide what tasks we should put you on." He winked.

"Hey! Don't push it. I might like helping, but demand too much of me and I might not come anymore."

"Tom, take it easy on her," Garrett said. "We don't want her to leave."

"Right," Tom said. He picked up his cup and took another donut from the bag. "Well, I've got to finish cleaning saddles." He walked to the door.

"Wait," I called. He stopped in the doorway. "What should I start with?"

He shrugged. "If Garrett doesn't tell you what to do, look for me when you're done with your breakfast and I'll find something."

He left and I turned to Garrett. "What was that about?"

Garrett shrugged, taking the seat across the desk. "Beats me." He took a big bite from his scone. "These are good. I agree with Tom. You should skip classes and bring breakfast for us."

I scrunched my nose, as if the idea repulsed me, but that couldn't be farther from the truth. I loved being here. I wish I had planned on having classes only during the morning or the afternoon, so I could spend half of my day here.

"You always arrive this early?" I asked.

He glanced at the clock on the wall and I followed his gaze. It was not even eight in the morning, and he and Tom were deep into tasks when I got here.

"Yes. Though we come even earlier during the week." He sipped his coffee. "We don't leave before eight at night. Actually, I probably stay here until past ten."

"And you still manage to party. I'm impressed."

He stared at me, an amused expression on his pretty face. "I impress myself."

I squinted. "Please, you're not full of yourself too, are you?"

He tilted his head. "Who else is full of himself?"

"Your brother. Well, half-brother."

"Oh yeah, he is. I don't hold a candle to him in that aspect."

In that aspect. What aspect did he hold a candle to Jonah? Good looks? Check. Athletic body? Check. Mysterious demeanor? Check. Powerful eyes? Check. Way to make me tingle? Check. However, I doubted he was talking about any of those.

"I don't get you," I muttered.

"I don't get you either."

I smiled and he showed me that lopsided, closed-mouth grin of his. I bet he was even more handsome with a full-fledged smile. For some reason, I wanted to make him show me one. How? I didn't know.

"Well, do you want to get me?" I asked. He quirked an eyebrow at me, and heat flooded my cheeks. "You know what I mean. If you're curious about something, ask. I have nothing to hide."

He threw his empty cup in the trash can under the desk, stood, and walked around the desk, his eyes on me.

I gulped. Noticing he wasn't stopping, I stepped back. He continued coming. I took another step back. And another, and another, until my back was against a tall shelf and Garrett was right in front of me. He raised one arm, grasping the shelf behind my head, and leaned in. I inhaled deeply.

"I like the whole mystery thing," he muttered, his breath washing over my face. It smelled of coffee, cinnamon, and mint, as if he had chewing gum before I got here. And I got a sniff of his scent too. Woodsy, spicy, and just his. I took a deep breath, leaning closer to him. He stood still, but his eyes flicked to my lips.

I placed a hand on his chest, and I swear I heard a low growl coming from his throat.

A loud crash rattled the walls, and Garrett jumped away from me.

"Oh crap," Tom cursed.

Without looking at me, Garrett rushed out of the office. "Everything all right, Tom?"

"Yeah, yeah," I heard Tom saying from the stable main corridor. "Just knocked a wall down."

"What?" Garrett asked, his voice a higher pitch.

I took a couple of deep breaths to steady my racing heart and followed them to the tack room. An entire wooden panel came down, spreading pieces of wood and tack everywhere.

"How did this happen?" Garrett asked.

Tom rubbed his neck. "I may have put more hooks and hung more stuff than I should have."

Garrett shook his head. "Sometimes I think your head is going cuckoo, old man."

"You know, some cultures respect and idolize their elders."

Kneeling on the floor beside the fallen wall, Garrett snorted. "Elder. Are you living in a fantasy or sci-fi movie?"

I pressed a hand over my mouth to hide my laugh.

Tom shrugged. "Well, I'm the main character, so if I want it to be fantasy, then deal with it."

This time, I couldn't hold it in and laughed. They both stared at me.

"Are you two always like that?" I asked.

"Like what?" Tom asked.

"Like two young boys arguing about who is going to kick the ball first."

Tom humphed. "I'm fifty-seven years old, Miss Fernandes—"

"Bia."

"What?"

"Miss Fernandes is too formal. My friends call me Bia."

He smiled. "Bia. Okay. I like it." He looked around. "What was I saying?"

I heard a low chuckle from Garrett, but he had his back to me, rescuing tack from under the mess, and I couldn't see his face. I bet he almost had a full smile on. *Droga.*

"Was this wall part of the structure?" I asked.

Garrett stood with bridles and reins in his hands. "I don't think so, but we should fix it before we have a chance to find out."

I nodded.

"Someone has to feed the horses, make sure they have water, and then set up for the first riding group in about—" Tom glanced at his cell phone. "—seventy minutes."

I wanted to volunteer to help fix the wall, because I was sure that was what Garrett would be doing, but I also didn't want to push it. What happened in the office would happen again if it were meant to be. Besides, he rushed out of there so fast, he probably needed some time away from me right now. But why? Was he regretting having me cornered, saying that he liked how mysterious I was? He wished he hadn't done it? More reasons to be away from him right now.

"I can do it," I said.

"But—" Tom started.

"It's okay, Tom. I got it. If I realize time is flying and I'm behind, I'll ask for help."

He frowned for a second. "Okay, okay. You win."

I smiled and winked at him. "I always win."

11

I FED THE HORSES, MADE SURE THEY HAD PLENTY OF water, asked Tom which horses to get ready, and after he spat out the names of eight of them, I got them tacked and into the arena.

The guide, Larry, a man of about forty with sand-blond hair and a mustache, arrived five minutes before the first customer did and he didn't even say thanks for all I did.

By the time the group left, I was exhausted. I went inside, grabbed some water from the fountain inside Tom's office, and sat on the second to last step of a flight of stairs directly across from Midnight's stall. I could hear hammering and cursing coming from the tack room, but honestly, I was too tired to move a muscle, let alone stand to go see if they were all right.

Midnight stuck his head out of the stall and nickered at me. He had tried catching my attention all morning, but the most I did was pet him while I checked on his food and water.

"Hey, big boy. How is it going?" He moved his head up and down, and I smiled. "Sorry. Can't move. Give me a few minutes and I promise I'll pet you, okay?"

He nickered again and I watched him. He was so beautiful, so strong, so alive. If I were in any condition, I would be tacking him right now and taking him for a ride.

Tom came out of the tack room cursing.

"How is it going in there?" I asked.

He cursed some more and walked past me. He went into his office and came back a minute later, carrying a box of nails and a hammer. He branded it in the air. "Broke the other one."

"What?" I laughed.

He glared at me. "It's not funny." He disappeared into the tack room.

I stayed seated on the stairs for over fifteen minutes, while hammering and cursing echoed in the background. Finally, I was able to move again. Midnight nickered as soon as I stood. Smiling, I approached him and embraced him. He nipped at my hair and nuzzled my neck.

"Are you gonna make out with the horse?" Garrett asked.

I turned my face to his voice. He was under the doorframe of the tack room. "He's not my type."

Garrett raised an eyebrow. "What type is your type?"

Boldness filled me. "I like tall guys, with strong arms, who usually wear cowboy boots and hats. Oh, my kind of guy also rocks dirty jeans and a sweaty T-shirt."

The corner of his lip curled up, and he shook his head. "Too much bark, not too much bite."

I let go of Midnight, turned around, and leaned against the horse stall, staring at him while Midnight poked my back with his muzzle.

"Come closer and we'll see about that."

His eyes darkened and his jaw popped. He took a step toward me. Then Delilah entered the stable.

"What are you doing with my horse?" she asked, putting her hands on her hips.

Garrett sighed and I hung my head low, almost chuckling. That was twice that I thought something might have happened between us, but we were interrupted.

I glanced at his half-sister. "Good morning, Delilah. Come to practice?"

"Why should I answer you? I have no idea who you are."

"Delilah, her name is Bia and she's my friend," Garrett said. "Be nice, please."

"Friend?" She raised her eyebrows at me and gave me a disgusted look as if I wasn't worth a penny. "Yeah, right."

"What are you doing here?" Garrett asked.

"Came to see *my* horse," she said, walking toward me. I stepped to the side, granting her access to Midnight. He neighed and retreated to the back of the stall.

I didn't blame him for not liking her. Besides her pretty face, there was nothing there to like. The girl was too mean, and no amount of beauty compensated for that.

"How is he doing?" she asked.

"He's well," I answered.

She snapped her head to me. "I'm not talking to you."

"Delilah," Garrett hissed. "In the last two days, Bia has done more with your horse than any of us."

"I don't remember daddy hiring you," Delilah spat. "You don't work here. You have no right to spend time with my horse. I don't want you near him."

Whoa, Audrey version two, but instead of obsessing about a guy, she was obsessing about a horse.

"He responds well to her, better than to anyone else," Garrett said.

She tsked. "I don't care. He's my horse and I say who gets to deal with him, and you—" She pointed her finger at me. "—have no right to touch my horse."

My mouth hung open, ready to pounce at this spoiled brat. However, Garrett cleared his throat, and when I looked at him, he shook his head, his eyes on mine, pleading with me to leave this alone.

I swallowed the insults on the tip of my tongue and rolled them in my mind for release, but it wasn't the same. After she left, I would yell them, even if it were to the wall.

She turned to Garrett. "Make sure he exercises for half an hour today. *You* ride him."

Garrett nodded. "Yes, Delilah."

"I'll be back for practice tomorrow." She flipped her long hair at me, giving me the stink eye, and then sashayed out as if the stable corridor was a catwalk.

Garrett approached me. "Sorry about that."

I raised my finger at him, asking for a moment. When I heard the tires of her car squealing out of the parking lot, I opened my mouth and let it out. "*Filha da puta, mimada, china, invejosa, rapariga sem vergonha, piriguete, recalcada.*"

"Whoa." Garrett took a step back, pretending to be afraid of me. "What was that?"

"A lot of bad names. In Portuguese."

"You were cussing my sister in Portuguese?"

I couldn't help the smile that took over my lips. It felt good to let that all out. "Yeah, I guess I was. Sorry."

He shook his head once and that lopsided grin appeared on his mouth. *Credo,* he was handsome, and when he fixed his eyes on mine the way he was doing now, it took my breath away.

I wasn't going to force it, though. If he were supposed to kiss me, it would happen naturally. However, *Meu Deus*, I was rooting for it to happen.

I turned to Pepper's stall. "Do you think she needs some exercise?"

It took him a full minute to answer. "Um, probably, yeah."

Without another word, I got Pepper ready and took her to the trail.

PEPPER AND I RODE PAST THE LAKE. *DROGA*, I HAD forgotten my swimsuit again. It would have to happen soon, or I would have to wait until next summer.

I hadn't even survived one month away from home yet, and I was already thinking of next year. Good. That was how I was supposed to think. I wouldn't let lies stop me from doing what I wanted. And I wanted to be here. I wanted to finish pre-vet and go to vet school. I wanted to spend a lot of time at this ranch.

I took a deep breath, feeling peaceful. Even with all the bad stuff, life was good.

After forty minutes, I brought Pepper back in. We exited the trail and headed to the arena ahead of us—a new riding group was setting up with the same horses from the previous group. I hoped that the horses weren't too tired.

Among all the cars, a big black truck was parked in the parking lot beside the stable. I prayed Delilah wasn't back or worse, Jonah. I didn't want them to ruin my mood right now.

The riding group set off. Some waved at me as I neared the stable. It was odd how friendly Americans were. Everyone said hi or morning or evening to everyone, even if you had never seen them before. People in Brazil were friendly too, but only to their friends or acquaintances. We never walked around our neighborhood and said hi to anyone we found on our way.

Just outside the stable, I brought Pepper to a stop and jumped off her. I could hear Garrett and a new voice, but I couldn't make out the words. Curiosity gnawed at me but I walked away. I tied Pepper to the fence. The voices still reached me here.

"Delilah isn't happy," the man said, his tone harsh. "She said Midnight isn't collaborating. Is something wrong with that horse? He comes from a great lineage. There shouldn't be anything wrong with him."

"There isn't anything wrong with him," Garrett said, his voice strained. "He's just too young to be jumping."

"We've already discussed this. His age is not the problem. I can only think that the problem concerns you. She complained you're not training her well. Midnight must be picking up on that."

"I'm doing the best I can."

"Apparently that's not enough. I'm paying you to be the best trainer she ever had. Do you want me to hire someone else? Because I will."

"No, sir. I can do it."

"You better. She *has* to win the next competition. She *will* win the next competition. Got it?"

"Yes, sir."

I turned around and glanced past the open gate. Garrett had his hands knotted at his back, and his head slightly lowered as a man I had never seen before stood in front of him. The man was almost as tall as Garrett, with dark brown hair under a black hat. He adjusted the collar of his white T-shirt.

"This isn't a game, Garrett," the man continued. He picked a packet of cigarettes from the inside pocket of his fancy black jacket. "This ranch isn't a playground. I don't need it anymore. I don't make any money off this place. Hell, I actually put more money in to keep it running than I get back. However, I keep it because Delilah needs a place to train. If she loses the next competition, if she stops jumping all together, I have no use for this place, and I will sell it. And you know what that means for you, don't you?"

Garrett nodded, his gaze still low. "Yes, sir."

The man turned to Midnight's stall, and I returned my focus to Pepper.

"Hey, there."

I jumped and suppressed a yelp. Tom was right beside Pepper and me.

"Want to scare me to death?"

He grinned. "Not really, but I thought it would be fun. For me."

"Crazy old man," I muttered, reaching for Pepper's reins.

"That I am." He reached under Pepper and unbuckled her saddle. "So, you met Mr. Hudson. Well, not met, but now you know who the owner of this place is."

My mouth formed a little O. "That's Garrett's father."

"Yeah. And Jonah's father, and Delilah's father, and Stella's father."

"Stella?"

"Yeah, the oldest of the trio." He stared at me seriously. "She's older than Garrett too."

"Wait. If she's older than Garrett ..." I started and Tom nodded. "I thought Garrett was from a previous marriage or relationship."

"No. Mr. Hudson cheated on Mrs. Hudson with Garrett's mother."

"Oh."

It didn't make sense. Why was he here? I mean, if my father ever cheated on my mother and showed up at home with another kid, I probably wouldn't acknowledge the other kid. I would probably be mean to the other kid, without really intending to. Well, Delilah was mean to him. Nevertheless, he was still here. With the other family.

"Where's his mother?" I asked.

Tom took Pepper's saddle off. "She died when he was sixteen. He was going into foster care, but social services found his father and he took Garrett in."

"You mean they forced Mr. Hudson to take Garrett in?"

"No. I don't think they can force a parent to take in a child. Mr. Hudson could have signed away parental rights and left Garrett to the foster care system. I think he didn't want that though. Mr. Hudson might not love or care for Garrett that much, but I don't think he's cruel."

"Wow."

"Indeed."

Tom walked to the stable as Mr. Hudson exited the other side. He rushed to his big truck and drove away. I stayed outside, unsure what to do. Should I stroll inside and act normal, as if I hadn't learned a bit about Garrett and seen how harsh and rude his father was to him? And how submissive Garrett was with him—what was up with that? He had never given me the impression he took crap from others.

I checked my phone. It was almost noon; I should probably go. As much as I wanted to, I couldn't stay here all day.

To my surprise, Garrett exited the stable with the gray mare, Felicity.

"Going for a ride?" I asked, trying to sound nonchalant.

"Need to blow off some steam," he said, his expression still hard. I bit the inside of my cheek, unsure what to say to that. He stopped by my side and checked Felicity's saddle. "I would invite you to come with me, but I really need a few minutes alone."

Again, I wasn't sure what to say. "This is the second time I've seen you with her." I gestured with my chin to the mare.

That alluring half-grin spread on his lips. "She's mine."

Smiling, I reached to her and stroked her chin. "She's beautiful."

He nodded, looking at me. "She is. There are plenty of beautiful things around here lately."

My hand stilled. Taking a deep breath, I decided to play it cool. "Any new customers I haven't met yet?"

"No. Not a customer." He turned his body to me and I gulped, feeling the intensity and the heat coming from him on my skin. "Some brown-haired girl with an easy grin and too much charm."

I couldn't help but smile. "I thought you liked having me here because I do half of your tasks."

He brushed a strand of hair out of my face, grazing his fingertips on my cheek. I stopped breathing. His fingers splayed down my neck and he leaned into me. "That is an added bonus." He leaned closer.

I vaguely lifted my chin, angling myself to him as my mind spun. What was his interest in having me here if it wasn't because I helped with the chores? I wasn't dumb. I mean, he could be interested in me, but I found it impossible he didn't have a girl. He was too handsome and sexy to be alone. Well, there was Jennifer. I had seen her all over him before, though I had no idea what was going on between them. Besides, why would he want anything with me after the lies Audrey had been spreading?

Droga, that was it!

His breath teased my lips. I inhaled and stepped back.

"Is there something wrong?" he asked, his eyes shining with confusion.

"I ... I'm not sure." I frowned. "I don't think you

have the right idea about me." And kissing him this easily would add to that misconception.

I had had my fair share of kissing because the guy was cute and it had been fun, but this wasn't the time or the place. Not with all the lies. What if I kissed him and he told his friends? And his friends told everyone at The Bat? And that went to the ATN? By the time the news got there, it would have grown. They wouldn't be talking about Garrett and me kissing; they would be talking about us having sex in an empty stall. That would be ammunition for Audrey, and she would use it against me. And this time, I wouldn't even be able to defend myself, because she wouldn't be lying, not completely.

As much as I wanted to kiss him, I shouldn't. I took another step away from him.

A knot appeared between Garrett's brows. "What do you mean?"

I shook my head. "I better go." I patted Felicity's neck. "Have a nice ride."

I turned around and ran.

12

───────────

Monday was a long day. Molly ignored me, and Phoebe couldn't make it to our lunch date. I thought my mood couldn't get any crappier. Until Audrey stepped between my dorm building and me.

She took a step toward me, towering over me because she was in five-inch heels. "I thought I warned you to stay away from my boyfriend."

Seriously? "As far as I know, you don't have a boyfriend."

"Jonah came to the house last night to talk to me. I was so glad he was coming to his senses, until he opened his mouth and started talking about you. He asked me to tell you nothing is going on between us. I couldn't believe my ears."

"Audrey—"

"I didn't know how to answer him, but I think he misunderstood my shocked silence for consent. But I'm not ready. I'm not ready to give up. He's perfect for me and I'm perfect for him. I won't let you, a Brazilian slut—"

"Watch it."

"—spoil what we have. So, I'm begging you. Stay away from him. Discourage him. Make him believe you truly don't want anything with him."

"But I don't."

"Then make him see that."

"Why would I do anything for you?"

"If he believes you, if he stops this obsession with you, I'll do my best to put an end to the rumors spreading around campus."

How insolent. "The ones you started?"

She waved her hand. "That's beside the point. The fact is, I can make them go away."

"How?"

"I have influence and people believe me quite easily. I can quickly start a new rumor of how wonderful and kind you are, and how everything before that was a misunderstanding."

I wasn't sure I believed her. "What if I can't convince him to stay away from me?"

She offered me an evil grin. "Then I'll start a new rumor, much worse than before."

"Wow, Audrey, you're so nice."

"Test me."

I shook my head. "You're crazy." I walked around her.

I knew I could take this to the college dean, claiming harassment, but that would be like a child running to hide behind her mother's skirt. That would be viewed as a weakness, as me being weak, and I didn't want that. If she weren't expelled, she would use it against me.

No, I wouldn't denounce her. Not yet.

"Stay away from him!" she yelled at my back. "I'm warning you!"

Without turning around, I flipped her off and kept marching away.

"Here he comes," Phoebe whispered.

I had told her about Audrey's warning during our first class this morning. What I wanted was to send Audrey to hell, but I was trying to make a life here. I wanted to stay here and make friends. I couldn't declare war and let Audrey turn everyone against me. Besides, I wasn't interested in Jonah. I might have thought he was cute the first week, but now I thought he was cute and conceited. And I hated conceited guys.

I kept on staring at my notebook, afraid that any eye contact would encourage him. Apparently, he didn't need to be encouraged.

Jonah flopped down in the seat beside mine and leaned toward me with his charming smile. "Hi, Brazilian girl."

"I have a name," I retorted, my tone not too kind.

"I know, but calling you Brazilian girl is more fun."

Well, better than when Audrey called me Brazilian slut.

Thankfully, the professor arrived and I had an excuse to ignore the guy beside me. Not that he didn't try catching my attention during class, with smiles, whispering, and even notes.

Meu Deus, I felt like I was in high school.

When the professor dismissed us, I rushed out with Phoebe, but Jonah followed close behind. Once outside the classroom, he stepped in my way, making me halt.

"I talked to Audrey and she seemed okay about us going out."

I shook my head. "I'm sure you misinterpreted her."

"No, I'm positive. She said nothing and, when she's mad, she always throws a fit. This time, she didn't."

"Jonah, I don't—"

"There's a new Italian restaurant fifteen minutes from campus. I was thinking we could try it out tomorrow night, and consider a movie later. Wait, you like Italian food, right?"

"Jonah, this isn't a good idea."

His smile faded from his face. "Why not?"

"I ... I'm not into you. I'm not interested in you like that. You shouldn't waste your energy on me. I'm sorry."

He looked at me as if I had punched him in the stomach. "Brazilian girl, the first girl on Earth to say no to me." He shook his head. "I won't take no for an answer."

Wow, and Audrey said he wasn't conceited.

"Sorry, but no. I'm not going out with you."

"All right. You can say no now, but I like a challenge. It will be my mission to have you say yes to me before the Halloween Ball next month." His smile came back. "See you later, Brazilian girl." He winked before walking away.

I stared at Phoebe. "Um, I guess convincing him to back off didn't work."

She laughed. "You're so screwed."

I WAS HALF-EXPECTING AUDREY TO COME MARCHING with her pointy finger at my face any minute after Jonah told me he wouldn't take no that easily. Or she didn't hear about it, or she was having a long freak-out by herself, because by the next evening, I hadn't seen her on campus.

After my last afternoon class on Wednesday, I went to my room. Molly was there, getting ready for some Greek events that involve all the houses. I didn't pay attention to those anymore.

Without as much as a simple hi and bye, or even looking in my direction, she finished getting ready and left. I thought I would relax after she was gone, but the air was still thick inside our tiny room.

I missed sitting on my parents' porch and walking around the estate, inhaling the fresh air, and feeling free. The only place I could go here to feel a similar sensation was the ranch, but it was already too late for that.

On Friday, I weighed the good and the bad of

going back to the ranch. In the end, I decided to go because one, I was in need of being someplace where I felt like me, and two, who cared if Garrett had been after me, thinking I was the slut Audrey made me look like? Plus, it was a Friday night. I knew for a fact that The Bat had a mixer with the ATN, and that guaranteed a boy-less night.

I arrived at the ranch a little after five.

Tom was brushing Autumn's coat. "Where are my goodies?" he asked in a teasing tone.

"Only for breakfast."

At the sound of my voice, Midnight stuck his head out of his stall, his ears high.

Tom chuckled. "I swear, this horse is in love."

I smiled and scratched Midnight's chin, earning a nicker. "Hi, big boy." I wish I could take him for a ride, but I didn't want to cross any lines. Delilah was his owner, and if she wanted me away from him, well, I wouldn't stay away from him that much, but I wouldn't push my luck and ride him either. I turned to Tom. "Can I take Pepper out for a quick ride?"

He glanced at the clock on the wall. "The last riding group of the day is at five-thirty." That was in fifteen minutes. "If you help me put the horses away after the class, you can take Pepper out for a while."

I smiled. "Deal."

As Pepper and I set out on our path, I felt the weight of everything melting away. Here, Audrey and her lies couldn't touch me. Here, I could be me.

I closed my eyes and inhaled, enjoying the smell of fall coming from the trees and bushes. The sun was setting, disappearing behind the hill and giving everything a faint orange tint. It was so pretty here, almost as pretty as home.

Times like this one, I wondered why I bothered. Why I bothered going to school and, in this situation, enduring Audrey and Jonah. Why didn't I go home and ride all day? Or help at my parents' stable? Or Hannah's? I could do that for the rest of my life and focus on being happy.

But I knew why I was doing it. I was doing it for me. For my ego, for my pride. I needed to be someone other than the rich girl who lives in the shadow of her family. I loved horses—what would be better than to care for them on a level outside of tacking, grooming, and riding?

I was doing the right thing, even if it didn't feel like it sometimes.

The ride ended too fast, but it did wonders for my soul. I felt lighter and stronger at the same time.

Tom was in the arena, untacking the horses from the last riding group.

"Be right there," I told him. I jumped off Pepper, pulled the reins over her head, and guided her back to the stable.

I was opening her stall when Garrett jumped down the stairs. I couldn't help but stare and take him in. He looked ready to go out. Neat jeans, a black button-down shirt with folded sleeves, his usual boots, but no hat. His hair was purposefully messy, and his face was shaved clean. Shame. I would miss his five o'clock shadow.

I shook my head. What the hell was I thinking?

"Hey," he said. "Didn't expect to see you tonight."

"Yeah, I just needed to get out for a bit." *And I thought you wouldn't be here.*

I closed Pepper's stall and brought her a bucket of water, then left for the arena. I busied myself taking off the horses' saddles while Tom hosed them down.

"There you are," Tom said to an approaching Garrett. "Get in here and help out."

Garrett groaned. "I've gotta go."

"The party won't go anywhere," Tom said.

"But I'll smell like horse manure."

Tom grinned. "Some girls like that."

"Yeah, right." Garrett joined us in the arena. "Twenty minutes. Then I'm out."

"Yes, lover boy," Tom teased.

Garrett rolled his eyes. He picked a saddle from the fence and took it inside.

I tilted my head. "Tom, does he have a girlfriend?"

He raised his eyebrows at me. "Why do you ask?"

My cheeks warmed. "Well, you just called him lover boy, so I assumed ..."

Tom chuckled. "If he has a girlfriend, I don't know about it. The last time I saw him with a girl was ... two years ago? He had a girlfriend back then."

"What happened?"

"She finished school and left. He stayed."

"Oh."

"But don't worry. It's rare to see him all fancied up, so I just call him lover boy to mess with him."

The warmth in my cheeks turned into burning. "I'm not worried."

"Right," Tom whispered, eyeing the stable from the corner of his eyes.

I followed his gaze. Garrett was back. He picked up another saddle and took it inside. If the customers cleaned up after themselves, Garrett wouldn't be here with a huge frown.

"You know, Tom," I started. "My brother's girlfriend owns a ranch in Santa Barbara, and she makes the riders tack and untack their horses. Otherwise, she won't let them ride. You should demand that from riders too."

"That's an interesting idea," Tom said.

"Isn't it? I mean, they get to know a bit more about horses and their equipment, and they will probably connect with the horses. Besides, it would shorten your to-do list."

"I vote yes," Garrett said, taking one of the cooled horses' reins.

I chuckled. "Of course you would vote yes." Garrett led the horse inside, and I turned to Tom again. "You just gotta ask them to be here ten minutes before their scheduled time."

"I'll consider it," Tom said as he started hosing off the last horse. "Mind if I ask, how do you know so much about horses?"

"My family owns a horse farm in Brazil, and my brothers have played polo since they could walk."

"That's why you moved to the United States?"

I nodded. "To California. My brothers and my cousin have a big contract there."

"And you moved all the way to Colorado?"

"To go to school."

"Aren't there any schools in California?"

I almost laughed. *Meu Deus*, the curiosity of this man! "What's with the twenty questions?"

He shrugged. "A pretty girl with a sexy accent driving a fancy car, rocking the cowgirl look, and who isn't afraid of getting her hands dirty? I'm curious." He looked over his shoulder, and I followed his gaze. Garrett was still around and he seemed to be paying attention to every word. "I'm not the only one," he whispered. This time, I snorted. Yeah, right. "So, are you going to tell me? Why didn't you go to school in California?"

I glanced to the side. Garrett paid attention to the horses. "I guess I wanted to get away from my family. My brothers' career is everything, and I was just supposed to follow them around."

He nodded. "You wanted to live your own life."

"Yes."

"Sounds like a good reason." He turned the hose off. "But is it worth it? Family is everything."

I agreed with him, but my relationship with my family was becoming strained because of all I had to give up coming to the U.S. That part, I decided to keep inside.

We took the rest of the tack and the horses inside.

"I'm off," Garrett said.

"Bye," Tom said, sounding uninterested.

"You remember I have tomorrow off, right, old man?"

That made me curious. Garrett had a day off. Why? What was he going to do?

What the hell was I thinking? Of course, he could have a day off. He should have a day off; everyone should.

Tom grabbed a few empty buckets. "Yeah, yeah, I remember."

"Okay, good." Garrett's eyes met mine. "Good night."

"Have fun," I said. I felt guilty for wishing he didn't really have fun.

He nodded and walked out.

Tom filled buckets with grain. When he had two filled, I picked them up and put them inside the horses' stalls.

"Do you plan on coming tomorrow?" he asked.

"I do."

He smiled at me. "Good

13

Saturday morning, I arrived at the ranch at seven sharp with coffee and the donuts Tom liked so much.

"Girl, I'm not kidding," he said, taking the coffee from the tray and a donut from the bag. "I'm gonna get used to this." He gestured with his chin to the food in his hands. "To the treats and your help. Then when you're gone, it'll hurt like heartache."

I laughed. "So dramatic. Don't worry, Tom. Unless you kick me out, I plan on coming here for a long time."

"I should probably start paying you, then."

I shook my head. "No. I don't need money. Besides, being here makes me feel like me. I need this."

He narrowed his eyes. "You aren't you all the time?"

"Unfortunately, no."

"Want to talk about it?"

"Not really." I finished my coffee and threw the travel cup in the trash. "What can I start with?"

"Take Midnight for a run."

My eyes widened. "I can't. Delilah forbade me to ride him. I don't care about her, but I don't want Garrett to be in hot water with her, or his father."

"I know, but he isn't here, and as far as I know, she won't be here today."

I bit my lip. "Are you sure about that?"

"No, but someone has to ride him and he doesn't really like me."

He didn't need to do much convincing. I was all for riding Midnight. "Are there any riding groups scheduled for this morning?"

"Not until eleven, why?"

"Nothing." I shrugged. "I'm going to take Midnight out now, then."

Before getting Midnight ready, I raced to my car to grab my bag with my swimsuit and a towel. With no riding groups soon and with Garrett out of the picture, I could stop by the lake and swim for a couple of minutes.

"Hey, big boy," I said, approaching Midnight's stall. He nickered, watching me. I showed him the halter in my hands. "Want to go for a ride?"

He nickered again and I took that as a yes. I got him tacked and ready, and left with him. We followed the main trail down to the lake. It wasn't as warm as the previous week, but I didn't think I would freeze in the water. Well, I would soon find out.

It was as if Midnight could read my mind or sense me, because I didn't need to steer him off the trail to the lake. He simply turned toward the lake. He stopped on the bank and lowered his head to drink water.

I jumped off him and tied his reins to a low tree branch. After looking side to side to make sure there was no one around, I stepped between two thick trees shadowing the lake and quickly changed from my jeans and tank top into my dark blue bikini.

I dipped my toes in the water and shivered. "*Puta que pariu.*" It was cold, really cold. Midnight snorted, as if laughing of me. "What? Do you think you can handle it?" He nickered, tugging against his reins. "All right. I get it."

I took off Midnight's saddle, untied him from the branch, and taking a leap of faith, let go of his reins. He stomped into the lake, spouting water everywhere and soaking me. I gasped as the cold seeped into my skin.

"Oh, you." Using my hand as a scoop, I threw water at him. He snorted and stomped some more before going in deeper. I just watched. "You like to swim, big boy? Who knew?"

I dove in after him and met him in the middle of the lake. The cold wasn't too bad here, but it was probably because I was getting used to it, and the water wasn't too deep, but I had to paddle to stay above water. He poked his wet muzzle on my shoulder before crossing to the other side of the lake.

For some reason, I wasn't worried he would run away.

While playing, I told him about Preta. "I miss her," I said, floating on the water beside him. "She's a dark gray mare with a strong temper too. You would like her." He snorted, poking my waist with his wet muzzle. "I mean it. Maybe someday you'll meet her."

I swam for a couple of minutes, while Midnight played close to the shore.

I dove and swam to the bank, close to where

Midnight played. I just didn't grab his legs from underwater, because on instinct he would stomp on me, so I jumped above water a few feet from him.

He neighed and reared. I laughed and he charged me, poking his muzzle in my ribs. I fell in the water, laughing, and he pushed and shoved me.

"Having some fun, Brazilian girl?"

I froze and Midnight neighed again.

Reaching for the horse's reins, I turned and found Jonah on a brown horse at the edge of the water.

"What are you doing here?" I asked, hiding behind Midnight. The last thing I needed was Jonah ogling me.

"I came to check on Midnight for Delilah, but Tom said you had taken him for a ride, so I decided to catch up with you." He licked his lips. "I'm glad I did."

"Isn't it a little early for you?"

"I had to get up early for an international meeting my father had. He wanted me there." He tilted his head, trying to see me behind the horse. "I had no idea you were still coming here. Why didn't you tell me?"

Because I didn't want you knowing, dumbass. I

shrugged. "Didn't occur to me." I started walking to the bank, pulling Midnight with me. "You shouldn't be here."

"Hmm, why? This is my father's ranch."

"That's not what I meant." On the bank, I picked up the towel and wrapped it around myself, then tied Midnight to a tree branch. "Audrey is out for my blood, and I really don't think you should be anywhere near me."

He jumped off his horse. "I told you I talked to her. She knows there's nothing between her and me anymore."

"She didn't accept that, Jonah. She told me that herself. She asked me, not very politely, to stay away from you, and honestly, I wish you and she would stay far away from me."

His flashy grin took over his features. "You don't mean that."

"What do I have to say for you to get it? I don't want anything to do with you. I'm not gonna go out with you."

"Who's talking about going out?" He took a few steps toward me. "We could just go back into the lake, or lean against a tree here."

My jaw fell open. So, that was what he wanted with me. "What happened to the date and getting to know me part?"

"Well, I thought being polite and cute would be the best approach, but you refused that. Maybe if I'm more myself, rough and direct, you'll like it." He reached his hands to me. "I promise you won't regret it."

I slapped his hands away. "Don't! Step back, Jonah, or I'm going to scream until I burst your ears."

"You do realize nobody would hear you, right?"

Fear flooded my senses, making my blood turn to ice. He wouldn't do what I thought he would, right? "Leave me alone, Jonah. I mean it."

He sighed, losing the smile. "I'm crazy to have sex with you, but I won't force you. I'm not that kind of guy. But ..." He wrapped his fingers around my wrist and pulled me closer. His lips brushed my ear. "You'll come begging me, Brazilian girl. I'll make sure you do."

He let go of me, hopped on his horse, and trotted away.

Anguish erupted in me, and I fell back into the grass, gasping for air, tears brimming in my eyes.

Meu Deus, what just happened?

I closed Midnight's stall door and Tom entered the stable with two doggie bags.

"Lunchtime," he said, jerking his head to his office.

Smiling, I followed him in. He set the bags on the table and sat down on his chair. I took a seat across the table.

"I hope you like sandwiches." He handed me one of the bags.

I opened it and found a chicken salad sandwich and bottled orange juice. "I do."

He had a tuna sandwich and grape juice. We ate in peaceful silence for about two minutes. I tried keeping my encounter with Jonah out of my mind before I freaked out.

Thankfully, Tom distracted me with questions.

"So," he started, eyeing me over his half-eaten sandwich, "you don't like polo?"

"I do. I used to play with my brother when we were younger."

"I don't really follow polo, though I think it's a great sport. Are your brothers doing well?"

"You could say that."

"How well?"

"My twin is ranked first in the world. My other brothers, Ricardo and Pedro, are ranked tenth and seventeenth respectively, and my cousin, Gui, is twelfth."

"Whoa, that's ... they're famous."

I nodded. "Yes, but being famous in the polo world doesn't mean stepping out of the house and having paparazzi on your tail." Unless one of them was involved with drugs, or stopping another famous polo player from killing a woman. But I wouldn't mention that.

"That's good. I mean, being famous but not that kind of famous."

"I guess it is."

"How about you? Is Colorado turning out to be everything you expected?"

"No." My voice didn't disguise how miserable I was.

"I thought you were after freedom. You should be free and happy right now."

If only it were that easy. "I wish."

"What happened?"

When I thought about answering that, I felt childish. My problems felt childish. Why didn't I just stand up and faced them headfirst? It wasn't as if I was going to die. Maybe my reputation would, and my pride, but those were already sinking fast.

"It's just ... each time I go through an obstacle,

there are more fences in my way, you know. The course never ends."

He nodded, his expression serious. "It never will. There will always be challenges and problems you'll have to face."

"I was hoping I could take a breather between problems, but they keep coming at me, escalating." And making me change into someone I didn't really like, someone weak and submissive.

"Want to talk about your problems? Specifically?"

I shook my head. "Tell me about you instead. How did you become a cowboy?"

He laughed. "I'm not a cowboy, not anymore. Garrett has the title of the ranch's cowboy right now."

I stilled. I wanted to take advantage of the fact that Tom had mentioned Garrett, and ask more about him, but I was concerned about what that would look like.

To my surprise, Tom continued on his own. "Garrett wasn't always into horses, you know. When he first arrived here, he had never seen a horse up close. It took him a while to get used to horses, but once he let them in, he was taken."

"Mr. Hudson sounds very ..." I grasped for a word.

Tom filled in for me. "Harsh? Cold?"

"I wasn't going to say that."

He nodded. "But Mr. Hudson is harsh and cold, especially with Garrett."

"I bet it was hard for all of them, when Garrett came to live here."

"It was. Mrs. Hudson was mean to him, and Stella too. Jonah seemed glad. I guess having another guy close to his age meant he would have a buddy, and in the beginning, they were buddies. Now they are friends, but not very good ones."

"What do you mean? They seem like great friends."

"Believe me. It's not all that it seems."

Odd. They were always together around campus. I would have said they were still buddies, but Tom knew more about that than anyone, I guessed.

"I heard Garrett was pre-vet for his undergrad but didn't go to vet school."

"Yes, he graduated last year, almost sixteen months ago. It took him a while to finish since he had to take fewer classes."

I frowned. "Why?"

"Because he had to work full time to pay for his tuition."

"Mr. Hudson didn't pay for it?" I asked. Tom

shook his head. "But I bet he pays for Jonah's."

Tom snorted. "He does. And he paid for Stella too, and I know he will pay for Delilah's."

"That's unfair."

"I know."

"Why is he still here? I mean, when he turned eighteen, wasn't he considered an adult and he could leave?"

Tom paused, looking at me with a wary expression. "He has his reasons."

"Won't you tell me?"

"I think I already gossiped too much about his life. If you want to know more, you should ask him."

"I won't ask him."

"Well, then you won't find out more."

"Maybe I will. Can you tell me where he lives?"

He cocked an eyebrow. "Planning on visiting him?"

"Yeah, right." I slapped his arm across the table. "It's just I see him around here a lot, and I was wondering if he lives here."

"If you're asking if he lives at the mansion, no. He has never even set foot inside."

"No." I pointed my finger up. "I mean here. I saw him coming down from upstairs."

"Oh. We have a spare room upstairs, but we

only use it when someone has to stay when a mare is about to deliver. No, Garrett doesn't live here. He has his own place, and that's all I can tell you about it."

I pressed my lips closed, but the question jumped out anyway. "Why?"

"Because where he lives is connected to your previous question, why he's still here. Again, if you want to know those details, you gotta ask him." He stood, put the waste in the garbage, and halted by my side. "Let's get back to work."

For the next couple of hours, I helped Tom all over the ranch. Around four, I stopped to rest a little. Although, I rested while humming a country song and brushing Midnight's coat. My mind was on Garrett, of course, and everything I had learned about him.

Poor guy. It must not have been easy living with his father's family and being pushed aside.

Tom stopped in the main aisle and narrowed his eyes at me. "I don't get you."

"It isn't the first time I've heard that."

"The few things I have heard about Brazil involve soccer, samba, and women. I guess there's more to it than that."

"Much more."

"You're not much different than us. I mean, I

thought Brazilians would be different from Americans. Besides your accent, sometimes I forget you're not from here."

"We're different, but I guess that when living here, a person starts to change. I guess that happens to any foreigner in any country."

"How different is it?"

"Too many things to actually list, but like here, each state has its own traditions and culture. People have different accents and manners. I'm from the south, and we are one of the proudest states in Brazil. We always say our men are the manliest and fearless, and our women are the prettiest and most intelligent." I shrugged. "Normal state rivalry."

"I can definitely attest to the beauty of one woman from the south of Brazil." Tom winked.

I shook my head. "Careful, old man. I'm going to think you're a creep."

He laughed before walking in the tack room. Talking about my country made me miss it. An idea bloomed in my mind and excitement bubbled inside me.

I kissed Midnight's muzzle. "I hope they like it."

I LOOKED AT THE SPEEDOMETER, CAREFUL NOT TO GO over the speed limit too much. Excitement filled me and it was hard. I wanted to sink my foot on the pedal and get to the ranch right this instant.

I parked my SUV beside Tom's old truck at 6:56 a.m. I hopped out of my car, and skipping, I grabbed the basket from the passenger seat and entered the stable.

"Someone is in a good mood," Tom said from his office.

I joined him inside. "I am."

He jerked his chin to my arms. "What's in the basket?"

"Brazilian things."

His brows arched up. "Like what?"

I placed the basket on his desk and pulled the plaid towel from over it. "Like food."

The sweet smell from the basket spread almost instantly, and Tom practically moaned. I pushed some of the towering paper aside and began spreading everything on his desk. The sound of tires rolling on the stones outside brought butter-flies to my stomach. I didn't know why I was wor-ried about what Garrett would think of all this, but I was. I kept organizing our banquet while hearing his approaching footsteps.

Garrett halted by the door and inhaled. "Is this heaven?"

His gaze went to the goodies on Tom's desk before settling on me. He wore his worn hat, a light blue and white plaid shirt, faded jeans, and his brown boots. His hair looked like it hadn't seen a comb this morning, and he hadn't shaved in a couple of days. *Meu Deus*, he was something. Something that made my heart beat faster, something that brought lust with full force into my veins.

I cleared my throat and broke the stare. "Close." I waved him in. "Yesterday—"

"You were here yesterday?" He took two large steps and stood by my side.

"All day," Tom said.

I thought Garrett would comment on that, but when he shut his mouth, I continued, "Yesterday, Tom asked me a few things about Brazil, so I thought about showing you both a few things instead." I pointed to a bowl with bread rolls. "These are called *cacetinho*. Wait, that's only in my state. In other states, it's called *cervejinha*." I pointed to the next thing. "This is *goiabada*. It's made from a fruit. You guys call it guava, I think. It's sweet and we like to eat it with cheese. Next—" I pointed to another bread-like roll. "—is *Pão de Queijo*, or cheese bread." I pointed to the next plate. "These are called *sonho*. It's Portuguese for dream. They are made with a fried sweet dough and filled with, in this case, *doce de leite*." I picked a closed jar of *doce de leite*. "It has the same consistency as peanut butter, I guess."

"What's that?" Tom pointed to the thermos beside the basket.

"That's hot water for the *chimarrão*."

"Chima-what now?" Tom asked, wrinkling his nose.

I chuckled, reaching for the *cuia* inside the basket. "This is called *cuia*. We fill it with this herb." I grabbed a packet from inside the basket. I opened the packet and filled half of the *cuia* with the green herb under curious surveillance. I tilted the *cuia* to the side, covering its opening with my hand. Carefully, I took my hand off, leaving the *cuia* slanted, placed the *bomba*, which was like a metal straw, and filled it with hot water. "Now, we leave it to soak a little, because the herb will absorb half of the water." I dropped the *cuia* on the desk. "The ones I bought came with a flat base, otherwise I would need a stand for it."

"And then what?" Garrett asked.

"You drink it."

"Is it legal?" Tom asked, examining the herb.

I chuckled. "Yes. It's an herb, like a tea herb, though this one is bitter, not sweet."

"Bitter tea?" Tom asked.

The water was already gone, so I filled it up and drank the first one. Then I filled it again and offered it to them. "Who is going to try it?" They looked at each other. "*Meu Deus*, you two are babies. Just try it."

Garrett took it from me. "I just drink it through here?"

"That's called *bomba*, and yes, you drink it through there."

He shook his head once and took a long sip. His nose wrinkled and he pulled back. "Oh, God, this is bitter."

I laughed. "Nobody likes it the first time they drink it. Nor the second. But it gets better. And I guess it's a matter of getting used to it. My parents always drank it twice a day. Growing up, I started drinking it with them. Nowadays, I barely drink it, but I miss it."

"Interesting," Tom said.

Garrett finished it and passed the *cuia*. "I don't want any more."

I filled the cuia with more water and offered it to Tom.

He raised his hand in defense. "No, ma'am, I'll wait until the next time."

"I'll hold you to that," I said. "Now, the songs." I let go of the *chimarrão*. I pulled a small speaker from the basket, plugged it into the wall, and connected my iPhone to it. "The songs you're about to hear are from the south of Brazil." I picked a magazine from the basket. "And these are the typical clothes we use while performing these dances." I opened the magazine and showed them a gaucho with *bombacha*—a type of pants—a shirt, thick belt, boots, hat, and scarf. Beside the gaucho was a *prenda* in a dress with a full skirt and lots of frills and laces. Her hair was tied with a bow or flower. Tom and Garrett repeated the words *gaucho* and *prenda* several times, testing them out. It was almost funny. "Depending on which town you visit, you may see people wearing this kind of clothes on a regular basis. Especially men." I approached Garrett and held his hands. "Ready?"

His brows shot to his forehead. "For?"

I smiled. "Dancing."

"Um, I don't know this dance."

"I'm gonna teach you." I put his right hand on my waist and my right hand in his left hand. "Hit play, Tom."

He did and the rhythm reverberated through the walls.

Tom tapped his foot to the beat of the song. "It's nice. I like it."

"It's two steps to your left, one to your right. Meanwhile, we circle the dance floor."

"What dance floor?" he teased.

I rolled my eyes. "Just do it." I tugged his arm and we started moving. In the first few steps, he was too slow and tried to pick it up on the last second. He looked down at our feet, too worried about space, rhythm, feet, and all that. "Hey, Garrett." I squeezed his hand, and he finally looked at me. I slid his hand from my waist to my back, making his body touch mine. "Relax."

His eyes on mine, he nodded and then took a deep breath. After ten seconds, he was visibly better and didn't feel too tense.

He gave me a half-grin. "This isn't too bad." Becoming bolder, he took me for a wider spin on our fake dance floor. "So, people listen to this kind of music down there?"

"Only in the south and it's not many. I only listen to it on Sunday mornings, when my father likes to put it on and sit on the porch with his *chimarrão* before breakfast. And on special occasions like balls and such."

"But everyone knows how to dance?"

"In the south, most do. It's like samba. Every Brazilian girl knows how to samba, even if she's not a fan of it."

"You aren't a fan of it?"

I shook my head. "Not really."

He tilted his head. "Sometimes I wonder if we'll ever stop learning new things about you."

I smiled. "Possibly never."

Garrett spun me under his arm, then held me close and tipped me back. He angled his torso to me, putting his face inches from mine. His hazel eyes sparkled and my breath caught. "That's kinda exciting," he whispered. He pulled me up, keeping his head close to my neck. I heard a sharp inhale. Was he sniffing me? "I like your perfume."

"Thanks," I whispered, stunned.

Tom cleared his throat. "So, how about we actually eat all this food?"

Tom's words broke the spell. I stepped back, away from Garrett's arms. He watched me with a knot between his brows. *Meu Deus*, what wouldn't I give to know what was going on his mind right now.

Taking a deep breath, I forced my attention to Tom. "Yeah, sure."

14

MIDTERMS WERE HARDER THAN I THOUGHT THEY would be. Maybe it was because my mind was so scattered, or that I didn't study as much as I should. I had always been a good student, but I guess being away from college for over a year had made me lazy.

I had six exams and two massive papers due between Monday and Friday; I felt like I didn't have a breather. I also didn't get a breather from all the crazy guys hitting on me. Seriously, what was up with that? If I were paranoid, I would think it was Audrey's doing. She was paying them to come bother me. However, that would be too insane.

By the time Saturday morning came, I was more than eager to get to Rock Hill.

As usual, I took breakfast to Tom and Garrett. They teased me it wasn't the Brazilian stuff; they wanted more. I promised I would buy more soon. Or, if they found me a range, I could cook for them.

After lunch, I sat behind Tom's desk and sorted through his papers. This morning I had asked him if he would like to have all the paperwork organized. When he said yes, I told him I didn't mind organizing the mess for him if he didn't mind me seeing the paperwork—some of them were bound to have the price of things Mr. Hudson wouldn't be too happy with strangers get a glimpse of.

"I trust you," Tom said.

An hour later, I had the paperwork organized in stacks separating them by subject. The next step was to organize them by dates—the ones that were from a long time ago and could go into the file cabinet, the new ones that needed to stay within reach, and the future ones, which needed action. In addition, several things needed to be entered into the computer system, and some payments were past due. I was sure money wasn't the problem here, only disorganization.

I estimated that I would be working here twenty-four-seven for the next three weeks.

I was separating the overdue bills so I could

show them to Tom later when my phone rang. I fished it from inside my jeans pocket and glanced at the screen before answering.

"Hi, Leo," I said, smiling.

"Hi, *irmãzinha*."

I shook my head. I was born two minutes after him, but still he insisted on calling me his little sister. "What are you up to?"

"Nothing much. Practicing, going to tournaments, winning."

"Spending quality time with me," Hannah shouted into the speaker.

I chuckled. "Of course."

"How are you?" he asked.

Once upon a time, I would have been painfully honest with him. Things had changed. Time passed. We grew up, and I moved away. As much as I would love to share all my problems with him, he was too far away to comfort me. Not to mention, he would want to hop on the first flight here to fix everything. I couldn't let him do that.

"I—"

"You hesitated," he said. "What's wrong?"

"There's nothing wrong."

"Of course there is. You're always bubbly and talkative, and you say whatever is on your mind.

You're not doing that, which means there's something wrong."

"There's nothing wrong, Leo."

He paused. "Okay. If you say so. I'll find out soon enough."

"What do you mean?"

"Montenegro has a fundraiser game in Denver in three weeks. I've been trying to arrange it since you left, you know, to go visit you, but I didn't want to tell you before it was happening. And well, it's happening."

I smiled. "That's great."

"You'll come see us, right?"

"I don't know. With Dad there, I'm not sure I should."

"You will let a misunderstanding with Dad stop you from seeing me?"

"Is Mom coming?"

"No."

"Hannah?"

"No. It's just the guys."

I let out a long breath. "Without Mom or Hannah, there won't be a buffer."

"All right. Who are you and what have you done with my feisty and big-mouthed sister?"

I laughed. "I guess moving out can change a

person." That and everything else said person had to go through.

"Wow, I thought I would never see the day. I will miss the old Bia."

I missed her already. "Okay, back to the game. Just for one day?"

"We'll arrive in the morning, play at two in the afternoon, and take the flight back at eight."

"You guys are crazy."

"As long as you come to see me, I'm happy being crazy."

Garrett walked into the office holding some papers.

"All right, I'll come see you," I said.

He stopped with the papers in his hands and stared at me. A crease settled between his brows.

"*Ótimo*," Leo said.

"See you there."

"*Eu te amo.*"

For some reason, I answered in English. "I love you too." Garrett's brows shot up. I ended the call and turned to him. "Those papers are for me?"

"Um, yeah." He handed me them. I thought he would rush out. But he stayed, looking at me. "So, was that your boyfriend?"

I laughed. "I don't have a boyfriend. That was my twin brother. He just told me he's playing a fundraiser game around here in three weeks and asked me to come see him."

"Oh."

Was it relief in his eyes?

I cleared my throat. "Can I help you?"

He cocked his head. "In about an hour, I'm going to take Felicity on the main trail. She needs the exercise. I was wondering if you want to come too. With Pepper. You know, Pepper needs exercising too."

I smiled. "I would like that."

That cute lopsided grin tugged on his lips. "Great."

***

"Did you buy her, or was she born here too?" I asked, pointing at his light gray mare. With the stables behind us, we steered the horses around the arena, toward the main trail.

As if knowing I was talking about her, Felicity nickered. Garrett leaned over her and patted her neck. "I bought her when she was three months old."

Jealous, Pepper shook her head and I patted her too. "How old is she now?"

"Seven."

So, he bought her when he was eighteen. "What's up with her name?"

"What do you mean?"

"Hmm, it's kinda girlie for a guy to name his filly Felicity."

He looked at the pasture. "My mother loved horses. She never took me riding, but she talked about horses frequently. Once she said one of her dreams was to own a beautiful gray mare. She said she would name her Felicity."

"Oh."

"So, when I got involved with horses and learned to love them on my own, I searched for Felicity."

I smiled. "That's sweet."

He nodded. "How about you? Do you have any horses of your own?"

"Yes. Her name is Preta."

He frowned. "Preta?"

"It means black in Portuguese, but the word is also used as a sweet nickname, like calling someone sweetheart or darling. Some people call their loved ones preta."

"That's odd."

I tried seeing it from his point of view. I guess it would be odd for any non-Brazilian. "I guess it is."

"Where's Preta now?"

"At Hannah's ranch. She's my twin brother's girlfriend."

"Wait. Did you buy her here in the U.S.?"

"No, I brought her from Brazil."

His eyes went wide. "Wow."

"My family owns a farm in Brazil. We have polo teams and breed polo horses."

"Right. Your family is big on the polo scene."

"Yeah. Well, my brothers' and cousin's horses are all from our farms. We brought them with us."

"That's quite the move."

I nodded. "They want to stay so they had to bring everything."

"And the farm in Brazil?"

"I'm not sure what my father's plans are for that. He'll probably try to keep it running from here, I guess."

"That won't be easy."

"Nope."

We fell silent and I looked around. The path was narrower here and the trees formed a brief but beautiful canopy. A gentle breeze ruffled the trees and the leaves bled colors as they changed from summer to late fall.

"How are you liking Colorado so far?" he asked, breaking the silence. I grimaced, unsure how to answer. I couldn't be honest with him, could I?

"It's not bad."

"It has been only two months since classes started. You'll learn to love this place with time." He sounded so sure, but I wasn't. "Do you miss Brazil?"

"I miss the rest of my family, I miss my friends, I miss my family's ranch, I miss the food, but I don't miss much more. It's a great country, a beautiful country with so much to give and so much to offer, but it's messed up. The government is messed up. Even though I think the United States has its flaws, I find it's easier to live here."

"Even with all the rumors going around campus?" he asked and I tensed. "Sorry. I shouldn't have mentioned that. It was out before I could stop and think about it."

"It's okay, I guess."

"I see how the rumors affect you."

"Do you believe them? The rumors, I mean?" For some reason, his opinion mattered to me.

He averted his eyes. "I don't know."

"Tell me what you've heard."

"I'm not sure you want to hear."

"Please, I want to hear."

He sighed. "I heard about that first mixer, that

you tried giving a lap dance to one of the actives at The Bat, and when Audrey tried to stop you from acting like that, you argued with her. Then, I heard you are—were—after Jonah. You followed him; you threw yourself at him."

My mouth hung open. "You still believe that?"

He shook his head. "I'm starting to believe it's the other way around. Jonah is after you, and Audrey is spinning lies about you as a way to get back at you. Crazy girl."

I blew out a long breath. "That's exactly what's happening. The first time Jonah came on to me, I didn't know Audrey and he had been an item, and she freaked out. That's when she spread the lap dancing lie." I shuddered. "*Meu Deus*, how I hate her." One corner of his lips curled up. "What?"

"It's cute when you say words in Portuguese."

Heat spread over my cheeks. "I can't shut it off."

"I know and I don't mind." He tilted his head, locking his eyes on mine. "I'm sorry Audrey is making your experience here such a terrible thing."

"I hope that if I stay quiet it'll die down eventually. Even if it happens again next semester, it has to die down."

"I'm glad you don't have something going on with Jonah."

My breath caught. "Why?"

"He's my brother and he's on my side most of the time, but he can be a jerk, especially to girls. He was a jerk to Audrey, but she keeps coming back. I think she actually likes it, or he was too good in bed and she can't get over it."

I shuddered, not wanting to imagine Jonah in bed. "Thanks for putting the picture in my head. Yuck." A low chuckle came from him, and I looked at him again, hoping to see a full smile. Nope. Just his regular closed-mouth, lopsided grin. "How about you?" I asked. "You guys seem like you get along well."

"Sorta. Not always. We used to be closer when we were younger. Now we're too different."

Strange. I refrained from asking why. Why didn't he get along with his half-brother? What happened between them that set them apart? Instead, I asked something else. "You lived at The Bat and have a pre-vet degree. Aren't you going to apply for vet school?"

He shrugged. "Unfortunately, not everyone is cut out for greatness."

"What do you mean?"

"It's complicated," he muttered. I wanted to ask

him to explain, but I sensed his tension and decided it was better not to push my luck. "Tell me something about Brazil, something that is different from here," he asked, continuing the conversation.

I launched in a long speech about schools. Most schools in Brazil weren't divided by grade—elementary, middle, and high school. In Brazil, you could stay in the same school from pre-school to high school. Your parents enrolled you in the one they thought was best, or the ones they could afford—public schools were rare and not the best. There was no school district. You didn't have to go to a certain school because of where you lived. If your parents wanted to drive an hour to take you to school, they could.

I also told him that teenagers only got their driver's licenses at eighteen. We could also drink at eighteen, and we could vote at sixteen—and voting was obligatory. There was no way around it.

I told him girls in Brazil were becoming too direct and out there for my taste, but still not at the point of being sluts or whores like everyone thought they were. Of course, there were exceptions—like in any place.

"The country of beer, *Carnaval*, soccer, and

beautiful women," he said. "That's what we always hear when someone mentions Brazil."

"I hate beer so I can't tell you about that."

He nodded. "Whiskey girl."

"Exactly. I don't really like *Carnaval* that much. People can get crazy. They drink too much. It's as if *Carnaval* is an excuse to be a drunk asshole for five days. As for soccer, I don't watch too many games, especially since we moved here, but we have our teams and we're kind of fanatics when it comes to them. Unfortunately, once again, some people go to extremes. There were several bad fights after the fans left the stadiums, which is a shame."

"That kind of people exist everywhere."

Exactly. I thought the same about the lies Audrey spread about me. She was basing them on the fact I was Brazilian. She was applying a stereotype to me. She couldn't be more wrong.

"As for beautiful women, you just need to take a look at Victoria's Secret models. I think most of them are Brazilian."

He stared at me, his face serious. "I have proof of that right here."

My cheeks flamed and I averted my eyes. What was wrong with me? I had never felt or acted coy. I guess Audrey's lies were getting to me. I was too worried about making everything worse that I was denying being me. Even here, at the ranch, where I promised myself I would be me and only me.

"Sorry, I didn't mean to put you out there."

"I know," I whispered.

I wanted to tell him I wasn't this shy, that I didn't overthink everything I did. Not the real me. That me was hiding somewhere and I couldn't bring her out even when I wanted to. I missed being loud and carefree and happy. I hoped Audrey and her lies didn't shoo my real self away for good.

The real me would have answered him with something witty, and then, if or when we stopped the horses, she would make a move. She wouldn't have kissed him, but she would let him know in a subtle way that he could if he wanted to. I inhaled a deep breath and tried finding her. She was too well hidden, or she really had run away.

The lake appeared on our right.

"Come on," Garrett said, steering Felicity's reins toward the lake.

Pepper and I followed them. Close to the lake, he jumped off his mare and tied her reins on a tree branch. Garrett brushed his hand under Felicity's chin and gave her a kiss. She nickered, clearly happy he was giving her attention. At that moment, I was jealous of a horse.

"Weren't you teasing me for kissing a horse the other day?" I asked. He showed me the lopsided grin and shrugged. I tied Pepper alongside Felicity, and then turned to him, a little wary. "What are you doing?"

I hoped he didn't plan on taking off his clothes and jumping in the lake. Well, not that that was a bad idea, really, but I had had one bad experience with this lake already. I didn't need to repeat it.

He extended his hand to me. "Come with me."

A little flutter spread through my chest, and I took his hand. He guided me through a few low rocks, then a large tree with branches that extended over the lake.

He circled the tree, until he was before low branches that formed steps.

"Wow, is it natural?" I asked.

"Yup." Garrett started climbing it, without letting go of my hand.

When we reached the last step, he let go of my hand and hugged the trunk. He scooted around the tree, until he was on the other side, stepping on one of the thick branches that hung above the water. He leaned around the tree and offered me his hand again.

"Come on."

I took his hand and he helped me to the other side. Then, he sat down and scooted until he was in the middle of the branch, several feet over the water, and enclosed under a dome of the tree crown.

He looked at me. "Aren't you coming?"

"What if the branch breaks with our weight?"

He chuckled. "Then we fall into the water. Are you afraid of getting wet?"

"I'm not made of sugar." I had heard Hannah say that before and it stuck with me.

His eyes shone. "Some would argue with that." What did he mean? What was up with him and these innuendos? "Are you coming or not?"

I shook that line of thought from my mind and scooted along the branch until I was beside him. From here, the water seemed too far below. I looked around, amazed by how secretive and magical this place felt.

"This is amazing," I whispered.

"Isn't it? I come here sometimes when I want to get away."

I looked at him. He was sharing his secret hideout with me. Why would he do that?

"I like it here," I whispered.

"Me too."

We stayed quiet for a few moments. I closed my eyes and took a deep breath. I imagined all the bad things—Audrey and the lies; Jonah and his sudden arrogance and directness; Delilah and her snob self; Molly and the way she kept ignoring me; my problems with my father; and the fact that I not only had to start over, but had to do pre-vet before going to vet school—leaving me when I exhaled. I repeated the process one more time.

I wasn't sure if it was the place, the company, the determination, or a mix of it all, but when I opened my eyes, I felt a little lighter.

"What are you thinking about?" Garrett asked, breaking a branch half the width of my pinkie from the tree.

"Nothing. And everything."

He broke a tiny piece off the branch and threw it in the water. "Care to elaborate?"

"I'm just tired of it all. I thought it would be easier to belong, but it's exactly the opposite. It's hard to get up in the morning knowing I have to walk around campus with people looking at me, whispering and spreading lies. I have to be careful with every word I say, with every look I give, with everything I do."

He threw another piece of the thin branch into

the water. "Sometimes I feel like I don't belong either."

"What do you mean?"

"Isn't it obvious? Mrs. Hudson hates my guts, and I can't even argue with her there. In her place, I would hate my guts too."

"But it wasn't your fault," I said. Then I slapped my hand over my mouth. He tilted his head to me; his eyes narrowed. "Sorry. Tom told me a tiny bit about you."

I thought he would be mad about it, but if he was, he disguised it well. "It wasn't my fault, but I'm a constant reminder of her husband's betrayal." He sighed. "My father is ashamed of me, and I believe Jonah puts up with me because he pities me. Thank goodness, Stella moved away after she got married, because that one was actually the worst. And Delilah has her days."

"I witnessed you two bickering a little, but I haven't seen one of those days yet."

"No, you haven't. Be thankful for that. She's her mother's daughter. When the woman is in a bad mood—worse than usual I mean—Delilah can be quite the bitch."

Once more, I wanted to ask more about it, but thought it was better if he told me on his own. I didn't know why, but I wanted him to trust me, to *want* to tell me everything.

The branch creaked and I froze. "*Meu Deus.*"

Garrett chuckled. "Maybe it's time for us to go back."

I scooted closer to the tree's trunk before I ended up in the water. "I'm going."

15

I ENDED UP SLEEPING IN SUNDAY, WHICH WAS actually a nice change. Even nicer when I noticed Molly had already left the room. The whole moving roommates thing wasn't going well. I knew she was still bothering the housing department about it almost daily. I guess nobody wanted to change to the Brazilian slut room. Whatever.

At my own pace, I browsed through my notebooks, making sure I was up to date with homework and other projects, and then put a quick lunch together.

It was just past one in the afternoon when I arrived at the ranch, carrying a tray with to-go coffee cups.

Tom stepped out from Autumn's stall with a shovel. "What, no pastries?"

I smiled. "Be thankful I brought coffee."

"Well, thank you." He grabbed a cup and entered Midnight's empty stall.

"Where's Midnight?"

He jerked his chin to the back gate. "At the arena with Garrett."

I dumped the tray in a trash can and walked out, holding the remaining two coffee cups.

Garrett was indeed at the arena, with his arms raised and shushing an agitated Midnight. I took a second to appreciate the beauty of the scene before me. The black horse ran side to side, snorting every few stomps, but his coat gleamed under the sun and his muscles rippled with each movement. Just beautiful.

And just as beautiful was the man trying to calm him down. Garrett, in his usual worn jeans and cowboy boots and hat, was the epitome of coolness. He didn't look bothered at all by the fact that Midnight, a thousand-pound monster, was stomping around him.

I halted along the fence as Midnight saw me. The horse nickered and trotted to me.

Garrett followed him and offered me a half-smile. "Coffee, good. I need it."

When I extended the cup to Garrett, Midnight snorted and trotted away.

"What happened?"

Garrett took a sip from his coffee before answering. "Delilah just left, and let's say she lost it a bit during practice."

"Oh no."

"Yeah. She yelled at him and he reared on her. It wasn't pretty."

I turned my gaze to him. "Now you're trying to calm him down."

He nodded. "Emphasis on trying. We have been here for almost thirty minutes, and I don't think he'll calm down any time soon."

I looked at Midnight. Poor horse. He snorted, flinched, and trotted back and forth as if a ghost was following him, tugging on his tail and wailing in his ear.

"Can I try?" I asked.

Garrett waved his hand to the center of the arena. "Be my guest." Before I handed him my cup, he wrapped his fingers around my wrist. His eyes fixed on mine. "Be careful." His voice was low and grave.

I nodded. He released me and took my cup from me.

As I walked toward Midnight, I could still feel

Garrett's touch, his warm skin on mine. A shiver ran down my spine. Shaking my head, I pushed those thoughts from my mind. I had to focus on Midnight. I wasn't afraid, but a bothered horse could be dangerous and I didn't want to take any chances.

Midnight saw me approaching, and he gaited to the other side.

"Hey, big boy. Why are you running from me? Didn't you just come to me a few moments ago?"

He snorted and continued moving away from me.

I never had to break a horse or train a crazed one like Hannah and Leo had done, but I knew a thing or two about horses. Granted, not all of them behaved the same.

In the center of the arena, I found a dandelion beside me. Smiling, I picked it up and closed my eyes.

I wish ... what did I wish for? What did I want most right now? For Audrey to stop bothering me; for the students to forget what Audrey was saying about me; for Molly to move out since that was what she wanted; for having more time with Phoebe; for good grades; for Delilah to go to hell and stop harassing her beautiful horse; for Midnight to stop jumping since he was still a baby; for

Garrett to find his place and be happy; and for the rumors Audrey spread about me to evaporate so I could actually allow myself to think I could go for Garrett—as if he would have me—and not care what repercussion that would have.

I sighed.

I wish for things to get better.

I blew on the dandelion and opened my eyes to see the white fluffs floating away. Behind them, I saw Midnight standing about eight feet from me.

I smiled. "Hey, big boy." He nickered, but didn't move. I took that as an opportunity. Slowly, I approached him. "I know you didn't have the best day. I'm sorry. How about we forget about that and start over? Let's pretend it's early morning. I just got here and took you out to play. How about that?" He snorted and took a step closer to me. I tried to contain the smile on my face to become a loud giggle. "What if I throw in a nice brush time and maybe some tickles?" We were less than four feet apart now. Carefully, I extended my hand, showing him what my intention was. He watched my hand with alert eyes. "Not good enough. Hmm, what if I add a massage to that package?"

Tom walked out of the stable door and shouted, "Garrett!"

Just like that, Midnight snorted and galloped away. I turned to Tom with murderous eyes.

"Damn it, Tom," Garrett said.

Tom raised his arms. "Sorry. I had no idea you were working on Midnight."

"I know," I said, watching as Midnight galloped along the fence.

Garrett turned to Tom. "What is it?"

"I need some help here," Tom said.

Garrett looked at me then back at Tom. "I would rather stay here in case Midnight goes crazy on Bia."

Tom nodded. "Okay. But I'll need your help soon, then."

"Duly noted," Garrett said.

"Sorry again, Bia," Tom said, retreating into the stable.

I looked at Garrett. "You don't need to stay here. I think I can do this without a babysitter."

His hazel eyes were serious. "I know, but I will feel better about it."

I tilted my head, wondering what he meant exactly. Feel better if Midnight went crazy and I needed another pair of hands to hold him down, or feel better in case Midnight advanced on me and I got hurt? Well, I didn't want to dwell too much on it, otherwise, I would think of impossible answers.

Sighing, I sat on the grass.

"What are you doing?" Garrett asked, taking a step toward me.

I stretched my hand, my palm turned to him. "Stay there. I'm gonna try something."

His brows knotted in what looked like concern. "I don't like it."

"Just trust me," I said.

He retreated to the fence, but the frown stayed on his handsome face.

I almost smiled. Was he really worried about me? My heart fluttered. That was too cute.

Midnight snorted, catching my attention, and I focused on him again.

I stayed there, sitting on the grass, quiet and almost immobile, waiting. Each one of his steps toward me dragged on for centuries. When he finally was within reach, I lifted my hand but didn't touch him. He sniffed my fingers and then poked my palm with his wet muzzle.

Smiling, I ran my hand under his chin. He took a final step and touched his muzzle on my shoulder.

"Hi, big boy. Are you better now?" He nickered and nipped at my hair. Still smiling, I stood and put my arms around his neck. "I have an idea. You're probably cooled down by now, but how about we play with the hose like that other day? That was fun, right?"

I grabbed his reins and pulled him with me toward the stable's back gate.

Garrett was still by the fence. He had a half-grin on. "Incredible."

I was feeling proud of myself too, though I hadn't done anything special. It had been all Midnight. For some reason, he liked me. And I liked him.

"I'm just glad he calmed down."

Garrett fell into step with me. "So, I heard about that deal you tried making with him. Brush, tickles, and massage. Are you still offering that?"

I turned to him and a blow hit my chest. He had this teasing shine in his eyes and a goofy half-smile. I slapped his arm and he chuckled.

"No, that's just for cute horses."

He lost the smile and tried pouting. "Damn."

Damn me. I could bite those lips.

WEDNESDAY WAS HALLOWEEN, MY SECOND ONE IN the United States. Last year though, we had dinner at Hannah's, and since she lived on a ranch, no kids knocked on her door.

I couldn't help but smile while I walked across campus. Everything was decorated, and 90 percent of the students and professors were dressed up for the occasion. It was odd.

During the day, I counted sixteen guys—one Prince Charming, one Round Table Knight, one Egyptian warrior, one Luke Skywalker, one magician, one Indiana Jones, one soccer player, two zombies, three vampires, and four I had no idea what or who they were supposed to be—who came on to me and asked me to accompany them to the big Halloween Ball tonight.

Right, because I was going.

I wanted to go, but not with them. Of course, how could I? If sixteen guys hit on me during the day, how many would do it during the ball? Besides, I knew Audrey and Jonah would be there, since this was one event hosted by the Greek houses. I really didn't want to bump into them there and cause another scandal that surely would be the spark for Audrey to spread more lies.

I sipped my coffee, low in a corner booth at the coffee shop, when a few ATN girls sat at a close table. They hadn't seen me yet, and hoping not to be found out, I turned my face away and pulled my scarf over my hair.

"Audrey said that." I recognized the voice. It was Evelyn, one of the new pledges.

"Yeah," another girl said. "She was specific about it."

"What else did she say?" a third girl asked.

"That the Brazilian slut is out to get all of our guys," girl B said.

What the hell? They were talking about me. I didn't want to hear them talking about me. However, there was no way I could get out of the booth without them seeing me.

I pulled the edge of the scarf over half of my face and glanced at them.

"The Brazilian slut can't possibly bag all of them," Evelyn said.

"She's going to try," a girl with red hair said.

A blond girl got something from her purse, looked at it, and then shoved it inside again. "She would have to sleep with half a dozen every day to accomplish such thing."

"According to Audrey, that's normal for her," Red said.

What? They couldn't believe that. That was impossible. Who would sleep with six different guys every day? Even one different guy each night? Who even wanted that? *Credo*.

And why the hell was I hiding? I had nothing to hide. They could say whatever they wanted about me. I had my sacred place to go to cope with whatever they tried to say or do. I pulled down the scarf and sat straight.

"Worse than her throwing herself at our guys is how they are after her," Evelyn said. "Joana's boyfriend and Kimberly's boyfriend broke up with them. They have been after the Brazilian slut ever since."

"I know," Red said. "It makes me sick to see them all hitting on her day after day."

"Wait." Blondie stopped, searching her purse as Evelyn reached to the side to fix something on her sandal. She saw me, and her eyes went wide. "Isn't that strange? Audrey says she'll sleep with all the guys, and the guys are coming after her, but we haven't heard about the b—"

Evelyn slapped Blondie's hand. "Shhh."

"What?" Blondie snapped.

Evelyn jerked her head toward me. The others turned to my table, and her eyes matched Evelyn's.

Without taking my eyes from them, I stood and walked to their table. "Glad to see how much you girls care about me that you can't stop talking about me."

Mimicking them, I flipped my hair and walked out of the coffee shop. I rushed to my dorm building, afraid that if Audrey or any other ATN girl appeared before me, I could do some real damage.

I was about to enter my building, to retreat into my room for the day and pretend I didn't know about the ball when a girl stepped in my way. She wore a huge red wig, a lacy mask, and a fancy dress.

"Excuse me," I said.

She laughed. "It's me. Phoebe."

I stared at her. Now that she said it, I could see the traces of her face, but if she hadn't mentioned it, I would have never known. "*Meu Deus*, you're unrecognizable."

She took off her mask. "Precisely my point."

"What?"

She gestured to the large bag in her hand. "I've got something for you right here."

I TWIRLED BEFORE THE MIRROR HANGING FROM THE wall in Phoebe's dorm room, not believing my eyes.

"Told you it would work," she said in a proud tone from behind me. Her reflection stared back at me from the mirror. With her hands on her hips, Phoebe admired her work.

It totally did. With a blond wig, a black mask, and a fancy dress like hers, nobody would know it was me, unless I told them, let my accent slip, or took off my mask.

"You're a genius!"

She smiled. "I know."

"Kevin doesn't know about it, right? I mean, you didn't tell him I'll be in a costume like yours?"

"No. I told him you were staying in."

"Good. It's not that I don't trust him, but you know, the less risk ..."

"I know. Don't worry. I won't tell."

"Thanks."

She squealed. "I can't believe we will be able to dance and drink and laugh together. Hmm, we should come up with a fake name for you, and how I met you, in case Kevin asks who you are."

"Oh, good thinking. I'm just some random girl from one of your classes. How about you call me Liz?"

"Simple. I like it. Now, Liz—" She offered her arm to me. "—are you ready to go to a ball?"

I took her arm. "Totally."

16

I WAS HALF EXPECTING THE BALL TO BE IN A GYM, since that was where high school proms were—I watched too many American movies. I was glad to be wrong.

Phoebe and I entered the administration building and followed the crowd to the ballroom on the first floor. Big, double doors opened to a large room with a tall ceiling, fancy chandeliers, and hardwood floors. Black, purple, and orange streamers hung from the ceiling, reaching the tables—also with black, orange, or purple cloth—bordering the dance floor, forming a cozy canopy enveloping the disco ball. Across the room, the band—in ghost or skeleton costumes—played a popular song on the stage.

The place was quickly filling up and I was amazed, watching everyone wearing costumes. Witches, fairies, devils, angels, princesses, doctors, naughty nurses, pirates, Disney and Pixar characters, and everything in between. If we were in Brazil, most people would wear normal clothes.

"Let's grab some punch," Phoebe said, tugging my arm to a long table to the left. People milled around it, grabbing finger food and drinks.

There was spiked punch, for those older than twenty-one, and regular punch. University employees stood close to it, carding when they felt necessary. Of course, Phoebe and I were carded, and Phoebe had to go for the non-alcoholic version. We would remedy that soon.

"Thank you," I said, taking the plastic goblet from the man who served me. I waited until Phoebe had hers and extended my goblet to her. "To having a good time."

She smiled. "To having a great time."

I took a sip of the drink, savoring how it began sweet, and then turned into a slight burning, one that begged to be repeated.

I hadn't drunk alcohol since that party at The Bat—when all this mess started. I hadn't been out, danced, or had a good time since before that. I sighed in delight. It had been too long and I missed this.

Phoebe took my hand. "Let's dance."

She dragged me to the dance floor as the band began playing "Gotta Be Somebody" by Nickelback. We moved to the beat, doing our best not to spill our precious drinks. The ground thrummed under me, and I felt the rhythm in my veins. Bah, I really had missed this.

When the song changed, I realized her man was missing. "Where's Kevin?"

"He had a late class. He'll text me when he gets here." She waved her cell phone at me. The time she had with me, she would spend watching her phone, and then he would arrive and they would be all over each other, and I would be alone.

I wasn't mad at her. I probably would have done the same if I had a man of my own. That was why jealousy made its way into my chest. Because I wanted a man of my own.

No, no. No time for pity parties now. This was my only night out in God only knew how long, and I wouldn't mope around.

My eyes wandered around the crowd. I didn't recognize anyone. However, that didn't mean much since, one, I had not met a lot of people here, and two, they all wore crazy costumes and makeup, making it difficult to recognize them.

After three songs with empty glasses, I leaned close to Phoebe and yelled over the music, "Going to get a refill."

Nodding, she handed me her glass, and I weaved to the table/bar. The place had noticeably more people now than twenty minutes ago. Would they limit the number of people entering? The ballroom was huge, but I doubted it could host one-eighth of the student body living on campus.

There were three older men handling each punch bowl now. I stopped at the end of the line and waited my turn. With nothing to do, I swayed to the music and looked around.

I regretted it the moment I saw a flock of the ATN girls entering the ballroom wearing matching pink schoolgirl outfits with the sorority logo on the left side of the shirt. Audrey and Sarah led them, and I couldn't help but gawk at their costumes. The baby pink shirt was tied in a knot under their breast, most of the buttons undone, and the plaid skirt barely covered their butts. They had on hooker heels and high baby pink socks, ponytails, and too much makeup. Everything about them screamed DO ME!

And they called me slut.

Shaking my head, I started turning away, but The Bat caught my attention. They entered the ballroom right behind the ATN and they were all —wait for it—dressed as bats. Black pants, black T-shirts, a cape that was supposed to pass as wings, pointy ears, and fake fangs. So original. I hoped they didn't wear this every year, but I had a feeling they did. Like a signature thing.

However, one guy among them was in a different costume, though I knew it wasn't a costume at all. Beside bat Jonah, Garrett strolled in wearing jeans, a plaid T-shirt, a thick belt, cowboy hat, and boots—with spurs.

I ducked behind the guy next in line, but then remembered he wouldn't recognize me unless I spoke to him. And I wasn't going to speak to him. Letting out a long breath, I relaxed. Ten seconds later, it was my turn and I got two refilled goblets. Weaving through the now heavy crowd with two full glasses was a feat. I almost spilled all of it over me more than once.

By the time I finally made it to Phoebe, Kevin was with her. He had his hands around her waist, and they looked at each other as if there was no one else in here. Once more, jealousy assaulted me.

Feeling ashamed of my feelings, I downed one

of the drinks in one big gulp. I was about to turn and go hide in a corner, or leave and go to my dorm, when Phoebe clutched my arm and pulled me closer.

"Hey!" She disentangled herself from Kevin and took the full glass from me. "What took you so long?"

I smiled and gestured around. "Have you seen this place? It's full."

She nodded and then introduced me to Kevin. We began dancing again, and soon, a couple of Kevin's friends joined us. One of them tried to catch my attention, but I kept glancing around, looking for some other guy.

I finally found him at the edge of the dance floor, close to the stage and to the table with the alcohol goodies. He stood beside Jeff and Jonah, each with a drink in hand, scanning the crowd.

As if he knew where to look, Garrett's eyes found mine. I ducked to hide in the crowd.

"What happened?" Phoebe asked.

She was Kevin-less. "Where's your man?"

"He went to grab us more drinks. Now tell me what happened."

"Jonah and Garrett are here."

"Oh. Where?"

"Over there." I pointed with my finger, making

sure it was hidden from anyone else. Of course, she elongated her neck and tried to find him. I pulled her down. "Don't look now!"

"They won't see me, and even if they do, they won't recognize me."

"True, but I don't want to make them wonder. All I need is for them to be curious about us."

"Well, one of them can go to hell, I agree, but the other." She grinned. "The other can take you to paradise."

I slapped her arm playfully. "Phoebe!"

"What? I call it how I see it."

My cheeks warmed. "Is it that obvious?"

"To me, it is. I bet the others don't notice it, since you're always so careful not to show anything about you."

When she put it that way, I felt like there were fences—built by me and by everyone in my life—around me. Fences carefully placed to keep me safe or to drive me crazy. Family misunderstandings, insecurities, living alone, fake friendships, stereotypes, and lies—my fences.

It wasn't as if I didn't want to show myself, but because of a misguided stereotype and lies, I couldn't be me. I could only imagine if I had shown up dressed like the ATN girls. They were envied and glorified. The men drooled and the other girls wanted to be them. If it were me, I would have been crucified on the spot. They would call me slut, whore, relationship wrecker, and much more.

Kevin came back with our drinks, and I downed mine again. I could feel the buzz building, slowly but steadily, and if I kept drinking at this rate, I would have to be carried to my dorm. And since I didn't have anyone to do that, I should stop.

"I'm going to buy a bottle of water," I told Phoebe.

She nodded and I zigzagged through the crowd. I stepped off the dance floor and the maze opened up a little bit, but I halted. Garrett was seven or eight feet from me, beside a table where Jonah and Jeff and some other guys and girls were seated. Wearing the same barely there outfit as her sisters, Jennifer from ATN stood in front of him, her hand on his arm, and her chin turned up to him.

I ordered myself to breathe and keep going. A step at a time. I could do this.

One step. Two steps. Three steps.

Not resisting the fight in me, I kept checking on him, afraid he would wind his arms around Jennifer and lean over her. He nodded to something she said. She blabbed, and he took a sip of his drink—whiskey, I would bet—before looking around. As if pulled by a magnet, his gaze fleeted over me, but he did a double-take and paused, narrowing his eyes at me.

Heat crawled across my cheeks and I turned my head, pulling the blond hair to hide my face. I joined the line and prayed for the line to move fast.

Why was I so afraid he would recognize me? Did I think he would tell the others it was me? Not really. I mean, I would like to think I knew him well enough to trust him with that, but I wasn't sure. I didn't really know him that well.

I paid for my water and turned around, focused on not looking his way, not wondering what he would do to Jennifer, not caring either. As soon as I reached Phoebe, Kevin, and his friends, I shoved my water bottle into a guy's hands, grabbed Phoebe's half-full glass, and downed it, knowing Kevin would have given her spiked punch.

With wide eyes, Phoebe leaned close to me. "Hmm, what happened?"

"Saw Garrett talking to Jennifer."

"Oh." She smiled at her boyfriend. "Baby, could you please refill our glasses?"

He shot me an annoyed look before smiling at

her and nodding. He said something to the guys and then disappeared through the crowd.

"Tell me," Phoebe asked.

Rage and jealousy surged through my veins as I told her how he was flirting with Jennifer, but he looked at me as if he knew me.

I had no right to feel this way, but it hurt. Seeing him flirting with some girl hurt. I wanted to write a sign that said "unavailable" and hang it around his neck. However, the sign was a lie. Just because I was drawn to him, just because I felt something for him, didn't mean he wasn't free to flirt, kiss, and do whomever he wanted to. He was completely and absolutely free.

When Kevin returned with the drinks, he gave one glass to Phoebe and one to me. I sipped it while dancing—and scanning the crowd for Garrett—because I really didn't need to be drunk in less than thirty seconds.

A shove pushed me forward, and I bumped into one of Kevin's friends.

"Sorry," I mumbled, stepping away from him.

I turned to yell at whoever had pushed me, but froze when I saw it was Jonah and Audrey.

He took a step away from her, and she grabbed his arm, pulling him back.

"Come on, Jonah," Audrey said, her voice slurred. "You can't just not want me anymore."

"Why is it so hard to believe?" he asked, his tone harsh.

With a grin, she gestured to herself. "Have you seen me?"

He rolled his eyes and started moving again and looking around as if searching for someone. He hadn't taken three steps before Audrey stopped him again. "Audrey, let me go."

Audrey dropped her hand from him and put them on her waist. "She's not here."

"Who?" he asked, feigning innocence.

"Do I need to say her name? That Brazilian slut."

"How do you know?"

She shrugged. "I would have known. I know almost everyone here, and they would tell me if she had come."

I pulled my huge blond hair over my face for good measure and continued listening.

"What's your interest in it?" he asked.

She leaned closer to him. "So you won't fall into temptation."

He showed her that same cocky smile I had seen before. "She's the one all over me, Audrey."

I gasped. If the music from the band weren't

loud enough, they would have heard me. I pressed a hand to my mouth.

"You have to back off, Jonah. I don't care about any of it." She clutched his arm. "Please, give up. Tell the others you're out. Don't ruin what we have."

"We have nothing. We haven't had anything in a long time."

"We could have it again. Remember? It was great. So good. Please, don't sleep with her."

"Enough." He pulled his hand away. "Go bother someone else. I want to enjoy this party."

He walked away and she stood there, watching him, her eyes filling with tears. It was like watching a train wreck in slow motion, but just when one expected the impact and the screams, she took a deep breath, wiped her hands under her eyes, and strolled the opposite way, her head high.

Shocked, I finished my drink.

"What the hell was that?" Phoebe asked me, right behind my shoulder.

"I have no idea," I said, turning to face her. She stared at my face and handed me her untouched glass. "You didn't drink anything."

"I'm not much of a drinker, and I know you probably need it right now."

I did need it. Without ceremony, I took the glass from her and drank half of it in one gulp. "Thanks."

She smiled. "Anytime."

By the ... how many drinks did I have? Not sure. But it was not even midnight, and my head was buzzing. I laughed. In Brazil, parties started at midnight, and I couldn't remember one time that I went home before the sun was up. This was quite different.

It was nice though, to drink and forget. To let the alcohol take over and be someone else, do something else. To forget who I was, to forget everything.

Maybe I should do it more often. Invite Garrett to the lake late at night with a bottle of Johnnie Walker Blue Label. Would he refuse that?

And that was not forgetting him.

Another shove sent me, once again, into one of Kevin's friends. A little tipsy, I clutched his forearms to steady myself. Almost instantly, his arms were around me. He smiled. Poor guy, I didn't remember his name. I smiled back, but retreated, not wanting to give him the wrong idea.

Seriously, now I needed water this time. Otherwise, I would be too careless and someone would find out about me. Or I would trip on my own feet and I would reveal myself. Yeah, not what I wanted.

"Gonna buy water," I told Phoebe before sashaying through the crowd.

I tried not looking around but that was impossible.

Jonah was right in front of the stage with Jeff and two other guys. Audrey was with Sarah, Molly, and two other girls from their sorority near the table/bar, watching Jonah, of course. And where was Garrett? He had probably left with some girl by now. Maybe Jennifer.

I pressed a hand to my belly, feeling sick. Jeez. I never felt sick. The line to buy a bottle of water was too long, and I would never drink it before this sick feeling left me. Literally.

I turned to the left and rushed to the corridor leading to the bathrooms. I pushed inside the women's bathroom, which was full, of course, and headed to the sink. I cupped my hand under the faucet and drank tap water. Not the best, but it would have to do.

Some girls stared, and I was glad I was wearing a mask and wig. If they had heard Audrey's lies, and almost everyone on campus had, they would know who I was, and if they saw me, nearly drunk, trying to abate my sickness with tap water, more lies would ensue and tomorrow everyone would have heard, what? That I tried to fuck a guy in a corner, and when he said no, I was so hot, I went to cool down in the ladies' restroom. I bared myself and practically laid over the sink.

Credo.

I drank slowly but steadily, taking deep breaths between each swallow. Soon, the sickness was gone. However, my head was nowhere near clear yet. Without rush, I exited the restroom and turned back to the party. I could endure the rest of the night now; I just couldn't drink anything else.

Once back in the ballroom, I paused. My head wasn't good, and I still felt tipsy. Maybe it was time to leave.

I turned to the end of the room with the intention of walking around the outer walls, close to the curtain-closed windows. It was darker and had fewer people, which was odd since, hmm, shouldn't there be couples making out in the dark? I wouldn't mind them; I just wanted to avoid the crowd. I took a step into the darkness and halted.

Garrett stood before one of the large windows. The curtain was pulled to the side enough for a thin streak of moonlight to seep in. With his hands on the windowsill and his torso slightly forward, Garrett looked up. To the stars? The moonshine illuminated his face, creating shadows under his chiseled jaw and chin.

I sucked in a sharp breath. *Meu Deus*, he was handsome.

His kissable lips seemed relaxed into his usual half-smile, as if he enjoyed being here, away from the others, and admiring the night sky. I could bet his hazel eyes were bright, and I ached to check them out. To check all of him out.

The old Bia would have walked to him, hooked her hand on his neck, and pulled his mouth to hers, and she knew he wouldn't resist her.

Warmth spread through me, followed by my old boldness. The old Bia wanted to break free. She wanted to take down the fences, if only for a moment. *He won't know it's you*, she said.

She took over me and I didn't even fight it.

I marched until I was standing two feet from Garrett. Noticing my presence, he whirled to face me.

"Um, hi," he said, frowning. "Do I know you?"

I stepped into his personal space and looked at him, loving how tall and wide he was compared to me. I kept out of the moonlight, hoping it was enough for him not to see my eyes—which were a dead giveaway of who I was. The mask didn't hide their unique color—and slid a hand around his neck. Even in high heels, I was still shorter than he was, so I tugged him down. He resisted.

Oh no, he wouldn't. I scratched my nails on his nape, and he took a sharp breath. The frown deepened, and he turned his face to my arm. He closed his hand around my forearm and pulled it closer, making me lose my grip on him. He inhaled before placing a soft kiss on my wrist.

I shivered and warmth ran low in my belly.

Slowly, he turned his eyes to mine and placed my hand back around his neck. However, he didn't move. Not to me, not away from me. He just stared at me, his eyes darkening, his chest rising and falling faster.

I tried it again. I took another step, pressing my body to his, and tugged his neck down. This time, he met me halfway. I brushed my lips against his, and shock raked my body. *Meu Deus*, if a simple peck could do this to me, what would happen if—?

His hands landed on my hips, his fingers digging into me through the fabric of this ridiculously heavy dress, and his mouth claimed mine. His lips were soft but demanding, and I wanted to give him all he asked. I parted my mouth, and his tongue took charge, drawing a moan from my throat. Groaning, he deepened the kiss and whirled us around, pushing me against the window and trapping me with his hard body. One of his hands slid up, purposely brushing against my breast—and making me gasp in his mouth—before continuing up. He clutched my shoulder, wedging his fingers under the dress. That simple touch, his skin grazing mine, sent another powerful jolt down my spine. I entwined my fingers with the hair on his neck and snaked the other hand around his back, pulling him closer, as if there was any space left between us.

Garrett propped his knee between my legs, but the full skirt of the dress caught in the way, and suddenly, I wanted it off. The dress was not helping! He bit my lower lip, sucking hard, and I thought I would melt at his feet, because there was no way this was real. It felt too good, too right.

He dragged his mouth to my jaw. His lips and his hot breath on my skin were a deadly combination, and I was ready to combust. I clutched his shoulders, arched my back, and threw back my head, granting him access. He planted a kiss on my neck and inhaled, sending another shiver sweeping through my body.

Then he whispered against my skin, "You're so sweet, Bia."

I froze. What did he say?

Noticing my tension, he straightened to look at

me. There it was, written in his eyes. He knew. He knew who I was.

My throat went dry. I dropped my hands from him and stepped back.

He held on to my waist. "No, Bia. Wait." I pushed his hands away and continued retreating. He reached for me, but I raised a hand and he stopped.

I opened my mouth but nothing came out. I wanted to scream at him, but scream what? I had been the one who came to him. I buried my face in my hands, mortified. "*Meu Deus.*"

Now he had proof that I was the slut Audrey painted me as.

His hands enveloped my wrists and pulled my hands away from my face. "Don't hide." He didn't let go of my wrists and drew me closer. "Talk to me."

"Let me go," I said, my voice barely above a whisper.

"Bia ..."

I cleared my throat and said louder, "Let me go."

Sighing, he opened his hands, and I withdrew my arms.

I whirled on my heels and ran into the crowd. I didn't look back to see if he was following me. I didn't stop. I didn't slow down. I just weaved through the bodies, counting the seconds until I was out of the ballroom, out of the building, and running across campus. I only stopped once I was inside my dorm, with my back against the closed door.

My tipsiness gone, I pulled the mask and the wig off and let out a deep breath.

Meu Deus, what had I done? How could I have been this stupid? Yes, I missed partying, I missed drinking here and there, I missed kissing guys and feeling like they appreciated me, but one kiss, one really good, really hot, really perfect kiss could throw everything I was working so hard to erase to the wind.

What if he told Jeff or Jonah about it? What if they told more friends, who told more friends, who told Audrey? Tomorrow, there would be at least one more big lie about me hovering over my head and crushing my soul.

I couldn't let this happen. I couldn't slip this way. My life, my reputation, my future here were on the line.

My phone dinged, and I was reluctant to look at it, afraid to see his name on the screen. However, it wasn't him.

Phoebe: *Where are you?*

Me: *Sorry. I'm in my dorm.*
Phoebe: *Everything all right? Why did you leave?*
Me: *Wasn't feeling well.*
Phoebe: *Want me to go there?*
Me: *No. No need. Enjoy the party. I'll see you tomorrow.*
Phoebe: *Okay. But call me if you need anything.*
Me: *I will. Thanks.*
Phoebe: *TTYL*

I set the phone on my nightstand and stripped off the dress. I hid it, in case Molly saw it and recognized it. I didn't want her knowing I was there—even if it were likely she would know soon enough.

I slipped into my pajamas and under my covers. Closing my eyes, I tried to imagine a green pasture under a warm sun. Preta and Midnight running free, playing with each other, while I laughed, happy to see them happy. Then Garrett stepped into my daydream.

"Bia, wait," he said, reaching for me.

The simple thought of him touching me, resting his hand on my arm, sent a wave of heat through my core. I recoiled in my bed, aching for more than a kiss, but knowing it couldn't happen. The kiss couldn't have happened.

I dragged my hand over my belly and under my panties. Reliving the moment we shared at the ball, I touched myself, imagining it was Garrett's hands on me instead of mine. My heart rate sped up; my breathing came out into little rasps. Heat swarmed in me and my belly clenched. I was about to come, and I knew I would scream his name when I did.

The door opened and Molly stumbled in, giggling.

My hands stilled and the heat seeped out of my body. She didn't even look my way while she changed from her skimpy costume to her pajamas, tripping over her feet several times.

Groaning, I rolled to the side, giving her my back, and tucked my hands under my pillow, hating her for interrupting such a glorious daydream.

17

FRUSTRATION, DISAPPOINTMENT, AND EVEN ANGER simmered in my chest, and I fought the urge to scream every few seconds. If I was feeling bad about everything that was happening, now that I had kissed Garrett and he had recognized me, I felt much worse. Why, *meu Deus*, why was I so weak? Why did I throw myself at him? After all, I went through to make him believe I wasn't like that.

On Thursday and Friday, I avoided being out of my dorm. I only left to go to classes and grab food. On Saturday and Sunday, I thought I would have to tie myself up so I wouldn't go to the ranch.

Maybe it was silly, avoiding the ranch because

Garrett and I had kissed, but I couldn't get past it. How was I supposed to face him? What could I say? I hadn't heard any new rumors yet, but that didn't mean there weren't any.

It was silly, and it made me anxious and agitated. What the hell was I supposed to do with myself? Study. I could study. I hadn't done well with my midterms, I was sure, and it wouldn't hurt to start prepping early for final exams. However, each time I sat down and started reading my books, my mind zoned out. My thoughts flew across everything and anything, except whatever was written on the pages before me.

Finally, on Sunday evening, I gathered the courage to leave the room and take a walk off-campus. I wasn't much of a reader, but with nothing better to do, I wandered inside a bookstore and stopped by a shelf with plenty of books with horses on the cover. I fingered through some, trying to find out if they were fiction or nonfiction.

"If it isn't the Brazilian girl." Jonah stopped by my side.

I cringed and glanced at him. "What are you doing here?"

He leaned on the shelf, turning his torso to me,

and smiled. "I was walking to the bar across the street with the guys when I saw you entering the bookstore. I couldn't pass up the opportunity to see you."

I put the book I was holding back on the shelf and stepped back. "Um, you just saw me. Now you can go."

"How about you come to the bar with me? Let me buy you a drink while we talk. You never gave me the opportunity to actually sit down and talk." He reached over and ran his finger up my arm. "To get to know each other."

I stepped back once more, out of his reach. "I'm not interested."

He held my gaze. "I promise you. Give me five minutes. I'll make you interested."

What did a girl have to do to make a guy give up? Sighing, I walked away. I actually had hoped he would let me go, but hope was a fickle thing. Jonah caught up with me as I stepped outside the bookstore.

He halted in front of me. "Okay, let me ask you a question. Why don't you want to give me five minutes of your time? What is it that makes you say no to me? Not to sound vain, but I know I'm not hard on the eyes, I'm rich, I'm smart, and I like to think I'm a good friend. I don't see why you wouldn't want to at least try to get to know me."

That was my answer. His arrogance. And Audrey. I really, really wanted to stay far away from her, and if that meant never being friends with Jonah, I was okay with that.

"Goodbye, Jonah." I whirled around and started walking away.

"I'll see you soon, Brazilian girl," he said.

I really hoped he didn't.

THE SUN WAS WARM, BUT NOT ENOUGH AGAINST THE chill of the second weekend of November. I pulled my turtleneck over my chin and tugged my jacket tighter against me.

An older woman sat beside me. "Beautiful day, isn't it?" she asked, touching her pearl necklace. "If it was a few degrees warmer, it would be perfect."

I watched the bright green field before us. Leo had emailed me a VIP pass so I could sit in one of the fancy chairs right in front of the field. This club wasn't as fancy as the one my brothers and cousin played for, but it looked bigger. The people walking around, talking to friends, and searching for their places were well dressed.

I looked down at my clothes. A thin sweater and jacket, black slacks, and black boots—unfortunately, these weren't cowboy ones. During the summer, I usually wore dresses to these events, but when it was chilly like today, I wouldn't dare leave my legs bare. Who cared if I was a bit under-dressed? Surely, not me.

"It is. A great day," I said.

The truth was that I felt anxious and frustrated. I had managed to avoid the ranch since the Halloween Ball ten days ago, and Jonah since the encounter at the bookstore last Sunday. It wasn't easy though. Everything in me screamed to go to the ranch, even if I had to turn my back on Garrett and pretend he didn't exist each time he came in the stable. However, I wasn't that strong. Not anymore. My feelings had been all over the place, and with all my other problems, I would crumble if I pushed a little too hard. And facing him would be pushing too hard.

I almost went there this past Friday. I knew The Bat was having a mixer and Garrett was bound to be there—as well as Jennifer. The ranch would be Garrett-less, and I could use a couple of hours submerged in that world to forget the rest. Once again, my new fears won and I stayed in my room.

My phone dinged.

Leo: *Where are you?*

Me: *Already seated.*

Leo: *What? Why aren't you with us?*

Me: *I better wait until after the game.*

Leo: *Because of our father?*

Me: *Yes. If we argue again, it'll weigh on you guys and I don't want to ruin your game.*

Leo: *This isn't a tournament.*

Me: *I don't care. You have to win anyway.*

Leo: *No pressure, huh?*

Me: *None at all.* Boa sorte.

Leo: Obrigado.

I pocketed my phone and it dinged again. However, this time it wasn't Leo.

Tom: *Where are my coffee and my donuts?*

Me: *Sorry, Tom. I can't come today.*

Tom: *You didn't come last weekend either. What did Garrett do?*

I smiled, but it was a sad little effort. If only he knew.

Me: *I'm out of town, actually.*

Tom: *Everything okay?*

Me: *Yeah. My brothers and cousin are playing in Denver.*

Tom: *Yeah, I remember now. Garrett mentioned the polo game.*

Me: *Yeah.*

Tom: *Well, have fun, and come visit me soon.*

I wouldn't make any promises.

Me: *Bye.*

I was pocketing my phone again when my family strolled to the other side of the field. The guys saw me and waved. I waved back.

The woman beside me looked at me. "Do you know them?"

"Yes," I said, suddenly proud. "I'm their sister."

Her eyes widened. "Oh."

Not long after, the game started, and, as I expected, Montenegro won by a landslide.

After they celebrated their victory, greeted their opponents, talked to people who I was sure were from the club's administration, I walked over to them.

Leo saw me coming and opened his arms to me.

I scrunched my nose and slapped his hands away. "Ew, you're all sweaty."

Big arms enveloped me from behind. "*Oi*, little sis," Ri said.

I yelped, jerking away from him. "You too! All sweaty!"

Noticing what was going on, Pedro turned to me. "Come here, Bia."

"Don't you dare!"

By his side, Guilherme laughed.

Until my father squeezed in our circle.

"Beatriz," he said, nodding his chin at me.

"*Oi, pai.*" I forced myself to calm down and act as if nothing had happened. "How are you?"

"*Bem.*" He turned to the guys. "Pedro, you slacked when Lewis opened on the left. You should have taken the ball from him. Guilherme, you lost that goal because you would rather smile at the fans. Don't be cocky. Ricardo, you improperly crossed the line of the ball twice. Two faults. Don't let that happen again. Leonardo, your ride-offs are extremely risky."

"That's the point in doing them." Only Leo would interrupt my father during a post-game lecture.

My father's face grew hard. "I'm talking, boy. Respect me." He sighed. "There are more effective ways to steal the ball," he continued. "We'll talk about it at our next practice. Other than that, good game."

He turned on his heel and started walking toward the horses.

Leo nudged me with his elbow. "Go on. Talk to him."

"And say what?"

"Anything? I don't know. You can't run away from him forever though."

Maybe I could. I just needed to add that to my things-to-run-away-from list. The damn list was growing at an alarming pace.

Guilherme saved me. "Hey, when are you coming to visit us? I miss my party partner."

I smiled. I didn't even go out with him that much, and it usually was a problem because girls thought we were together. "Not sure."

"Thanksgiving for sure," Leo said.

"We don't even celebrate Thanksgiving."

"We celebrated it last year, and Hannah plans on doing the whole thing again for us. So you better be there."

That actually didn't sound like a bad idea. Other than the fact that I would have to spend three or four days at my father's house. Well, I could always sleep in Hannah's guest bedroom.

"I'll think about it," I said.

Leo raised an eyebrow at me. "Why wouldn't you come? Everyone will probably go away to spend the holiday with their families. The university will be practically empty."

Ri gave me a funny I-know look. "She has a boyfriend."

All four guys stared at me with huge eyes.

"What? No! There's no one." Unfortunately.

"Then there's no reason for you to miss Thanksgiving with us," Pedro said.

I sighed. "Like I said. I'll think about it."

"Nu-uh. I'm buying your plane ticket tomorrow," Leo said.

I shook my head. "Okay, are we going to stand here in the middle of the field, or are you going to take me someplace nice to eat?"

"At four in the afternoon?" Ri asked. "You know we never have dinner before seven."

"Seven-thirty," Gui said.

"Preferably at eight," Pedro added.

Ri nodded. "Exactly."

"I wasn't talking about dinner, *idiotas*. I want a huge piece of cake and plenty of coffee."

"That I can do," Gui said.

"Wait." Leo raised his hand. "Only after you talk to *pai*."

I groaned. "Childish much?"

"Me or you? Cause I think you're the one avoiding him, not me."

I wanted to throw at him the many years he avoided our father while wasting his life, but it was too cruel. I wouldn't remind him of how terrible his past was.

Instead, I swallowed that response and lifted my chin. "Fine."

Trying to stay calm, I scanned the area and found my father talking to a man on the other side of the field. I had seen that man greeting the guys after they won the game. He had graying hair and wore a blazer with the name of the club embroidered on the left side.

I took a step and Leo held my arm. "Try to be nice," he said.

"When am I not nice?"

He looked at me with an are-you-going-to-make-me-say-it expression. "Plenty of times. The guys and I will take a quick shower and change. We'll meet you in the parking lot in a few."

I nodded and he let go of me.

My father saw me walking toward him and excused himself. He turned to me, his face as hard as a rock.

"What is it?"

"I just wanted to say hi."

"You already said hi."

I sighed. "Are you going to treat me this way every time we see each other now?"

"You defied me. Without even telling me about it, you left my house, you practically ran away." There they were again, those two words. "And you're asking me to treat you, how? Like you are my little girl."

"*Pai*, I'll always be your little girl."

He pressed his mouth in a thin line. "No, Beatriz. My little girl would have listened to me. She would have sat down and talked to me about everything. She would have told me how she felt about following her brothers and cousin around. She wouldn't just come to me and tell me she was leaving, and expect me to be okay with that."

That was how he saw this? Because I didn't. I tried talking to him, I tried making him see it from my point of view, but he was too busy with the guys. He didn't have time to talk, and each time I tried, it was rushed and I was never able to express myself completely. In a way, he pushed me away.

"I'm tired of arguing," I said. "Hopefully time will erase this misunderstanding from our minds, and we'll be able to be father and daughter again one day." He stared at me with wide eyes. I stepped back. "Goodbye."

Once more, as I walked to the parking lot, I felt like I was running away.

I slipped inside my car and turned on the stereo, hoping the lyrics of a country song would drown the thoughts in my mind.

However, it was impossible. There was too

much on my mind. My father, Garrett, Midnight, Delilah, Molly, Audrey, Jonah, and even poor Phoebe. She was so adorable and nice to me, but she had been spending a lot of time with Kevin. The jealousy in my heart was all wrong. I wasn't an old friend she was shoving aside for a guy. She had met him and me practically at the same time. Of course, she would prefer him to me. Besides, she had been a great friend so far, even with a new boyfriend taking a lot of her time.

The passenger door opened and Leo slipped in. "Where are you?" he asked. He knew me too well.

"Nowhere." I smiled. The other guys slipped inside the backseat. "What time do I need to bring you back?"

Ri answered, "We told *pai* to meet us at the airport, so you can drive us there by seven."

"All right." I put the car in reverse. "Where to?"

"Anywhere with a huge piece of cake and plenty of coffee," Pedro said, repeating my previous words.

I smiled at him. "That's my boy."

He laughed. Not five seconds later, Guilherme started telling us one of his bizarre tales, and just like that, I felt light. It was as if I was home, but outside home. These crazy guys made me feel home wherever they were.

Guilt assaulted me. I had left to get out of their shadows, but I missed them way too much. I pushed the guilt away. Tomorrow I would revel in it. Right now, I would enjoy their company.

18

WITH A TO-GO CUP OF COFFEE, I MARCHED TO MY dorm building, seeking the shelter it provided. I had succumbed to my desire of getting out and ended up regretting it when a guy openly hit on me while I waited for my coffee. I almost ran off without the coffee. I would have if the girl preparing it hadn't called my name at the last second.

There were days when I wondered why the hell I was still here. Why I still submitted myself to this torture. Was it worth it? I didn't know anymore.

I was half a block from my dorm when I saw Garrett's truck parked on the street—odd spot for him, since I knew he had a guaranteed space in The Bat's driveway each time he came over—I had heard Jennifer commenting about it before I stopped hanging out with her and the other girls.

Garrett leaned against the closed door, scanning the area. I shrugged into myself and turned my shoulders the other way. Not that I thought he was here for me; he hadn't come after me since our kiss two weeks ago. Why would he come after me now? However, I didn't want to be seen.

I heard approaching footsteps and rushed mine.

"Bia, wait," Garrett called.

I could act like a stubborn child and pretend I didn't hear him, but I was tired of running. Groaning, I slowed down, and he easily fell into step with me.

He shoved his hands in the pockets of his faded jeans. "Can we talk?"

I kept my gaze on the path. "I'm busy."

"I know you don't have any more classes this evening."

A knot formed between my brows. "How do you know that?"

He looked away. "Jonah. He knows your schedule, and I was able to get that information from him."

I shuddered. Jonah was creepy. Seriously. "I have to study," I lied.

He hurried his steps and halted before me.

Gasping, I skidded to a stop, being extra careful not to spill my coffee on us both. "*Eita*."

I dared look up and he had that cute half-grin on. "I told you I like hearing you speak in Portuguese, didn't I?"

I took a step back. "What do you want?"

The smile faded from his face. "I want to know what is going on."

"What do you mean?"

He cocked his head to the side. "You know what I mean. I can take a wild guess as to why you haven't come to the ranch for the past two weekends, but why?" He advanced a step. "Was it that bad to kiss me?"

I gulped and asked what had been on my mind since he whispered my name. "How did you know it was me?"

"Your perfume. It's ..." He pressed his lips tight for a second before continuing. "It's unique. And then, I saw your eyes right after calling your name and I knew I was right."

"Oh." My cheeks flamed while I remembered him telling me he liked my perfume a few weeks ago.

"Tom thinks you're not coming because I did something wrong, and he's giving me hell for it."

Of course, that was the reason he was here asking me why I hadn't come by lately. Because Tom was bothering him about it. Or ... "You just want me to go back so you have fewer chores to do."

The lopsided grin was back. "Maybe." He lifted his hand, his fingers coming close to my arm, but he dropped it before any contact. My stomach flopped. "Come back. It was fun having you there. Tom misses you. Midnight misses you." He ran a hand through his hair before pocketing his hand again. "I miss you."

I fought against the smile wanting to explode on my lips. "Okay."

His eyes widened for a brief moment. "You'll come this weekend?"

"I will."

He nodded. "Good. I'll see you then." He leaned into me and kissed my cheek, his soft lips grazing my skin and robbing me of air. "Good night," he whispered.

He walked to his truck while I remained frozen in place, my hand on my cheek.

FRIDAY, I DROVE TO THE RANCH AS SOON AS MY LAST class was over. It was only because I missed the ranch. Nothing to do with the fact Garrett had asked me to go back. What if he had a party to go to and wasn't there? My belly twisted in knots and my palms sweated.

Credo, this wasn't me. I wouldn't become one of those lovesick girls who were like puppies following guys around. I focused on breathing and remembered Midnight was there too. I could spend a little time with him.

Holding a bag from Panera, I entered the stable. Tom was nowhere to be seen, and Garrett was brushing Felicity in her stall.

He half-smiled when I stopped outside the stall. "Hey, there."

"Hi." I felt heat crawling up my cheeks and looked around. "Where's Tom?"

"In the round pen."

Midnight snorted, looking at me from over his stall's door. "Hi, big boy." I dropped the bag on a bench and turned to the beautiful horse. "How are you doing?"

"He's not doing too well today, actually," Garrett said.

As I ran a hand over Midnight's face, I glanced at Garrett over my shoulder. "What do you mean?"

He exited the stall and dropped the brush on the shelf along the wall. "Delilah was here earlier and she kinda freaked out on him, causing him to freak out on her."

"Oh." I patted Midnight's neck. "Everything is okay now, big boy." He poked my stomach with his muzzle, and I embraced him. "You'll be okay."

Garrett walked toward us. "It's incredible. Until a few minutes ago, he was still twitching and neighing inside his stall. Driving us crazy. Now, look at him. I swear he's in love."

I smiled. Good. At least someone loved me around here.

Garrett lifted his hand to caress Midnight, but the horse snorted and pulled away, almost knocking my head with his muzzle in the process.

"Whoa." Garrett stepped back, his hands up. "I won't touch you if you don't want me too." Midnight snorted once more before turning his back to us. "See? He's cranky since practice."

I frowned. "I'll try to calm him down later, but now—" I grabbed the bag from the bench. "—we should eat. I brought dinner and it's getting cold."

His half-smile appeared again and my heart fluttered. "You really like spoiling us, don't you?"

I wiggled my brows. "Maybe."

He held my gaze and I held my breath, amazed

at the intensity of his eyes. It was as if he wanted to pass a message directly to my brain. I was dying to decipher it.

He cleared his throat and stepped back. "I'll call Tom."

Why did he pull away? I thought he had asked me to come back to continue what we had started the other night. Why wouldn't he? Scanning through the possibilities in my mind—he had not liked the kiss; he didn't think I was pretty; he was interested in someone else and only wanted my help at the ranch, etc.—I walked into Tom's office. I pushed back a few papers and set up our improvised dining table.

Tom crossed through the door and rushed to me, putting his arms around me. In total surprise, I stiffened.

"Kid, if you ever stay away this long again, I'll personally hunt you down."

Feeling a little awkward, I patted his back. "Maybe I should put that to the test."

He stepped back, his index finger pointed at me. "Don't you dare." I laughed, and he stared at the to-go boxes on the desk. "What do we have here?"

"I didn't really know what you two preferred, so I chose chicken panini and iced tea for everyone." I reached inside the bag and took more things out. "There are also chips, bread, and apples."

"A banquet," Tom teased.

I rolled my eyes. "Hardly."

We ate in awkward silence. It was hard to avoid looking at Garrett when he was seated on a chair beside mine. Once we were done, we threw all the plates, boxes, and bags in the trash, and moved to the aisle.

"Is there anything I can help with?" I asked.

Tom shook his head. "Not really. I was just thinking about doing a check run. Check water, check if all the tack was brought inside. That kind of stuff, then closing and leaving." Midnight stomped his hooves on the hard ground. Tom sighed. "Delilah wasn't very nice today."

"Garrett told me," I said, sharing a quick glance with Garrett.

He cleared his throat. "How about you try to calm him down, like you said you wanted, while I help Tom with the check run."

"Sounds like a plan." I turned to Midnight's stall, but Garrett's hand around my wrist stopped me. I faced him. His jaw popped band his eyes had a dark glint.

"He's in a crazy mood. Be careful."

"I will," I muttered, unsure how I had the ability to talk under the intensity of his gaze.

As he let go of me, he nodded. He and Tom left the stable through the back gate, and I turned to Midnight.

"Do you have any idea what is happening here, big boy?" I smoothed my hand on his soft coat, letting him get used to my presence before entering the stall. "Because I don't. If you have any idea or even suggestions, I'm all ears." As if mocking me, Midnight snorted and shook his head once. I chuckled. "That's what I thought."

THE NEXT MORNING, MOLLY AND I ARGUED ABOUT the time she came back last night and the time I got up this morning. She complained she couldn't sleep. Well, I couldn't sleep while she stumbled through our room, giggling and tripping on her own foot, trying to get her clothes off and put on her pajamas at two in the morning.

I was about to explode again, so I shoved jeans, a thick sweater, and my black and white boots on, and stalked out of the room before I punched her.

I drove to the nearest Starbucks for breakfast, then to the Rock Hill ranch. On the way, I recalled what happened last night. Or what didn't happen.

I was able to calm Midnight, and until we left, he was acting more like himself. Still a very hot-blooded colt, but more manageable. He didn't even twitch or snort when Tom and Garrett approached and petted him.

On the other hand, I twitched on the inside each time Garrett approached me—and did nothing. Each time he got close to me was for a reason. Or was it an excuse? Still, it didn't look like he was trying to get close to me to be close to me. Other than when he held my arm to warn me about Midnight, he didn't touch me, he didn't lean into me, and he didn't try to kiss me again. Though I caught him staring at me with darkened eyes a few times, nothing else happened.

I pushed through the disappointment boiling in my chest. *Credo,* hadn't I said I wouldn't be this kind of girl?

At the ranch, Tom came to meet me at the door. "Glad to see you came back."

I gestured to the bag in my hand. "This is all you want."

He put a hand over his heart and gasped. "I can't believe you think that." But once I was beside him, he smiled wide and snatched the bag from me. "Give me that."

I laughed as we entered the stable and sat around his desk. "Where's Garrett?"

"Today is his day off." Tom took his donut from

the bag. "Why were you avoiding him? Did something happen?"

"N-no. It's just ... he's a pain in the butt and I prefer being here when he isn't."

Tom laughed. "All right. I'll pretend I believe that."

The disappointment from last night returned with a vengeance. Garrett asked me to come back, and then he wasn't here. See, all he wanted was for me to do his work.

Tom and I had developed a rhythm when working together. It was nice and I felt useful here. Once more, I wondered why I even bothered going to school. I should probably give up and work on a ranch. Wasn't it where I felt more at home?

I was brushing Pepper when Delilah entered the stables followed by a tall woman with the same blond hair, though the woman had sharper angles and eyes. She spared a glance at me before raising her nose and walking on.

What the hell was wrong with these people?

Tom came rushing out of his office, where he finally was going through some paperwork. "Mrs. Hudson, I wasn't expecting the two of you today."

"Delilah has a competition in a little over a month," Mrs. Hudson said. "There's no better time to practice than the present."

"But ..." Tom looked at me with wide eyes for a brief second. "Garrett isn't here."

Mrs. Hudson waved him off. "We don't need him for a quick practice. Get the horse—" She wrinkled her nose. "—and meet us outside."

She put a hand on Delilah's shoulder, and like models on a catwalk, they sashayed to the arena.

"Shit," Tom muttered.

"What's the matter?" I asked, stepping out of Pepper's stall.

"If I knew they were going to be here, I wouldn't have let Garrett take the day off."

"Maybe Mrs. Hudson is right, and they can handle a quick practice without him?"

Tom faced me. "You've seen Delilah practicing before, right?" I nodded. "Haven't you paid attention to how much she irritates that horse, and how Garrett is able to calm him down a little? Well, what do you think will happen without Garrett here?"

He had a point. "I can calm Midnight. I think."

"Delilah forbad you to be near him. She won't let you calm him down, which will only frustrate him more."

I shook my head. "You have to talk to them."

He laughed. "Right. Because I want to be fired at fifty-seven. Not a chance." He went into the tack room, and four seconds later was back with a bridle and saddle. "You get Midnight ready." He dropped the saddle in my arms.

I looked down at the tack. "What?"

"He doesn't like me, but he adores you. Just tack him. I'll take him to her."

Biting my lip, I turned to Midnight's stall. As soon as I approached his door, he came to meet me. "Hey, big boy." I dropped the tack on the ground and opened the door. "You'll have to do a favor for me today, okay?" I smoothed my hand over the soft coat of his neck. He nickered. "You need to be a nice big boy, okay? Just for an hour tops. If you behave, I'll give you half a dozen carrots after the practice." He nipped at my hair and poked his muzzle on my neck. "I promise."

I hugged him, and he rested his heavy head on my shoulder. I swear I could feel him relaxing when close to me. I was starting to believe we had a special connection, though I wasn't sure what to do about it.

I tacked him and handed him to Tom, who took Midnight outside, where Delilah was waiting for him. She checked her boots and affixed her helmet, looking bored.

As soon as Tom gave her the reins, Midnight's body tensed. She jerked the reins to have him follow her to the jumping poles, but he didn't move. Trying to control the urge to go forward and help, I sat on the fence and watched. Tom leaned over the fence beside me.

After fighting with him, Delilah hopped on him.

I bit my nails—something I never did. "I have a bad feeling about this."

Tom nodded. "Me too."

Mrs. Hudson rested a hand over her pearls, which were neatly resting over an expensive-looking cream blouse. She coordinated it with brown slacks and pumps. Who in their right mind wore pumps in an arena?

"Are you ready?" Mrs. Hudson asked. Delilah gave her a thumbs up. "Then wow me."

Delilah kicked her heels at Midnight's sides, startling him. He balked and started a slow gait. Meanwhile, Mrs. Hudson watched her daughter and Midnight like a hawk.

"Does she understand anything about horses and jumping?" I asked Tom in a low voice. Mrs. Hudson wasn't close, but I didn't want to risk her hearing us.

"Not really, but she has loads of money and that's enough to make me bow out."

I wanted to be mad at him for that, but I also

understood. What he said about being fifty-seven and not wanting to be fired stayed with me. He wasn't a young guy anymore, and it wouldn't be easy for him to find another job. He knew Midnight was too young to be put through training, and he knew that practicing while Garrett wasn't here was a bad idea, but he couldn't go against his boss's wife. Still, I wish he would stand up for what he believed was right.

Delilah started with low jumps to warm up. After a few laps on the circuit, she asked Tom to raise the poles. I helped him. She gave me the stink eye but didn't say anything about it.

Delilah prepared to start at the new height.

"Fly!" Mrs. Hudson shouted as Delilah and Midnight leaped over the first poles. She tensed, making Midnight tense too. His hooves hit the pole, knocking it down. "What was that?" the woman asked, gesturing to the pole on the ground. "That's not acceptable. Start over and don't let him touch the poles."

Tom quickly put the pole back in place and nodded for Delilah to go ahead. She tapped Midnight and they set out.

"You can do it!" Mrs. Hudson shouted, and the same thing happened again. Delilah tensed, Midnight tensed, the pole fell, and Mrs. Hudson verbalized her discontent. "What are you doing? Why aren't you controlling that horse?" She pointed at Midnight and took a few steps closer. "You have to do better, Delilah. You're my daughter. I know you can do better. And this horse? What's the matter with this horse?" She approached them. "Is that stable boy working on him? I don't think he's doing a good job. This horse needs someone with an iron fist."

She jabbed her finger at his neck.

And he reared.

I jumped off the fence and ran to them.

Mrs. Hudson scurried away from Midnight's powerful hooves. "See what I'm saying?" she yelled. "That horse is a menace!"

Irritated, Midnight reared again. Delilah screamed, trying to hold the reins. With my hands high, I approached him.

"Whoa, big boy. Shhh, calm down."

But Delilah and Mrs. Hudson kept screaming.

Delilah slapped his neck. "Stop it, stupid animal."

Midnight kicked his hind legs high. Delilah got a hold of his mane and yelled.

"Midnight, look at me," I said. He did. I held his stare. "Calm down, big boy. Everything is okay. Just let Delilah get off."

"Take this brute animal away from here," Mrs. Hudson shouted, coming to my side.

Neighing, Midnight reared again. Delilah, still holding to his mane, lost her footing and fell back. Midnight fell with her, and they crashed onto the nearby poles.

My heart stopped.

Mrs. Hudson screamed some more while Tom and I rushed to them.

Thankfully, Midnight hadn't fallen on Delilah, but the pole under them was broken, indicating how hard their fall was. Delilah was unconscious and Midnight twitched, trying to get up. His eyes were wide and his breathing was accelerated.

Tom looked at me with big eyes. "Go pick up Garrett."

"What?"

He fished his cell phone from inside his pocket. "I'll call 911 and the vet, but I need you to get Garrett."

"Why? Why can't you call him?"

He dialed a number and pressed the phone on his ear. "There's no cell reception where he is, and he'll kill me if I don't let him know what happened."

My mind was spinning. "But I don't want to leave Midnight."

"Please, Bia, I beg you."

My heart weighed in my chest. "All right. All right."

He told me how to get where Garrett was, and I ran from the arena, my heart staying there.

I jumped in my SUV and squealed out of the parking lot. I followed Tom's instructions. Exit the property, turn right. Go for five miles, turn on the next right on a dirt road. Go for another two miles, turn left, go for seven miles, and I would find him.

I stopped my car before a big lot with lush green grass. The frame of a big barn stood out in the center, and several yards to the left, trees flanked a small cabin.

With low-riding jeans and an open shirt, Garrett was on top of the structure, holding what looked like an industrial stapler. He stopped working on the structure when he saw my car approaching and jumped from post to post until he was on the ground.

With a frown, he walked toward me.

I lowered the window from my car and yelled, "Come quick. It's Delilah and Midnight."

He stopped, his eyes going wide. He turned and picked up a hand towel and his jacket from beside a big toolbox and rushed to my car. He barely sat in the passenger seat before I tore off.

"What happened?" He wiped the sweat from his face and arms. I peeked at his taut torso before he buttoned his shirt. Yup, he had a nice chest and abdomen. Too nice, actually. "What happened?" he repeated.

I shook the momentary distraction from my mind. "Delilah and her mother showed up to practice. Tom didn't like the idea because you weren't there, but Mrs. Hudson insisted." I groaned. "Mrs. Hudson is one irritable woman."

He snorted. "You're telling me?"

I glanced at him again. I wondered what the history there was. He was the constant reminder that her husband had cheated on her. That was probably not nice. However, he wasn't guilty, and it was probably not nice for him either.

I went on. "Delilah was taut and stressed, which made Midnight taut and stressed, and then Mrs. Hudson started yelling, and I really mean yelling and saying terrible things to Midnight. The woman really spooked him. He reared, and they fell over one of the obstacles."

His eyes went wide and his body stiffened. "How is Delilah? And Midnight?"

"I don't know. I wanted to stay to help, to be there when the vet arrived, but Tom begged me to come pick you up because you would kill him if you didn't know about it right away."

He nodded. "He was right. I would." He glanced at me. "Thank you for picking me up."

"You're welcome."

In a couple of minutes, I was parking my car beside an ambulance at the ranch. I barely stopped the car, and Garrett jumped out. He ran to the arena. I killed the engine and ran after him.

Two paramedics wheeled Delilah on a stretcher while her mother cried by their side. The girl was awake though, and she seemed mad.

Garrett stopped by her side. "You're going to be okay."

She nodded. "Ouch. Can't move. Hurts."

"It's okay." He looked at the paramedics. "How is she?"

"We don't know for sure yet, sir," one of them answered. "We think she has a few contusions, but we'll take her to the hospital to get checked out to be sure."

He nodded and let the paramedics go. Side by side, we approached where Midnight had fallen. He was still in the same place and the vet was over him. He saw me and jerked.

"No, no," the vet said, pressing his hand on his sides. The horse tried to stir again. "Don't move."

He looked at us. "I gave him a sedative, but I don't think it has kicked in yet."

"He wants you," Garrett said to me. "Go to him. Calm him down."

I stepped between Tom and the vet, and knelt beside Midnight's face. "Hey, big boy. I'm here." He reached his muzzle to my hand. My eyes filled with tears.

"How is he?" Garrett asked.

The doctor had his stethoscope on Midnight's chest. "It was a nasty fall. I won't know the extent of the damage until I can take some x-rays, but by the way he cries each time he tries to move, I'm thinking he broke something. Also, see this pole?" The vet pointed to one half of a broken wooden pole. "We can't see the end of the other half, so I'm thinking it might be under him. From his position, it probably pierced him."

"That's not good," Garrett muttered.

I brushed my hand under Midnight's chin and leaned my face to his. "Don't listen to them," I whispered. "You'll be okay. I know it." I kissed his forehead. He tried to turn his muzzle to me, but I pressed him down. "No, big boy. Stay still, please. It's better for you."

The ambulance carrying Delilah off caught my attention, and I snapped my head to the driveway.

Mrs. Hudson stepped out from the stable and marched to us.

Her mascara was running, but she still looked unbreakable. She pointed a finger at Garrett. "This is your fault."

He stepped back. "What? I wasn't even here."

"You're their trainer. You're this horse's trainer. The horse should have been prepared; he should know what to do. He shouldn't hit any poles. He should be perfect! But he isn't and it's your fault." She flipped her hair the same way I had seen her daughter doing. Garrett clenched his fists but somehow stayed quiet. "Haven't you noticed by now that a lot of the bad things that happen around here are your fault?" She spun on her heels and marched away.

Garrett let out a long, loud breath. "Well, the show is over," he snapped. "Pay attention to the horse."

The three of us focused on Midnight. His breathing had slowed, and his body seemed more relaxed and I assumed the sedative had kicked in. Poor big boy. The vet arranged a trailer to take Midnight to his practice, and soon the horse was being driven away.

Garrett turned to Tom and me. "I want to stay and help clean up, Tom, but I should probably go to the hospital, check on Delilah," he said, his voice low.

"Go." Tom nudged me in the arm. "I know Bia will be a trooper and stay with me and help me out around here. Right?"

My wish was to go after Midnight, but he wasn't my horse. What if Delilah found out I spent my free time in the waiting room of a veterinary practice? Not that I minded what she thought, but I was concerned about what she could do to the horse because of my affection for him.

"Right," I answered.

Garrett nodded and started walking away. His usual high chin pointed to the ground, and his perfect posture and open shoulders slacked to the front as if he really was responsible for what happened.

Wait. Did he think he was responsible for it?

I rushed after him, and only realized what I was doing when I closed my hand around his wrist, making him stop and face me. As soon as his bright but now sad hazel eyes locked on mine, I let go of his arm.

"Y-you know it's not your fault, right?"

"I know," he said in a low tone.

"Send news, please. Tom and I would like to know how Delilah is." I paused, biting my lip and wondering if I could ask for more. "And if you hear anything—" I closed my mouth, regretting having started the sentence.

"If I hear anything about Midnight, I'll let you know."

"Thanks."

He nodded and resumed walking away.

I heard Tom's boots crunching the grass before his hand rested on my shoulder. "They will be fine. Delilah, Midnight, and Garrett."

"I hope so," I whispered.

"Come on." He gestured toward the stable. "We won't hear anything for a few hours and nothing like immersing ourselves in work to make the time fly."

20

I woke up early and pondered if going to the ranch the day after the accident was a good or bad thing. I was worried about Midnight and Delilah, but I didn't want to intrude.

Garrett had sent a couple of messages yesterday evening saying Delilah would be fine. She had a concussion and had twisted her wrist, but it wasn't bad. She would be back to practice in about a week.

Midnight wasn't doing so great though. When he fell over the poles, one of them broke in the middle and pierced his left stifle. Thankfully, it had been superficial and fixable with a few stitches and rest. However, he had twisted his pastern and torn a minor ligament. His prognosis was good, and with care and rest, he would be able to ride and jump again. Just not in time for the competition Delilah and he had been practicing for.

Garrett didn't say much about it, but it was clear Delilah was furious about it. When first told that Midnight wouldn't be competing, Delilah had such a freak out that the doctors had to sedate her so she would calm down.

After that, Garrett stopped sending updates to Tom and me, and that had been only six in the evening, more than twelve hours ago. I was dying for news but didn't want to sound curious or nosy. It really was none of my business, even if I liked Midnight almost as much as I loved Preta.

I wasn't sure if Garrett had another day off, but I made up my mind to go and help Tom. Besides, it beat staying holed up in my dorm room, or walking around campus under staring and whispering.

After a quick stop at Starbucks, where I bought extra coffee and pastries in case Garrett or Carl were there, I drove to the ranch. I almost made a U-turn in the driveway leading to the parking lot when I saw Jonah's truck parked beside his father's truck. With the accident, I had almost forgotten how much of a creep Jonah was being lately. Almost.

I shoved my nerves aside and marched in the stable with my head high. Who cared what he had done and what he thought? I didn't. I wouldn't let whatever game he was playing shake my core. Having to play coy and be quiet on campus was one thing. On this ranch was another. I had found my peaceful little paradise here, and he wouldn't undo that for me. Nor would his father.

I stopped short once I heard loud voices coming from inside.

"I don't care!" Mrs. Hudson yelled. "I don't care if he's your son. I want him out of here. I want him out of our lives. I want him far away from my children."

"Virginia," Mr. Hudson said in a warning tone.

"No, no. I won't keep quiet anymore. I tried being patient, I tried being civilized, but enough is enough. He almost ruined our marriage. Twice. He's poison and he'll soon infect our children."

"Mom, please," Jonah said. "I understand your position, but he *is* my brother."

"*Half*-brother!" she screamed. "I don't understand how any of you can't see how he is breaking us apart, little by little."

Jonah said something in answer, but he had

lowered his voice and I wasn't feeling like snaking behind the door to listen.

"Tom," Mrs. Hudson continued. "Arrange for him to be fired today. I don't care where he finds a new job, as long as he stays dozens of miles from our properties."

I heard footsteps and rushed to my car, pretending I was just arriving. Mrs. Hudson marched past me without even looking my way. A full minute later, Mr. Hudson and Jonah walked out of the stable.

Smiling, Jonah slowed down. "Hi, Brazilian girl."

I nodded. That was the best greeting he would get from me.

Mr. Hudson turned. "Jonah, are you coming to the hospital?"

"I'll be there soon."

Mr. Hudson looked from his son to me and frowned. "Don't be late. Your sister will like to have you there when she's discharged."

"Yes, sir. I'll be right behind you."

Mr. Hudson nodded and left with his wife.

Holding the cardboard tray and the brown bag, I walked around Jonah, but he stepped in front of me. "Excuse me." I took a step to the right and he followed me. I took one to the left and he followed me again. "Let me pass," I said through gritted teeth.

"Someone woke up on the wrong side of the bed."

An urge to punch him assaulted me. "Get out of my way."

"Only if you agree to meet me tonight." I groaned and stepped to the side. He followed me again. "Meet me at The Bat after the party."

Appalled, I halted and gawked at him. "What do you take me for?"

"For a Brazilian girl." He ran his finger up my arm, and I jerked him away.

"Don't touch me."

He grasped my arm. "You don't want me yet? That's impossible."

"Conceited much?"

Grinning, he leaned over me. "I have proof that I'm impossible to resist."

"Well, I'm glad to take that proof away from you." I jerked against his hold, but he didn't let go.

"One kiss and I'm sure you'll be at my mercy."

I gritted my teeth and strained against his grasp. "Let me go."

He put his other hand on my neck. "I'll show you."

I opened my hand and let the brown bag fall

on the ground. I closed that free hand over a coffee cup and flicked my thumb, opening the lid. Then I threw the hot coffee in his face.

Screaming, he jumped back. "Bitch!"

"Stay away from me, creep!" I yelled, stepping back. I bumped into something and tripped, but strong arms grasped my waist, keeping me up. My heart tightened. "Thanks," I whispered to Garrett.

Brows furrowed, he stared at his half-brother. "What's going on?"

"Nothing," Jonah said quickly. He took off his jacket and used the inside of it to wipe his face. "She tripped and almost let go of the tray. I tried helping but only got a coffee bath." He didn't look at me.

"Lucky her," Garrett said, his voice devoid of emotion. He picked the brown bag up from the ground and held it.

"I should go," Jonah said. "I have to be there when Delilah is discharged and I still need to stop by the house—" He gestured to the white mansion atop of the hill. "—to change."

"See you later." Garret's jaw ticked.

"Bye." Jonah turned on his heels and headed to his truck. He didn't look at us as he backed away and exited the property.

Expression softening, Garrett faced me. "Are you okay?"

"How much did you see?"

"Enough."

I looked around. His truck was parked in the back of the lot beside a thick tree. "I didn't hear you arriving."

He sighed. "I arrived before you, but my father, Mrs. Hudson, and Jonah were already here, so I parked in the back and waited."

"Oh." My cheeks flamed. He had seen me eavesdropping.

"They were talking about me, right?"

"Yes."

"I'm not sure I want to know what they were talking about exactly." He took a step toward the stable. When I didn't go along, he stopped and glanced at me. "Aren't you coming?"

I shook my head. "I'm not sure I should be here."

"What do you mean?"

"I ... This isn't my ranch, but I keep acting like I'm part of it. I've been working here, not that I mind. I don't mind. I like it, actually, but it's not my place. I don't want to impose. I keep stumbling into conversations I shouldn't hear and—"

"What other conversation did you hear?"

I bit my lip. "You and your father. He was telling you Delilah has to win the competition, and it's your job to make sure she does."

His expression hardened. "Well, that's out of my hands now."

"What are you going to do now?"

"I don't know," he said. I handed the tray of coffee to him. He frowned at it. "What?"

"Take it. I bet Tom will like it, and I think you'll like it too. I can stop by and buy more after I leave."

"You don't need to leave."

"But ... You and Tom must be tired of the little brat sticking her nose where she's not supposed to."

He showed me that lopsided grin and my heart skipped a beat. "One, you're not a brat. Two, you're not sticking your nose where you're not supposed to." With his eyes one mine, he stepped to my side. "And three, we're not tired of you." He put a hand on my back, pushing me forward. "I'm not tired of you."

My breath caught. "Are you sure?"

The corner of his lips turned up. "I'm sure. Come on."

"I CALLED THE VET WHEN I WOKE UP," GARRETT said. Tom demanded news as soon as we stepped into the stable. "He said Midnight is doing well. He had surgery this morning to fix his torn ligament, and now they're giving him a strong pain medication, which makes him sleepy. He has to keep off that leg for a few days. Hopefully, he'll be back here in about a week."

I set the tray and the bag on Tom's desk, and sat in one of the chairs around it. "And his stifle?"

"The cut was superficial, but he'll have a big scar there."

"Poor Midnight," I whispered, handing the to-go cups to them. Garrett tilted his head at me. My cheeks heated under his scrutiny. "What?"

"I'm just wondering how and why you fell for that horse."

I shrugged. "I believe everyone comes into your life for a reason, and that includes animals."

"Interesting," he said. His gaze was making me too self-conscious.

Tom cleared his throat. "Well, I have news to share with you too." He reached for a donut from the bag.

I shrank in my seat, wishing I wasn't present for this part. Or maybe I should be here. I should be here for Garrett. He was a good ... friend? Or something like that. I cared about him, that was what mattered, and I wanted to be here if he needed a shoulder.

Garrett sighed. "Spill."

"Mrs. Hudson demanded to have you fired today. She wants you out of here and away from their property."

Garrett snorted. "That would be hard to accomplish."

"I know," Tom said. Knew what? I didn't get it. "Anyway, she left in that rabid queen manner of hers, but Mr. Hudson stayed behind and told me to ignore her. He said to keep you here for now. But be advised, you're under probation. Anything wrong or even not perfect, he'll fire you."

Silence fell over Tom's office.

Garrett snatched a cinnamon scone from the brown bag and stared at it for a few minutes. I exchanged a few what-do-we-do-now looks with Tom, but he shook his head, and I kept my worries in.

Finally, Garrett bit into his sweet, but then he pushed it aside. "I'm going for a walk." With his to-go cup in hand, he stood and exited the room.

"Should we go after him?" I asked Tom in a low voice.

The old man shook his head again. "Not yet."

Tom and I finished breakfast rather fast and started working. An hour later, Garrett wasn't back from his walk and I was starting to worry. Tom promised that if Garrett didn't come back in another hour, he would let me go after him.

I tried distracting myself with chores. I mucked out stalls, I checked the horses' water, I helped set up a riding group, and then I took Pepper, Autumn, and Felicity to the pastures. I leaned on the white fence, crossed my arms over it, and rested my head on my arms.

As much as I liked riding horses, I liked watching them too. My heart raced more than watching a parade for *Sete de Setembro*—Brazil's Independence Day.

I bent my knee to scratch an itch on my ankle and saw a dandelion. With a smile, I picked it up and closed my eyes.

Garrett deserves better. I wish for Garrett to receive all he deserves.

Opening my eyes, I blew on the flower and the white petals flew away. I followed them with my gaze. In the distance behind them, Garrett walked toward me. My heart skipped a beat.

He paused, knelt on the ground for a second, and then resumed walking to me. As he approached, I saw what he had in his hand. A dandelion.

He halted by my side. "What do you do with this?"

I smiled. "I close my eyes, make a wish, and then blow on it."

"Do you believe it'll come true?"

I shrugged. "I don't know. I just know that wishing and working for better things usually puts me in a better mood."

He arched an eyebrow at me before closing his eyes. Five seconds later, he opened his eyes and blew on the dandelion.

He leaned on the fence beside me. "What now? Just wait for it to come true?"

"I guess." I glanced at him. "What did you wish for?"

"Isn't it a bad thing if I tell you?"

"I thought you didn't believe in it."

"But you do," he said with his half-grin. He turned his eyes to the horses running around the pasture. "I wished to find my home."

A painful jolt ran through my heart. "Don't you have a home?"

He chuckled. "I do. But I don't feel *at* home, you know. I haven't felt at home, like I belong somewhere, since my mother died."

I turned my body to his, leaning my shoulder on the fence. "May I ask a question about that?"

"Ask anything, but I'm not sure I'll answer."

Honest, I liked that.

"Why are you still here? Why haven't you packed and left them behind?" Not that I wanted him to leave. One of the good things about spending so much time at this ranch meant that I also spent time with him.

"When I was born, my father tried buying my mother's silence. She was young, only eighteen, and her parents didn't want anything to do with her. So, she accepted it. He gave her some money, but for some reason, they agreed it wasn't enough, but he couldn't take more without having to explain to Mrs. Hudson where the money was going. So, he wanted to sell a piece of his land and give her that money. My mother asked him for the land instead, not the money. She told him she would sell it later, when she needed the money, and he believed her. Many years later, she got sick and told me who my father was and that he had given her a piece of his land."

"That place I picked you up yesterday."

He nodded. "When she died, the land became mine, and when I came to claim it, Mrs. Hudson found out about me. I won't enter into details of the war that went on for many months. I was six-teen then, and the court suggested my father take me in, take care of me, so I wouldn't go to foster care. He offered me the room above the stables and work at the stable, to keep me occupied."

"You didn't go to school?"

He shook my head. "Not after moving here, no. I took the GED a few years later. When I turned eighteen, I wanted to leave, but I had no money. I had a talk with my father, and he started paying me to keep working here. I was able to save a little to buy Felicity and pay for college, but not enough to move out. My goal was to get a scholarship for a vet school somewhere else, so I could move out of here, but my grades weren't that good since I worked more than I studied, so I got in none, not even at the school here. That's when the idea of making something of my land presented itself to me."

"The barn you're building."

"Yeah. I built the cabin first, before I graduated from college and had to move out from The Bat house, so I would have a roof over my head."

"And before going to college. Where did you live?"

He pointed to a tiny white dot past the man-sion atop the hill. "That's where most of my father's employees live. The ones working with his cattle. It's much like a dorm building, and one of those rooms was mine."

My heart sank. "Oh."

"Anyway, I'm building the barn, and then I want to build a small stable and buy a couple of horses. I hope that I'll open my own ranch in a couple of years. And with that, I'll be free of Rocky Hill."

I rested my hand on his arm. "I'm sorry about what you went through." His gaze followed my hand. "But I'm glad you're able to keep your head high, and you're doing something for yourself."

He lifted his gaze and his eyes met mine. "Thanks. Sometimes I have doubts about what I'm doing, and hearing that helps a lot."

I pulled my hand away. "Say, I don't need to work here all the time. Let me know your days off, and I'll help you there if you want."

"I can't pay you for that."

"I'm not asking to be paid for what I do here. Why would I ask to be paid while working at *your* ranch?"

He smiled. He actually smiled. A huge, all teeth, true smile. The shine in his eyes matched his smile, and my heart skipped several beats. *Meu Deus*, he truly was even more handsome when he smiled for real. Now that I had seen it, now that I had experienced it, I wanted more. I needed to make him smile more.

"I'll take that into consideration," he said.

I shook the shock off my system and nudged him in the ribs with my elbow. "Come on, you would love to have my help. Admit it."

The wattage of his smile diminished, but it was still more than I had ever seen from him. "You're amazing." Heat crawled up my cheeks and I shook my head. He brushed a strand of my hair away from my face. "You really are amazing."

My gaze flicked to his lips, and I remembered how great they had felt against mine. My heart beat faster, and I inhaled sharply.

He hadn't shown any interest in me since the first and only time we kissed. I wouldn't be the one to beg. Besides, even if he wanted something, that something could be to get between my legs and nothing else. After having the attention of dozens of men on campus, but knowing they had one thing in mind, I couldn't tell when a guy was interested in me, or just my body.

I averted my eyes and he let his hand fall beside him.

"Did I say something wrong?"

Did he? No, he didn't. In fact, he hadn't said

one thing wrong the entire day. Being here with him, hearing him opening up, was fantastic. Some of my old boldness slipped into me, and I relished in it. I embraced it. I called it forth and begged it to take me over.

I turned my face to him and found him still looking at me. Without hesitation, I leaned closer to him, stood on my tiptoes, cupped his cheek with my hand, and put my lips on his. He stiffened for a second, as if not expecting my sudden change of heart, but soon enough, his soft lips moved with mine and his hands rested on my hips.

I opened my mouth and his tongue didn't waste time. It plunged in, exploring each corner of my mouth and drawing a moan from my throat. His arms slid around my waist, and with one big hand splayed on my back, he drew me closer.

Pulling away, he whirled us around and pressed me against the fence, drawing a gasp from my lungs. He stared at me, his eyes shining with lust. I shivered.

His arms snaked around me again before he dipped his head and met my lips with his. His mouth was harder this time, and when I slid a hand under his shirt and grazed my long nails on his back, he groaned before deepening the kiss.

His lips seemed to have been made for me, and

his kiss made every nerve in my body feel alive. He brushed his thumb under the hem of my thin sweater, and that simple act made me shiver. He smiled against my lips. With a smile of my own, I bit his lower lip before sucking on it. He groaned again.

"I want to be on top of you," he whispered.

I knew what he meant. Imagining him on top of me brought desire burning in my veins.

He kissed my chin before grazing his tongue along my jaw and down my neck. He left a trail of fire whenever he touched me, with his hands or his lips, or any part of him. He gently bit the soft spot between my neck and shoulder, and I gasped, sinking my nails into his back.

I turned my face to his and inhaled, savoring in his spicy, woody scent. It was so much better when this close, when my body was pressed against his, when his hands were all over me, when his mouth was on me. He lifted his face, crushing my lips with his again.

Until the fence creaked behind me and we froze.

"*Meu Deus*," I whispered.

Garrett stepped back, pulling me with him.

He buried his face in my neck and laughed. "Thought I would let you fall?"

"I don't know. Would you?"

"Depends. If I fell over you, it might be worth it."

Heat swam in my body, and I slapped his shoulder.

"Garrett!" Tom called.

We sprang apart, as if we had been two teenagers sneaking around behind our parents' backs to make out.

"Yes?" Garrett asked, turning to the stable.

Tom peeked out the back gate. "Help me in here, please."

"Sure." He glanced at me but didn't do anything. He didn't nod, he didn't cock his brow, and he didn't smile. Had he regretted kissing me already?

He walked away from me and into the stable.

Careful to avoid the creaking wood, I collapsed against the fencepost.

21

I SETTLED IN THE COFFEE SHOP AFTER MY LAST Monday class—alone, since Phoebe had ditched me to go to the movies with Kevin—and opened my history book. Phoebe, Jonah, and I hadn't started our damn paper yet, and I didn't want to leave it for the last minute. It was hard to research when my mind was somewhere else.

And it wasn't only one thing—it was crazy Audrey, creepy Jonah, missing Phoebe, injured Midnight, bitchy Delilah, and hot Garrett. After the kiss yesterday, he kept busy with chores. He didn't stop for one minute, and since I wouldn't play the whiny, needy girl, I didn't hang around waiting for him to look at me. However, I didn't want to look like I was running away either. So, I stayed and got busy too. I only left in the middle of the afternoon with an excuse that I had to study. Which I had to do, but wasn't in the mood to.

I took a long breath and imagined myself riding through green pastures, the sun warming my skin, the wind wiping my hair. That cleared my mind, and I turned my focus to my book.

Until my phone rang. I saw Jonah's name blinking on the screen and pressed the end button. So much for clearing my mind. The phone rang again. I pressed the end button again, and muted it before the people at the coffee shop started complaining about it.

When the phone rang a third time, I knew he wouldn't give up.

"What do you want?" I answered, my voice harsh.

"Hi, Brazilian girl."

"Stop calling me that."

"But aren't you a girl? Aren't you Brazilian? I think it's perfect."

"What do you want?" I repeated.

"I bumped into Phoebe after class, and we agreed we should stop delaying and work on our essay."

"All right. When should we meet?"

"Right now."

"Wait. No. Phoebe went to the movies with her boyfriend."

"No, she canceled it. She's here with me."

I let out a frustrated breath. "Okay, okay. I'm on my way to the library."

"Not the library. We're at The Bat."

I paused. "Why?"

"Because we were close to here, and I told her we had plenty of brownies and pumpkin spice latte that our maid made this afternoon. She said she couldn't pass it up."

That traitor. "I would rather meet at the library."

"I want to see you convince Phoebe of that. She's buried in the kitchen right now, and I think we'll have a hard time talking her out of there."

I sighed. "I'll be there in ten."

"Great."

I hit the end button and sent a message to Phoebe.

Traitor.

She didn't answer right away, because she was probably stuffing her face with brownies. I liked brownies too, but I would rather go to Panera or Starbucks and buy one than eat one for free at The Bat.

I closed my book, packed my stuff, and

marched out of the coffee shop. The walk to The Bat took only six minutes, and one shove to a guy with grabby hands. *Meu Deus*, when would they leave me alone? I was tired of walking around feeling like a porn star or something.

I stopped at the door and reached my hand to the bell, but then remembered all the movies I had seen that showed fraternity houses and their unlocked doors. Not surprisingly, I turned the knob and the door opened. A little wary, I stepped into the foyer.

The house didn't look like it was in a full party mode, but it wasn't quiet either. Guys milled in the living room, watching a football game. They shouted at the TV as if the players could hear them. On the other side, a trio of guys was seated by the bar, drinking at five in the afternoon. *Ótimo*.

I went to the kitchen at the back of the house. There were more guys there, seated around the island, drinking beer. They stopped talking when I stepped in and stared at me.

"Hey, it's the Brazilian girl," one said, standing from the stool. His gaze ran the length of me. "Come to play?"

"As if." I tried remaining calm. One guy didn't scare me, but a house full of them could definitely send me into a panic. "Where's Jonah?"

"Oh, don't be like that," another one said. He licked his lips. "Jonah won't mind sharing."

I groaned and turned on my heels, exiting the kitchen to the sound of catcalls and wolf whistles. Really? Men.

My will was to leave, but Phoebe was here. I wouldn't leave her alone inside a house full of horny guys. I reached for my phone and was about to call her when Jonah appeared on the landing atop the stairs.

"There you are," he said, smiling.

"Here I am." I slipped my phone back into my pocket. "Where's Phoebe?"

"In my bedroom."

I raised my eyebrows. "Really? What a convenient place to study."

"If you want peace and quiet, it is." He pointed to the doors on each side of the foyer. The living and the dining room. Point taken.

With gritted teeth, I climbed up the stairs and followed him to the third floor. He led me down a long corridor and opened the last door for me. His bedroom was large and neat. A queen bed against the wall, an open closet door, a desk and chair, a tall dresser, and many posters of horses and cow-girls in skimpy outfits.

And no Phoebe.

"Where is she?" I turned to him.

He closed the door behind him and smiled at me. "Not here for sure."

Fear crawled up my spine. "What do you mean?"

"I lied. I didn't meet with her, and I have no idea where she is."

"What?" I grabbed my phone and stared at it. I had sent her a message, and she hadn't answered. Of course. It wasn't because she was stuffing her face with brownies or with her nose in a book, but because she was at the movies with her boyfriend, as she said. My hand fell to my side, my grip tightening around my phone. "Are you delusional?"

He took a step closer to me. "It was the only way to make you come here."

"Y-you got that right. Now, excuse me." I started walking around him, but he held my arm and pulled me back. "Let me go."

"Not yet, Brazilian girl. I said you were going to want me, and I'll make you want me right now." He pulled my tote from me, threw it on the floor, and pushed me against the bed. I fell, seated, on it. "In five minutes, you'll be screaming my name."

What the hell was wrong with him? "Yeah, right."

He stepped toward me and I rose, pulling my knee up and smashing his precious dick.

He let out a loud groan and doubled over. "Bitch."

I pushed him back and he fell on his knees. "Listen, you bastard. I'm not a slut. Most Brazilian girls aren't. If you don't know, there are sluts in the United States too. Want proof of that? Go on spring break at some fancy beach. You'll find plenty, and they will do whatever you want them too. As for me, I'm off-limits. I'm a nice girl and I won't let you or Audrey spoil that. Do you hear me?" He groaned. "You don't get to touch me; you don't get to speak to me anymore. Look at me in a way I don't like, and I'll knee you again in front of the entire campus."

"You'll pay for this," he croaked.

"As if I care." I picked up my tote and rushed out of the room, climbing down the stairs three steps at a time.

I crossed the hallway to the sound of hollers and cheers.

"Jonah won?" one asked.

"I think so," another said.

"Jonah won!" a third one yelled.

What did he win? Me? The guys probably thought Jonah had gotten some. Ugh. The things they thought of me got worse by the minute. Tears brimmed in my eyes, and I hurried out the door. I bumped into a wall, and I would have fallen back if Garrett hadn't clasped his hands around my upper arms and held me up.

"Bia? What happened?" he asked. I shook my head and swallowed the tears, the terror, and the anger. His grasped softened and one of his hands slid up, cupping my face. "Hey, talk to me."

I stepped back and out of reach. He was just like Jonah, only a little subtler. Soon, he would be like his half-brother, only instead of trying to get me alone in a bedroom, he would lock me in the tack room at his father's ranch.

"I'm okay," I said, willing my voice to stay strong. "Excuse me."

I walked past him, but he followed me. He stepped in my way, making me halt. His jaw hardened. "Did someone do something to you?"

I forced my head up and stared at him. "No."

"But something happened. Why won't you talk to me?"

"There's nothing to talk about. Now, please, let me go."

He stayed in the same spot for a full minute until he finally stepped aside. "Fine."

I could feel his eyes on me as I walked by him

and continued my march down the street, in the dorm's direction, but I didn't look back or slow down. I wanted to be as far away as I could from men like them.

Graças a Deus, Molly wasn't in our room, and I was able to throw myself on my bed and hug my pillow. I fought hard, but a couple of tears rolled down my cheeks. Perhaps I wasn't as strong as I thought I was. Perhaps this new Bia wasn't as strong as the old Bia.

My phone dinged. I weighed looking at it and decided to surrender to it. Whatever it was, I would see it later anyway, so why not get it over with?

Phoebe: *I just left the movies. What did I do?*

It took me a moment to remember I had called her traitor in my last message. If only she had responded earlier.

Me: *Nothing. I was teasing Hannah and I sent the message to you by mistake.*

Phoebe: *Oh. Good. How are you?*

Me: *Good.*

What a lie.

Phoebe: *Great. I'll see you in class tomorrow.*

Me: *Yeah. Have fun.*

Phoebe: *Thanks.*

I tossed my phone at the wall, and I was kind

of pissed when it didn't smash into several pieces.

Tuesday was cruel. As usual, guys and girls looked at me and whispered and pointed and chuckled or looked at me with disgust. I was getting used to that. I didn't like it, I wanted to do something about it, but I was getting used to walking around like the clown of the university. Getting used to having only one friend.

However, the day felt cruel nonetheless. I wasn't sure if it was harder because of the whole almost-sexual-assault from Jonah yesterday, or the kiss with Garrett on Sunday, but something had changed in me, and I felt vulnerable.

Molly wasn't completely ignoring me anymore, but she still wasn't speaking more than some necessary words here and there. As for switching rooms, she gave up trying.

My first class went by in a blur. I couldn't focus and I couldn't stop my mind from racing. I was sick and tired of Audrey's lies, I was sick and tired of Molly's cattiness, I was sick and tired of others staring at me and whispering, and I was so sick and tired of caring about any of that.

Suffocated. That was how I felt. It was as if

every little thing came barreling down on me, and I could do nothing to stop it. Having to start college over, being among younger students, living in a tiny, ugly, and cold dorm, not having my mom's cooking, having near to zero friends, and dragging poor Phoebe down this road. Having an accent and not knowing perfect English. Being away from my crazy brothers and cousin. Being away from Hannah, and even her sister Hilary, whom I got to know a little since Leo and Hannah started dating. Missing my friends in Brazil. Hating that I didn't miss more of my country and feeling guilty about it. Walking across campus as if nothing affected me, no lies, no stares, no gossip. Not punching Audrey's face each time she was near me. Having kissed Garrett twice and having it lead to nothing. Being alone. All of those things were my fences. The fences in my path, the ones I couldn't jump over. The ones closing in on me, suffocating me, and squashing my self-confidence.

Never before had I felt like curling up in my bed and sleeping until everything settled down. The thing was, would it settle down? I hoped it would. Next month, next semester ... It had to settle down. They had to forget about me at some point, and I would be able to be myself again.

I hoped.

When the class was over, I stepped into the hallway and a hand closed around my forearm, pushing me back to the wall.

"Hey!"

Audrey's face was inches from mine, her brown eyes spitting rage. "Who do you think you are?"

"*Meu Deus*, here we go again." I pushed her back, but she only staggered a foot away from me. "Didn't we have this conversation already?"

"I warned you. Stay away from him." Her voice was loud, and she drew everyone's attention around us by flailing like a crazy person. "But what did you do? You offered yourself to him."

My eyes widened. "What?"

She turned to the others with a wicked smile. "That's right. She knows Jonah and I are a thing, but this girl—" She pointed her thin finger at me. "—couldn't stay away. She went after my man. She told him she didn't care that he was in a serious relationship. She just wanted one good night with him."

A crowd gathered around us, and they all stared at me with more disgust in their eyes. *Meu Deus*, I hated this girl.

"That's not true!"

She raised her voice to drown my protests.

"What would you do after you had him? Chase another guy? What if the next guy also has a girlfriend? Oh, wait, you don't care about that."

"Audrey, that's enough! Stop inventing lies. I didn't do anything."

"Friends, she's Brazilian. If the university regulations allowed, she would probably parade around wearing those carnival clothes women down there wear. Those shiny, feathery things that cover *nothing*!" I gritted my teeth. It was *Carnaval*, not carnival. She didn't even get the facts straight before accusing me. "Don't you all know Brazilian women are easy? This one isn't just easy; she also goes after our men."

Nothing I said would make this situation better, so I pushed away from the wall and walked away. However, she didn't leave me alone.

"Yes." Audrey chuckled, a sick sound that knotted my stomach. "Run away and don't come back. Take that big ass of yours and stay away from our men, whore."

Oh, that was it.

I spun around on my boots and was in her face in three steps. Her eyes widened. She wasn't expecting me to turn back. Well, she wasn't expecting what I was going to do next either.

I pulled my arm back and punched her pretty, plastic nose.

She yelled, putting her hands over her face.

Screams, laughter, and hoots filled the hallway.

Droga, what had I done?

"You'll pay for this!" Audrey yelled as I rushed out of the building.

ON WEDNESDAY, I WALKED INTO THE HISTORY CLASS with ten seconds to spare. I knew the campus was abuzz with news that the crazy Brazilian girl had broken precious Audrey's nose, so I didn't give them time to talk to me, to ask me about it, to bother me.

The professor eyed me with a frown. Maybe he noticed I had always been here and ready for class by the time he entered the classroom, and this time was different.

I approached his desk and handed him a thick stack of paper.

"What's this?" he asked, taking the papers.

"Our essay. Phoebe's, Jonah's, and mine."

"But it isn't due for another month."

"I know. But we wanted to cross off our long to-do lists, so we worked hard this weekend to finish it."

He glanced at Phoebe and Jonah, seated in the back row. I fought the urge to glance back and hoped they didn't look surprised.

"All right," the professor said. "Very good." He faced the class. "Everyone should take that as an example."

Phoebe watched me with wide eyes, but I shook my head and, instead of sitting beside her as I usually did, I took a seat in the first row, beside a nerdy kid. He stared at me as if he was thirteen and seated beside Gisele Bündchen.

I ignored him and class started.

My phone vibrated in my pocket. *Ainda bem* that I remembered to put on silence mode.

Phoebe: *Why did you do that? And why are you sitting there?*

Me: *I'll explain later.*

Phoebe: *You better.*

Like yesterday, this class went by in a blur. The professor dismissed us and, five seconds later, Phoebe was by my side.

"What's going on?" she asked.

I stood, glancing at the back. Jonah was still in his seat, but his eyes were on me. "Can we talk outside?"

"Sure."

Side by side, we walked through the hallways, and out of the building.

Ten steps after, Phoebe held my arm and stopped. "Tell me—" Her eyes widened. "Haven't you been sleeping well?"

"Um, why do you ask?"

"You have dark circles under your eyes."

I pressed my fingertips under my eyes. "I didn't sleep the past two nights, trying to finish the essay."

"Why? Why weren't you in our first class? Why did you do it all alone? And why didn't you ask me if that was okay?"

"I'm sorry, okay. I'm really sorry. I just ..." I sighed and told her about Monday and Tuesday—about Jonah's plan and how I punched Audrey—as fast as I could. I didn't want to spend much time on details, reliving it.

"I can't believe he did that!" she said, her voice louder. A few students walking around turned their heads to us, and she slapped her hand over her mouth. "Sorry."

"It's okay." I shrugged. "I just wanted to be done with it, so I don't need to spend any time with him."

"Do you think he's telling everyone that you slept with him?"

I shuddered in disgust. "I don't know, but Audrey heard about it, so I'm assuming more people heard about it too."

"That's crazy."

"Tell me about it."

"Bia."

I heard Jonah's voice—calling me by my name for once—and stiffened.

"Oh, boy," Phoebe whispered.

He stopped beside us. "We need to talk."

I glared at him. "Um, no, we don't."

"Yes, we do," he insisted, shooting out his hand toward me.

Phoebe pushed his hand away. "Hey, creep. Stay away from my girl."

I smiled at her.

Jonah glowered at her. "I don't take orders from anyone, little girl."

She gulped. "Well—"

"Jonah."

My heart skipped a beat. It was Garrett and he was approaching us fast.

"What are you doing here?" Jonah asked.

Garrett jaw tensed. "Can I talk to you?"

"I'm busy right now," Jonah said.

"I wasn't talking to you," Garrett said. He faced me. "Can I talk to you?"

I opened my mouth and closed it again.

Jonah clenched his fists. "Why do you want to talk to her? Because she hasn't brought you coffee in the mornings?"

"How do you know that?" I asked.

"Wait." Phoebe raised her hand. "You're bringing him coffee?" She pointed to Garrett. "And you didn't tell me about it."

"It's not like that."

Jonah crossed his arms. "It isn't? Then what is it like?"

I glowered at him. "This is none of your business, creep. Keep your distance from me, or I'll find a way to get a restraining order."

He laughed. "Right."

I took Phoebe's arm and started walking away. "I'm dead serious."

Phoebe stayed close to me, and I glanced at Garrett. He was watching me with a hard expression, but he didn't stop me from leaving, and he also didn't come after me. Again.

When we were out of hearing range, Phoebe leaned into me. "What is happening with the cowboy?"

I shrugged. "I have no idea."

"Sure you do."

"I— It's complicated, I guess."

"Lucky for you, I have the next two hours open, and we're going to the coffee shop, where you'll tell me everything."

I opened my mouth to tell her I had to study for a test. With all that had happened, my mind had been elsewhere, and I hadn't really paid attention in my classes.

However, wasn't it yesterday that I was complaining about not having anyone to talk to? Here Phoebe was, offering me her time and attention.

I hooked my arm with hers and smiled. "I'm in."

22

———

TELLING EVERYTHING TO PHOEBE HAD DONE wonders for my soul. I still felt restless, frustrated, and upset, and I was still lusting after Garrett, but at least now, I had someone to run to, to call, even to text when I needed to talk. Shame on me for not telling her any of this months ago.

It was past nine when we walked out of the coffee shop and to our dorms. Approaching my building, I rummaged through my tote, looking for my car keys. It was late, but I wanted to go out and grab something to eat. Preferably not fast food. I could stop by Olive Garden and order something to go.

I looked up, watching the sidewalk so I wouldn't trip and fall on my face, and saw Garrett leaning against the wall a few feet from the front door. I halted. He had his hands in the pockets of his jacket and his eyes fixed on mine.

"What are you doing here?" I asked.

"We gotta talk."

Now he wanted to talk? Or had he just come here to kiss me then disappear? I looked around. A few students walked past us. I jerked my chin toward the dark parking lot and walked to my car. Garrett followed me.

I opened the door of my car, threw my tote inside, and leaned against the frame. "About?"

He stopped two feet in front of me. "What were you doing in Jonah's room?"

His question caught me off guard, and my mouth fell open for a second. Then I clamped it shut and my hands closed into fists. "He didn't tell you?"

"His version doesn't make much sense. I want to hear yours."

"What did he tell you?"

"Your version first."

I clenched and unclenched my fists. Anxiety and rage filled my chest. I didn't want to relive that moment. "He tricked me into believing Phoebe was at The Bat working on our project with him. I went there and ..." I pressed my lips together and crossed my arms.

"He tried something with you," he finished for me. I nodded. "Son of a bitch," he said through gritted teeth. "What happened then?"

"I kneed his goods and fled. That's when I bumped into you. I was fleeing." Garrett closed his eyes, and I wasn't sure what to make of it. "What did he tell you?"

He ran a hand through his hair. "That you showed up at his door, offering yourself. He refused because he wanted to take you out on a date first, but you kept pushing him. That's what I mean about not making sense. Knowing him, he doesn't really care about taking girls out on a date before taking them to bed."

I shuddered. "I'm sorry, but his version is twisted." However, Jonah was his brother. He would probably defend the guy before believing a Brazilian slut.

He erased half the distance between us. "I know. I believe you."

"You do?"

He reached for me and uncrossed my arms. "I do."

"But why?"

"Because I think I know you better than they do."

The old Bia would have done one of two things. One, she would have kissed him right then, or two, she would at least start the we-kissed-now-what conversation. But this Bia? This Bia was afraid of blinking because it could be interpreted the wrong way.

I wrapped my arms behind my back and entwined my fingers on my lower back. "How is Midnight?"

Garrett cocked his head to the side, and his expression told me he was calculating if I was bipolar or not. "Recovering. If he keeps making progress, he should be back at the ranch by Friday. Or, if it slows down a little, next week."

"I might visit him."

"At the vet?"

"No, at the ranch."

"Why wouldn't you? I mean, you're there every weekend," he said, making it sound so casual. I averted my eyes. "Wait. What is it? You were thinking about not going to the ranch this weekend, weren't you?"

"I still am," I whispered.

"Tom will be disappointed."

Once more, he talked about how Tom would

miss me, or how Midnight would miss me. But not him. No. The only time he mentioned something like that was to help him with his chores.

"Tom will survive."

He sighed. "Is it because of me? If you don't want to go because things are awkward between us, I have a solution for that. I'm going to Santa Fe tomorrow morning to look for a new horse for Delilah. You should bring breakfast on Saturday to Tom and spend some time with Midnight, if he's better."

"Wait. What? Delilah is buying a new horse? What will happen to Midnight?"

"I don't know yet. Right now, the only thing we know is that he can't compete and she needs a new, trained horse ASAP."

Needs a new horse. Couldn't she sit this one out and help her horse recover?

"When will you be back?"

The lopsided grin split his lips. "Why? Will you miss me?"

I rolled my eyes. "No, so I won't be there when you come back."

The grin faded. "Why are you avoiding me?"

I could shrug and tell him he was a pain in the ass, but that couldn't be farther from the truth. Deep down, in a dark place inside me, where I didn't like to admit things to myself, I had hopes that Garrett really liked me for me, not just for my pretty face and nice body. I had hopes of Garrett and me together, making it work even through all the lies Audrey spread. That was only a dream. Yet, if I never opened up, it would never come true.

I sighed. "Because I don't want to give you the wrong impression about me. It's enough what Audrey put in everyone else's minds."

He braced his arm on the doorway and leaned closer, his eyes on mine. "The only impression of you right now is that we kissed, and I wouldn't mind doing that again."

My cheeks flushed and I averted my eyes. "Tell me when you'll be back."

"Sunday night, if I get a new horse fast. Otherwise, I'm staying there until I find one."

That meant I could go to the ranch Friday after my classes, and Saturday and Sunday all day.

"Tell Tom I'll be there Friday."

He shook his head. "I would have said I was leaving town last time you disappeared if I knew that's what it would take for you to go back."

I smiled. "That would have brought the old Bia back, and she can be very mean."

"Is that the same one that kissed me at the Halloween Ball and last Sunday?"

I nodded. "I do my best to keep her hidden."

"Why?"

"Because she was more carefree, more alive, more out there. Not like Audrey makes me look like, but certainly my behavior would have fed her lies. Everyone would look at me and believe her."

"I hate to tell you this, but I don't think they doubt her now," he said. I knew it, but hearing that hurt a little more. "You shouldn't change because of that."

I poked his stomach in play, but regretted it. His abs were rock hard. My cheeks warmed a little more. "Um, you like this Bia. Plain and quiet."

Garrett grabbed my hand, and he leaned into me, pressing my back against my car. "I do, but I think I would like the other one too. I've seen glimpses of her, and I do like her."

He liked me? Before I could think about what he had said, he slid a hand around my neck and lowered his face to mine. His lips brushed mine. My breath caught. He started pulling away, but I fisted my hands on his jacket and pulled him to me. I melded my mouth with his. He sighed and relaxed, opening his lips to me, letting me in. He leaned into me, winding his other arm around me and pressing my chest to his. Desire, want, and lust swarmed through me, and I almost fell headfirst in it. I almost clung to him for dear life, pulled him into my car, and climbed onto him. Or invited him back to my dorm. Almost.

A flicker of reason sparked in my mind, and I remembered where we were. Other students could see me, could see us, and add fuel to Audrey's fire.

I broke the kiss and turned to the side, hiding my face under my hair.

"Hey, don't," Garrett said, brushing my hair from my face. "Don't run away again. Don't hide."

Really? I had run away the first time, yes, but last Sunday, he was the one that kept his distance from me. He had been the one running away.

"I-I need to go," I lied. Yes, I was hungry, but I had nothing scheduled. I could eat later, or not eat at all. Still, this felt inappropriate.

He sighed and pulled his hands away. "I'll see you when I get back, right?"

"Maybe," I said in a low voice.

"Maybe is better than no."

I shook my head, hiding a smile, and looked at him. "Bye, Garrett. Have a safe trip."

He stared at me for a moment before answering. "Bye, Bia."

He walked around the car, toward The Bat house, and I drove out of the parking lot. I had lost my appetite and ended up driving around for half an hour before stopping by a McDonald's, and going back to my dorm to sulk.

———

KNOWING GARRETT WAS AWAY, I DIDN'T EVEN THINK if going to Rocky Hill was an option or not. I loved going to the ranch. It was the only place where I could clear my mind and be a little more like myself, but things between Garrett and me were odd. I tried not caring, but it influenced my decisions.

This time, it was a no brainer. Right after my Friday afternoon class, I rushed to my room, dropped my tote, picked up my cowboy hat, and drove off-campus.

The last two days had been complicated. The only bright side was seeing Audrey walking around with a huge bandage over her broken nose. Still, I felt a little guilty for feeling good about having done that.

Wary, I parked my car beside Mr. Hudson's SUV. The thought of leaving crossed my mind, but what the hell? If he asked about it, I was a frequent client.

The door to Tom's office was closed, and I could hear voices coming from inside, though I couldn't hear exactly what was being said. And I didn't even want to.

On instinct, I approached Midnight's stall. A pang ran through my heart at seeing it empty. I knew he was recovering well, even though he wouldn't be able to ride for a long time, but the pain was also from missing him. Beside Midnight's stall, Felicity nickered. I extended my hand to her and let her sniff me before running my fingers along her smooth coat.

"Hey, girl. Missing your man?" I asked. She snorted, and I laughed as if she had answered me. "I sorta miss him too." She poked her nose on my arm. "All right. I miss him. A lot." I sighed. "You know him better than I do. Got any advice on dealing with him?" She lowered her head, going for the water bowl. "I thought so."

Noticing her water was low, I got busy by giving her more water and checking the other stalls and doing the same. I was halfway done when Mr. Hudson stepped out of Tom's office. He saw me leaning over Autumn's stall and frowned. Tom exited the office and Mr. Hudson turned to him. They exchanged a few hushed words before Mr. Hudson straightened his jacket and left the stable.

Tom rubbed his hand on the back of his neck as he approached me.

"Hi," I said, a little worried about why Tom looked worried.

"Hi," he answered, his voice small.

"Want to talk about it?"

He halted beside me. "There's not much to talk about. Mr. Hudson isn't happy with the way things are going between Delilah and Garrett. He hopes Garrett can find a new horse and make a champion out of Delilah in record time."

"That's ... not impossible, but not likely to happen."

Tom raised his eyebrows. "It *is* impossible and we both know it."

I bit the inside of my cheek. "What will happen then?"

"I don't know." He sighed. "Let's hope Garrett can perform a miracle."

I wasn't the praying type, but this was a matter worth praying about. Even if things never worked out between Garrett and me, I didn't want to see him kicked out of here, or worse.

"And just now?" I asked. "After Mr. Hudson saw me. What did he say to you?"

"He asked me if I had hired new help without his knowledge."

"Oh. What did you tell him?"

"That I would never do that. I told him you're a client and that you're becoming attached to one of our horses. You come early to spend a little time with the horse."

I nodded. "You didn't tell him which horse."

"If I told him, he would find it strange, wouldn't he? I mean—" He gestured to the empty stall behind us. "—Midnight isn't here at the moment."

"Thanks."

"No worries." He picked up a halter from the bench along the wall. "Now, are you here to work or what?"

I smiled. "You're abusing my goodwill."

He shrugged. "I'm taking what I can."

I kicked his shin lightly, and he feigned it hurt. "Ouch, that is going to leave a scar." He limped a step.

I shook my head. "Such an old man."

23

———

"WHAT TIME DO YOU PLAN ON LEAVING?" I ASKED Tom when he entered his office. It was just past six and I was thinking about turning in. Yeah, too early for a Saturday, but since I didn't party anymore, six was a good time to settle down, eat something, and curl up in bed with a good book. Besides, I had stayed here until late last night and had arrived here early this morning.

"I'm not sure, why?" he asked me.

"Because I'm hungry, and I thought you probably know a great typical American diner nearby to take me to."

He raised his eyebrows at me. "Are you asking me on a date, Miss Fernandes?"

I rolled my eyes. "Sure I am," I teased.

"Well, ma'am, I do know a great diner with a greasy burger you have to try."

"Great." I smiled. "What time are we leaving?"

He glanced at his cell phone. "Not soon."

"Why not?"

He averted his eyes. "I'm not supposed to say anything."

"What does that mean?"

"Nothing."

"Tom!"

He raised his hands and stepped back. "My lips are sealed." He rushed out of his office.

"Tom!" I called again, but he didn't come back.

Oh no, he wouldn't get away with it. I stood and ran after him, but the sound of tires crushing the driveway stones made me halt.

Curious, I walked out of the stable. Garrett's truck parked right in front of the stable with a horse trailer on the back.

He opened the door and jumped out from his truck, tipping his hat at me. "Howdy, ma'am."

I crossed my arms. "Weren't you supposed to be back tomorrow night? Or maybe after that?"

He half-smiled and my heart skipped a beat. "Yes, but I worked hard and found a great horse in record time."

"And why was that?"

He rushed to me and kissed my cheek. "Because I knew you would still be here." Then he turned and marched to the trailer. I hated it when he said things like that and then just dropped it.

Tom appeared from inside the stable, smiling.

That was when it clicked. "You knew he was arriving."

"Yup. He asked me to make sure you were still here."

My mouth fell open.

"Hey," Garrett called, opening the trailer's back door. "You two going to keep gossiping over there, or are you going to help me?"

"As if you needed help to unload a horse," I said, walking toward him.

"True," he said, smiling. "But that doesn't mean I don't want you close." My cheeks warmed. Embarrassed, I glanced over my shoulder, but Tom was gone. Garrett lost the smile. "You don't need to be ashamed of Tom. He's actually rooting for us to get along."

"What?" Had they been talking about us? I shook my head. "Wait. I'm not ashamed."

"Then why did you look back at him?" he asked, and I shrugged. He stepped inside the trailer, and two seconds later, came out pulling a dark brown horse. Another Thoroughbred, almost as tall and big as Midnight, and just as beautiful.

I stepped closer and ran my hand over his smooth coat. The horse turned his muzzle to me and nickered.

"Don't tell me this one will also fall in love with you," Garrett said.

I smiled. "What can I do? I'm a horse magnet."

He leaned in and whispered in my ear, "Not just of horses."

I slapped his shoulder, and he kept on pulling the horse out of the trailer.

"What's his name?" I asked.

"Golden Racer."

"You're kidding?" I asked, and he shook his head. "When is Delilah coming to see him?"

Garrett led the horse inside the stable. "Tomorrow. She wants to practice already."

"Shouldn't she get to know him first?"

"Tell her that. With the accident, she already lost a week. She can't afford more or she won't make it to the competition."

It still pissed me off. I knew this competition was important, but there were plenty of smaller competitions all the time. She could go to any of those, and then go to another big one.

Garrett walked in with the new horse. For a

few minutes, he ran around the place, making sure the new horse had plenty to eat and drink, that he was comfortable and set up.

"All right," he said. "I think he should be okay for now." He turned to me. "Tom told me you want me to take you to the Horseshoe Diner."

"What?" I looked around for Tom, but he was nowhere to be seen. Typical. "I asked him if *he* wanted to take me to a diner."

Garrett raised an eyebrow. "You're telling me you asked Tom out on a date?"

I fought the urge to roll my eyes. "Yeah, exactly that."

He loomed over me. "Come with me. I'll take you there."

"Is it close to campus?"

He frowned. "No. It's just outside town."

I considered it for a minute. I was hungry and he could show me a typical American diner. I had never been to one and I was curious about it. Besides, I was dying to eat a big, greasy burger. Bonus points for not being close to the university. Chances were nobody would see us together.

"Okay," I whispered. He took my hand and led me out. He turned to his truck, but I stopped, slipping my hand from his grip. "I'll take my car." He frowned. "Driving back here to get my car after would be wasted time." Not that I didn't have time to waste. "I'll just follow you."

He nodded before walking to his car.

I followed him to the Horseshoe Diner and parked beside him.

He opened the front door for me. I walked past him, and he put a hand on the small of my back, stepping beside me. That simple touch sent a rush of heat through my entire body. With a slight pressure of his hand, he led me to a corner booth.

"You want the American experience," he said, once we were seated and looking over our menus. "Then you'll let me order for you."

I lowered my menu and looked at him across the table. "Okay."

He half-smiled. "Good."

The waitress, who batted her fake lashes at Garrett, took our order and brought our drinks. Thankfully, he didn't seem to notice how flirty she was.

I was getting used to being this close to him and not doing anything. Just being there, side by side, in comfortable silence. Still, my mind wandered through several topics we could talk about. Or not. There wasn't really anything I wanted to talk about other than enjoying Garrett's company.

A few minutes later, the waitress brought our

food. The burger Garrett had ordered for me was bigger than my head, and the portion of fries could feed a soccer team.

"How am I supposed to bite this?"

He chuckled. "It's supposed to be messy."

I didn't really enjoy messy. It took some time and tries, but I finally bit into the burger.

"*Meu Deus*, this is delicious." I could eat this every day. Shame it wasn't healthy.

He nodded. "I know."

I took another bite and moaned. Garrett stopped chewing and watched me with hooded eyes. My cheeks heated, and I forced myself to chew and swallow before I burst into flames. Without taking his eyes from me, Garrett resumed chewing and swallowed.

"We need to talk," he said, putting his burger down.

"About?" Pretending ignorance wasn't my forte.

"You know what. The kiss. Or better, the kisses. You and me. Us."

What was it with him and the need to talk? Guys were the ones who usually avoided the subject, not girls. "Do we need to talk about that? Can't we just forget it? Pretend it never happened?"

"Do you want to forget about it?"

Not really, but I didn't have room for that right now. There was too much going on. And, as much as I would like to think I was brave and could be strong enough to parade around campus with a boyfriend, I really wasn't. Not anymore.

"Look, Garrett, I'm not ready for a relationship right now."

"Who is saying anything about a relationship?"

I leaned back in my seat as if he had delivered me a blow. "Oh." So what did he want? To kiss here and there? To fool around? Just like the other guys who asked me out every day. No, I wouldn't make an exception for him. He might make my heart beat faster, and take my breath away every now and then, but I was better than this. I deserved better than a hookup and some hidden kisses. I deserved a guy who saw through my bullshit and insisted on being with me even when my mind betrayed my heart.

Besides, this was too confusing. Even if he wanted something more serious—which didn't seem the case—I was sure Audrey would spin it into something outrageous and spread more lies.

I looked down at my half-eaten burger. "I don't really want to talk about this."

"Why not?"

It stung. The way he wanted to talk about this,

whatever *this* was, in a casual manner. As if it didn't matter. Excuse me, but this was my life and it did matter.

The old Bia would have slapped him, cursed him—in Portuguese—and dumped his drink over his head. She would have done something to release her anger, her indignation.

"I thought you didn't believe Audrey's lies," I hissed, clenching my fists. "I'm not the whore she says I am and I won't start now."

His mouth hung open, but one second later, he clamped his lips together. "Where did Audrey come from?"

"Okay, forget about Audrey. So what now? If you don't want a relationship, then what do you want? I bet it isn't to make out here and there."

He ran a hand through his hair, averting his eyes. "I don't know what I want."

Why did he bring this subject up, then? Boys! "But you know you don't want anything serious."

He turned serious eyes to mine. "I didn't say that."

"But you didn't deny it either."

"You're the one who said you're not ready for a relationship right now."

I opened my mouth to tell him to go to hell but quickly shut it again. He was right. I had said that.

It was true. Although, when I thought of a relationship with him, I kind of wanted it. But he was right. It wasn't the time for a serious relationship.

Realizing I had overreacted—or better, acted like the old Bia—I swallowed the embarrassment and forced the new Bia—the calm and quiet Bia, the I-don't-bitch Bia—to resurface.

I opened my purse and took a twenty out from my wallet. "I just remembered I have an essay due tomorrow." I slapped the money on the table. "Thanks for bringing me here."

"Bia?" Garrett asked, his eyes shining with something similar to concern. I scooted out of the booth. "Bia, where are you going?"

I hurried my steps, exiting the diner and jumping in my car in a matter of seconds.

The worst part of it all? As I backed away from the parking lot, I could see Garrett through the diner window and he hadn't moved from his seat.

I hadn't expected him to come after me, of course.

Only, I kind of had expected exactly that.

24

———

"HEY, PRETTY GIRL." I RAN MY HAND OVER MY mare's face. Preta nickered and I smiled. "I missed you too." I leaned into her and she nipped at my neck. "I really did miss you. I missed Leo and Hannah. I missed the guys. I missed home."

My twin brother and his girlfriend picked me at the airport this afternoon, and brought me to their house at Hannah's ranch. Leo tried convincing me to go to our parents' ranch, but I wasn't in the mood to face them. Not yet. I knew I would have to tomorrow, during Thanksgiving dinner, and that would be enough. So, I just teased he didn't want me in the house because I would interrupt their naughty schedule.

He reddened. "That's not it."

Hannah and I laughed, and he relaxed. As soon as Leo's SUV parked in front of the house, I flew out of the car and ran to the stable, but Preta wasn't there. I walked into the arena and saw her in the pasture with Argus and Minuano. I whistled and her ears perked. The moment she turned to me, she pushed into a happy gallop, until she was pressed against the fence.

Smiling, I climbed over, flung my legs to the other side, and jumped beside her.

I kissed her face. "If I told you everything, you wouldn't believe me."

Last night, Phoebe had come to my dorm—thank goodness, Molly had been out—and I had told her about the latest problems. She barely believed Garrett would be such a jerk and practically suggested we just fool around. A horse would believe me even less.

In turn, Phoebe told me she thought she was in love with Kevin, and she was considering a big night after Thanksgiving break to tell him. I felt happy for her, but I also felt jealous. And guilty and terrible for being jealous.

"I might," Hannah said. She leaned on the other side of the fence. "Do you want to talk about it?"

Did I? Part of me wanted to ramble, to scream,

to punch something hard, but another part of me wanted to be quiet and forget.

"Not really. Not now, at least."

She nodded. "I understand. But you know I'm here, right? I mean it."

I smiled. "Thanks." I patted my mare's neck. "Are there any plans for tonight that I need to get ready for, or can I just tack her and go for a long ride?"

"Ri, Pedro, and Gui said something about coming by later. I'm not sure. But don't worry. I won't serve dinner for at least two hours, so take your time."

Graças a Deus. I jumped over the fence again. I didn't want to leave Preta's side for one second, but I had to go get the tack from inside the stable. "If they come early, call me. I'll have my phone with me."

She walked to the stable beside me. "If they come early, I'll give them Coke and appetizers and turn the TV on some random soccer game. That should keep them entertained for a bit."

I nodded, amazed at how well she knew them. And me. Well, sort of. She had known me well, until I went to that damned university and became a messed up, wimpy little girl.

"I'm glad Leo found you," I said, feeling a little jealous too.

She paused in front of the tack room door. "Bia, are you feeling well?"

I chuckled. "I know, right? Me, emotional?"

"Yeah, not something I see every day. Or, well, ever." She touched my arm. "Are you sure you don't want to talk?"

I patted her hand. "Not now. I need to go riding first."

She nodded and gestured toward the tack room. "Do you need help with it?"

I gave her an are-you-mad look. "Really?"

She shrugged. "Just being polite."

I nudged her ribs with my elbow. "Sometimes you're too polite."

She tease-curtsied. "I do what I can." We laughed. "All right. I'll let you to it. Go relax."

"That's exactly what I'll do."

She winked and I waved her off, before entering the tack room. I grabbed all I needed and headed out again. Preta was still in the same spot, waiting for me. She nickered and stomped her hooves when she saw me approaching her.

She twitched as I ran a hand over her soft coat. A little to her right, a lonely dandelion caught my attention. I picked it up. "What should I wish for, pretty girl?" She nickered and I chuckled. "Exactly that." I closed my eyes. *I wish to be happy.* If only that was simple. I blew on the flower and watched as the white fluffs flew away. "All right, let's get you ready. You excited, pretty girl?"

I tacked her, and once I was up and ready, she set out in a beautiful gallop and we rode around the ranch. The wind in my face, my hair flying behind me, the setting sun, all of those were the same things I wished for at Rocky Hill Ranch, but the horse made all the difference. When I was riding Midnight, it felt almost the same. Almost. He wasn't mine, but Preta was. And she would always be my mare, my partner, my friend. She was gentle, loyal, and respectful.

If only more humans were like her, life wouldn't be so complicated.

THE GUYS CAME AND ALL WE DID WAS DRINK COKE, eat whatever food was available, talk shit, and tease each other. *Meu Deus*, how I missed them. Seeing them, them wanting to know how I was, what I did, saying they missed me, even if it was "I missed teasing you" made me realize I hadn't appreciated them enough. When I left, I was only worried about me. I wanted to get out of their shadow, be by myself, live my life, but never for one second did I stop to think that maybe I would miss my life with them. They weren't just my blood; they were my friends.

By this time last year, Ri, Pedro, and Gui had their own apartment in Santa Barbara, leaving me alone at my parents' house. I didn't mind much, especially since I knew I could crash at their place, or Hannah's and Leo's place, any time.

To entertain us, Gui told us about their wild parties, and the events they hosted at their place. Apparently, they had been partying more and more since I moved away.

The get together was so fun that they left after two in the morning, and only because Leo kicked them out.

"The horses will wake up early no matter what," he said, shoving them out the door. "And I gotta be up with them."

Graças a Deus, I didn't have anything to do until the afternoon the next day, because I really wanted to sleep in. However, the banging of pots and pans coming from downstairs woke me up. I buried my face under my pillow, but now I couldn't get back to sleep.

Grunting, I switched my pajamas for sweatpants and a long-sleeved tee and trudged downstairs. Hannah was in the kitchen, but it could have been the middle of a war. There were three pots going on the range; the oven was on; steak on a cutting board; potatoes in a bowl; onions and tomatoes in another; flour, sugar, and baking soda on the counter; and eggs, butter, and milk out of the fridge. Her laptop was open on the island, and she looked like a lost chicken in her own kitchen.

"What happened?"

Startled, she whirled on me and almost knocked me out with a wooden spoon. "Sorry. Good morning. Sleep well?"

"If you're trying to ask if I heard you and my brother, no I didn't."

Her fair cheeks got a red tint as she stirred something in a pot. "That's not what I meant."

"Okay, seriously, what happened here?"

"Well, it's almost noon, and I'm trying to cook lunch and get ahead with tonight's dinner, but I'm starting to regret it." She sighed. "I should have focused on lunch first, then dinner, even if I spent all day in the kitchen."

I glanced at the clock on my phone. Shit, it really was almost noon. I had slept a lot after all. "Leo isn't helping you?"

"He was, but he went to check on the horses. Jimmy is off today."

I pulled my hair into a ponytail. "I can help you. Just tell me what to do?"

"I'm making *carreteiro* with leftover steak from *churrasco*—"

I laughed. One and a half years ago, who would have guessed Hannah Taylor would cook Brazilian meals? And she wasn't half-bad. On my goodness scale, she only lost to my mother. Even though I knew how to cook, I bet I lost to her too.

"Are you trying to please me?" I asked, pulling a clean cutting board from a cabinet.

She shrugged. "I figured you were eating a lot of fast food and missing a homemade meal. A *real* homemade meal."

I winked at her. "Is it during this meal that you declare your love for me and ask for my hand in marriage?"

She laughed. "Oh, no, *guria*, you gotta work more for that." She slapped my butt before turning to the steaks.

"Hey." I poked her with my foot, and she jumped to the side to get out of my reach.

Chuckling, I stepped closer and poked her with a spoon. With a squeal, she slapped the spoon away and tried to stomp her foot on mine.

Leo barged in the kitchen through the back door and gaped at us. "Am I interrupting something?"

"Yes!" we answered together, which made us laugh more.

"*Bom,* I'm hungry, so whatever you two are doing can wait. *Morena,* tell me what to do to help."

She handed him the bowl with potatoes. "Peel."

He stared at the bowl. "All of them?"

"There will be eleven adults here tonight. What do you think?"

"*Credo,*" he muttered, grabbing the bowl. "I think we should put everyone on a diet."

"Right," I said. "Because you, Ri, Pedro, and Gui can eat any less than a horse."

"We can. We just don't want to."

I snorted. "Convenient."

The teasing slowed down, and soon we were each focused on our tasks. An hour later, Hannah served lunch and we took a break.

With nothing to occupy my mind, I thought of Garrett and Midnight. Was Midnight well? How was his recovery? When would he be able to jump again? I hadn't known anything about his health for quite some time and was worried. I wished he had a quick recovery and that Delilah regretted having asked Garrett to buy her a new horse. What was Garrett doing right now? Did he have anyone to spend Thanksgiving with? My heart squeezed. *Meu Deus*, I hadn't thought of this before. To me, this was the biggest American holiday, and he was probably alone at his cabin and barely there barn. An urge to take the first flight back to Colorado assaulted me, and I gripped the table to avoid getting up and running to the airport.

Leo's hand rested on my arm, and I jumped. "Hey, you okay?"

I forced a smile. "I'm great."

He exchanged a look with Hannah. "If you say so."

I knew he didn't believe me, nor did Hannah, but I wasn't asking them to. All I wanted was for them to respect me enough not to push it. I was finally feeling well again. I was finally feeling like me, like the loudmouth, hotheaded girl I had always been. And that was all I needed right now.

AT SIX IN THE EVENING, HANNAH'S DINING ROOM was exploding with people. Hannah, Leo, Hannah's parents and Hilary, my parents, Ri, Pedro,

Gui, and me. We were all around the dining table, drinking and talking and munching on appetizers.

My father and I had barely said hi since they arrived, and we certainly hadn't exchanged any looks or smiles.

When dinner was served, the guys went to eat at the kitchen table and I went with them.

Ri served a big spoonful of sweet potato casserole to his plate. "When are you going to talk to him?"

I didn't need to ask who "him" was. I shrugged. "I don't know. Not now, if I can help it."

"Why?" he asked, passing me the spoon so I could serve myself.

"I don't want to talk about this."

"You should," Pedro said from across the table. "If you're not gonna talk to *pai*, then you should talk to us."

"We're all ears." Gui nodded. "You know, if Leo is getting along better with your dad, you can too."

I glared at them. "Are you guys rallying against me?"

"If it's the way to get you to talk to *pai*, maybe." Ri winked.

I sank into my seat. "I don't even know what I would say to him."

"Just reach out to him," Ri said. "Maybe he'll do the talking."

Then we would fight again. I knew we would.

We ate the rest of the meal in silence. Hilary and I helped Hannah to take the dishes back to the kitchen, while everyone else gathered in the living room. Soon, Hannah served dessert and more drinks.

I was about to go to the living room with the rest of them when my father stepped out in the hallway, and we almost bumped into each other.

"Beatriz," he said as if my name hurt his tongue.

"*Pai*," I said, imitating his tone.

He looked at me with his hard hazel eyes. "I'm glad you came back."

"Me too."

"I didn't think this adventure would last this long."

"*O que?*"

"I thought that after a month, you would be back home. *Bem*, took you three months, but I'm glad it ended."

My jaw fell open. "It didn't end. I came for the holidays. I'm leaving Saturday evening."

His face blanched. "You're going back?"

"Yes, I am."

"Why, Beatriz? Haven't you proved your point to me already? I know it now. You'll do whatever *porcaria* you want to without my approval. I get it."

"That's not the point. There isn't a point. All I want is to do something for me. To be myself." Once I said those words, it struck me like a punch. All I wanted was to do something for me and be myself, but I wasn't being myself. Not in Fort Howell. And only sometimes at Rock Hill Ranch. I wasn't myself anywhere.

"Did I ever stop you from being yourself?"

I shook my head. "It's not that, *pai*."

"What is it, then?"

"I already told you. A thousand times. But you never listen."

"You think I'm not listening."

"Then you just don't care, but I've been saying it for a long time."

"Stop being childish, Beatriz."

Irritation and frustration seeped into my chest. He would never understand because he would never listen to me. Not really.

I walked around him. "Good night."

"Beatriz," he called me. "Where are you going?"

"It's none of your business." I opened the front

door, pretending the living room wasn't right there and everyone was watching me, and marched out of the house.

Fighting the angry tears brimming in my eyes, I ran to the stable and into Preta's stall.

25

ON FRIDAY, PRETA AND I WENT RIDING BEFORE eight in the morning.

I actually had woken at six and wasn't able to go back to sleep, so I threw myself into action. Better to do something and occupy my head with mindless thoughts than obsess about my life. Even if I wanted to, I didn't have the energy for it.

With a slice of bread with butter and a to-go coffee mug, I tiptoed out of the house, honestly hoping Hannah and Leo would sleep in and rest a little. They worked hard on this ranch and deserved some peace.

I fed the horses, checked their water, released a few of them into the pasture, and got ready to muck out their stalls, but decided against it, afraid that the sound of scraping the shovel on the ground would wake the happy couple.

The jealous feeling came back and I pushed it away. What the hell? He was my brother and she was one of my best friends. I was happy for them. A little jealous of what they had built for themselves—even though their beginning had been rough. Well, kind of terrible, actually—of how strongly they felt for each other and showed it any moment they could.

I shook my head of those thoughts, tacked Preta, and went out with her.

Preta and I only returned after I got several messages from Hannah, Leo, and Ri, asking me to come for lunch. The guys were over and promised me I would have fun. How could I say no to that?

With Leo's help and a copy of my mother's cookbook, Hannah made *feijoada*, and for dessert a cake of *negrinho* and *branquinho*—what we called it in the south of Brazil. The dessert made from sweetened condensed milk was called *brigadeiro* and *beijinho* in the other Brazilian states. She was truly becoming a Brazilian master cook. If Leo wanted proof that she really loved him, he didn't need to look further. However, I was sure he knew it, and that he loved her that much too.

Later, we drove to my parents' ranch and played with the trucks in the field. If my father saw us coming, I didn't know, and honestly, I hoped he pretended he didn't. Hannah went with Leo, and I hopped in Ri's truck. Pedro wanted to drive his truck, but the game was too difficult with four trucks, so he joined Gui with the promise that they could switch at some point. When they switched, I nudged Ri until he let me drive for a bit.

After everyone went home and showered, we met again in a restaurant/bar downtown. *Meu Deus*, it felt so good to dress up and go out.

We gathered around a round table in a corner. Ri and Hannah sat by my side, with Leo on Hannah's side, Pedro on Ri's side, and Gui directly across from me. This time, Leo gave us the okay to order alcoholic beverages. I hated drinking in front of him, but I could use a good dose of whiskey and Coke. Being considerate, Hannah, who I knew loved whiskey as much as I did, stayed with plain Coke with him.

They told me all about them. The practices, the tournaments, the new faces around the polo scene, the ones who looked like serious threats, the ones who would probably be out in one year or two. It was all about polo, of course. I felt like a hateful bitch. I loved polo, probably almost as much as they did, and I had run away from them as if it hurt me. That was never the case.

I just had to find myself. I thought leaving home would be the solution, but so far, everything had gone wrong. When I was in Fort Howell, I wasn't myself. It wasn't right, and I had to do something about it. Maybe go back to Brazil? Gui's parents and his sister, Gabriela, were still there, as were my real, old friends. There, I could be myself again. I could pick up vet school where I left off, without worrying about starting over. I would still be older than the rest of my class, since I had been away for almost two years, but at least I wouldn't have to go through pre-vet, then apply for vet school, hope I was accepted, and study for another four years. In Brazil, I would graduate at twenty-five. Here, I would graduate when I was twenty-eight.

"What's the matter?" Ri asked, leaning closer to my chair. I wasn't sure if it was because he was the oldest at twenty-six and had his head on the straightest, but he was the most perceptive and the peacemaker. Whenever Leo and my father had one of their warlike arguments, Ri had been the one to break them apart.

Now it seemed like it was my turn to be in the war zone with our father.

Noticing I had been frowning and gripping my glass tightly, I relaxed. "Nothing."

"Right, because you have been loud and opinionated, like always."

I snorted. "Is it that noticeable?"

"You're telling me you didn't notice you're different?"

I shrugged. "It's not a big deal."

"Bia, I know Leo has always been closer to you, and now Hannah, but you don't seem to want to open up to them, and they're worried about you. They aren't bugging you though because they think you'll react badly and distance yourself even more."

"Aren't you afraid I'll distance myself from you if you push me?"

He grinned. "Maybe that's exactly what I want."

I slapped his arm. "*Chato.*"

He chuckled. "I've heard worse."

I frowned, swirling my glass. The golden liquid slushed close to the brim, but not too close to spill. "How have *you* been?"

He lifted one eyebrow at me. "Changing subjects, huh?"

"Maybe? Seriously, though, I want to know. We haven't really talked in—" I did the math in my head. "—three months, and I know you were still hurting from ..." I didn't continue. It wasn't worth it mentioning Joana.

Last year, all hell broke loose. Hannah's ex-boyfriend Eric found out about Leo's past and spilled the beans to the local newspapers to get Leo away from Hannah by making her mad at him. We found out Joana had been involved. The reporters dug up what they could in Brazil and, mad that Ri had left Brazil—and her—to come to the United States, Joana told the reporters all she knew about it. And since she had been with Ri for a long time, she knew a lot. If she had known Ri was ready to propose to her and ask her to come live in the United States with him, she probably would have held her tongue, but it was supposed to be a surprise. How would she know? Still, the fact that she would gossip about our lives like that made all of us mad at her, especially Ri. After that incident, they never talked again.

He ran a hand through his light brown hair. "Better, I think."

"Still think a lot about her?"

His bright blue eyes darkened. "Not really. What stayed with me is the hurt. The way she just opened her mouth and told the world all of our secrets will haunt me for a while."

Understandable. I hoped what Joana had done didn't mark his life though. I wondered if he would ever be able to trust another woman again.

I reached over and held his hand. "As long as you don't let it consume you." He shrugged, and I could see they already did consume him. *Droga.* I squeezed his hand. "I bet you'll meet a girl who will knock you off your feet soon enough."

He scoffed. "No serious relationships for me anymore. Right now, I'm Gui's clubbing partner."

I frowned. "Please, tell me you didn't become a manwhore?"

"That would be going too far." He looked away. I thought about how to make him keep talking, because he looked like he needed it more than I did, but he raised his hand and motioned for the waitress to refill our drinks. Then he turned to me, his face impassive. "Now it's your turn. Going to tell me what's bothering you?"

"Do I have to?"

"Not really. Is it that bad?"

I laughed but it was missing humor. "I don't know. Honestly, it's kinda hard to judge anything lately. It seems that being a Brazilian girl is causing me problems. There's this girl who likes this guy, but they broke up some time ago. The guy hit on me, she got mad, and started spreading lies about me, using my citizenship as an excuse. You know, because all Brazilian girls are sluts."

He tsked. "That's ridiculous."

"You're telling me? But it only gets worse. Now, each time I do something that remotely reminds her of someone who likes going out or who likes guys—" I widened my eyes. Come on! I did like guys! "—she adds more details to her lies."

"You shouldn't have to put up with it. What did you do?"

"Um, I dumped coffee on her head, and punched her face."

He almost spat out his drink. "Ha, I would have loved to have seen that. Did you break her nose?" I nodded. "Nice. I mean, not nice. But yeah, nice."

"Yeah, but none of that helped my case. It only made her hate me more and spread more lies."

"Well, I never saw Beatriz Fernandes cower because of lies."

Me neither, and that was what bothered me. Why the hell did I care what they thought of me? Being here, it was easy to tell myself I wouldn't let that happen anymore. That I would lift my chin and confront them headfirst. That feeling was bound to die once I was back there though. I knew that. I would be alone, in a strange place that didn't feel like home, and the old Bia would slip away from my grasp again. It wasn't easy to keep my head high in a place I didn't feel welcome.

I opened my mouth, about to tell him all of that, when a guy stepped behind us. "Hey, the Montenegro crew and—" His dark brown eyes looked at Hannah then me. "—their cheerleaders."

"Evening, Malcolm," Ri said, turning to shake the guy's hand.

Everyone chipped in, greeting Malcolm. I couldn't help but notice he looked like my brothers and cousin. Not his physical appearance —his eyes were dark, his skin fair, and his hair black—but the way he posed himself, and his Tommy Hilfiger cowboy attire.

Guilherme leaned closer and whispered, "He joined the club two months ago, with the Knight House."

Since Eric had been locked up after trying to kill Hannah and Leo, the club had been after a re- placement for him. They had been on the fourth guy before I left. Apparently, this was the fifth.

Leo cleared his throat. "Malcolm, this is Bia, my twin sister."

Malcolm smiled at me, offering me his hand. "Sister, uh?" I slipped my hand in his and he shook it, maintaining a firm grip. "I'm relieved. The last thing these guys need is another cheerleader."

"Hey!" Hannah called out. "Who are you calling a cheerleader?"

I smiled at him. "Just because I'm their sister, it doesn't mean I'm not a cheerleader. I'm just not—" I scrunched my nose. "—that kind of cheerleader."

The shine in his dark eyes shifted. "That's good enough for me."

Pedro spoke up. "Do you want to join us for a drink, Malcolm?"

"Unfortunately, I have to pass." He gestured to a table on the other side of the restaurant. "I'm here with my team and we've been discussing gameplay." He turned his wide smile to me. "Nice to meet you, Bia. I hope to see you at the club."

I was going to tell him that wouldn't happen since I moved away, but for some reason, decided it wasn't worth it. Why did I have to tell him that? I would be back here in about three weeks for winter break.

"Nice to meet you too," I said simply.

He said good night to the others and walked away.

Leo stared at me. "What was that?"

"What was what?" I feigned innocence.

"Malcolm looked interested in you," Pedro said.

"And you seemed interested in him," Ri added.

"Oh, grow up, guys. Can't I flirt a little?"

"No," all four of them said together.

See? That was why I left. I loved them so freaking much, but they suffocated me. I was twenty-two years old, and they still acted as if I was fifteen and just now starting to go out and discovering how men can be jerks. Spare me.

"Thank goodness you aren't in Colorado with me," I muttered, lifting my glass to my lips.

Leo's jaw clenched. "What's that supposed to mean?"

Hannah placed a gentle hand on his arm. "Leo, don't. We're here to have a good time."

Ri slapped his hand on the table. "Hannah is right. How about we play a game. Whoever says something depressing or upsetting has to take a shot of tequila. Except for Leo. I'll make him drink Dr. Pepper, which he hates."

Ugh, he knew we all didn't like tequila, but it should be fun to see where this went.

"I'm in," I said, determined to resume the good time with my family. "But can we order dessert along with it?"

Ri winked. "You read my mind."

SATURDAY WENT BY TOO FAST. I SLEPT IN AND WOKE up to find Ri, Pedro, and Gui helping Hannah and Leo in the kitchen. Hilary arrived right before Hannah served us another Brazilian dish for lunch.

I couldn't help but stare at Hannah's sister. At eighteen, the blonde with green eyes was too beautiful for her own good. I hadn't really known her before Leo and Hannah got together, but rumor had it, she had been a spoiled brat with a loud mouth that rivaled mine. Well, old Bia's mouth. But the incident with Eric changed her. I got to know her as our families grew close, and she was a quiet, timid girl, who seemed in excruciating pain whenever she was alone with one of the guys. She went to a therapist who specialized in sexual assault victims twice a week, and apparently, she was doing better.

Hilary smiled at my brothers' and cousin's jokes, but she never laughed. When we sat in the living room to watch a movie, she took the farthest armchair and turned it in diagonal, so half of its back was turned to the rest of us.

After the movie, we all rushed to the stable. Hilary followed us there and even patted Belle, but not being a big fan of horses, she left before we were done tacking the horses.

Gui watched as she walked out of the stable. "So young and pretty, and so damaged," he whispered.

I nodded. Poor girl. I prayed she got better and moved past the events that haunted her life.

We rode around Hannah's estate most of the afternoon, and only stopped because I had to get ready for my flight.

Before I took a shower, the guys headed to the airport to meet me there. When I stepped out of the bathroom with my hair dripping wet, I yelped and almost slipped on the hardwood floor.

"Wow," my mother said with her sweet voice. She was seated at the edge of the bed. "I know I'm getting old, but I'm not that bad, am I?"

Right. The woman didn't look a day over thirty-five, and her oldest son was twenty-six. Everyone said she could be our sister, which made her glad, of course.

I tightened the towel around me. "*Mãe*, what are you doing here?"

"I came to wish you a good trip."

"Is *pai* here?"

She shook her head. "He's still upset. But he

wasn't going to keep me from seeing you. In fact, he seemed relieved I insisted on coming."

Why would he? He didn't really care about anything I did, thought, or believed in. Okay, maybe that was an exaggeration, but I was upset too.

"I appreciate it." I grabbed my clothes from beside her and rushed to the bathroom. "*Um minuto.*"

I quickly shoved on my jeans and sweater, and wrapped a towel around my head, before joining my mother in the guest bedroom. It felt awkward to have her here, watching me, and not having much to talk about.

"So," I started, sitting down beside her. "How is everything around here?"

"The same. Practice, tournaments, horses. Dealing with issues from the farm in Brazil." She watched me as I put on my socks and cowboy boots. "Bia, I want to apologize for your father. He has a short temper, like you, and you two against each other is almost worse than when Leo was ..." She sighed. "I don't like seeing you both like this, but I also know neither of you will give in."

"It's not just that, *mãe*."

She raised her arm. "Let me finish. Deep down, I believe your father is proud of you, for going after your dreams, for following your heart, but he'll never admit that. I know you must be hurting from the argument on Thursday, but I hope when you come back for winter break, you will be calmer and I hope you're able to see the situation more clearly. You're the only girl among three boys. Make that four since Guilherme is practically a son to us and a brother to you. And you *are* the youngest."

"Leo and I were b—"

"I know, only two minutes apart. I was there, you know?" She smiled and I rolled my eyes. "The fact is, even if Leo was a little younger than you, there are still three older boys before you. You're your father's only daughter, and he still sees you as his little girl."

"I'm twenty-two!"

"He'll feel that way even when you're fifty."

The same thing Leo said a few months ago. That wasn't helping. "I can't do whatever he wants me to, *mãe*. I need to have my own life. Hell, I'm way past that. Here, most young people leave their parents' house when they are eighteen to go to college."

She nodded. "I know, but you have to remember he didn't grow up here and he won't change now. You also didn't grow up here, but you're young and I understand your necessity to adapt and feel a part of this country. But your father won't change, *querida*. He's too old for that."

He wasn't that old, but I got what she was saying. "I know." I sighed. "I'll try to come back for winter break calmer and with an open mind, but don't expect me to accept whatever he says or wants."

"I'll work on him. Hopefully, he'll be better, more accepting when you're home again."

Home. My parents' house was supposed to be home, but I hadn't been there during this holiday.

A pang ran through my heart when I realized the saddest fact. Right now, no place felt like home.

26

I DIDN'T KNOW WHAT CAME OVER ME, BUT A TEAR escaped and rolled down my cheeks when Leo, Hannah, Ri, Pedro, and Gui decided to give me a group hug. Why the hell did I want to leave again? Honestly, right now, I wasn't sure. They were here, my parents were here—even if my father and I had our differences right now. He was still my father—and my horse was here. If I was so set on going to vet school, why didn't I find one closer? If there wasn't one in Santa Barbara, I could find one close enough to drive back every weekend. That would make me feel better, and more like myself. I could have my independence and still be a part of their lives.

During the flight, I sketched a plan. I would

finish this semester the best I could, ignoring everyone but Phoebe. It was just three more weeks. I could go from class to my dorm and nowhere else for three weeks. Meanwhile, I would look for pre-vet courses around Santa Barbara and apply for a transfer. I hoped that I would be able to start the spring semester at the new university and have a fresh start. Nobody would know who I was, and hopefully, I wouldn't mistakenly upset a hormonal bitch who loved to spread lies and wreak havoc.

My heart tugged. I would miss Phoebe and Midnight Dream and Garrett. However, Phoebe had Kevin and her other friends. Midnight had Tom and Garrett, and some of the time, Delilah. And Garrett, well, Garrett was a grown man and could take care of himself. Besides, he made it clear that he didn't want anything serious with me, so why should I care what he ended up doing? He had been okay so far. He would still be okay.

I arrived Saturday late at night and was immensely glad my roommate hadn't made it back yet. I took advantage of Sunday to organize my stuff, making sure I had all my homework and essays and projects ready for the end of the semester, and looked for universities in and around Santa Barbara.

When Molly arrived Sunday night, already bitching, I missed my family even more. Perhaps Santa Barbara was my home now, even if I hadn't realized it when I left for Colorado. Perhaps, if I got my own place in town, went to college there, and saw my family whenever I wanted, I would finally feel at home again.

With that positive thought in mind, I shut out Molly and went to bed.

FINALLY, PEOPLE SEEMED TO START FORGETTING ME after Thanksgiving break. Maybe they were still hungover from partying so much, or too excited about having only three more weeks of classes. Either way, I wasn't complaining.

After coming back from California, the cold got to me. I mean, it was chilly before Thanksgiving break, but after enjoying the nicer weather in Santa Barbara, it was like the temperatures had gone down twenty, thirty degrees.

The week went by with a little less problem. Phoebe and I hung out after our classes, Jonah didn't bother me as much, I didn't see Audrey anywhere, and only six guys asked me out.

Friday evening, I was able to stay away from

the ranch and pretend to study. After all, final exams were coming. Saturday morning was another story though. I was able to ignore the voice inside me begging me to go to the ranch, imploring me to go ride at least for ten minutes, but it was too painful. I had to go.

I stopped by Starbucks and grabbed the usual breakfast, including Garrett's favorites, though I hoped he was off today. However, when I arrived there and Tom told me Garrett was indeed off, I wasn't ready for the sharp pang in my heart. All right, I was, but I preferred to think I wasn't. I shouldn't have been.

Tom opened the lid of the travel cup, lifted it close to his face, and inhaled. "Ah, paradise."

I chuckled, patting Midnight's head. He had stuck his head out of his stall the moment I set foot inside the stable. Such a sweet horse.

"How's he doing?" I asked. I hadn't seen him since the accident, and I hadn't had any news since I stopped talking to Garrett two weeks ago. Midnight had a soft cast around his ankle and moved slowly.

"Better, but he still takes pain meds, and needs lots of rest. He won't be able to be ridden again for a couple of months."

"Has Delilah spent time with him?"

He snorted. "Right. Because that's just like her. Of course, she didn't. She hasn't even looked at him since the accident." He adjusted his hat. "In fact, she doesn't want to see him anymore."

"What do you mean?"

"She asked Garrett to sell Midnight."

I gasped. "What? Garrett can't do that."

"He doesn't have a choice. Mr. Hudson approved Delilah's request, so now Garrett is looking for a buyer."

No, no way. What if he was sold to a bad owner, worse than Delilah? What if he ended up with an owner like Argus's previous one, who beat him and let his dogs bite him? I hoped they checked the background of whoever offered on him. My heart squeezed. *Meu Deus*, Midnight would be gone soon and I couldn't bear the thought.

Which was ridiculous because I was leaving too.

The will to ride faded. All I wanted to do was spend my day with Midnight. Without a word to Tom or an offer to help, I grabbed a brush from the tack room and entered Midnight's stall. I brushed his coat and he nickered.

"Do you like it, big boy?"

He nickered again and I smiled. When I turned

to brush his neck, he poked his muzzle on my arm. "I missed you too." I wound my arms around his neck and rested my cheek on his soft coat. "I'll miss you."

I sighed, still not believing Delilah was so cruel. How could she sell him after all he went through? She was throwing him away as if he was a piece of trash and that infuriated me. I hoped she didn't show up here today, because only God knew what I would do to her. With all the pent up rage inside me, this was the cherry on top, and I would certainly explode in her face.

"You really like this horse," Tom said.

I glanced over my shoulder. He still stood behind the stall's closed door.

I smiled. "I do."

"And he likes you just as much." He tsked. "I don't understand. Garrett and I have been here, giving him attention since he was born. Why would he prefer you, a newcomer, to us?"

Garrett had posed a similar question a couple of months ago. I shrugged. "There's no way to explain how two people, or an animal and a person, connect. I guess it's just like when you fall in love. You don't choose the person you fall in love with. It just happens."

He tilted his head at me. "Have you ever been in love?"

I frowned. "I don't think so. I had a boyfriend in Brazil, but we broke up when I came to live in the U.S. I thought I would miss him too much, but the truth was, I didn't." He nodded. "How about you?" I asked.

"I had a wife, but she died of breast cancer a long time ago."

"I'm sorry. No kids?"

He shook his head. "We had plans, but the sickness took us by surprise."

When didn't it?

"I'm sorry," I repeated.

"It's okay. I miss her, but it has been so long, I guess I'm used to being by myself."

Nobody should be used to being alone. Not that being alone wasn't okay. It certainly was. However, a person was made to love and be loved.

The sound of tires rolling over the parking lot pavement caught our attention. Tom walked to the door and spied.

"It's Delilah. You better get out of there."

I shook my head and stood my ground. "I won't. She wants to sell him, which means she doesn't care about him. If she tries to bitch at me about it, I swear I might punch her."

A smile split Tom's mouth. "I would love to see that."

Delilah marched inside the stable holding her head high. "Tom, where's the list Garrett made of potential bu—" Her eyes shifted from him to me and her words died. Her body tensed. "What are you doing in there?"

I continued brushing Midnight. "Giving attention to *your* horse."

"Didn't I tell you to stay away from him?"

I snapped my head to her. "Now you're authoritarian? Weren't you just asking about his buyers?"

She crossed her arms. "That's none of your business."

"Then let me be." *Before I break your pretty nose too.*

Tom appeared by her side with a sheet of paper. "Here it is," he said, his eyes darting from her to me and back to her.

She ripped the paper from his hands and huffed. Without another word, she tossed her hair aside and marched out of the stable.

I gaped at Tom. "What a bitch."

Tom shrugged. "What else is new?"

After a restless night, I woke up on Sunday with a heavy heart.

Molly was passed out on her bed, so I got ready in silence and left the room. I exited the dorm building and sat on the front stairs. It was only eight in the morning—seven in Cali—but hopefully she would be awake.

The phone rang three times before she picked up.

"Bia, hi, girl," Hannah answered with an energetic voice. "What are you doing up so early on a Sunday? Didn't you party until late last night?"

I snorted. "Yeah, right."

"Why not?"

"I had a big paper to work on," I lied. Better than telling her the truth. "And why are you this chipper so early?"

"Leo and I just came back from a ride with Argus and Minuano. And later, I'm taking Preta for a run. She misses you."

"I miss her too." I had just seen her last week, but it felt like an entire year. "But she's well, right?"

"Yeah. She really likes Argus, and even Minuano has been nice to them."

I laughed. Horses could be so temperamental. "I'm glad she's well."

"But you already knew that. I mean, it's not as

if I'll let her not be well. And if she weren't well, you would be the first to know. So, since you knew she was well, I'm guessing this call is about something else."

"It is."

"Should I be worried?"

I laughed. "Not really."

"All right. Then tell me."

I took a deep breath. "I need a favor from you, and a favor from Leo."

"Here is your continental breakfast." I placed the tray and the brown bag on Tom's desk.

After hanging up the phone with Hannah, I drove to Starbucks, then to the ranch in record time. *Graças a Deus*, there were no cops along the way, because I was sure I had gone over the speed limit.

Tom looked up from the check he was filling out. "Hmm, it smells so good."

"Great." I spied out the door. "Is Garrett here?"

"Yeah, I guess." Tom pulled a donut out of the bag. "What's up with you?"

"What do you mean?"

"You look ..." He waved his hand as if trying to find a word.

I smiled. "Excited? Happy? Crazy?"

"All of the above."

"I guess I am all of the above." I fished my phone from my pocket and found Garrett's name on my contact list.

He answered on the second ring. "Hi."

"Where are you?"

"Um, at the round pen with Delilah's new horse." His tone was flat. "Why?"

"Didn't you see me arriving?"

He paused. "I did."

"I brought coffee and cinnamon scones."

"I'm not hungry."

I sighed. "Garrett, please drag your butt here. I need to tell you something."

"I'm busy right n—"

"It's important and it won't take five minutes. I'm sure Delilah's horse can take a quick break."

He sighed. "Be right there."

Smiling, I pressed the end button.

Tom was looking at me with a concerned frown. "I don't remember seeing you this excited before."

"I haven't felt this excited in a long time," I admitted.

"Girl, you're making me nervous. Sit down, please."

I rolled my feet from the heel to my toes and back. "I can't sit down."

"Can I ask what you want to tell Garrett?"

"I'll tell you once he's here." I winked.

"Okay, I'm worried. Did you go out last night? Did you drink from someone else's cup? Because, you know, you look high."

I laughed. "Tom, you're funny."

Heavy footfalls entered the stables and I tried to hold still. Garrett appeared under the doorframe, his face serious, the muscles in his neck tense. What bit him?

"I'm here," he said, his voice strained. "What is it?"

I bit my lip to suppress the squeal I wanted to let out. "Okay, are you two ready?"

Tom groaned. "Say it, Bia!"

"I want to buy Midnight," I blurted out.

Garrett's eyes bulged. "What?"

"Aren't you trying to sell him?"

"Yes, but ..."

"I'll be the buyer."

Tom chuckled. "That's great."

Garrett didn't share our enthusiasm though. "Why?"

"Excuse me?"

"Why do you want to buy him?"

"Because I like him? Actually, I love him. I want that horse."

He narrowed his eyes. "Are you sure?"

"Jeez, Garrett, you look happy for Midnight. And me."

"It's just—"

"Just tell me your price. Let's negotiate."

"He's very expensive."

"Good for you. My family has plenty of money and a huge love for horses, especially expensive ones." I grabbed the coffee I had bought for him and pushed it toward him. "Here, let's celebrate."

He stared at it for a moment. Then he took the cup, a half-smile on his lips. "Let's celebrate."

27

GARRETT AND DELILAH LEFT FOR HER COMPETITION Monday morning. I would probably not be all over their itinerary if Tom hadn't messaged me each new thing he learned.

Tom: *They arrived.*

A couple of hours later:

Tom: *Garrett says Golden Racer is nervous. This is his first competition.*

The next day:

Tom: *Delilah didn't score well on the first showing.*

On Wednesday:

Tom: *They just had a big fight. Why don't you call him? I think he listens to you.*

Right, because all he needed now was to hear

my voice. No. I kept out of it. On Friday, I didn't even read his texts anymore. I just deleted them.

My plan to keep my head down and only go where I really needed to go was working. Students weren't pointing at me and whispering as much as they used to. Even the rate of the guys halting in my way and asking me out diminished.

I used my free, alone time to research colleges around Santa Barbara. Some didn't have pre-vet, but they had biology and chemistry, which could be used as a pre-vet major. I ended up applying for five different places. I hoped to be accepted into at least one; otherwise, I didn't know what I would do. I didn't want to stay here anymore and I didn't want to waste another semester waiting for the time to apply again. Although, I knew it was a close call. Applying in December to start in January? Only with lots of luck. Still, it was all I had.

On Thursday night, I wasn't in the mood, but Phoebe dragged me to her dorm—her roommate was out on a date. She made loads of popcorn and put on some chick flick for us to watch. Even though I cried at the end when the couple finally declared their undying love for each other, it was good being out and doing something with a girlfriend.

After the movie, we stayed in her bed and

talked. She told me about Kevin and how great things were going, and I told her I bought Midnight and that I was leaving once classes ended.

"What?" she sat up. "But ... why?"

"Do you need to ask that?"

"I know, no. I mean, yeah, I know, but still." She clung to my arm. "You can't leave me!"

Chuckling, I flung a pillow at her and she let go, falling back on her bed. "You'll be fine without me."

"Maybe. But will you be fine without *me*?" she teased.

"I'll survive."

"Serious now, are you sure about this?"

I sighed. There was no point in staying here. There had been no point in coming here in the first place. "I considered all options and that's the less painful one. The less complicated one."

"I understand, I guess." She pouted. "I'll miss you."

"I'll miss you too." I flung the pillow at her again.

I PROMISED MYSELF I WOULDN'T CAVE, BUT THE competition was supposed to end Sunday evening.

Being holed up inside my dorm was driving me crazy, even if it was working. Against my better judgment, I woke up early on Saturday, stopped by a Starbucks, and drove to the ranch.

Tom smiled wide when I walked into the stable before it was eight in the morning, armed with breakfast.

"My savior," he teased, grabbing the tray and brown bag from me.

As if sensing my presence, Midnight stuck his head over his stall's door. I caressed his chin and placed a kiss on his face. "How are you, big boy? Doing better?"

"He looks like it," Tom answered, coming to stand beside me. "You know, Delilah wasn't too happy you bought him. When I told her, she threw a fit. After a few minutes, she started yelling you should pick him up right that instant, but I told her you were paying for boarding. If her father wasn't here, she would probably throw another fit at that, but he said he didn't mind, as long as you had another plan for him soon. I told him you had." Frowning, he stared at me. "Do you?"

I nodded. "I do."

"I know it's none of my business, but can you tell me what it is?"

My hand stilled on Midnight's neck. For a moment, the thought of lying to him crossed my mind, but why? I didn't owe him anything.

"It's not a done deal yet, but I applied for a transfer to—"

"Wait, what?"

"—several colleges around Santa Barbara. My family is there, and my mare is there too. I'll take him with me and he'll stay with my mare at my family's ranch."

He gaped at me. "You're leaving? Why?"

I pressed my lips tightly and stepped back from Midnight. I didn't want him to feel the tension in my body right now.

"It's not working here. And when I was there for the holidays, I realized I missed them. All of them, even my father and our arguments."

He didn't say anything for a moment, but then his expression softened. "I understand. I mean, if I had family anywhere, I would probably try to stay close to them too." He tsked. "Garrett will be devastated."

I snapped my head back to him and gave myself whiplash. "Excuse me?" Shaking his head, Tom retreated. "Tom, what does that mean?"

"I shouldn't have said anything. I mean, I'm not even sure. It's just ..." He wandered off.

"Oh no, Tom. Now you gotta finish it."

"I don't know exactly what happened or is happening between the two of you, but I'm not blind. The way you look at him and the way he looks at you? There's more there than you both want to admit. I can see it on the days you don't show up. He is like a hawk, watching the parking lot. Every time we hear a car approaching, he looks at it and I literally see him deflating when it's not your red SUV. He might not say it, but I know he feels something for you." He smiled, but it didn't touch his eyes. "And you have feelings for him too."

I shook my head. "You got it wrong, Tom."

He tsked. "We'll see."

I TRIED BRUSHING MIDNIGHT'S COAT, BUT HE turned his head to poke me every ten seconds. I considered tying him, not because he was bothering me—I liked it when he was being this silly—but because he wasn't still a hundred percent healed and I didn't want him moving around too much.

I longed to take him out and ride him for an entire morning. There would be time for that later, when he was healed and well. When we were living in California. Both sadness and happiness washed over me, if that was possible. I was sad I was giving in and running away to my family. Maybe, just maybe, I was a tiny bit sad about leaving Garrett without trying something more. And I was happy because I could try again, a fresh start. I would be near my family, my best friends, and I would have both my horses with me. I had to believe it would be perfect.

The sound of a car approaching made me stiffen. This early on a Sunday morning? There were no riding groups scheduled until the afternoon, and Garrett wouldn't be back with Delilah until tonight. I could only think it was Mr. Hudson coming to check the ranch. And I was here. The fixture he didn't install.

Footsteps sounded louder, and I stuck my head out of the stall to greet Mr. Hudson. My throat went dry. To my surprise, the person who entered the stable was Garrett. He halted in the doorway and looked at me. The shine is his eyes was dull, the corners of his lips were turned down, and he looked beaten.

"Hey," I said.

He took off his hat with a loud sigh. "Hey."

Tom rushed in the stable from the arena with a big smile. "What are you doing here this early? We weren't expecting you until this evening."

"I know," Garrett said, his tone sharp. "Delilah lost last night. I was driving all night. Just left her at the manor."

"What?" Tom asked, his eyes wide. "But ..."

He ran his hand through his hair. "I know." What the hell were they talking about? Garrett gestured toward his truck and the trailer. "Golden Racer has been twitchy since Delilah yelled at him repeatedly day after day. I might need help taking him out of the trailer. Tom?"

"Yeah, sure."

I frowned as they walked out. What the hell happened? I had heard Mr. Hudson talking to Garrett before, and I dreaded what the older man meant by saying Garrett knew what to expect if Delilah didn't win. Well, she didn't win and now fear flooded my system.

Why was I fearful for him? Just because I was a good person? That wasn't a good enough answer. Since he made it clear he didn't want anything with me, Garrett was like any other nameless guy I didn't care about. Or that was what I told myself.

The horse fought them the entire way. At some point, I helped, holding the reins while Garrett joined Tom in trying to calm him and make him take one step after another. *Meu Deus*, what did this girl do to her horses? Scare them to death? It wasn't right.

We shoved him inside a stall, and Garrett slammed the door closed, leaning against it.

He let out a long breath. "That was brutal."

Still in fight or flight mode, Golden Racer charged the door, probably targeting Garrett. Tom yelled his name. I reached forward, closed my hand around his arm, and jerked him forward with all I had. Startled, Garrett bumped into me, his chest crashing against mine. We tripped a couple of steps back and the horse bit air. I grasped my hands around his biceps, and his fingers sank into my waist, looking for balance.

His eyes locked on mine, and I forgot to breathe. His nearness warmed my core, and I had to fight not to lean close to him and inhale his delicious scent. The hazel in his eyes turned a dark brown and his gaze fell to my lips.

Meu Deus, I was going to combust.

Tom cleared his throat. "That was close."

Like a bucket of water being dumped over my head, I sprang apart from Garrett and looked everywhere, but his way.

"Yeah. Thank you," he said, his body still angled toward mine.

I glanced at him. "Sure." Inside the stall, the

horse thrashed and trotted, bumping against the walls. He would hurt himself if he kept that up, or break down the walls. "What's wrong with him?"

Garrett sighed, looking at the horse. "Let's just say Delilah had a panic attack after losing and lashed out at the poor horse. He has been agitated since we left last night."

"We'll take care of him," Tom said. "Why don't you go sleep, Garrett?"

He nodded again. "I will, right after we sedate the horse."

"Tom and I can do that," I said.

His eyes, serious and concerned, met mine. "You just saw how crazed he is. For this, three is better than two."

We stood in front of the stall, in awkward silence, while Tom gathered the sedative. It was a pain in the ass, but after almost thirty minutes fighting with the horse and almost getting bitten several times, Garrett injected the sedative in his system, and he settled down almost instantly.

"Hopefully, he'll wake up calmer," Garrett said, exiting the stall.

I closed the door, looking at the horse standing on the back of the stall, his chest moving up and down in a steady rhythm. Poor animal.

Tires rolled in the gravel, the sound of a car entering the property.

"Any riding groups this morning?" Garrett asked.

"No," Tom answered.

"Shit," Garrett cursed under his breath.

We waited for the new arrival in the stable aisle. When Mr. Hudson stepped in with furrowed brows and tight lips, Garrett didn't look surprised. He stuffed his chest and met the stare of his father with a raised chin.

"Good morning, Mr. Hudson," Tom started, trying to break the awkward vibe with a chipper tone.

Without acknowledging his employee or me, Mr. Hudson gestured to the office. "Let's talk."

The man entered the office and Garrett followed suit. If he was afraid or concerned, he didn't show it and I envied that. In situations like this, I was never able to contain my loud mouth, my temper. Or tears, depending on my emotional state.

The door was slammed closed and I turned to Tom. He shrugged before walking into the tack room. I was about to go with him and ask him what he wanted me to do, but harsh words coming from the office stopped me. I couldn't make out what they were saying, because it was clear they were trying to keep it down, but it was nearly impossible. Even not knowing the words, I could hear the venom coming out of their mouths.

I knew Garrett was able to defend himself, but for some reason, I wanted to play Prince Charming and come barging in and save the day. A smile tugged at my lips.

Their voices rose. "I can't put up with it anymore, Garrett. Virginia can't put up with it anymore. And Delilah can't even hear your name at the moment. I warned you. I told you what would happen if you failed."

"I know and I accept that, but before I go, I have a few things to say. One, I never wanted this. Any of this. It's not my fault I was born. It's yours and my mother's. But I am sorry I was shoved into your life after she died. I'm sorry I put a strain on your perfect marriage. I'm sorry Delilah is such a brat that she scares away her horses and there's nothing I, or even the best trainer in the country, can do to make her a star. She isn't meant to ride. Hell, she isn't meant to be close to horses. So do everyone a favor and stop pushing her to it."

"What the—?"

"Oh, and one more thing. I'm sorry I wasn't and never will be a son to you."

With that, the door opened and Garrett

marched out. His darkened eyes found mine, and I held my breath. He pressed his lips together, and his jaw tensed. I stepped toward him, wanting to touch him, to hold him, and to tell him everything would be okay, but I caught myself before it was too late.

He gave me his back and all but ran from the stable.

Tom peeked out of the tack room.

"Should I go after him?" I asked in a low voice, afraid Mr. Hudson would hear me. "I should go after him."

Tom shook his head. "He needs some time to cool down. If you go after him now, he'll blow up on you."

I understood that, but what if he was blind with rage and he drove directly into a tree? Worse than seeing him in this state would be seeing him in a hospital. Or in a coffin.

Mr. Hudson exited the office, his face impassive. "Tom, we need a new trainer. I know you have contacts. Talk to them before putting any ads out there."

I clenched my hands. If I knew I had any chance of success, I would have jumped at his throat and slapped him hard.

"Sir?" Tom asked, his head low. "What about Garrett?"

Mr. Hudson adjusted his jacket. "Garrett is no longer with us."

"But, sir—"

"Tom, don't make it harder than it needs to be."

Tom nodded. "Yes, sir."

Mr. Hudson looked at me, then back to Tom. "I have to head out now. Have a good day."

Tom wished him the same and I didn't answer. I just stared at the door, wishing I was strong enough to go after Garrett, just to make sure he was okay. What the hell? Why wasn't I strong enough? Of course I was strong enough.

"Bia, I have something for you to help me with," Tom said, slamming down my brief boldness.

Feeling the moment was gone, I faced him. "Shoot."

28

I left the ranch around four in the afternoon and headed toward campus. I turned the volume up and Tim McGraw blasted from the speakers, drowning the thoughts that plagued me since I decided it was time to go back to my dorm.

You should go see him. Just to make sure he's okay.

Who was I kidding? I *knew* I was driving to his half-built barn, even if I didn't want to acknowledge it. To myself. So pathetic.

I followed the instructions Tom once gave me, and my heart raced, knowing I would see him soon. At least, I hoped I would. I had no idea where else he could be.

As I drove down the dirt road, I saw his truck parked in front of the barn.

Then I saw him. With a plaid shirt open and the sleeves rolled up to his elbows and fitted jeans, swinging an ax and cutting a log in half over a tree stump. Sweat glistened from his taut chest ... oh my. My stomach clenched and my mouth watered.

I parked my SUV beside his truck and stayed there. He stopped, ax in hand, and stared at me. My breath caught with the intensity of his gaze. I broke the stare, because I couldn't help it, and my eyes wandered down his chest and abdomen again. *Meu Deus*, he was too hot, too handsome for his own good. I licked my lips and swallowed hard.

Okay, I had come here to check on him, not to stare at him from inside my car as if he were a piece of meat. Even if he was a fine piece of meat.

I slipped out and forced my eyes to look at something, anything, other than him. The barn seemed like a good thing to stare at. Even though the structure was still a wooden frame, it had new additions. Half of the roof was put on, and wooden panels covered the back of the first floor walls.

I jerked my chin to the barn. "I see you've been making progress."

He shook his head once and placed a new log over the stump. "What are you doing here?"

"I wanted to see how you're doing."

He let the ax fall. The log broke apart and two

perfect halves tumbled to the ground. "I'm great." The sarcastic tone of his voice was something new.

"I'm sorry," I whispered.

"For?"

"For what happened."

"It's not your fault."

"Still, I'm sorry it happened."

Garrett picked up another log from the pile, his muscles flexing and popping with his movements. My mouth went dry and heat spread down my body. He placed the log on the stump and cut it in half, pulling the ax with more force than before.

He straightened and picked up another log. He was about to put it in place when his gaze locked on mine. A shine fleeted in his hazel eyes, something I couldn't decipher, and I licked my lips. Groaning, he set the log down and let the ax fall on it with too much force.

"Hey," I called, taking a few steps closer. "Talk to me. I can see there is a storm inside you. Let it out."

His half-grin took over his lips, but it didn't have its usual pull. This time, it was a sarcastic one. "Believe me. You don't want to see my storm coming out."

"I do."

He groaned and grabbed another log from the pile. "Don't you have someone else to bother?"

"Unfortunately, no, I don't. And I'm not here to bother you. I promise I'll leave once I know you're okay."

"I'm okay," he said through gritted teeth.

"Yeah, and I'm the Fairy Godmother."

He raised an eyebrow. "Are you granting wishes?"

I scoffed. "Genies grant wishes, not fairies."

"Damn."

He cut the log, and I could see it was his way of burning off some steam. He was letting his anger and frustration out with each slash of the ax.

"Garrett, what are you going to do now?"

That stopped him. He looked at me, his eyes harsh. "I don't know."

Curiosity tugged at my gut and I glanced at the cabin. It looked so old and too small. Did it have everything he needed? Wouldn't it fall on his head?

I walked to the cabin, went up the two front steps, and opened the door. The place was dark, with only two windows, rough wooden walls, and a course stone floor. The kitchen—a couple of cabinets, sink, small fridge, and even smaller range— was in the right corner. A small fireplace that was lit and warming the place, a tube TV, a low wooden table, and a sofa occupied the left corner. In the back, a queen bed, a nightstand, and a tall drawer completed the place. Past the bed, a door led to what looked like the bathroom.

My heart tugged. He deserved much more. The worst part? Knowing his father could have given him everything and didn't.

"What are you doing here?"

Startled, I jumped and placed a hand on my speeding heart. I hadn't seen him following me in. I turned to face him and found him close, looming over me with hooded eyes.

"I told you. I came to make sure you're okay."

"No. I mean here." He gestured to the cabin. "Inside."

I opened my mouth to speak, but nothing came out. Why was I inside the cabin, looking at where he said he would be sleeping? Besides making me hurt and want to help, what else did it do? Anger him, that was what it did. By the tension radiating from his shoulders, neck, and jaw, and the harsh shine in his eyes, I knew he was mad at me right now.

"I'm sorry. I didn't m—"

"Stop feeling sorry for me," he hissed, clenching his fists. "I don't want your pity."

So this was his new game? To frighten me so I would stay away. This was probably his new game for everyone. He had been hurt before. By his mother when she died and left him alone, by his father when he refused to be a father to him, by Mrs. Hudson when she was a bitch to him, by Delilah and her fake righteousness. I bet even Jonah had let him down one way or another. Add a broken heart or two to that equation, and I knew he was on the brink of closing down for good.

"I don't pity you, Garrett, but I hate this situation. I wish I could do something to help you. You're a good man and you deserve better than this." Taking a long breath, I rested a hand over his heart and he went still. "I want to be here for you, and you won't scare me away with your harsh words and brooding mood."

A pained shine crossed his eyes, and his heartbeat accelerated under my palm. I couldn't ignore how wonderful and warm his skin felt. I wanted to run my fingertips up and down his chest, tracing each of his muscles, feeling them contract and expand with my touch.

My fingers twitched and I licked my lips. His gaze followed my tongue, his eyes darkening. He pressed his eyes shut and growled.

Feeling bolder than when we kissed the ball, I

took a step into his personal space. The heat of his body brushed against my own, even with the half foot between us.

I gave in and let my fingers trail south, contouring his pecs, then the six-pack on his abdomen, and that V muscle leading down into his jeans. My other hand followed suit and when my fingertips grazed the waist of his jeans, Garrett inhaled sharply and wrapped his hands around my wrists, stilling my fingers.

He opened his eyes, and the anger and frustration in them were gone, replaced by lust. Raw lust. My knees went weak, but before I could melt to the floor, Garrett tugged my wrists and pulled my arms up and around his neck. Slowly, he slid his hands over my arms, around my shoulders, and down my back. He splayed his fingers on the low of my back and pressed me against him, drawing a loud huff from my lungs. He leaned into me and I tilted my head toward his. My heart raced as I waited for his mouth to be on mine, but he paused an inch away.

"What do you want, Bia?" His voice was barely above a whisper, and his breath washed over my skin. *Meu Deus.* I grasped his shoulders for support. "Tell me what you want?" His lips grazed my chin, and I whimpered. "You gotta say it."

I pushed this frail Bia aside and forced the old Bia to emerge. "I want you," I said, hoping my eyes conveyed exactly how much I wanted him.

A growl rumbled from his throat, and he closed the distance. He brushed his lips over mine once, twice, three times, as if he needed to test the waters before actually jumping in deep. *Meu Deus*, but then he jumped in, his mouth moving with a rough want against mine. I matched his rhythm, showing him I was ready for whatever he wanted to give me. For whatever *way* he wanted to give me. His tongue invaded my mouth, dancing with mine, and I moaned. With a groan, he knotted his hand in the hair at my neck, pressing me to him even more, as if there was any space left between us.

His other hand slipped under my shirt, and I shivered with his touch on my skin. He brought his hand around me, until his thumb grazed the lower edge of my bra. I gasped against his mouth, and he took advantage of my surprise to kiss me deeper. I fell, not caring what was at the end of this cliff. I just needed to fly, to feel, to let him ravish my body, even if it ended up mangled on the other side.

Painfully slow, he slipped his entire hand

under my bra and cupped my breast, pinching my nipple. I moaned, sucking on his lower lip.

"Hot damn," he whispered.

Without breaking his hungry stare, I pushed his shirt down his arms and pulled my sweater over my head. I reached to my back to open my bra, but he gave me that lopsided grin.

"Let me," he said, his voice husky.

With pleasure.

His eyes on mine, he advanced. The intensity in him, in his stare, in his powerful body, had me almost stepping back. However, I stood my ground. I had never been with a man that could bring me to my knees with one simple touch—and I wanted to. I wanted *him*.

He reached around me, his chest an inch from mine. *Meu Deus*, the heat coming from this man would drive me insane even before he had done anything to me. I bit my lower lip. The thought of what he would do to me made me desperate.

He glanced at my mouth. "I'll bite it," he whispered, bending toward me and taking my lower lip between his teeth and making me whimper. Letting go of my lip, he unclasped my bra and threw it to the side.

"You should lose the pants too," he said, tugging the waistband of my jeans. He popped open the button and the zipper, then pushed my jeans —and my panties—past my hips, and down my legs. I helped him and stepped away from them. He threw them in the same direction the bra and the top had gone. Then he stood there, watching me with those incredible hazel eyes, not close enough to touch, but close enough to burn me. His eyes raked every inch of my body, as if he wanted to etch my image into his mind so he could never erase it, even if he wanted to.

I should be embarrassed by standing naked in front of him, but I wasn't. I could see it in his eyes that he liked what he saw and that brought more boldness to me. I stuffed my chest and stood proud as his gaze burned my skin and coiled my belly.

He lifted his hands, but didn't touch me. He hovered close to my skin. "You're so beautiful," he whispered. I shivered.

Incapable of standing this close to him and doing nothing, I put my hands over his and guided them to me. One cupping one of my breasts, and the other on my hip. His gaze intensified, and I was sure he could make me come just like that.

He brushed his thumb over my nipple, and with the other hand, dug his fingers into my skin, pulling me to him. I gasped at the full contact of his chest with mine. He let go of my breast and snaked that hand to my back, pressing me to him.

"This feels so good," he said, before taking my mouth with his. His kiss started slow and deep, but when I entangled one of my legs around his, he groaned and his kiss became rougher, as if he couldn't get enough of me.

He slid his hands down to my thighs and tugged them. I wrapped my legs around his waist, and he lowered us to the bed. He kept an elbow on the mattress so his weight wasn't crushing me, but that was exactly what I wanted. I tugged his ass with the heel of my foot, pressing him closer, and he groaned, but dropped the elbow and buried his face in my neck. He inhaled before placing a sweet kiss on the soft spot between my neck and shoulder. I shivered again. Chuckling, he bit that same spot, making me shiver yet again.

I was about to protest that he still had his pants on, when his hand trailed a path to my inner thigh. I stopped breathing, suddenly aware of how bad this could go, how involved I could become, how taken I would be, but I was not capable of stopping right now.

He propped himself on his elbow and looked at me. His fingers neared my entrance, and I arched my back, closing my eyes.

"Look at me," he said. I opened my eyes, but as soon as his finger rubbed against my tender flesh, I closed them again. He withdrew his finger. "Look at me, Bia."

I sucked in a breath and forced my eyes open. My reward was his entire finger inside me. I cried out, closing my eyes in the process.

He pulled his finger out. "Bia."

I shot my eyes open. "All right. All right."

He chuckled, placing a soft kiss on my chin before locking his eyes on mine again. This time, he thrust two fingers inside me, and somehow, through the immense pleasure flowing through me, I was able to keep my eyes open, to stare into his dark pools, those hazel eyes that shone with lust.

He rubbed his thumb on my clit and I cried again, digging my nails on his shoulders. He drew circles around me while sinking his fingers deeper, sending fire rolling in waves in my veins. Moans escaped my throat, but that was something I couldn't control, especially when Garrett was watching me with his mouth slightly parted, his breathing heavy, and his eyes shining as if I was the most beautiful, the most delicious thing he had ever seen.

My toes curled and I arched my back, feeling

the pleasure built up, so close to exploding.

Then he stopped everything.

"What ...?" I asked, but he raised a brow at me and started moving down on me, placing tiny kisses on my neck, shoulder, breast, belly, and hip. My breath caught. *Meu Deus*.

He spread my legs apart and leaned into me. He teased me with his hot breath along my inner thighs, making my belly clench in anticipation. Then his tongue lashed out on my clit, and I cried his name. I fisted the sheet around me, afraid I would break into a million pieces with each stroke of his tongue. Then he slid two fingers inside me hard while circling his tongue around my clit, and I was done for. My body tightened and pleasure broke loose like a dam, making my body quiver uncontrollably.

For a moment, I was in a blissful daze, and when I came down from my high, but not down enough, *Graças a Deus*, I found Garrett with a foil package hanging from between his teeth while he took his pants and boxers off. I looked at his erection and swallowed hard. He was huge, and I couldn't wait another second before he was inside me.

"Are you just going to stand there, or are you going to do something about it?

"I'm coming," he said, kicking his pants to the side.

"I hope so," I said with a naughty smile.

I didn't know if he caught the double meaning of my words, but he showed me that half-grin, and pure lust radiated from his eyes as he rolled the condom on. Slowly, he crawled over me. Keeping most of his weight on his elbows, he rested his forehead on mine, and as I spread my legs, he positioned himself over at my entrance. I grabbed his biceps as he entered me, robbing me of air and filling me completely. When he was deep inside me, buried to the hilt, he stilled.

"Fuck, this feels good," he muttered.

I wrapped my legs around his waist and kicked his fine ass. "Garrett, I'm going to die if you don't move."

His lopsided grin flashed on his lips before he brought them to mine. Kissing me, he pulled back, all the way out—I instantly felt his absence—and then sank back inside me. He did it again and again, going faster and deeper with each stroke, making me scream louder and louder.

This was too good, *Meu Deus*, just too good. Sex had never been this good. I didn't know what it was, but I felt so close to him, so connected to him. He kissed my neck, his warm breath on my skin and his delicious scent filling my lungs, sending a shiver up my spine.

He bit my neck. "God, so good," he said in a growl. "I could eat you up."

Oh, please, do.

With each thrust, my body tightened with pure pleasure, and I was sure that if he kept that rhythm I wouldn't last much longer, and damn, I wanted this to last. Surprising him, I pushed him to the side and flipped us around. His eyes widened as I sat straighter over him.

I smiled and then he smiled. A full on smile. Just for me. My heart stuttered.

His hands landed on my waist and, with my eyes locked on his, I started moving. I pulled up, then down hard. He groaned and his fingers curled in my skin.

"Fuck," he mumbled as I moved up and down, harder and faster.

Even swimming in pleasure, I couldn't *not* appreciate the view under me. He was too hot, too handsome. His abs, chest, and biceps were taut. His chin and jaw chiseled, his cheekbones high, his parted mouth swollen and kissable, his hair soft and messy, messier than usual. His hazel eyes bright, staring at me. I had no idea what was written in them; I just knew that I couldn't stop. I couldn't stop staring at him, and I couldn't stop moving. Faster and harder.

"Bia, please, don't stop," he said, his hands on my hips, guiding me over him.

I leaned over him, wanting to be close to him, as close as we could be, when we both came. I placed a soft kiss on his lips, but then his hand was on my neck, locking me there. I wiggled my hips while moving them up and down, feeling my pleasure at the edge, and he groaned.

"Like that?" I asked, wiggling again.

"Oh, fuck yeah," he whispered.

He nudged my neck lower and took my mouth in his, plunging his tongue in and caressing mine. I wiggled one more time and lost it. I exploded but didn't stop moving. Although, with two more strokes, Garrett went still for a second, before trembling under me. He wrapped both arms around me as he rode down the high, and I smiled, glad I provided this moment of pleasure and relaxation to him.

When he stopped trembling, he ran a hand through my hair and kissed my forehead. "That was ..."

I crossed my arms over his chest and propped my chin on them, looking at him. "Amazing?"

He craned his neck and I met him halfway for a brief kiss. "More than that," he said.

"Agreed."

We stared at each other. I was unsure why I fought against this so hard, but I was glad I finally gave in and came to him on my own.

The glow on his face faded, and he pushed me to the side.

"Um, I'm hungry. Are you? How about I drive somewhere and bring us food?"

I frowned. Maybe it was me, but it seemed like he realized what a mistake he had made and was now looking for a way to get rid of me. A pang ran through my chest. As much as it hurt, I wasn't a clingy girl, and I wasn't going to complain or ask why.

I forced a smile. "Yeah, sure."

He shot up, got dressed, and then knelt on the bed beside me.

"I'll be right back." He placed a sweet kiss on my lips and then rushed out of the cabin.

29

I leaned on the driver door of my SUV, asking myself why I didn't just leave. I mean, he all but ran away from me after we were done. Obviously, he didn't want me here. As soon as I heard his truck driving down the road, I shot up and got dressed, determined to leave. However, as I walked out of the cabin, I realized that would be childish. We couldn't just pretend nothing happened. Well, maybe he could, but I couldn't. I liked him way too much to pretend. Besides, would I run away from another thing in my life? No, I would stay right here until he got back, even if he took his sweet time cursing himself for sleeping with me before manning up and coming back. He probably thought that if he stayed out for a long time, I would get tired of waiting and would leave.

I confess, I almost hopped in my car and drove away several times. *Droga*, that option wasn't out of the question yet. If he took much longer, I really would leave. Final exams started tomorrow, and I hadn't started studying yet.

I hugged my jacket and looked up, knowing it was about to snow again. Another half hour passed. The hell with it. If he didn't want to talk to me, then I didn't want to talk to him either. Apparently, we were taking the childish path.

I opened the door of my SUV and I was slipping inside when I heard the sound of a car driving closer. I turned and saw his truck approaching. He parked beside me, exited his truck, and walked around it, looking at me with a frown.

"You're leaving?" he asked, shoving his hands in the pockets of his jeans.

I jumped out of my SUV but leaned against the doorframe. "I thought you weren't coming back." He opened his mouth, but before he could say anything, I continued, "Listen, Garrett. If you didn't want me here after we had sex, you should have told me. I'm not a child and I'm sure not clingy. I won't whine or complain. You should have told me you needed space or some other half-lie like that and I would have left. Okay?"

I turned to enter my car again, but he grabbed my arm and turned me to face him.

"I admit," he started, "I needed some time to think, but I was—I am—hungry, so I took advantage of that time to think."

I tugged my arm and he let go. "Glad to see you manned up and came to tell me the truth."

"About what?"

"All right. I'll just spare you, okay. No need to tell me what a mistake it was, and that it won't happen again. The message is loud and clear."

I turned to my car again, but this time, he shot his arm out and blocked my way in. "Wait a minute, you think it was a mistake?"

I crossed my arms. "You clearly do."

"Bia, do you think it was a mistake?"

"It doesn't matter what I th—"

"Answer the damn question. Please."

"N-no, I don't. But like I said, I'm not clingy and I won't bother you again."

He took a step closer, making me retreat a step. My back pressed against the side of my SUV, and he loomed over me, so close I could feel the tension in his body.

"Bia, I don't think it was a mistake."

I gaped. "Then why did you leave?"

"For one, I really am hungry, and after being away all week, there's nothing to eat. The last time I ate was five o'clock this morning, before arriving in town. I haven't eaten anything since and was about to leave to grab something when you arrived. Two, I really needed to think, not about how to ditch you, but to understand what I'm feeling."

I bit my lip, trying to keep the question in, but it was stronger than I was. "And what are you feeling?"

"Honestly, I'm not sure yet, but all I know is that I don't want you to leave." He grazed my cheek with his knuckles. I leaned into his touch. "Stay."

I shouldn't stay. Not because I didn't want to. *Meu Deus*, I wanted to. However, I had to study. With all that had happened, I hadn't done well with my midterms and I needed to do well on the finals to end up with a good GPA. After all, my grades would transfer when I did.

Garrett's knuckles slipped down my neck, making me shiver. Who was I kidding? Even if I went back to my dorm, I wouldn't be able to focus on studying now, would I? Hell no.

I nodded.

A lopsided grin adorned his lips before he pressed my body against the car with his body, and brought his mouth down to mine. I let him control the kiss and didn't regret it. His lips moved slowly and deeply, and his tongue caressed mine, making me moan.

Groaning, he broke the kiss and whispered in my ear, "I want to hear you moan and scream for me again, but first—" He took a step back. "—let's get out of this cold and eat." He opened the passenger door of his truck and pick up a large brown bag and a tray with sodas from the floor. "Come on." He jerked his chin to the cabin and started walking that way.

I followed him, and in those sixty seconds of silence, my mind raced.

What the hell was I doing? I should be at my dorm studying, and more than that, I shouldn't be getting involved now that I decided I was going back to California. I mean, not that we couldn't have a hot affair in the remaining week I still had here, but that was putting my heart on the line for something I was sure wouldn't last.

Not to mention, if Audrey found out that Garrett and I slept together, she would probably find a way to spin this story into one of her terrible lies and make me look like a slut.

Even if I was able to convince myself to leave, it was too late now. With all the time we spent together and the way I knew him, I was already too attached.

Garrett sat on the couch and started pulling the contents from inside the bag. "I hope you like pasta." He placed a to-go plate of fettuccine Alfredo and another one of spaghetti a Bolognese on the wooden table in front of him. Lifting his chin to look at me, he patted the free spot beside him. "Won't you sit down?"

"Yeah, of course," I said, sitting beside him.

He grabbed napkins and plastic utensils from the bag. "Do you prefer regular plates and a fork? I have it."

"This is fine," I said. He gestured to the plates and I shrugged, not very hungry. "I like both, so I'll let you choose."

"Okay." He grabbed the Bolognese plate and handed me the other one.

I opened the lid and played with the food while he dug in. After a minute of silence, I finally opened my mouth. "Are you feeling better? I mean, I came to find out if you were okay and I still don't have an answer."

He finished swallowing before answering. His eyes darkened. "I thought you had noticed, but I was pretty okay earlier, when we were in bed."

Heat crawled across my face and I slapped his shoulder. "That's not what I meant."

"I know. I just wanted to tease you. I like when you blush."

Of course, that made my face hotter, and I was sure my cheeks were bright red. "I'm serious. I am worried about you."

His expression hardened. "Don't. I'm okay. I'll be okay."

I wanted to prod, to make him talk and open up because there was no way he was okay after all that happened the past two days. Delilah lost the competition, and he saw her lashing out at her new horse. He drove back through the night—which reminded me, how the hell wasn't he sleeping on his feet—and had to stand before his father while the man literally kicked Garrett out of his life. His insides were probably bursting with rage, frustration, and concern. I knew I would be.

I set my barely touched plate aside. "You said you drove all night and got here this morning." With a mouthful, he nodded. "You're probably exhausted."

Relaxed, he raised an eyebrow and swallowed. "I guess the events of the day kept me alert."

I lifted a brow at him and chuckled. "Excuse

me? Usually, I'm ready to fall asleep after sex. In your state, I don't know how you didn't."

He lost the amused mien and frowned. I practically saw the tension spreading through his body, and the walls going up as he shoved his empty plate inside the bag, picked up mine, and put it inside the bag too. He clenched and unclenched his hands.

Meu Deus, what now?

I leaned closer to him and took his hands in mine, stopping them from opening and closing. "I can see something is bothering you. Talk to me."

He let go of my hands and stood, immediately pacing the small area. "I know Audrey's lies are that, just lies. Fortunately, I got to know you and you're nothing like how she paints you to everyone." He stopped and faced me. "But you just … it's just … Have you been seeing someone else?"

Where did that come from? "No."

"Then were you seeing someone else?"

"No." I stood in front of him. "Why are you asking me that?"

"You just practically implied you were having plenty of sex."

I gaped at him and raked my brain. *Usually, I'm ready to fall asleep after sex.* "*Meu Deus*, no." I almost chuckled, a little too happy about his jealousy. "I meant in the past. I haven't been with anyone in nine months or so, and even then, that was a mistake. I didn't feel anything for the guy, and I'm sure he didn't feel anything for me either." I slapped my mouth shut. I had just blurted too much information, which I knew guys hated. But it was the truth. I had gone out with Ri, Pedro, and Gui during a tournament in France. I met a guy at a bar and took him to my hotel room, which is as slutty as it gets, but I really didn't do that. Not often, anyway. In the morning, I shooed him off before my father woke up and came to call me for breakfast.

Garrett stepped toward me. "Are you saying you feel something for me?"

My cheeks warmed. "I-I ..."

He chuckled, reaching to me and placing his hands on my hips. "You don't need to be embarrassed." He pulled me to him and leaned into me. He whispered in my ear, "I care about you too." My heart rate went through the roof. He did?

"What about Jennifer?"

He stared into my eyes. "Jennifer and I used to spend some time together, but there's nothing going on with her. Not since last spring break." He ran his fingertips from my cheek, down my neck, to my shoulder. "Right now, there's only you." Before I could say anything coherent, he pushed us back until I was pressed against the wall. "Let me show you what I mean."

He cupped my face and kissed me, as if he was searching for the essence that gave him energy, which sustained his life. His tongue ravished my mouth and my knees weakened. I clasped my hands around his shoulders before I fell. But I wanted to. I wanted to fall headfirst.

No, Bia, you can't. You're leaving soon, and you aren't planning on coming back.

Garrett trailed kisses down my neck and over my collarbone. He stopped long enough to pull my sweater over my head, and then he kept going, kissing around my breast and down my belly. He unzipped my pants and pulled them down before standing straight, shrugging his shirt off, and pressing his body against mine.

I gasped when his mouth met mine, and he thrust his hips on mine, his erection rubbing against me, making my core hotter and hotter. His hands slid around my leg and teased the edge of my panties. I whimpered and he smiled against my lips. He rubbed his finger on me through the panties, drawing a moan from me.

"Do you want it?" he asked, his voice throaty. I dug my nails on his skin and gasped when he pulled my panties aside. "Do you want it?" he asked again.

"*Sim, por favor.*" Realizing I had just spoken Portuguese, I added, "Please."

He sank a finger inside me and I moaned. He buried his head on my neck and groaned with his mouth on my skin. "Fuck, Bia, you're so wet."

He slipped his finger out and then thrust two in. I arched my back, trying to give him better access to me. I didn't know what was better, the combination of his hot breath on my skin, the hand digging on my hips to keep me steady, his naked chest flush against mine, his erection running against my leg, or the way he was touching me, driving me to the edge.

"So good," I whispered.

He rubbed his thumb on my clit and I burst. I trembled and whimpered, but he didn't let it go. He increased the pressure and kept on thrusting those fingers inside me. I wanted to crawl inside myself, inside him, because there was no way I could survive this much pleasure, this much heat. A new wave hit me, and I screamed his name as I came.

With deft hands, he pulled a condom from the back pocket of his jeans. I reached to him and worked on his zipper, my eyes on his. I pulled his pants down enough to free his massive erection and closed my hand around him. A shiver assaulted his body, and a low growl rumbled from his chest.

He bent forward to kiss me, but I leaned back, wanting to look at him while I stroked him, while I gave him pleasure. I ran my palm over him a couple of times more before snaking my hand down and pushing his jeans all the way to his feet.

I sank to my knees and his gaze went wide. I smiled before clasping his hips and licking his erection from head to shaft and back.

"Oh fuck," he muttered, knotting his fingers in my hair.

I took him into my mouth, sucking hard, and he cursed some more. I felt him tensing, his fingers curling into my scalp, with each stroke of my mouth, with each swirl of my tongue. I changed the rhythm, taking him in deeper and slower.

He shuddered. "Bia," he gasped. I felt him coiling, his body stiffening, and I knew he was close. He cupped my face and pushed back, then pulled me to my feet.

I licked my lips. "I would have finished it."

His gaze followed my tongue and he swallowed, finally ripping the foil package. "I know, but we can do that another time. Right now, I want to come inside you."

I shivered with his words, with the raw desire in his eyes. He slipped the condom in place and leaned into me. His arm wound around my waist and he pressed me against the wall again. Not breaking his stare, I wrapped my legs around his waist, and he entered me, none too gentle. I cried out, arching my back to take him deeper, wanting, needing the mix of pleasure and blissful pain.

"God," he muttered as a shudder ran through his body. He closed his mouth over mine and assaulted me with his tongue. "I can't get enough," he whispered against my lips. "I can't get enough of you."

His words thrilled me in a way they shouldn't.

Just then, his thrusts became harder and deeper, and I forgot about what I should be worried about it. All that mattered was this. Us. Together at this moment. I knew I was moaning a little too loud, but who cared? There was no one for miles.

The heat wave was back and threatening to take me over any second now. *Meu Deus*, I wanted it to take me over. I wanted Garrett to take me over right now.

"Garrett," I gasped. "Please, don't stop."

He growled and bit my neck. Somehow, his thrusts became rougher, and I thought I was going to break into a million pieces of pure bliss. Then I did. My ecstasy exploded and my legs turned into goo. With one more thrust, Garrett joined me on the other side. He held me tight while his body convulsed, his head buried in my neck.

His quivers faded, and he brought his face to me. He kissed me long and gentle, taking my breath away. He didn't break the kiss while he lowered us to his bed, and we lay on our sides.

He placed butterfly kisses over my neck and shoulder, then sat up and reached for the covers. He brought them over us and lay on his back, tucking me under his arm. I rested my head on his shoulder and my hand on his chest. His heart still raced. I tilted my face to him and found him watching me.

Heat spread through my cheeks. "What?"

He kissed my forehead and tightened his arms around me. "Nothing." He sighed. "It's just ... if you hadn't come here, I would probably still be outside, working to death. Or I would have gone to a liquor store, bought plenty of whiskey, and spent my night with a bottle. I was really upset when I left the ranch this morning. Now I'm not anymore. Not too much, at least."

"I'm glad I could take your mind off your problems."

A half-grin broke onto his face. "Me too."

I didn't really want to bring it up now, but if it weren't now, when would I talk to him about it? I was leaving in less than a week. He had to talk to someone.

"What now?" I asked, my voice low, afraid he would be mad at me.

He stared at me with those bright hazel eyes. "I don't know. I don't want to stop this—" He pointed to him and me. "—but I haven't been in a relationship for a while. I'm not sure how to be in one anymore. How about we take it slow? By the way, are you going to California for the holidays?"

Wow, his answer took me by surprise. I propped my body on my elbow so I could look at him better. "T-that wasn't what I meant."

"Oh. Why? You don't want to take it slow? Or you don't want anything, period?"

I wasn't sure I should answer those questions. After the events of this evening, every decision I had made these past couple of weeks seemed frail. My plan to leave for California for good looked like an insane one right about now.

"I meant, about you. Your future. What are you going to do now?"

His forehead creased. "Um, I don't know. Find a job somewhere, anywhere, and try to finish the barn as fast as I can. It would be great to have it ready for spring. I have contacts; know a lot of people. Hopefully, I'll open the ranch and already have riding groups scheduled and some horses coming for boarding."

"What if you don't find a job? Not right away?"

"I have a little money saved. I was using it to build this place, but if it comes down to it, I'll use it to pay bills and such." Running his hand through my hair, he closed his eyes. "Don't worry about me. I'll be fine."

He was strong and determined. I knew he would be fine. However, that didn't erase my worry.

I pressed a soft kiss on his chin. "Sleep. You're probably about to die of exhaustion." I started disentangling myself from him.

His hands splayed on my back, keeping me in place, and his eyes shot open. "Where are you going?"

"Finals start tomorrow, and I should probably sleep in my dorm so I won't be late."

"Don't go," he whispered, the shine in his eyes pleading. "We'll put an alarm clock for a little earlier, so you have plenty of time to get there, just don't go."

How could I resist that?

Smiling, I lay over him again. "If you want me to stay."

He placed a finger under my chin and angled my mouth to his. "I do. I want you to stay."

30

I raced across campus, bumping into everyone and everything. I rushed through the building's door and into the classroom, taking my seat with ten seconds to spare. The professor looked at me with an annoyed amusement.

I mouthed, "Sorry."

He grabbed a pile of papers and started passing the stack around.

Of course, when the alarm rang this morning, I ignored it. Until Garrett shifted over me and did things to me that brought heat to my body even now. I pushed those memories back. This wasn't time to have a meltdown. I had an exam to focus on, which was hard to do knowing I would see Garrett again tonight. The fraternity houses were holding the second to last mixer tonight, but he told me he would rather not go and spend the night with me at his cabin.

Once again, I reprimanded myself for not choosing to study, but how could I? Finally, Garrett and I were together. Finally, we were working things out. If I didn't study, I wouldn't fail. I just wouldn't get great grades. Well, I would try to compensate for that next semester.

After I was done with my exams, I stopped by my dorm to take a shower and change clothes.

Molly was seated at her desk, studying. "Where were you last night?"

Damn. I hadn't thought about her noticing I hadn't been here. "It's none of your freaking business."

Her eyes widened. "You were out with a guy."

I rolled my eyes. I could let it go, but then she would tell Audrey, and the bitch would come bother me about it. Not to mention the new rumors she would spread. Seriously, my last few days here could be rumor-free.

"I was with Phoebe. We studied until late and I slept in her room." Before she asked more, I raced to the bathroom.

However, I didn't escape the questions after my shower, while I slipped into jeans and a sweater, and packed my toothbrush and toothpaste.

She raised her eyebrows. "Are you going to sleep at *Phoebe*'s again?" The way she said Phoebe told me she didn't quite believe me.

"Yes, I am." I shoved the small toiletry bag inside my purse and slung it over my shoulder. "Good night."

I left the room under her suspicious stare. Whatever. There were only four more days in this hell. She could tell whomever she wanted whatever she wanted. I didn't care anymore.

The drive to Garrett's cabin seemed longer than the twenty-seven minutes it really was. Maybe it was because my heart was already racing and I couldn't wait to be with him again.

Damn, what I was doing? I was lining my heart for a major heartbreak, and I didn't seem to care.

I parked my car beside his beat-up truck. I walked to the cabin, careful with the thin layer of snow, and as I climbed up the front steps, the front door opened.

"Hey, there." Garrett stood in the doorway in a plaid shirt—the sleeves rolled to his elbows and most of the buttons undone—jeans, and barefoot. His hair was more rumpled than usual and a half-grin took over his handsome face.

I halted and swallowed hard. Yeah, it would definitely be hard to leave. "Hi."

He beckoned me over, and like a silly girl, I stumbled to him. Once I was within reach, he grabbed my arm and pulled me hard against him. After taking my purse from me, he leaned in and kissed me. His lips were soft and gentle, and I melted in his arms.

He wrapped an arm around my waist and hoisted me inside the cabin without breaking the kiss. He pushed the door closed and retreated to the couch, still not breaking the kiss. He pushed my jacket down my shoulders and threw it aside, then lowered us to the couch.

The kiss mixed with his weight pressed against my body warmed my core. I wrapped my legs around his waist and pushed his hips into mine.

He growled and broke the kiss, burying his face on my neck.

I wedge my hands between us and reached for his shirt. I wanted it off. I wanted all of his clothes off. Now.

He propped himself on his arms. The cute half-grin was stamped on his face. "Aren't we in a rush?"

My face flamed. "Well, it's not like you were helping."

He chuckled, lowering his face to mine again. He brushed his lips on mine, taking my breath away. "As much as I want to rip your clothes off and abuse your hot body right now, I have other plans first."

He shot off the couch. Feeling ignored, I sat straighter and ran a hand through my hair. "Yeah, and what are your plans?"

Garrett walked to the kitchen. "I noticed how you were divided when I invited you over. I know you have to study for finals, so we'll compromise. You'll study while I cook dinner." He gestured to the pans and pots on the range. "But after that, you're mine."

I shivered, imagining what wonderful things he would do with me later. The shiver gone, my body warmed, especially my heart.

"You're gonna cook dinner for me?" I didn't even know he could cook.

With a lopsided grin, he tipped an invisible hat. "Yes, ma'am."

My heart skipped a beat. *Meu Deus*, what was he doing to me? How considerate of him, letting me study for a little, feeding me, and not just sleeping with me. I could see this, us, going far if I stayed here.

No, that wasn't an option. I wouldn't change

my plans again. I would enjoy my time with him and then leave. Simple as that.

I stood and walked to the door.

Garrett was beside me in a flash. He pressed his hand on the door so I couldn't open it, and faced me with huge eyes. "Where are you going?"

I was able to keep my cool, but internally, I was grinning like a little girl. "My tote with my books is in my car. I was going to go grab it."

He let out a long breath. "Oh, okay. Stay here, I'll grab it for you." He placed a quick peck on my lips and shoved his boots on. He exited the cabin and closed the door behind him.

I stare at it. What was that?

I didn't analyze his actions much; I just reveled in the content feeling stirring in my chest. It looked like he really wanted me to stay.

Garrett was back in less than a minute. He took his boots off and ran a hand through his head, brushing flakes of snow off his hair. "Started snowing again." He extended my tote to me. "Here." I took it, but he held my arm and stepped into my space. He kissed me quick but hard. "Now, go study. I have a dinner to cook."

He turned to the kitchen, and in a daze, I retreated to the couch.

How was I supposed to study after that? Practically fanning myself, I sat on the couch and took my books out of my tote. I opened the book on one of the chapters that would be on the exam and started reading it.

Not ten seconds later, I heard the spark of the range turning on, the clink of spoons on pots, pans and lids being opened or closed, water running, a knife slicing. There was no way I could resist the allure of peeking at him.

Garrett looked like a master chef, moving with precision and expertise around his tiny kitchen. He peeled potatoes, while steaks were marinating on the counter, and water boiled on the range. His brows were slightly furrowed, and he seemed really into it.

I smiled. *Meu Deus*, I was doomed. I would leave Colorado and I was sure my heart would stay behind. It worried me, yes, but not enough to run away from this. I wanted this. I wanted to experience this. I wanted to share these moments with him.

He caught me spying and tsked. "You're not studying, Miss Fernandes."

I fought against my smile and lowered my head to my book. *Meu Deus*, this was going to be hard.

Thirty minutes later, Garrett placed two goblets of wine beside my books on the coffee table and wedged himself between the couch and me.

I glanced at him. "What are you doing?"

"Pretend I'm not here."

"How about dinner?"

"In the oven. You have another thirty minutes to study before I serve you dinner." He wrapped an arm around my waist and pressed my back against his chest.

"You want me to study with you this close to me?"

He kissed my neck. "If you don't, I'll go back to the kitchen."

Groaning, I looked back at my book and he chuckled.

I read my notebook, but I wasn't sure how much I was absorbing. It was hard to when his thumb drew circles on my belly, and his breathing teased my neck. However, I wanted him to stay close, so I pretended to study, hoping something was making sense and sticking to my brain. Perhaps I would be surprised tomorrow and would remember everything.

Yeah, right.

When I finished reading my notes, I flung my notebook on the coffee table. "*Credo*, how can this be so boring."

He glanced over my shoulder. "History?" I nodded. "History is interesting."

"I agree. I used to like history, but this book. Ugh. This book is terrible. The author was sleeping or dying when he wrote it."

He chuckled. "I remember books like that. I had a biology one that sounded more like politics. Don't ask me how. It was horrible." He pulled me closer and I relaxed my back on his chest, resting the back of my head on his shoulder. "Sorry you have to take so many core curriculum classes this far along. That is boring."

I sighed. "In the beginning, it was hard to accept I would have to go over all of this again, but now I'm okay, I guess. I mean, I don't like it, but it has to be done. There's no way to trick the system, so that's that."

He brushed his lips over my neck and under my ear, making me shiver. "I know I told you this before, but you're amazing. You know that, right?"

I turned my face to him, searching his eyes. He was serious and that brought a new wave of emotion rushing through me. I leaned into him and captured his mouth with mine. I turned around and straddled him, pressing my hips against his. He groaned and his fingers dug into my waist.

I worked my hand under his shirt, about to pop the buttons open, when the oven dinged.

"Great timing," I muttered.

Chuckling, he picked me up as if I were a porcelain doll, stood, and then deposited me on the couch again.

"You can come to the table," he said, walking to the kitchen.

I took a minute to compose myself, then joined him in the kitchen and sat at the table. He placed the plates on the table. Warm bread rolls, steak covered in bacon, and mashed potatoes.

"It's garlic and pepper mashed potatoes," he said, sitting across the table from me. "I usually put a lot. I hope you like it."

"I'm sure I will." I watched as he served us.

I took a big bite of the steak and mashed potatoes, and had to hold in a moan. *Meu Deus*, the guy could cook.

"So, how many girls have you wooed with your cooking skills?" I asked, taking a piece of the bread roll.

He stopped cutting his steak and looked at me, his hazel eyes serious. "None."

Oh. Not even his ex-girlfriend? That was unexpected. I played it cool though. "I'm the first, then."

"If you want to look at it that way. To me, I'm just feeding a hungry girl." He winked, trying to lighten the mood.

"Starving," I said.

After we were done, I grabbed a few plates and took them to the sink. I turned around to grab more plates and help him clean up, but Garrett was right there, in front of me.

"There's dessert," he said, placing his hands on my waist and pushing me against the counter. "But that will come later."

He kissed me and I almost forgot my name.

31

AGAIN, I ARRIVED IN THE CLASSROOM WITH TWO seconds to spare. Garrett had given me one hell of a night and morning. I probably slept only three or four hours. Later, I would require a nap.

Even though there were still three days of finals, celebrations started early. Besides the fraternity mixer on Monday, there were plenty of festivities going around. On Tuesday, the party was at the Bull Bar. I wasn't going to go, mainly because I had to study, but Phoebe kept harassing me, saying she would drag me there if I didn't go. And then when Garrett sent me a message saying Jonah was giving him hell and he had to go to try and keep the peace, I made my decision.

I put on a short jean skirt, red cowboy boots, a

lace red blouse that hugged my body, and a red leather jacket. I brushed my hair until it shone and applied a little makeup. As I looked at myself in the mirror, I wondered if Garrett would like what he saw. Once more, I berated myself for caring about what he thought.

Careful not to slip on the snow accumulating on the ground, Phoebe and I walked to the bar. Once there, she met Kevin. He had his friends with him again, and they kept trying to chat with me while I scanned the crowd, searching for Garrett.

No sign of him, but I could see Audrey, Sarah, Molly, and other ATN girls on the dance floor. Jonah, Jeff, and other guys from The Bat had taken two tables right in front of the bar. Some girls mingled with them, shaking their asses in their faces. And they called me a slut.

One of Kevin's friends slid a hand on my back, and he would have taken it south if I hadn't stepped away.

"I'm going to grab a drink," I said to Phoebe.

"Are you okay?" she asked.

"I'm fine, why?"

"You look a little upset."

"Just your boyfriend's friends. They should keep their hands to themselves."

Phoebe laughed. "Well, hon, dressed like that, I would be all over you too."

I looked down at my outfit. "It isn't that much." I jerked my head to where Audrey was dancing in a short, tight pink dress. The cleavage was so low, I had no idea how her breast didn't pop out. "Not like that."

"That—" Phoebe pointed to Audrey. "—is trash. She needs all the help she can get."

"That's not true. She's pretty."

"Yeah, but you're more than that. You're beautiful, stunning, and when you put clothes that accentuate that, even if only a little, there's no competition."

I felt myself blush and shook my head at her. "I think you had a little too much to drink."

She laughed again. "I haven't had a drop of alcohol yet."

"Well, that is about to be remedied. What do you want?" She rattled the name of a beer brand. "Be right back."

I weaved through the sea of bodies and reached the packed bar. While waiting for a spot to squeeze through, I couldn't help myself and looked for him.

"What can I get you, beautiful?" the bartender asked me.

"Whiskey and Coke," Jonah answered, squeezing by my side.

I frowned. "I can order my own drink, thank you very much."

He smiled wide. "You're welcome."

Jerk.

I caught the attention of the bartender and ordered Phoebe's beer too.

"Glad to see you out and about," he started. "Do you want to dance?"

I glared at him. "Excuse me? If it depended on me, you wouldn't come within a mile of me."

He pressed his lips together. "Look. I realize I crossed the line, but I was hoping you would realize I had a moment of weakness or craziness or whatever you want to call that, and forgive me."

The bartender returned with my drinks. "But I know it wasn't a moment of weakness, craziness, or whatever. So, no, I don't forgive you." I stepped away from the bar, and his hand clasped my wrist, stilling me.

"Wait."

"Let me go," I said through gritted teeth.

"Just dance with me. One song. We'll talk and you'll see I'm not a monster."

I jerked my arm, but he held on to it. "Take your hands off me."

"Bia—"

"Oh, now I have a name." Something past Jonah's shoulder caught my attention. Garrett, entering the bar. He scanned around and found his friends right beside us. I glared at Jonah again. "I don't want to have to scream. Please, release me."

"Not until you agree to dance with me."

I jerked my arm and he finally let go. "Don't touch me. Ever again," I hissed.

I turned to leave and found Garrett standing beside Jeff, not ten feet away. He watched Jonah and me, his eyes narrowed. I let out a long sigh and forced myself to push Jonah and all the bad feelings he brought me from my system.

I focused on Garrett. He was here and he looked incredible in jeans, a plaid shirt, suede jacket, and his cowboy boots. A small smile tugged at my lips, but he remained passive.

I was about to walk over to him, when I remembered I still had Phoebe's beer in my hand. I darted to find my friend. She was sucking face with her boyfriend, so I grabbed one of her hands and put her fingers around the bottle.

She pulled back from Kevin. "Hey, thanks."

"You're welcome." I stood on my tiptoes and tried finding Garrett through the crowd.

Phoebe took a sip from her beer. "Looking for something? Or someone?"

"Someone," I said.

"Oh, who?"

I found him. He had moved to the other table and was now speaking with Jonah. His brows were furrowed, and I could see the lines of tension in his neck. Jonah didn't look much different. *Droga.*

"You know who," I said before downing my entire drink.

I threw my empty plastic cup in the nearest trash and weaved toward Garrett and Jonah. For some reason, I believed they were arguing about me, and I wanted to hear what they were saying. Not to mention, I would love to see Jonah's face when Garrett put his arms around me, and I let him.

Still arguing with his half-brother, Garrett glanced in my direction. The frown deepened and, keeping his arm down, he showed me his hand. What the hell did that mean?

He said something else to Jonah, causing the guy to close his eyes for a second. Garrett glanced at me again and slightly shook his head, his hand still turned to me. Was he asking me to wait?

I halted a good fifteen feet from them, hating the mass of bodies coming and going, covering most of Garrett and Jonah from my view. I was growing impatient. Until Jonah finally threw his hand out, as if throwing a towel, and marched to the bar.

Garrett's eyes locked with mine, and I couldn't help but smile. He didn't smile back. Not even that half-grin of his. I took a step toward him, and he raised his hand again. What the hell?

Subtly, he nodded his head to the back before turning around and walking that way.

Something like annoyance and wariness made its way into my chest. I followed him to the back of the bar, past the tiny stage, and into a squared hallway that led to the restrooms. A wooden bench ran along most of the walls. A couple sat in a corner, kissing as if the world was ending. On the opposite wall, a group of girls chatted too loudly and giggled every three seconds.

Garrett leaned in a corner, the darkest one. Still wary, I halted in front of him, my arms crossed.

I stared at him. "What's going on?"

He ran a hand through his hair. "Bia, I know how it looks, but I'm not sure you want to be seen with me."

My heart faltered. "What I'm hearing is that you don't want to be seen with me."

"It's not that. I'm just worried about your reputation."

"That my reputation will taint yours?"

He shook his head. "I don't care about my reputation."

I took a step closer to him. "Then why, Garrett? Why don't you want to be seen with me?"

He opened his mouth, but nothing came out. On purpose, I uncrossed my arms and let my hands slide down my waist in a seductive manner. I had chosen this outfit with him in mind. He better look at it.

His eyes followed my hands, but he didn't stop at my waist. Slowly, his gaze ran down my legs and back. His eyes found mine and he swallowed hard. Seeing he was losing the battle, I took another step toward him, leaving two inches between us.

"I don't care about what others think." I tilted my chin up, angling my mouth to his. "Kiss me," I said, my voice low and throaty.

He groaned. "Fuck it, Bia." He clasped his hand around my neck and pulled my mouth to his.

His lips were soft and he tasted of mint, as if he had just chewed gum. However, there was where the subtlety ended. He kissed me with hunger and desperation. His fingers knotted in my hair, and his other hand splayed on my lower back, pulling me against him. I felt his erection coming to life and fought against a moan.

He slid his lips to my neck and inhaled deeply, as if savoring my scent. I wasn't done ravishing his mouth though. I tilted my face to capture his mouth with mine, but he stilled and pushed me back.

"What the—?"

"I told you, Bia." He glanced over my shoulder before meeting my eyes again. Pain flickered through his hard expression. "I'm not interested."

A pang ran through my entire body, from my head to my toes and back to my stomach, where it gutted me.

With his head low, Garrett marched around me and exited the hallway.

"But ..." I started, following him out until I bumped into Audrey.

Oh, *puta merda.*

She stared at me with her mouth hanging open, and her eyes wide but full of wonder, as if she had been given the best gift in the world.

She sneered. "I see you're not attacking only my man. You're after his brother too. Isn't one man enough for you?"

I shook my head. "Go to hell."

"Oh, mad someone turned you down?" Her

smile fell. "Wait. Why did he turn you down? He's in it. He wouldn't turn you down."

"What the hell are you talking about?"

"There you are!" Phoebe said, smacking into me. "I was looking for you, hon." Her words slurred and she swayed. How many beers had she had after I left her? "You know Ben, Kevin's friend. He said he's in love with you!" She squealed, and the amused expression returned to Audrey's face. "Isn't that so freaking adorable?" She grasped my hand. "Come on. I'll introduce you to him." She started to turn and saw Audrey. "Oh, hey, it's the bitch we hate."

Audrey glowered, and I matched her stare until we were out of sight. I let Phoebe take me, mostly because I had no idea what to do, what to think, what to feel. On instinct, I looked for Garrett, but couldn't find him anywhere. It didn't mean he wasn't here though. He could be seated around the table with his friends, or at the bar.

A lump rose in my throat. I had been considering changing my plans again, so I could be here next semester, so I could be with him. However, he had just told me he didn't want to be seen with me, *and* he had pushed me away in front of Audrey. My chest hurt; my head spun.

Phoebe turned me around to face Ben. "Here

she is," she said. "Now you can profess your love for her."

He looked at me with a smile. "Hey, um, I was wondering if you want to get out of here." He ran a finger over my arm and leaned into me. "You know, go to a place more private, where we can—"

"Excuse me?" I stepped back.

"Why not? You're Brazilian, right? That's not what they do—"

Something in me snapped, probably the rage mixed with frustration and disappointment, and I slapped him hard, cutting his words.

His face jerked to the side.

Phoebe gasped. "Bia!"

Kevin shouted, "What the fuck?"

His other friends looked at me as if I was crazy, and the rest of the people around us stared.

Ben turned his eyes to me, glowing with anger. "Why you little—"

Phoebe pulled me back. "Hey, don't talk to her like that."

Kevin turned to her. "Why not? The chick just hit him."

"She'll pay for it," Ben spat.

My head spun and my heart raced. This was getting out of control. I took Phoebe's hand and leaned closer. "I'm sorry about this mess," I whispered in her ear. I squeezed her hand and let go, stepping away.

"Bia, where you going?" I heard her calling me.

Keeping my head low so I didn't have to see all the disgust, the outrage, or the curiosity on every-one's faces, I all but ran from the bar.

32

I almost didn't get up the next day. However, finals were calling me. I didn't want to go, but I knew that I would regret it later, so I kicked myself in the butt and got up. Since I barely studied, I wouldn't get an A, or even a B, but getting a C or a D was better than failing the class.

For the first time since I arrived here, I had to put on makeup in the morning to hide the dark circles around my eyes.

After I left the bar last night, I ran across campus, trying to hold the tears until I was safely in my dorm room. I almost made it, but I broke down in front of the building. *Graças a Deus*, there weren't many people around and I was able to drag myself inside almost unseen.

I kept glancing at my phone or my door, expecting Garrett to come and explain to me what the hell happened, but the only messages and calls I got were from Phoebe. I messaged back, saying I was fine—what a lie—and that I would talk to her soon.

I fought hard, but the tears won and I cried until I fell asleep.

In the morning, I calculated the time so I didn't spend one extra second outside. I arrived in the classroom right when the professor handed out the exams, left as soon as I finished, and then dragged myself to my dorm again.

Of course, I noticed some students looking my way. The new lies from Audrey must have spread with the wind. Although, this time, I knew they weren't lies. Whatever she told the others, there was probably truth in them.

She probably told them I threw myself at Garrett, I begged him to take me, but he brushed me aside as if I were a cheap whore, one who he couldn't get away from fast enough. Where was the lie in that?

Phoebe called in the afternoon, but I didn't answer. Instead, I sent her a message, saying I wasn't ready to talk yet. Truth was, I was counting the hours until Friday, when I would leave right after finishing the last exam, and I wouldn't come back.

Good riddance.

At night, knowing everyone was at a party in the main courtyard, I took advantage of the almost empty building to start loading my car. The more I did now, the less I would have to do on Friday and the earlier I could leave.

I opened the trunk of my car and placed a box with books inside it. I turned to pick up another box when I saw someone approaching.

My heart stopped for a second.

His head low and hands inside the pockets of his jeans, Garrett walked toward me. I rushed to shove all the boxes in the trunk and close it before he got near. Shaking with nervousness and hurt, I dropped one of the boxes and books scattered on the dirty pavement.

"*Puta merda*," I cursed, placing a hand over my eyes. Luck really wasn't on my side lately.

"I like it when you speak in Portuguese, even if it's cursing." Garrett's voice came loud and clear.

I spun around to find him right there, standing four feet from me.

I shook my head and crouched down to pick up the books. "Go away, Garrett."

He knelt beside me and started helping me. "We need to talk."

Hadn't I heard that before? And what good did it do?

I glared at him and took the books from his hands. "I don't think so." I threw the books in the trunk. I would organize them later. Right now, my mission was to pick them up so I could get away from here.

He reached out, but stopped himself. Instead, he grabbed another book from the ground. "I need to apologize for the way I acted last night, and I need to try to explain what happened."

"Try? Try to explain?" I shook my head. "I don't care. I don't want to hear it."

"Please, Bia."

I stared at him. "Once you told me you didn't believe the lies, but last night, you helped start a new mill of them. First, you tell me you don't want to be seen with me, and then you turned me down in front of Audrey. Audrey! Of all people in the world, you know she is the worst. You humiliated me, Garrett."

Frustration crossed his face. "I'm so sorry about that. I wish we could go back in time. I wouldn't have gone to the bar. But I thought you weren't coming. You said you had to study. If I had known you would be there, I wouldn't have gone."

I gaped. "*Meu Deus*, can't you see you're making it worse? You just said that if you had known I was there, you wouldn't have gone. Why Garrett? Because you just wanted to fuck me in the dark. Is that it?"

His eyes flared and he leaned over me. "What we did was more than a simple fuck, and you know that. You were there; you felt it too."

I swallowed the lump in my throat. "What is it, then? Why didn't you want me there, and why did you humiliate me?"

He flinched. "I swear it was never my intention to cause you pain. I never meant to hurt you."

I heard a succession of footfalls and turned to where I thought it was coming from. It was the end of the parking lot, and there was nothing there, not even a car, except for shrubs and a couple of trees.

To my left, a girl strolled from one dorm building to another. I must have heard her steps and, so confused, thought it was on the other side. My head was so messed up.

I picked up the last book, threw it in the trunk, and closed the door. "You're not making any sense."

Garrett pressed his mouth tightly. Finally, he said, "I can't really explain right now, and we can't be seen together."

"Again with that? Go to hell, Garrett. I'm not a call girl. I won't just be around whenever you want release."

I started walking away, but he grasped my upper arm and pulled me back, against my car. He leaned into me. "I just said it was more than that, didn't I?"

"But you also said you can't be seen with me."

He dropped his head on my shoulder, and his scent filled my lungs, twisting my belly and weakening my knees.

He lifted his head again, and I could see the frustration in his eyes. "Please, believe me, there's more to it, but I can't explain right now. You have no idea how much it pains me to say this, but we have to pretend nothing is going on until you're back from the holidays."

"I'm not coming back," I told him. Surprisingly, my voice was even.

His eyes widened, gleaming with shock. "What? What do you mean?"

"I'm moving back to California."

"When did you decide this?"

"When I came back from Thanksgiving."

"But ... that was before we slept together. Why didn't you tell me?"

"We weren't exactly on speaking terms back then."

"Why are you leaving?"

I snorted. "As if you didn't know. Audrey and her lies. The many weirdoes who hit on me every single day. Your creepy brother included." The fact that his jaw clenched when I mentioned the guys hitting on me didn't escape me. "You tell me you can't be seen with me, then humiliate me in front of my worst enemy. Shall I go on?"

"So, basically you're giving up."

"Right now, coming to this university was a mistake. I should have done what my father wanted from the beginning. Apply to a college there and stay close to home."

He frowned. "Are you saying I was a mistake?"

I sighed. I could lie, say it was, or be quiet and let him assume he was, but for some reason, I thought he deserved the truth from me, even if he didn't do the same for me.

"No." I reached over and cupped his face with my hand. "You were the best thing out of this whole experience." He turned his face into my hand and placed a soft kiss on my palm. I shivered, fighting to stay strong. "Well, you and Midnight."

His usual half-grin showed up on his kissable lips. "I'm losing to a horse."

I withdrew my hand. "There's no competition there. The horse wins."

"Hey, now. Let me kiss you, and then you tell me that again." He leaned into me.

I panicked but didn't move.

He brushed his lips against mine, probably making sure I wasn't bolting. Well, I wasn't bolting, and to show him, I wrapped my hands around his neck and parted my lips. Almost instantly, he closed his mouth on mine, and his tongue plunged inside my mouth. His hands tightened on my waist, and I wiggled my hips, adjusting them so I could feel more of him. He pressed his hips against mine, his hard rock erection brushing against my core, making me shiver. *Meu Deus*, I would miss this. I would miss him. I would miss the way he touched me, the way he was able to melt me, to turn me into mush.

I would enjoy it while it lasted, because I knew that, after this, after him, I would be lonely for a long while. I couldn't imagine trying to kiss someone else, trying to be with someone else. Even if I did, I knew it wouldn't be the same. Garrett and I connected in a way I had never connected with anyone.

I didn't believe in soul mates. I believed there were a handful of people with whom an individual could be perfect with, but on a planet with seven billion people, a handful was rare to find. However, I had found one of mine and I didn't want to go after any other. Still, I had to let him go. *I had to go.*

I broke the kiss, panting.

His breathing wasn't much better than mine, and that made me a little less sad. *Good. Maybe he'll miss me too.*

He pressed his forehead against mine. "Come to the cabin with me."

A sob made its way through my throat, but I clamped my mouth and kept it in. Here it was again. Didn't he see what he was doing to me? He just asked me to go *fuck* him, but be quiet about it. To be his obedient whore.

I took a deep breath, calming my nerves, and placed a soft kiss on his lips. Fighting against myself, I dropped my arms from him and pulled his from around me.

"Bia ..."

Stepping aside, I flashed him a smile. A sad one. "Goodbye, Garrett."

33

Thursday was a repeat of Tuesday and Wednesday. I went from my dorm to my finals and back to my dorm. To make things worse, I was eating only snacks or frozen stuff so I didn't have to go out for meals.

On the bright side, Molly wasn't around much —probably partying with her bitchy sisters.

Friday, I woke up feeling a bit better. I had one final exam in the morning, and then I was done. I just needed to take the last of my things to my car and drive away, leaving the lies, the heartbreak, and everything else behind me.

I hadn't told my family about moving back, but I was sure they wouldn't be opposed to it. In fact, I believed they would love it. I hoped that I would be able to make amends with my father, and everything would be right again.

Except for my heart.

I finished my final exam in record time. I wasn't doing too well, since I barely studied, but at least I would pass, and then I would study my butt off at the new university next semester to compensate.

I would be fine. I would be okay.

I exited the classroom and noticed several students laughing or gasping at something on their cell phones. What was so amusing? Justin Bieber got arrested again? Or he finally had been deported? Being a foreigner, I hated it when one toyed with his or her permission to be here.

I pulled out my cell phone and unmuted it. There were several missed calls and messages, from both Phoebe and Garrett. What the hell? The last one from Phoebe asked me if I had seen it yet. Seen what?

As I exited the building, several students looked from their cell phones to me, and sneered or laughed or snorted. My heartbeat sped. Whatever this was, I knew I didn't want to be a part of it.

I raced to my dorm, focusing on what I had to do: grab my bags, throw them inside my car, and go. However, I came to a complete standstill when

I saw Audrey, Sarah, Molly, Jonah, Jeff, and some others in front of my dorm building.

"There you are," Audrey said, loud and clear.

Students who came and went turned their heads to her. Apparently, she wanted everyone around us to hear her. Great.

I took two steps toward them. "Let me pass."

"In a minute," she said, smiling. "First, I would like for you to see when we deliver the prize."

"What?"

My cell phone rang. It was Garrett. I pressed the ignore call button and faced Audrey. "Get out of my way before I break your nose again."

She cringed, touching her nose. Recovering, she smiled and pointed to the phone in my hand. "I bet that was Garrett." I frowned. She glanced behind me. "And here he comes."

I turned around. Garrett was running toward us.

With flushed cheeks, he halted in front of me. "Don't believe anything she's saying."

Meu Deus. "She hasn't said anything."

"She's going to," he continued. "Please, don't believe her. Let me explain."

My heart sank.

"No," Audrey said, her tone harsh. "I'll explain."

"Bia—"

"Shut up, Garrett," Jonah shouted.

Garrett clenched his hands and took a step forward, but I raised my hand and stopped him before he could jump on his half-brother. It seemed I wasn't going to escape this. The faster it went—whatever it was—the faster I could leave.

I looked at Garrett. "Let her tell me."

"No, Bia, pl—"

"You heard her," Audrey started. "She wants to know, and I'm dying to tell her."

I crossed my arms and faced her. "Then tell me."

Her lips curled into a wicked smile. "There was a bet going on since your second or third week here. The guy who was able to take you to bed first would take the jackpot."

My stomach dropped. Oh, that was why I was constantly being hit on. All those guys wanted the money. What a low move. "Who started the damn bet?"

Audrey shrugged. "I have no idea," she said in a singsong tone.

I fought the urge to punch her again. "You're a sick woman, do you know that? Why don't you mind your own business?"

"But you weren't minding yours," she said,

losing the smile. "You went after my guy, and of course, being a Brazilian slut, all the guys wanted you. Including mine."

"I wasn't yours," Jonah snapped.

Audrey tsked. "For the moment. Everyone knows we'll end up together again." She winked and he shook his head.

"Let's clarify something here," I said. "One, I didn't go after your guy. I never wanted anything with Jonah, not even for a second. He, on the other hand, doesn't seem to know what the word no means. Two, Brazilians aren't sluts. Not all of them. Just like not all American girls are saints. I bet there are plenty of sluts around here."

"But we know you're one," Audrey said.

"I'm not!"

She grabbed an iPad from Molly and flipped it over to me so I could see the screen. She pressed the red triangle in the middle and a video started.

I gasped.

A headline appeared for five seconds. "He won," it read. Then it faded away and an image of Garrett and me appeared, standing almost in this same place, two nights ago.

We were beside my car and someone had recorded us talking. I glanced to where the person with the camera could be. The place where I thought I had heard something, in the back of the lot, near the bushes and trees. I knew there was something wrong.

In the video, I said, "I'm a call girl. I'll just be around whenever you want release. You want to fuck me again?"

"Yes, a simple fuck," Garrett said. Then we were kissing against my car. I tried not to look because the memory of that last kiss was still too fresh in my mind. "Come to the cabin with me."

"Right now," I answered.

The video ended and Audrey smiled at me.

Blood rushed in my ears and my head spun. Too shocked to do or say anything, I watched as, without ceremony, Audrey grabbed a thick yellow envelope from Sarah and extended it to Garrett.

"Ten thousand dollars to the winner," she said.

Garrett pushed the envelope back to her. "I don't want the money." He turned to me. "Bia, you hav—"

The fact that whoever filmed us had altered what we had said wasn't the main thing bothering me, the thing hurting me.

"You were in on the bet?" My voice wasn't much louder than a whisper, and it was laced with pain.

"You kn—"

"Answer the damn question," I said, my voice firmer. "Were you in on the bet?"

He lowered his gaze. "Yes, but—"

I stepped back as if he had physically hurt me. "Leave me alone." I faced Audrey and the others. "All of you, leave me alone."

I stormed past Audrey and Molly, shoving them both out of my way, and marched inside the building. My hands shaking, I fumbled with my keys. It took me a full minute to be able to unlock my room's door and step in.

I pushed the door back as hard as I could, but it didn't slam closed.

"What the—?"

An arm was wedged through the crack. Bracing the door, Garrett entered the room. "Bia, you have to li—"

"I don't want to hear anything you have to say. Please, get out."

He closed the door behind him and leaned against it, arms crossed. "No. I won't let you leave until you hear me out."

I sighed. The beginning of a headache throbbed in the back of my skull. It would be wonderful to drive seventeen hours to California with a headache. Maybe I would drive out of town and stop at an inn to take a nap. Or to cry.

I glanced at Garrett and calculated the possibilities. There weren't many. Every one of them involved hearing him, because really, he was standing by the door and he was too big for me to try and move him, and if I didn't want to jump out of the window, I would have to listen to him to get out.

At least I could finish packing while he said whatever he wanted to say.

I grabbed an empty box from under my bed. "Go ahead. Explain."

"You won't even look at me while I'm talking to you?"

"If I can help it, no."

He sighed. "Okay. Yes, I entered the bet, but please try to understand. I didn't know you then. I thought you were exactly what Audrey said you were, and I was in desperate need of money. I confess I felt bad about it, but you're beautiful and that made deciding to enter the bet that much easier. Right when you started going to the ranch, I was still invested in the bet. You must have noticed the insistent flirting. But once I started to get to know you, I realized you were so different from how Audrey portrayed you. I tried to get out of the bet, but they wouldn't let me. I tried getting out several times, actually, because I was falling for you. I have never met a girl like you. You're kind, generous, funny. You worked at a ranch and got your hands dirty just because you wanted to help, because you wanted to be around horses. You're filthy rich, but don't like to show it. You don't use your status to your advantage. You know more about me than anyone alive. And you're so beautiful that it hurts being here, standing in front of you, and not being able to touch you. I was falling, hard, and each time we kissed, it was harder because I knew I couldn't get involved with you. I also knew I wanted to sleep with you, not because of the bet, but because I wanted you for you."

My breath caught and tears brimmed in my eyes. Shoving my books and notebooks in the box, I swallowed hard.

He pushed away from the door. "That was why I didn't want you to be seen with me. Because they would know, and you would find out about the bet."

"Well, we were seen together, and I found out about the bet. How did they do that? Follow you and any other guy involved, filming whenever one got close to me? That was how they recorded us that night?"

"No. As far as I know, Audrey became suspicious of us after seeing us at the Bull Bar. She didn't understand why I was pushing you away, since I was in on the bet. So, when I was around campus on Wednesday, she asked one of her sisters to follow me."

I had one more question to which I needed an answer. "You said something about waiting until next semester. Why? Wouldn't the bet still be in place?"

He shook his head. "The deadline is tonight, before everyone leaves for the winter holidays." He took a step toward me. "Bia, tell me you forgive me."

Ignoring the last part he said, I closed the box with tape. "I heard you. You explained everything." I picked up the box in my arms and halted before him. "Now let me leave."

His eyes shone with desperation. "No, you can't go like that. Please, forgive me. I never meant to hurt you."

"And yet you did."

"If I could go back in time ..."

"You didn't know me then, and you needed the money. You still would have entered the bet."

He sighed. "Please, forgive me."

I inhaled, focusing on what I had to say. "Garrett, I'm leaving. For good. You'll never see me again. Take the damn money, use it to finish your barn, and move on with your life, because I'm moving on with mine."

I walked around him, but he stepped in my way. "Don't go, Bia. I like you. Really, really like you."

"If you really like me, you'll respect me, and you'll let me go."

He leaned over me. "You'll just go, pretending you don't feel anything for me too?"

I held my head high. "I'm not pretending anything. I'm hurting on the inside, because I do like you, but I'm trying to be strong." He reached for me, but I stepped back. "But liking you isn't enough. Now, please, let me pass before I scream my head off."

His eyes pleaded with mine, but I held on to my pride.

Finally, his shoulders sagged and he stepped aside. "I hope you forgive me someday."

I glanced at him one last time. "Someday, I might. But I hope that by then, I'm happy with someone else."

SEVENTEEN HOURS WAS A LONG TIME TO THINK. ADD the hours I stopped by an inn, took a shower, had dinner, and then slept, the drive easily jumped to twenty-five hours.

As soon as I left Fort Howell, I pulled over so I could catch my breath. Aka, let some tears fall and recover from the shock. The hurt would take much longer to recover from though.

On my first coffee break, I sent a message to Tom.

Me: *I'm leaving town for good. When I get back to California, I'll arrange for someone to pick up Midnight and bring him to me. Thanks for everything, Tom.*

He answered almost immediately, but I hadn't really checked his messages, afraid they would make me hurt or cry even more.

My first plan was to drive to Hannah's ranch and ask for her guest bedroom until I found an apartment. However, as I put distance between Fort Howell and me, the old Bia returned to me, and the old Bia never ran from a fight.

So, I drove to my parents' house instead.

I parked my car in the visitor's parking lot and rushed up the front porch's steps. I was about to knock on the door when my mother opened it, her eyes wide.

"Beatriz, you're here," she muttered.

"Hi, *mãe*." I hugged her and she ushered me in. "Is *pai* here? I need to talk to him."

She gestured to the door on our right. "He's in his office." I started for the door, but she held my hand. "Whatever you came to say, just, please, don't upset him more. I hate seeing you two fighting."

I kissed her cheek. "Don't worry about it, *mãe*."

I knocked on the half-open door, before sticking my head in. My father was on the phone, as usual, but his eyes bugged when he saw me, and he beckoned me in.

"Yes, March third. We'll be there. No, thank you." He hung up and turned to me, his face blank. "Beatriz. I wasn't expecting you."

"I know."

He pointed to one of the chairs across his desk. "Sit down."

"No, I'm good. This is going to be really quick, and then I gotta get going."

He narrowed his eyes. "Okay."

"I'm sorry if I disappointed you. It was never my intention. In fact, I wanted nothing more than the opposite. Being the youngest of three, or four, talented guys puts some pressure on me. I was never really talented in anything, and I didn't know what to do to be a star in your eyes too."

"Beatriz," he started.

I raised my hand. "Let me finish. I tried staying with the guys once we moved here, I tried following them around, but I was bored. Truly bored. I needed to do something for me, even if it wasn't as great as being a famous polo player. When I came home for Thanksgiving, I realized how selfish I was being. I mean, in some way, I blamed the guys' success for putting me in the shadows, and that's not fair. I love them and I'm so proud of their success. I shouldn't feel like this. I miss them. I miss you and Mom. And that's why I'm moving back."

His eyes widened. "Are you serious?"

"I'm moving back to California. I applied to a few colleges nearby and I should hear from them next week. I can transfer some of what I did in Brazil, and what I took in Fort Howell. If I'm not accepted for the next semester, I'll try again for next fall. However, I won't be living here anymore. I'm going to find an apartment for me, but I want to feel free to visit, to come over for lunches and family reunions. I don't want to feel like I'm entering a minefield." I sighed. "I won't ask you to understand or approve of my choices, because I know our visions are different. I just want you to respect me."

He frowned. "Beatriz, you're a strong girl and I respect you."

I tilted my head. "You have a weird way of showing it."

"I already said this, but you're my little girl. I know, I know. You're twenty-two, haven't been little for a long time, but it's hard for me. After three, or four, men, who have their own strong will, came a beautiful girl who is strong in her own way. If I could, I would keep you under my wings forever. I know I can't lock you up, but please don't ask me to be okay with releasing you into the wild alone."

I nodded. "I won't ask you to be okay, if you don't hold me back."

A soft smile adorned his worn face. "We can work on that. But I won't make any promises."

"I can live with that."

"Good. I'm glad you'll be closer to us from now on."

I smiled. "Me too."

EIGHT WEEKS LATER

SEATED ON THE FENCE, I WATCHED AS PRETA, Argus, and Minuano ran around the pasture. Soon, Midnight would be joining them. I had been two months, but finally Tom called me saying the vet had cleared Midnight to travel from Colorado to California.

I bit my nails—a habit I didn't have—eager to see my new horse. He would be happy here. At least one of us would.

I sighed. I wasn't unhappy, but I wasn't at my best place yet.

Being at Hannah's ranch with the horses brought the memories I was trying to forget in full force. I could feel Garrett's hand on me, his half-grin, his hazel-colored eyes, the way he cared about the horses, what that goddamned barn meant to him. I couldn't help but wonder how he was. If he had found a job and had finished the barn. If he had met someone. If he had already forgotten me.

A pang sliced through my heart.

One thing I didn't expect after leaving Colorado was how much my body, my soul, yearned for Garrett. I thought the hurt of what he had done, or everything I had lived through, would take precedent over how much I liked him, how much I liked being with him, how good he made me feel. My heart knew what I was feeling, but I ignored it. I couldn't think about love right now. It was too late.

No, I wouldn't go down that path. Even if tomorrow was Valentine's Day and everyone on campus, or even Hannah and Leo, were talking about their plans. My focus was on finishing prevet. I hadn't done too great last semester, and I was intent on doing great from now on. I had been accepted to college here and was doing better. I also had found an apartment close to Ri's, Pedro's, and Gui's, which meant I didn't have to worry about a roommate who had crazy friends.

In fact, so far I had only one friend. Laura and I clicked on the first day of class, much like Phoebe and I had. She was funny and outgoing, just like the old me—which I was working on bringing back. I had told her a tiny portion of my experience in Fort Howell, and I might have mentioned Garrett to her—and to Hannah too.

Other than her, I kept my mouth shut and didn't try making more friends. I wasn't ready to trust too many people at once again. Besides Laura, I had my brothers, cousin, Hannah, and Hilary, and that was already enough. More than enough.

My cell phone dinged, bringing me back to the present.

I fished it out of my pocket and glanced at the screen.

"Let me guess," Hannah said, approaching me from the stable. "Garrett again?"

"Ugh. His calls and texts have increased this past week." I deleted the message without reading it.

She sat beside me. "Bia, don't you think it's time you talked to him? He clearly cares for you. Otherwise, why would he make the effort?"

"I don't know," I whispered.

"He'll keep calling and texting until you answer him. Even if you plan on not forgiving him, then just answer and get this over with. Better to stop now than to give him hope."

"I'm not giving him hope."

"Until he stops calling, he still has hope."

I sighed. She was probably right, but I was afraid. Afraid of hearing his voice and falling into his trap again, of melting into the desire to see him, to have him again. To let myself love him. I shook my head. "I can't. Not yet."

Hannah glanced behind us. "I think Midnight arrived."

I followed her gaze and saw a truck and a horse trailer entering the ranch.

My heart squeezed. "*Meu Deus.*"

"What?"

I blinked once. Twice. Three times. But the truck—an old dark blue truck—continued the same. "It's Garrett."

Hannah stared at me with wide eyes. "Oh."

I jumped off the fence. "You go over there. Receive Midnight for me. Make sure he's all right. Pay Garrett for the trip, please. I'll refund you later, and—"

Hannah climbed down the fence and put her hand on my arm. "I love you like a sister, but no. I won't do it. In fact, I'm going to retreat into my house right now and let you deal with it."

"But—"

"Listen, Bia. You can solve this right now. Tell him to go away and leave you alone forever. Or you can listen to him. Think about it. He came all the way from Colorado just to bring you your horse? I doubt it." She patted my hand then dashed away.

"Hannah," I called, but she just waved her hand and headed to her house.

Taking a deep breath, I walked through the stables and out the front just as Garrett exited his truck. My heart skipped a beat at his sight. *Meu Deus*. I wasn't prepared for this. I wasn't prepared to see him again. The nice jeans hugged his legs, and a plaid red and blue shirt looked good on him. Too good.

Garrett took off his hat and closed the truck's door. "Hi."

I halted a safe fifteen feet from him. "What are you doing here?"

He jerked his chin to the trailer. "I brought Midnight."

"But why you?"

He scrunched his nose. "I thought it would be pretty obvious seeing as I am two states away from home," Garrett said, his tone even. His hazel eyes, though, seemed troubled.

I shook my head. "Garrett, I can't—"

"No, wait. Listen to me." He advanced two steps toward me, his eyes locked on mine. "I came to apologize, to ask for your forgiveness. I know I hurt you and I'm sorry. I never meant to. Once I realized I was falling for you, I didn't care about the money. I swear."

Tears of rage and frustration brimmed in my eyes. "No. You can't do this to me."

"Bia, I know I screwed up, but I need to prove to you that I regret it. I'll regret it for the rest of my life. But the truth is, I shouldn't have let you leave Colorado. I should have held on to you, fought for you, fought *with* you until you saw how much you mean to me, how great we are together."

No, no, no. Who did he think he was? He couldn't come here and expect me to forget everything that happened. I was still picking up the pieces from last fall, but I had built a life for myself here with a solid foundation. What was he thinking? That I would go back to Colorado with him, just like that? No. No more moving for me. I was here now and I wouldn't move.

"Please, stop. Nothing you say will change anything." I walked past him, toward the trailer. The sooner I got Midnight out, the sooner he would leave. "I won't move back to Colorado, and even if I forgave you, I can't imagine being in a long-distance relationship." I opened the trailer's gate and gasped. Midnight had company. I turned my eyes to Garrett. "What is Felicity doing here?"

A half-grin tipped his lips up. "You know the distance thing? That's all solved. I sold the land, and I'm moving here."

I gaped. "What? No, you can't do that."

"Why not?"

"Because of the land. Your mother left it for you."

Garrett stepped aside and plucked a lonely dandelion from a patch of grass. "I realized a few things. I don't think my mother left me that land for a greater purpose. That land didn't mean anything to her. She never stepped on it. How could it mean anything? She left me the land so I would have a place to land." He tucked the dandelion in the front pocket of his shirt, and then he reached past me, to Midnight, and untied him. "Maybe she wanted me to try to get close to my father, which I did and it failed miserably, but I don't think she had high hopes on that aspect." He handed me Midnight's reins. Twitching, the horse poked his muzzle on my shoulder when I ran a hand on his smooth coat. "Since the land didn't mean anything to her, I realized it didn't mean anything to me either. Therefore, I sold it to my father. I played hard to get, and to get rid of me, he paid twice what it was worth." He untied Felicity and took her reins. "Or maybe it was his way of giving me something and not feeling guilty for the way things were going between us. Who cares about his reasons? What matters is, I sold the land, got the money, and came here." He started walking toward the stable with Felicity. I followed him, taking Midnight with me. "I wanted to go after you the moment I got here, but I knew I had to build my case before barging into your life like that."

I put Midnight in an empty stall. "How long have you been here?"

Garrett pulled Felicity in another empty stall. "I first got here about two weeks ago."

I closed the stall's door. "Oh." My heart sank. Wow. He had been in the same town as me for the last two weeks and hadn't bothered to come after me. "Wait. You have been here for two weeks, and didn't bring my horse to me?"

Shaking his head, he exited the stall and closed the door. "I came to California two weeks ago, set up a few things, and then went back to Colorado to get my truck and the horses. I was there yesterday morning when Tom called you to let you know when to expect Midnight."

I frowned. "He knew you were the one bringing Midnight to me?"

"Yes," he said. Oh, I would call Tom and give him an earful. "I didn't want to show up here with nothing for myself but some money in the bank, which wouldn't last forever. So, I flew in a couple of weeks ago to search for a job and an apartment."

"A job?"

"I start at the Thompson's ranch on Monday. You know, just down the road from here."

My eyes bugged. "Yes."

He held the dandelion in front of him. "But I don't intend to stay there for long. I've been re-searching how to get my GPA up so I can apply for vet school and finish what I started." New tears burned behind my eyes. This time, he wiped them off, brushing his fingers over my cheek. He cupped my face. "I know I'm not a perfect man, not even close. I know I won't ever be rich or famous, but I want to try to be the best man I can be. I'll prob-ably have to work my ass off for the rest of my life. But when I look at the future and let myself imagine you by my side, I can't think of anything more perfect than that." He looked down at the dandelion. "Remember that day that I made a wish on one of these, and you asked me what I had wished for?" I nodded and he smiled. "Well, I wished to find a home. My home." He blew the dandelion. The plumes scattered around us. "You're my home, Bia. I ... I love you."

I put my hand over my mouth and suppressed a sob. Here he was, the man I loved, telling me he loved me back. And not only that, but he had sold the land his mother had left for him, he had moved to another state, he had found a new job, and was now thinking about applying to vet school. And it was all because of me. So he could be with me. So he could feel worthy of me.

My heart swelled. "Garrett," I whispered.

"Yes?"

"Just kiss me already."

He smiled, a rare full smile, making my heart flutter. "Yes, ma'am."

He lowered himself to me, and I shivered when his lips touched mine. Trial period over, he dove in and kissed me, really kissed me, taking the air from my lungs. I held on for dear life, fisting his shirt and pulling him as close as two people could get. *Meu Deus*, how I had missed his soft lips, his delicious scent, and his warm body against mine. With one hand on my waist, Garrett pushed me against the wall.

I chuckled and he pulled back a little. "What?"

"You always press me against something."

"Um, you know I can press you against a mat-tress, if you prefer." He touched his lips on mine softly.

Meu Deus. My stomach flip-flopped, remem-bering what he could do to me.

"Garrett?"

"Hmm?" He grazed his tongue under my ear and bit my jaw.

"I love you."

He stopped and stared at me, his eyes shin-ing. "I love you too." He dipped to kiss me again. My body trembled when his mouth claimed mine. This kiss was different. It was slower, deeper, as if it contained more meaning than the others. *Meu Deus*, what would it be like to make *love* to him? Warmth spread through my body.

Finally, out of breath, I broke the kiss. "What are your plans for tonight?" I asked, my voice throaty.

"Besides making up for being away from you for the past eight weeks?"

A shiver ran through my body. *Focus, Beatriz. Focus.* "I promised my cousin I would go to a din-ner-slash-party he and two of my brothers are hosting tonight. But that won't be for another—" I pulled my cell phone and glanced at the screen. "—four hours."

"I can abuse a hell of a lot of you in four hours." He kissed my neck. "As long as you promise we can continue it after you're back from the dinner-slash-party."

"Do you want to go to the party with me?"

He lifted one eyebrow. "Are you sure you're ready to introduce me to your family?"

I held his stare. "Yes." He smiled. A full smile again. Contentment filled my chest. "I'm not sure they're ready to meet you though."

Chuckling, he brushed his lips on mine. "I don't care. They can try to scare me away. I'll just hold you tight and never let you go again."

I smiled. "Works for me."

WANT TO READ MORE BOOKS IN THE BREAKING world? *Breaking Through*, Hil's book is next!

THANK YOU

If you want to see exclusive teasers, help me decide on covers, read excerpts, talk about books, etc, join my reader group on Facebook: Juliana's Club!

ABOUT THE AUTHOR

While USA Today Bestselling Author Juliana Haygert dreams of being Wonder Woman, Buffy, or a blood elf shadow priest, she settles for the less exciting—but equally gratifying—life as a wife, a mother, and an author. She resides in North Carolina and spends her days writing about kick-ass heroines and the heroes who drive them crazy.

Subscribe to her mailing list to receive emails of announcement, events, and other fun stuff related to her writing and her books: www.bit.ly/JuHNL

For more information:
www.julianahaygert.com

facebook.com/julianahaygert

twitter.com/juliana_haygert

instagram.com/juliana.haygert

goodreads.com/juliana_haygert

pinterest.com/julianahaygert

bookbub.com/authors/juliana-haygert

ALSO BY JULIANA HAYGERT

To find links and more info, go to:

www.julianahaygert.com/books/

Shorts

Into the Darkest Fire

Tested

Standalones

Daughter of Darkness

Rite World: Blackthorn Hunters Academy

The Demon Kiss (Book 1)

The Hunter Secret (Book 2)

The Soul Bond (Book 3)

The Shadow Trials (Book 4)

The Infernal Curse (Book 5)

Rite World

The Vampire Heir (Book 1)

The Witch Queen (Book 2)

The Immortal Vow (Book 3)

The Warlock Lord (Book 4)

The Wolf Consort (Book 5)

The Crystal Rose (Book 6)

The Wolf Forsaken (Book 7)

The Fae Bound (Book 8)

The Blood Pact (Book 9)

The Wyth Courts

Winter King (Book 1)

Spring Warrior (Book 2)

Summer Prince (Book 3)

Autumn Rebel (Book 4)

The Fire Heart Chronicles

Heart Seeker (Book 1)

Flame Caster (Book 2)

Sorrow Bringer (Book 3)

Earth Shaker (Novella)

Soul Wanderer (Book 4)

Fate Summoner (Book 5)

War Maiden (Book 6)